Praise for Daniel A. Rabuzzi's
The Choir Boats: Volume 1 of Longing for Yount

"*The Choir Boats* is *Gulliver's Travels* crossed with *The Golden Compass* and a dollop of *Pride and Prejudice* . . . An instant classic of fantasy . . ."

—John Ottinger,
Grasping for the Wind blog

"(A)n auspicious debut . . . a muscular, Napoleonic-era fantasy that, like Philip Pullman's Dark Materials series, will appeal to both adult and young adult readers."

—Paul Witcover,
Realms of Fantasy

"(A) fantastic and deeply entertaining debut novel . . . Part steampunk adventure, part classic fantasy, *The Choir Boats* might be earmarked for young adults, but anyone to whom this sounds like a rich ride will be surprised and delighted."

—Lincoln Cho,
January Magazine

"With full flanks ahead, *The Choir Boats* charts a magical course of verve and wit through a richly detailed nineteenth-century world, spinning off little arabesques of wonderment with every turn of the page."

—Matt Kressel,
host of *KGB reading series*,
founder of Senses Five Press

"*The Choir Boats* is the most underrated young adult title of 2009, although it's by no means limited to young readers. It's a gorgeous and light-hearted story, chock-full of clever words, characters, surprises, and one truly spectacular twist at the end. If you're seeking an engrossing and entirely unique world to sweep you off your feet, look no further."

—*The Ranting Dragon* blog

DANIEL A. RABUZZI

THE INDIGO PHEASANT
Volume Two of Longing for Yount

Illustrated by
DEBORAH A. MILLS

ChiZine Publications

FIRST EDITION

The Indigo Pheasant © 2012 by Daniel A. Rabuzzi
Interior illustrations and front cover woodcarving © 2012 by Deborah A. Mills
Woodcarving photograph @ 2012 by Shira Weinberger
Author cover photograph © Kyle Cassidy
Cover artwork © 2012 by Erik Mohr
Cover design © 2012 by Samantha Beiko
Interior design and hippocampus graphic © 2012 by Danny Evarts
All Rights Reserved.

This is a work of historical fiction. Apart from the well-known actual people, events and locales that figure in the narrative, all names, places, incidents and characters are the products of the author's imagination or are used fictitiously. Any resemblance to current events or locales, or to living persons, is entirely coincidental.

Distributed in Canada by
HarperCollins Canada Ltd.
1995 Markham Road
Scarborough, ON M1B 5M8
Toll Free: 1-800-387-0117
e-mail: hcorder@harpercollins.com

Distributed in the U.S. by
Diamond Book Distributors
1966 Greenspring Drive
Timonium, MD 21093
Phone: 1-410-560-7100 x826
e-mail: books@diamondbookdistributors.com

Library and Archives Canada Cataloguing in Publication

Rabuzzi, Daniel A. (Daniel Allen), 1959–
    The indigo pheasant / Daniel A. Rabuzzi; illustrations by Deborah Mills

(Longing for Yount ; 2)
Issued also in electronic format.
ISBN 978-1-927469-09-5

    I. Mills, Deborah A. II. Title. III. Series: Rabuzzi, Daniel A. (Daniel Allen), 1959- . Longing for Yount ; 2.

PS3618.A328I64 2012   813'.6   C2012-904098-3

CHIZINE PUBLICATIONS
Toronto, Canada
www.chizinepub.com
info@chizinepub.com

Edited by Samantha Beiko
Copyedited and proofread by Kate Moore

Canada Council   Conseil des Arts
for the Arts   du Canada

We acknowledge the support of the Canada Council for the Arts which last year invested $20.1 million in writing and publishing throughout Canada.

ONTARIO ARTS COUNCIL
CONSEIL DES ARTS DE L'ONTARIO

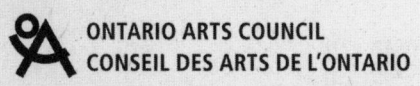

Published with the generous assistance of the Ontario Arts Council.

Printed in Canada

Dedicated to my wife, best friend, and creative partner: the artist Deborah A. Mills. She knows Yount in the crook of the osprey's wing, in the grain of the wood, in the flower-glow of twilight.

Continuing the story started in *The Choir Boats (Volume I of Longing for Yount)*, by Daniel A. Rabuzzi (Toronto: Chizine Publications, 2009). For notes to the text and more information about Maggie, the McDoons and Yount, see: *www.danielarabuzzi.com.*

Table of Contents

Prologue — 11

Chapter 1: Many Plans, or,
    The Most Superbly Ludicrous Project Ever Devised — 23

Interlude: Disjecta Membra — 42

Chapter 2: Many Meetings, or,
    A Long, Exact, and Serious Comedy — 53

Interlude: Videnda — 86

Chapter 3: Many Perils, or,
    The Profoundest Dangers of Air and Time — 101

Interlude: Qualia — 127

Chapter 4: More Perils, or,
    A Thousand Strokes of Mean Invention — 135

Interlude: Fontes — 157

Chapter 5: A Delayed Beginning, or,
    Brisk Entanglements of Wisdom and Folly — 167

Interlude: Indicia — 191

Chapter 6: An Awakening, or,
    The Publication of a Marred Peace — 201

Interlude: Cartulae — 233

Chapter 7: Battles Big and Small, or,
    Malicious Affections Roused — 236

Interlude: Vestigia — 282

Chapter 8: A Great Singing, or,
    The Fluid Signature of Joy — 286

Interlude: Farrigine — 342

Epilogue — 344

THE INDIGO PHEASANT

Prologue

"Thou, who didst put to flight
Primeval Silence, when the morning stars,
Exulting, shouted o'er the rising ball;
O Thou, whose word from solid darkness struck
That spark, the sun; strike wisdom from my soul..."
—**Edward Young,**
The Complaint: or, Night Thoughts On Life, Death & Immortality,
First Night, lines 35-39 (published 1742)

"The fowl digs out the blade that kills it."
—**Traditional Igbo proverb**

"The mother that bare them saith unto them, Go your way, ye children; for I am a widow and forsaken. / I brought you up with gladness; but with sorrow and heaviness have I lost you for ye have sinned..."
—**4 Ezra 2, 2-3**

"**B**lood," said Maggie. "I can see no other way, Mama—it needs blood. Blood to make it work properly."

Maggie emptied the afternoon ashes in the bin at the bottom of the garden behind the Sedgewicks's house on Archer Street by Pineapple Court. She listened to the bells tolling the end of the Lesser Feast of the Vicissitudes on a chilly day in May of 1816.

"Mama," she said to the growing shadows on the wall. For over a year, ever since the great singing with the white girl and the brown girl that brought the ship out of Silence, Maggie had been designing a machine in her head.

"I wish there was another way, I do," she thought. "Why blood? I fear it, I don't want it so. But I can taste it in my mind. Aceldama in the music, blood on the tonal fields."

A grey thrush landed on top of the wall, started his vespers.

"A musical instrument like no one has ever seen," Maggie said, admiring the fieldfare in song as the light turned wan.

She envisioned a structure larger than a house, with wires and gears, struts and enjambments, a tabernacular engine.

"Like in size to the organ at St. Macrina's, but much more . . . complex."

She arranged in her mind levers and pipes, knobs and buttons.

"The method of fluxions will not be enough," said Maggie, scratching out a calculation with a stick in the ash-kettle. "To build and steer this choir-boat, we will need Mr. Laplace's celestial mechanics, Mama, and something of his latest on probability—if only I knew French better. Not neglecting the monadology either."

Maggie had spent hours by candlelight alone in her tiny attic room dissecting a broken timepiece she got from the rag-and-bone man, contriving models made from scraps she found in refuse heaps and middens, drafting schematics and charts with pencil and a pale blue crayon. She read every book and paper on mathematics that she could convince Mrs. Sedgewick to buy or borrow for her. On her Saturday afternoons, she haunted the watchmakers' district in Clerkenwell, and once she spent a day's wages to visit the Mechanical Museum on Tichbourne off

Haymarket, having first been denied entrance at the Adelaide National Gallery of Practical Science on the Strand (serving as it did, "only the most esteemed and genteel elements of the Publick.")

Night by night, the plan became clearer.

"*Chi di*, we need seven singers," she whispered to the thrush. "Not you, little friend, but six others besides me. The white girl and the brown girl . . . they are two. I heard others when those two sang, but I cannot see them."

Maggie traced a pattern on the brick of the wall below the thrush.

"The ghost-stitches of our wanderings," she explained to the bird. "Another girl also sings alone, like me. A girl with black hair, very straight, and she has pale golden skin. I see her when I dream, I watch her sing, but I hear no music from her. She is very, very far away. I think she must come to me or else the great machine cannot work."

Maggie shivered and wondered if the machine needed the distant girl to be the seventh singer or to be something else.

"Ancestors—*ndichie*—help me," thought Maggie.

Only the thrush responded, singing more loudly as night fell and the moon rose.

"Seven singers . . . and blood to glaze the enamel, burnish the copper, oil the engine, to wax the casings. I wish, oh Mama I wish it wasn't so . . . but I see blood in the machine's making . . . I fear this, but the calculations are quite clear on the matter."

The head-maid called from the house, sharp words. Maggie sighed and hoisted the ash-pot.

"Here I am little better than a slave," Maggie said. "That Mrs. Sedgewick treats me like her pet, a fancy monkey who does tricks."

Maggie walked towards the house.

"White folks think they know us but they don't, not at all," she whispered. "Not sure but I should take my machine to Maryland, Mama, when I am through with it in the other place."

At that moment, a phantom echo—a shriek not heard but

felt in the marrow—crossed the moon and the thrush stopped singing. Maggie did not flinch. She shook her fist at the sky.

"You are not seen, but I feel you," she said.

Halting at the doorway to the house, she sensed that the thrush was gone from the wall. He would sing no more this night.

"No more pint o'salt," she said and went inside.

Sally had the carriage stopped at the corner of Mincing Lane, unable to go on.

"What is it, niece?" said Barnabas.

Sally could not say. Ever since landing at London's East India Docks that morning, on the Lesser Feast of the Vicissitudes, a chilly day in early May of 1816, Sally had felt uneasy. In the carriage, passing what should have been familiar places, she could not shake the feeling that something was—as Mr. Sanford would put it—"out of place."

"Figs and fiddles," said her uncle, when she confessed her fear to him. "Just getting your land-legs back is all, I reckon, after all our months at sea, first on *The Gallinule* through the foggy, complainin' places, now so many more months on an East Indiaman from the Cape."

Isaak stood with her two back legs anchored in Sally's lap, peering here and there and back again through the carriage window, face framed by her two front paws. Isaak lashed her tail, a threat and a greeting combined.

"Perhaps Uncle, and maybe," Sally said, holding Isaak by the belly. But she thought the streets of London felt even narrower and more askew than she remembered, the rooflines subtly unbalanced, the dome of St. Paul's minutely off centre. The rooks overhead seemed even shiftier and louder than she remembered.

"I fear a trick of the Owl," she said to Reglum and Dorentius. "Might he not have altered our course, magicked the Fulginator to send us to some *other* London on some other Karket-soom?

THE INDIGO PHEASANT *Volume Two of Longing for Yount*

"Especially with me so badly hurt, that's your thought is it not?" said Dorentius, shifting his amputated leg as the carriage jounced along a particularly poorly surfaced section of the Great East Road.

"No, no, dear Dorentius, I did not mean . . ." said Sally, putting her hand out to the place where his leg used to be, then withdrawing it with a little gasp.

"You could never offend me, Sally, you know that," said the Yountish chief-fulginator. "Only Reglum here can do that, given that he insists on Oxonian superiority in all matters!"

Sally smiled at the jibe, her heart full of relief and love for the brave Dorentius, whose leg had been shattered by a cannonball as *The Gallinule* escaped from Yount Great-Port. The night Afsana fell, shot by the Arch-Bishop's Guards . . . Sally's smile was short-lived.

"I do not doubt the Wurm has power to cozen even the leys and vortices of the Interrugal Lands, but I do not think our Fulginator played us false, especially not with both of you doing the fulginating," said Reglum.

"Could be just that we have been away so long," said Sanford. The others listened intently—his pronouncements were famously laconic. "Bonaparte's been defeated, for one. For the other, we McDoons have grown accustomed to being very nearly the only white people in our gatherings. It is strange to say it, but it is odd now to see so very few brown and black faces."

His speech at an end, Sanford settled back into customary silence, his eyes keen and bright as they surveyed the London cityscape through the carriage window. He looked for all the world like an old setter, nose outthrust.

"Why, 'tis true, of course, old Sanford has it precisely, in fact, I declare that I never saw so many pairs of blue eyes in all my life!" said Barnabas. "There, Sally, your fancy is nothing more than getting your senses reacquainted with what has now become foreign to us."

Still, Sally could not bring herself to travel the final hundred yards to the house on Mincing Lane.

Sally thought of Tom, as she did every day. She looked at Tom's boon companion Billy Sea-Hen, sitting quietly next to Mr. Sanford. She thought of Afsana . . . dead? She thought of Jambres, the Cretched Man. She thought of the Fraulein Reimer.

"She'll never come back," Sally whispered. "'The solace of salvation', that's what she put on the needlework. . . ."

"Ah, alas, well no, she cannot come back," said Barnabas, blowing his nose to hide tears.

"Dearest," said Reglum, clearing his throat, holding Sally's hand, offering a handkerchief to dry her tears. "I feel this to be London, the real and true London, not some Wurm's illusion . . . and surely you know London far better than I do."

"Dear, sweet Reglum," she thought, looking at Reglum, dabbing at her cheeks.

And then there *he* was, alive in all his pleadings, uncoiling in her mind: James Kidlington.

"James!" she shouted in her mind. "No, no, not you, James Kidlington . . . 'I speak not, I trace not, I breathe not thy name' . . ."

"Sally?" said Reglum.

Sally sat up, squeezing and then releasing Reglum's hand.

"'Tis nothing, dearest," she said. "Verily."

She folded Isaak to her breast, and said, "I can go on."

Sanford rapped on the roof of the carriage and the horses moved.

Suddenly there it was, their home on Mincing Lane, with its blue trim (recently repainted, as Sanford noted with satisfaction) and its dolphin door knocker. They had sent a messenger on ahead of them from the dock, so they were expected. The door to the house flew open even as they spilled out of the carriage and Isaak bounded up the steps.

"Salmius Nalmius!"

"Why, Mr. Fletcher and Mr. Harris in the flesh, looking very well indeed!"

"I must ask you straight away, lads, about my smilax root . . ."

Sally did not dismiss her fears even then, not until. . . .

THE INDIGO PHEASANT *Volume Two of Longing for Yount*

"Here now, you lot, let me through this moment or I will clout you black and blue!" said the cook, pushing her way past her niece and Mr. Brandt and all the others. A fleshy avalanche, smelling of dough and mustard-sauce, the cook enveloped Sally.

"Mr. Sanford, Mr. McDoon, sirs, it is good to have you back at last!" said the cook. "And here is our Isaak-tiger come home to us as well!"

The cook fair thundered her next:

"Best of all, may all saints and their servants be praised, sirs, it's Miss Sally, our own little smee! Welcome home, welcome home, welcome home!"

James Kidlington marvelled at his clean fingernails, at his fresh-pressed clothes, and the new hat on his head.

Standing on Effra's Bridge, where the Fleet River met the Thames, James shifted his attention from himself to the spectacle of London on a cold day in May of 1816. He followed the movement of barges and wains, loaded with coal and grain, and the rumbling of great carriages bearing travellers from as far away as Glasgow and Liverpool. He listened to a thousand voices raised in devotion to commerce, finding one among the clamour especially intriguing.

"Wheaten buns," sighed James, as he tracked the vendor who dodged and danced his way through the crowd. Not even the tannic stink of the rivers could blunt James's craving for a hot, blanch'd bun.

James made as if to approach the bun-seller but stopped at the sight of the tall figure next to him.

"Might I just pause for . . . ?" said James.

"No time," said the man. "No time, we are late enough as it is."

James sighed again, gave one last lingering look at the blanch'd bun, quieted his lust, and resignedly followed his escort. After all, the man had a gun and an evident ability to use it, while James was unarmed . . . and his hands were bound.

"Well," thought James. "No bun for now, but I had lost all hope of ever eating one again anyhow, so I can wait another few hours for that. In the meantime, I will at last be enlightened on the not-so-minor matter of my liberation. This fellow, and all the other guardians who have been with me every hour of every day since I was released from the . . . that hell-hole in Australia, they've all been as talkative as the dead, no word of explanation from them no matter how hard I tried. Not that I quibble, mind you, since I am free in comparison to where I was. But James Kidlington knows that no one is doing this as a favour. Oh no, oh no, the labour and the . . . torment . . . have not dulled my wits to that degree. What I want to know is: who is my 'benefactor,' and what does he want from me in return?"

With competence born of long practice, Mr. and Mrs. Sedgewick ignored each other as they breakfasted on the morning after the Lesser Feast of the Vicissitudes.

". . . back at last from their myriad adventures, the palmers return from the Land of Prester-John or the Golden Chersonese or wherever they may have been," said Mr. Sedgewick, contemplating the note just delivered from the McDoons. "And we are bid to see them this very afternoon, my dendritic day-lily."

Mrs. Sedgewick nodded, but listened more closely to her buttered toast than to her husband.

"Now we shall hear the truth of all the rumours and speculation," continued the lawyer, remarking naught of his wife's inattention. "Certainly and manifestly not lost like poor Mungo Park seeking Timbuktoo! So that's one hypothesis reduced to marmalade! But what transpired at the Cape? Did they, as some suggest, roam to India? To the wild Carmanian waste? We shall shortly hear all, direct and unimpeded from the mouths of the McDoons themselves. No longer will we rely on the hearsay of others. Nay, *nullius in verba* . . ."

Mrs. Sedgewick heard only the echo in her mind of the whispers she'd listened to in the dark. Of late she had dreamed of a man—at least something in a man's tall shape—dressed in a white fancy-coat, with cut-away tails reaching to his calves. He, or it, was tall but stocky, with a barrel chest and a power in his arms even as they hung at his sides. She could not fully make out his face, but thought it must be very round, plate-like, with two great unblinking yellow eyes.

The man muttered in the darkness, half-whistling in broken Latin, punctuating phrases with snappings, clickings, sounds of whetting.

Morning after morning she awoke, with a lingering image in her mind of this unwanted visitor, an abscess in the half-light. She could not tell Mr. Sedgewick; he would only scoff. Oddly, she thought of telling Maggie, but what sense could there be in confiding in a servant, no matter how skilled in arts and letters? Sally, Sally . . . she wanted to share this dream with Sally; Sally would know what it meant and perhaps how to end it.

"Yes, dear," said Mrs. Sedgewick to Mr. Sedgewick. "Yes, the Miss Sally, as you say, it will be very fine to renew my conversations with her. I am most glad she is back, you are as always quite and irrefutably right."

The Mejouffrouw Termuyden met her husband at the front-door of The Last Cozy House, as winter approached the Cape in May of 1816.

"Here you are, at last!" she said in English, less to her husband than to the three people he ushered into the house.

"You must be Mary," said the Mejouffrouw to the Chinese girl—twelve, maybe thirteen years old—standing before her. "You can have no idea how delighted we are to meet you. We have heard so much about you from our colleagues in the East."

"Her English is not good," said the lean young man standing close behind her. "I am her older brother. You can speak to me."

"Very well," said the Mejouffrouw, peering at the young man (perhaps eighteen or nineteen years old) for the first time.

"Her name is not Mary, it is Mei-Hua, but none of you have the tongue to say that, so you all say instead Mary. Misfortunate. Mei-Hua means 'Beautiful Flower.'"

The third guest—around sixty years of age— stepped forward and said, "Please forgive Shaozu. He sometimes forgets his manners. Allow me, please: I am Tang Guozhi, special sending from his excellence, the Jiaquing Emperor . . ."

All three Chinese bowed at the name of the emperor, prompting a bow and a curtsy from the Termuydens.

". . . Xie Shaozu and Xie Mei-Hua are my responsibilities. We thank you for receiving us. His heavenly Emperorship himself has much interest in this matter."

"We are indeed flattered, then," said the Mejouffrouw. "But it is we who forget our manners! Let us understand each other better over tea and small-cakes in our withdrawing room—the tea is genuine oolong, brought to us on an East Indiaman much like the one that brought you here yourselves."

An hour later, under the gentle ministrations of the Termuydens and the benevolent influence of The Last Cozy House, even the stand-offish Shaozu began to feel at home.

Offering Shaozu yet another slice of gingerbread, the Mejouffrouw said, "Tell us again about the wisdom Mary studies . . . we cannot pronounce it, I am so sorry . . . the . . . ?"

"The *luli yuanyuan* . . . it means . . . wait, I have written it down for you in English," said Shaozu, taking the gingerbread with one hand, while drawing a paper from his satchel with another. He gave the paper to his hostess.

"*Sources of Musical Harmonics and Mathematical Astronomy*," read the Mejouffrouw, her brow furrowed. "Ah, hmm, *precies* . . ."

"Mei-Hua is . . ." the young man paused. "I have not the word. She is the . . . she is special. She can do the *jie-fang-shen* in her head. That is what you call the al-ge-bra. Mei-Hua is blessed, that is the word. She can do *huan zhong shu chi* better than anyone in China, and that means the world."

The Mejouffrouw said, "That's what we were told as well. That's why we were asked to inquire about Mary. She is needed."

The emperor's emissary, Tang Guozhi, said, "The philosophers in The Forbidden City have studied these things for many lives. I remember their conversations with the English when the Lord MacCartney visited China."

"Ah, so you met Lord MacCartney," said Mr. Termuyden. "Did you know Sir John Barrow, his secretary? Sir John stayed here with us many times during his long stay in South Africa, after the end of the Chinese embassy."

"Yes, I knew Sir John a little," said Tang Guozhi. "I knew the boy best, the one who spoke Chinese so well: Thomas Staunton. He was then about the same age as our Mei-Hua is now."

"Curious thing, as you mention Staunton (Sir Staunton and now a baronet like his father); he is here in Cape Town as we speak," said Mr. Termuyden. "He is assistant-commissioner in Lord Amherst's embassy to China. Their two ships landed not a week ago for replenishment on the way to Canton. A curious coincidence . . ."

Tang Guozhi nodded but said nothing.

Mei-Hua broke the ensuing silence with a query in Chinese to her brother and Tang Guozhi.

"What Mei-Hua asks is . . ." began Shaozu.

"In my head," said Mei-Hua, speaking in English directly to the Termuydens. "What is the place I hear in my head? When I dream?"

The Mejouffrouw put down the tea-canister, and said, "Yount. It is called Yount, in English. We will tell you all you need to know. Your journey has, I fear, only just begun."

A dirigible he was, floating over endless plains of pocked and riddled dust and the frozen spume of long-dead volcanoes. In the distance were the teterrimous mountains, with peaks of sheared bronze. On the horizon, beyond the mountains, burned cold fires.

It might have been May of 1816, possibly on The Lesser Feast of the Vicissitudes. Here was all time and no time at the same time.

His shadow, sleek, loomed alternately larger and smaller as he flew over ridges, incising the earth with the shadow of his scissor-tail. That shadow, cast by the moon, lingered for a moment or two after he had sped on far above.

"I have seen Orpheus fail here," he said to himself, and his thoughts caused the dust down below to eddy upwards.

"No door will open easily here," he thought, and that thought became a whisper that became a wind through the mountains.

His vast whiteness sailed through the darkness, smothering any pretense of hope that distant atmospheres might conspire to insert into his domain.

Yet, he was troubled deep inside the sines and secants of his being. With his tympannic ears, he heard a humming, a very far-off music in many voices.

"Oh no, oh no," he boomed. "Orpheus could not do this thing, and neither can you!"

On he cruised, eyes seeing every grain of grey sand, every sliver of mica, every edge and ripple of every mountain-side.

On he cruised into the dark, straining to hear the music on his borders.

Chapter 1: Many Plans, or, The Most Superbly Ludicrous Project Ever Devised

"They who find themselves inclined to censure new undertakings, only because they are new, should consider, that the folly of projection is very seldom the folly of a fool; it is commonly the ebullition of a capacious mind, crowded with variety of knowledge, and heated with intenseness of thought; it proceeds often from the consciousness of uncommon powers, from the confidence of those who, having already done much, are easily persuaded that they can do more.

"Projectors of all kinds agree in their intellects, though they differ in their morals; they all fail by attempting things beyond their power, by despising vulgar attainments, and aspiring to performances to which, perhaps, nature has not proportioned the force of man: when they fail, therefore, they fail not by idleness or timidity, but by rash adventure and fruitless diligence.

"Whatever is attempted without previous certainty of success, may be considered as a project, and amongst narrow minds may, therefore, expose its author to censure and contempt; and if the liberty of laughing be once indulged, every man will laugh at what he does not understand, every project will be considered as madness, and every great or new design will be censured as a project. [......] Many that presume to laugh at projectors, would consider a flight through the air in a winged chariot, and the movement of a mighty engine by the steam of water as equally the dreams of mechanick lunacy."

—Samuel Johnson,
"Projectors Injudiciously Censured and Applauded,"
in *The Adventurer*, nr. 99 (October 15, 1753)

"We were the first that ever burst
Into that silent sea.

Down dropped the breeze, the sails dropped down,
'Twas sad as sad could be;
And we did speak only to break
The silence of the sea!

All in a hot and copper sky,
The bloody sun, at noon,
Right up above the mast did stand,
No bigger than the moon.

Day after day, day after day,
We stuck, nor breath nor motion;
As idle as a painted ship
Upon a painted ocean."

—Samuel Taylor Coleridge,
"Rime of the Ancient Mariner,"
Part II (published 1798)

THE INDIGO PHEASANT *Volume Two of Longing for Yount*

"We own you, Mr. Kidlington," said the one on the left, an angular man, a knitting needle come to life. "Understand me well. Notwithstanding the change last century in the laws of this United Kingdom, to wit, forbidding such things, His Majesty's Government in effect and for all intents and purposes . . . owns you."

Kidlington gazed coolly at the speaker, who was dressed in black but for a shockingly white, old-fashioned neck-cloth.

"How do you receive this intelligence?" said the one on the right, similarly dressed, rounder in outline, with enormous hands splay-gripping the mahogany table behind which he sat.

Kidlington adjusted his own neck-cloth and examined his own hands before responding.

"I thank m'lords for their candour," he said. "If I may be so forthright in return, I find all that has happened to me since your man plucked me from the shores of Australia to be wondrous strange indeed, a torquing of fortune that I can only be grateful for."

Kidlington hated his interlocutors as a matter of the marrow, his right by birth. He knew their type: the second sons of great landed families, bullied by custom and thwarted by the laws of inheritance, seeking retribution, recompense and glory on the backs of others.

"If, as you assert, I am owned still by the Crown, well, that is no change from my status on the wrong side of the Earth, is it?"

Kidlington looked from one to the other, and back again. "Needle and Ripper," he thought. "Dart and Harrow. That's what I shall call you."

"Still and all, 'tis yet a form of lenity contrasted with my most recent circumstance, so for that I thank His Majesty for his wisdom and his mercy."

The only immediate sound in the ensuing pause was the ticking of a large ormolu clock, flanked by ebony hippocamps, sitting on the mantlepiece behind Kidlington's two questioners.

... . . .

... . . .

From outside the Admiralty came dimly the cry of rooks, the muffled sounds of the Horse-Guard filing down Whitehall, the dull susurrus of movement from Birdcage Walk and St. James, of traffic on the Thames.

"Do you know why we called you hence?" said Needle.

"It is a curious tale, to be sure," said Harrow.

"I cannot say aught, m'lords, than that I am all ears for the hearing," said Kidlington.

"Indeed, you cannot," said Needle, smiling. His teeth were long and yellow.

"Mr. Kidlington, have you ever heard of a place called Yount?" said Harrow. "Ah, you have, we see the truth in your eyes, so do not deny it. No coyness in here, no need to pretend ignorance, we are His Majesty's most special branch, the Admiralty's bureau of inquiry and subtle response."

"The Crown's *agentes in rebus*," said Needle. "The House Venatical, his Majesty's most devoted hunters."

"The Office of the Caviards, the Arm of Redaction," said Harrow.

"In short: we seek, we find, we solve . . . if necessary, we erase," said Needle.

"Which brings us back to you and your case, and what that has to do with Yount," said Harrow. "We aim for panopticality, Mr. Kidlington, and this is what we saw: a promising young man, with a medical bent, who got himself imbricated with the worst sorts of people here in London, and who then further entangled himself with a highly respectable merchant and especially said merchant's niece, until you yourself could not differentiate where your loyalties lay, not until the whole wretched mess collapsed about your ears. Am I on the slot so far?"

Kidlington gave the barest of nods.

"Why would this sordid petty affair trouble His Majesty's Government?" said Needle. "Because we caught wind of Yount being somehow a thread in it. Ah yes, Yount . . . a whisper, a rumour, tales told by rummy old sailors in harbourside taverns, stories that also appear in learned texts, all the way back to Plato."

"Great Britain has an interest in discovering the truth about Yount," said Harrow. "*Raison d'état*, old chap, the needs of state: colonies, commerce, the expanding imperium, all the more so now that Napoleon is vanquished and our glorious nation has a window of opportunity through which to thrust."

Needle said, "A jailor at the Cape, on Robbens Island, passed along to the magistrate an odd tidbit (for money, of course; we do not assume all His Majesty's subjects are as selfless as those who serve the Admiralty). He revealed this—inadvertently, as we specialize in gleanings, half-truths and keyhole observations—to one of our men. In any event, the jailor overheard one day, from within one of the cells, a most queer sort of confession. By a young Englishman accused of larceny and unbecoming conduct towards a young lady . . . whose name was Sarah . . . Sally to you, yes? . . . I hardly need spell this out, do I?"

Kidlington shook his head once. "Not you, James Kidlington," rose through the walls of his mind's defenses; he used all his will not to slump in his seat—he would not give the Admiralty that satisfaction.

"Do not rebuke yourself too much, Kidlington," said Harrow. "We have long had certain individuals at the Cape under surveillance as it relates to Yount. Meaning those eccentric Dutch personalities, the Termuydens. Ah, that brings back memories for you, doesn't it?"

The clock ticked in the lull.

. . . . . .

. . . . . .

. . .   . . .

. . . . . .

"Oh yes, the Termuydens," said Needle. "Our propinquity goes back a long way. Why, the Second Secretary himself, Sir John Barrow, was their guest on many occasions in the nineties. Quite a file we have on the Termuydens, a long prolix archive."

"Do you wonder what happened to your Sally, to the McDoons, after your unfortunate detention?" said Harrow.

"So do we," said Needle. "We have pieced together bits of their story. A strange story, not to be believed . . . but we believe it."

"And now the McDoons have returned to London," said Harrow. "Ah, ah . . . you did not know this? But how could you? How does this revelation find you?"

... ...
... ...
... ...
... ...
... ...

"As we thought it would," continued Harrow. "Which is why we come now to the pith of the matter."

"We will have you reunited with the McDoons," said Needle. "Return of the lover wronged, of the resurrected hero. You *will* be a hero, won't you Kidlington? Such a turn—it is ludicrous, is it not? So sublimely ridiculous that only Jonson or Shakespeare—or His Majesty's most secret instrumentality—could concoct its like."

"We will house you in modest but respectable accommodations, just off Fenchurch, not far from Mincing Lane," said Harrow. "We remand you to the oversight of a lawyer we know, a Mr. Sedgewick. Talks in circles, does Mr. Sedgewick, but do not be fooled: he thinks in very straight lines, and the shorter the better. He has done Admiralty work for years, and is the essence of discretion."

Kidlington roused himself and said, "What am I to do? "

Harrow and Needle laughed.

"Nothing you have not done before and with agility! You will be a spy, of course," said Harrow. "Contrive to re-attach yourself to the McDoons, most particularly to the Miss Sally. Learn all you can covertly about their whereabouts once they sailed from the Cape. We find no record of them reaching Bombay or anywhere on the Malabar, nor the Bengal, nor Madras or any lesser port on the Coromandel. No trace of them exists in the Water Indies or on the Manilhase Islands or on any coast of China."

"They appear to have sailed, as the Bard puts it, to the equinoctial of Queubus, the torridity lying somewhere beyond three o'clock in the morning," said Needle.

"In an eggshell: we believe they sailed to Yount," said Harrow. "We want every sliver, every shard, of information you can procure for us about that."

Kidlington shrugged, his laughter laced with rue and hellebore, "Seeing as I have no other choice..."

"We knew you were a man of reason," said Harrow.

"Yount," said Kidlington. "Yount would seem a grail for others as well."

The two spectres of the Admiralty scythed Kidlington with their gaze, eyebrows raised.

"What I mean to say," said Kidlington, "is that the Admiralty is not alone in its investigation, even here in London, I think."

"Perspicacious, you are," said Needle.

"We know those others to whom you refer," said Harrow. "In fact, we extinguished your debts to them, as part of our arrangement. Would not do to have our chief informant found floating in the Thames, missing his eyes and tongue, would it?"

"Nevertheless, be wary still of those others," said Needle. "We eye them and they eye us, like a tiger and a leopard do, who encounter each other over a kill each claims."

"How shall I report?" said Kidlington. "What do I even call you?"

"Call us?" said Harrow. "We do not exist! We are the greyest of *éminence grise*—a grey that turns to white and then becomes transparent."

"If you must, think of us as Ithuriel and Zephon," said Needle.

"Sent by the archangel to discover Satan's whereabouts in the Garden," said Harrow. "With winged speed, leaving no nook unsearched, and all that. Protecting Adam and Eve."

"So, to you Kidlington, we are Mr. I. and Mr. Z.," said Needle.

Kidlington bowed his head slowly and just two inches.

"As for reporting..." said Harrow, picking up and ringing a small bell.

Almost immediately, a man opened a door on the far side of the room and entered.

"This is Lieutenant Thracemorton," said Harrow. "He will

be your handler. He is not of the smiling persuasion, so do not attempt japes, jests or jokes in his presence."

"He served with the famous Captain Sharpe in Spain," said Needle. "Salamanca in '12, I believe. He also assisted Maturin in Brest and other parts of France. You won't find better."

Lieutenant Thracemorton inclined his head but said nothing.

"Well, go on Kidlington," said Harrow. "Tick-tock, tick-tock."

Kidlington made to leave with the lieutenant. As the pair reached the door, the needle (was that Mr. I or Mr. Z.?) said, "Remember, Kidlington. We own you and we do not exist—you are the property of ghosts! *You* do not exist! Should you breathe a word of this to anyone. . . ."

... ...
 ... ...

". . . besides, even if you did, and we know you won't, who would believe you?" said Harrow. "They'd clap you in Bedlam as soon as Michaelmas."

Kidlington turned on his heel and, escorted by the unsmiling lieutenant, left the hidden room by an unmarked door in Admiralty House.

The harrow turned to the needle.

"What do you think of our newly sprung gamecock?"

"Useful. Highly intelligent. Motivated."

"Agreed. But also headstrong, cunning, untrustworthy."

"Agreed. In short: he's a poet, Childe Harold, a damned romantic."

The harrow rang the bell again. Another man entered the room.

"Captain Shufflebottom," said the harrow.

"Your humblest servant, m'lords," said Captain Shufflebottom, peering through grey-lensed spectacles.

"You will shadow those two," said the needle. "Unobserved, undetected even by our own lieutenant."

"At all costs, protect our asset," said the harrow. "He is not to leave our care, ever. Report only and directly to us, unless we are not accessible, in which case you may debrief with our confidential secretary, Mr. Tarleton."

"Keep Kidlington alive, using all your guile and all your strength," said the needle. "But, if conditions warrant it, if you cannot obtain our instructions prior, then you are hereby licensed to kill."

"I understand, m'lords," said Mr. Shufflebottom. "Off now to do your bidding, m'lords."

The door closed behind him. The clock on the mantlepiece ticked and tocked.

Then the harrow said to the needle, "We have waited a long time for this moment."

"Agreed. A profoundly long time."

"Lord Melville will be pleased. Sir John even more so."

"The French are well out of the game, at least for now. The Dutch and Danes likewise. No more interference from the Casa in Seville either. The Moghuls we have also sent to the sidelines."

"The Turks still dabble, and the Persians, but they are toothless old lions, content to gnaw bones under the shade tree."

"The Chinese, on the other hand . . ."

"The Chinese, . . . yes, but that's why we sent Lord Amherst on his embassy to Peking, so recently set sail . . ."

"And the . . . others . . . the strangers . . ."

"Still, this round goes to us today, I should think."

"Agreed. So long as our Mr. Kidlington is as we think he is."

"Oh, he will prove to be, you mark my words, Mr. I."

"We shall see, Mr. Z."

"Impossible," said Mr. Sedgewick. "*Affenspiele*. A mandrill's conspiracy."

He said this to his wife, ignoring Maggie who sat in front of them on the other side of the table. On the table, between Maggie and the Sedgewicks, sprawled the source of the lawyer's scornful disbelief: Maggie's latest model, three feet tall, a construction of wires and gears, the Tower of Babel in miniature.

Neither Mrs. Sedgewick nor Maggie responded right away. The ticking of the clock under the trumeau mirror pricked the silence. Outside, along Archer Street by Pineapple Court, and from elsewhere in the City, came the shouts of the water-seller and the scissor-grinder, of a huckster selling chapbooks ("read 'ere the mir'cles of Saints Florian an' Evaristus!"), of a carter berating a neighing horse. As always, threading their voices throughout the human cries of London, rooks cawed, magpies chacked and daws charked.

Mrs. Sedgewick stole a glance at Maggie while replying to her husband. She said, "You go too far, sir, with your accusations..."

He cut her off, his belly jouncing in agitation.

"Madam, do not presume..." he said. "What am I supposed to think, when confronted with this improbable monstrosity?"

Maggie choked back tears. "Mother guide me," she thought. "*Chi di*. This man, this so-very-white man, so learned, so self-respecting, so very high on his very tall horse, is so very wrong. I hate him."

Mr. Sedgewick was still belabouring Mrs. Sedgewick. "This is all *your* fault, you know, my dear. You encourage her in these whims and wigmaleeries. Or rather, you indulge and coddle her, as if she were your prize spaniel. But you raise up her hopes unjustly. You delude yourself and—worse—allow this girl to delude herself."

Mrs. Sedgewick, eyes glistening, made to speak, but Mr. Sedgewick slashed forward.

"No one can believe this child of Africa has made such a thing," he said. "Its sophistication, its refinement, ... no, 'tis not possible from such a mind as hers."

Maggie made to speak, but Mr. Sedgewick brooked no interruption.

"*Corchorus inter olea*," he said. "A weed among the herbs, that's what she is, and that's all she is."

"May this weed speak, master?" said Maggie, half-rising from her chair.

Mr. Sedgewick finally looked at Maggie, shifting the sesquipedality of his mind and belly in his chair.

"It seems I cannot stop you," he said.

"Whatever you believe you know, master, I *did* make this thing," Maggie said.

Mr. Sedgewick examined the model, fascinated despite himself. His gaze lingered on the intricate array of pipes and the series of cantilevered struts.

"I may begrudge you, oh cleverest of servants, the fact that you assembled the pieces," he said. "Nicely done, I admit, yet 'tis only insect architecture. Who instructed you? Whose was the mind that conceived this machine? Who imagined the design?"

"Must I forgive him?" thought Maggie. "Mother, he is so unfair."

"I did, sir, and only I," she said.

"Why do you persist so?" said Mr. Sedgewick. "Patently not true, girl! I have a reputation, this house has a reputation, and you sully it with lies! Now, tell me the truth!"

Maggie rose from her chair, her body so taut she thought she would break. Her tongue nearly cleaved to her palate. Her eyes stung.

"I did not steal this idea, I swear to Saint Macrina!" she said.

"There, surely that suffices, cease this interrogation!" said Mrs. Sedgewick.

"No, my dear, there is more here than your pet reveals," said Mr. Sedgewick. "She plays Caliban. I sense a Prospero in all this. That's it: I shall call her henceforth 'Calibanna.'"

Maggie stood as still as a pillar while her mind steeplechased.

"'I dare do all that may become a man; who dares do more is none,'" Maggie said.

"So you know the reference, do you? Well, do not quote *The Tempest* back to me," said Mr. Sedgewick. "You test my limits, girl."

As Maggie measured her own temerity, the clock ticked onward from under the mirror.

"It's not *The Tempest*, master sir," she said. "It's *Macbeth* I quote."

The lawyer heaved himself up, jowls quivering.

"Out, out, out!" he said. "I will not abide your insolence any longer, leave us now, back to the kitchen or wherever your duties require you!"

Maggie left, bumping into a small table as tears blinded her.

"Oh great Mother," she thought. "What am I to do? I cannot leave this house, it is all I have but I cannot stand that man. Show me the way, please help me."

But, if the Mother heard, deep in her ancient slumber, she gave no sign.

Mr. and Mrs. Sedgewick quarrelled long that afternoon. In the end, they declared a stalemate and Mrs. Sedgewick withdrew.

Alone, the lawyer contemplated Maggie's model and felt rising the checks of remorse.

"Perhaps you were too harsh," he said, looking up into the trumeau mirror. "Yes perhaps you were. She quotes Shakespeare. She knows the algebra and—*mirabile dictu*—even the calculus."

He poured himself a glass of sherry.

"Nay, this girl could not . . . she is a creature of Demerary," he said.

He inspected the model, with only the ticking of the clock for company.

"Ingenious," he said. "A bizarre clockwork, I make it. Tick tock. A meditation on torsion and balance, *multum in parvo*. But what is it for, I wonder? Beneath these salpincial tubes and nautiloid 'scapments, what is its purpose?"

He sipped his sherry.

"More to the point," he thought. "What is *her* purpose? Calibanna! *Fateor, paradoxa haec assertio*. Mystery walks with her, and something dangerous lives within her. If only I could tell Mrs. Sedgewick . . . which I must, and then the McDoons! But how?"

He looked at himself in the mirror again and spoke aloud.

"Diplomacy won't work here," he said. "The plainest of plain talk only. They must know what the Scottish court papers document, which I have validated by my own means: that this little daughter of Caliban is a member of the McDoon family."

There, I have said it aloud, and no devil or angel has stopped my mouth."

Mr. Sedgewick finished the sherry and said:

"Maggie is a cousin to Miss Sally, a niece of sorts to Barnabas. Whatever is the world become?"

"Beans and bacon, it will cost a considerable great sum," said Barnabas.

"Thirty-five thousand pounds at 25 pounds per ton," said Sanford. "And that with much hard bargaining. Copper bottoming, iron for the knees and braces, good Suffolk oak, scantlings more robust and spacious than is the norm . . ."

"Which only covers the ship itself," said Reglum. "Then there will be the cost of outfitting and victualling . . ."

"Precisely," said Sanford. "Say, another 4,000 pounds at the least on the one, and—with 120 crew and maybe 230 souls recruited by Billy Sea-Hen—that's, let's see . . ."

"Eighteen guns, at least," said Reglum. "With their ordnance . . ."

"It will take some years to complete," said Barnabas.

"Two years at the earliest," said Sanford. "If fortune favours us."

"It will mean a rigorous focus of our minds, a *menagement* of colossal proportions," said Barnabas.

"Especially as it will need be done in complete secrecy," said Reglum.

"Not to mention—oh, figs and farthings!—the cost of the Fulginator," said Barnabas.

"Which none of us knows can even be built, let alone the cost of building it," said Reglum.

Sally waited, holding Isaak in her lap.

After a long meeting, they had just bid goodbye to three visitors: the owner of the Blackwall shipyard on the Thames, his master marine architect, and the surveyor-general of the Honourable East India Company. Outside the house with its dolphin door-knocker on Mincing Lane, a woman hawked eggs and a linnet sang from the lone lime tree adorning the entire street. The endless traffic on Fenchurch, Cornhill and Leadenhall thrummed under one's feet, mixed with the distant lowing of cattle being driven to Smithfield and punctuated with the calls of rooks and choughs from the Tower. Inside the McDoon office ticked a clock framed by Prudence and Alacrity wrought in bronze.

Sally spoke, "Yet it must be done, whatever the expense, however long it takes, no matter the challenges of oversight and governance."

Barnabas, Sanford and Reglum nodded, with varying degrees of reluctance.

"Yes, of course, Sally dearest," said Reglum. "We're just considering the logistics."

"As we must," said Sally. "But not too long or with too much parsimony."

Sanford flinched almost imperceptibly.

"I'm sorry dear Sanford, I meant that not so barbed," laughed Sally.

"Oh, we'll stretch the shilling, to be sure," said Sanford, with one of his rare half-smiles. "But not at the risk of failure."

"Having said that, we cannot merely wish away the costs," said Reglum.

"Quite right," said Barnabas. "Hence the need to find investors. Quiet partners, investors who won't ask too many questions."

"The East India Company appears willing to commit," said Reglum. "And without probing too far into the nature of the voyage, so long as we guarantee them a specific profit."

Sanford clamped his jaws.

"The Landemanns and the Brandts will invest; they know all about Yount," said Barnabas. "Most likely our good friends Matchett & Frew also—they suspect we are up to something, and probably know more than they let on."

"The Gardiners don't know, but they trust us and will follow our lead," said Sanford. "Droogstoppel in Amsterdam, I'll wager, and possibly Buddenbrooks in Luebeck. Old Osbaldistone might take a punt. Chicksey Stobbles & Veneering, the drug merchants . . ."

". . . such snobs," said Barnabas.

"Yes, well, be that as it may, their money is solid."

"Those newcomers said to be risk-hungry, what is their name?"

"Dawes, Tomes Mousley & Grubb?"

"That's the very one!"

"We'll get the Anglo-Bengalee Disinterested Loan & Life with us, they won't delve too deeply. We could ask Domby but his son is so sick, I wonder . . ."

Isaak toured the office as the McDoons, including Reglum, debated investment strategies and ship design for the rest of the afternoon.

"We need a name for the ship," said Sanford.

"Sally, this is your conception," said Barnabas. "What do you propose?"

"Thank you. I have thought long on the matter. What keeps coming to mind are the birds that have inspired us on our journey so far. The *Gallinule*. The *Lanner*. All the ospreys. The nursery rhyme runs in my head: 'White crow, blue gawk, black swan, red hawk/ Fetch you home yon'digo pheasant.' So let it be the *Indigo Pheasant*."

The three men smiled and shouted, "Huzzah, huzzah! To the *Indigo Pheasant*! Godspeed the *Indigo Pheasant*!"

At that moment, the cook appeared in the doorway.

"Well, as a quab is a queen: call it coincidental, or call it what you will, but an indigo pheasant is printed on the pattern of the china plates I just laid out for your dinner," she said. "I am serving good English plaice in a butter sauce, with roast potatoes in their jackets and mashed peas. Come along now, all of you, tick tock, before your food gets cold."

Isaak followed them into the dining room.

"Ah, the echoes of this orb, the colliding humours of this world," said N.C. Strix Tender Wurm. He had just stepped through the casement of a long-case clock into a quiet house off Hoxton Square in London.

He moved his jaws from side to side, licked his lips. It had been a very long time since he wore this form. His words came out with a spilching sound.

His skin was the white of mutings and sputum and ash. His head was too large for his body, a great round head, bald, with enormous, yellow-tinged eyes set far forward. His lips were thin but a vivid dark red, a colour darker than brick, almost black. His legs were long, sheathed in tight silk the colour of an old tooth; his barrel chest stretched out a white coat with long, cut-away tails that reached well below his knees. Small black chevrons ran intermittently in hatched bands across the back and sleeves; his high stiff collar was cottised with the same.

Of the millions of worlds God created, the Wurm liked this one best, with its Cairo and its Delhi, its Peking and its London. Of the millions upon millions of species that Goddess created to inhabit those worlds, Wurm liked the ones on this world best. Humans, above all. Humans, who most closely resembled the creatures he imagined as his own children, step-children of his cold fever-dreams.

He loved (if such a word could be applied to the Wurm) the sounds here. He widened his ears and sucked in a river of human sound: the ceaseless murmurs, pleas, vain invocations, threats, idle boasts, a mussitation of folly, greed, lust, arrogance and every variety of venality, a chorus of cruelty interlarded with occasional notes of mercy ("ah, but 'nothing emboldens sin so much as mercy,' he thought, "To that extent, they know themselves full well.") He chuckled an awful wheezing chuckle.

He looked around his house. The long-case clock kept several forms of time, the time of London being only one of those. Its face was a dusky ozmilt-grey and featured white owls pursuing dryads and satyrs—at midnight the owls caught and devoured their prey. Inscribed around the clock in gold were "Ex Hoc

Momento Pendet Aeternitas" and "Qua Redit Nescitis Horam."

"'On This Moment Hangs Eternity' and 'We Do Not Know the Hour of His Return,'" he read the inscriptions. The Wurm chuckled again, at his own wit.

"Ah, I have returned, and soon you will know this hour all too well."

He looked around the house, long unused, only partly in this world, shielded from the eyes of all but the most perceptive. He sat in chairs, not having done so for so many centuries. He walked up the stairs to the second floor, just to experience again the sensation of human motion. He riffled through books and hefted cutlery. He opened drawers and doors and windows.

At the topmost window, he stopped and looked out over Hoxton Square. The sun was setting. He savoured the sounds of the street traffic: comings and goings at the fruiterers (he always liked their traditional sign, depicting Adam & Eve), drinkers at the Eagle & Child trying to out-sing their counterparts next door at the Boar & Bible, dogs whining, ballad-rollers and running patterers debouching their rat-rhymes and hornpipe verses into the evening air, pious folk gathering at the Three Cranes meeting house, lullabies sung by young mothers and old grans. He nodded at the rooks and magpies that swirled noisily around the rooftops, told them to hold their tongues and mind their manners or he'd have them in a pie for his supper. The birds flew off.

The Wurm sent his thought out across London. He touched on Little St. Helen's in Bishopsgate, on the workhouse at St. Leonard's in the Kingsland Road, on St. Anne's-upon-Hemsworth, and on the Geffrye almshouses. His mind swooped over the great hospitals in Whitechapel and by London Bridge, crossed Old Street, over Finsbury Circus and the Wall, soared down Fenchurch to pause at Dunster Court and finally hover over Mincing Lane.

"Hmmmm..."

The sky was moleskin black before the Wurm's thought left the airs above Mincing Lane. He could not see all clearly, his will was frustrated, but he knew his opponents were at home below.

"Machinations, plots and devisements...."

Nearby was another coney in its huddle, in the area of Pineapple Court, he thought, but the Wurm was doubly frustrated there—his thought could find no purchase, slipping and slitching around the flanks of an opacity he could not define.

"Nothing eludes me forever..."

He retrieved his winged thought into himself and turned from the window.

"The hunt is on," said the Wurm. "Here shall I gather my lieutenants. Except not the traitorous one, the one whose crimson coat I shall sear onto his body for all time when I find him. And find him I will."

The Wurm stretched his long, long arms and smiled with his razor-thin, deep-red lips. Even though his powers were greatly diminished in this world, encased in human flesh as he was, and needed to be, for entrance, his powers were nonetheless very great still. He relished the sense of cold empty force that flowed through his arms and out, like a bright ramifying darkness, into the space about him.

"A plan they have, the most preposterous and ridiculous project ever conceived—as worthy a piece of hubristic nonsense as I have seen since their forefathers sought to raise the city and its tower on the plains of Shinar. Hoo, hoom!"

He rubbed his long fingers together.

"The game is afoot. I shall call all my tribes of sullied santrels, pious imps, and minor mulcibers. Shamble forth noctambules and quasi-gorgons! Now is the time, tick tock tick tock."

His breath whistled and slurred. His teeth clacked.

"Come serpent-bearded Byatis and my wild-eyed Moriarty! To me, all you changelings, double-walkers, crafty men and conjure-wives."

Wurm shifted with precise and deliberate grace from one foot to the other, hunching his shoulders and thrusting his head forward and back in time to the clock.

"Tick tock, tick tock. I call the shoggoths and bear-ghasts, the gallows mannekin and *les dames blanches*. Arise Old Gammer Gurton and Saint Nycticorax, your time is at hand."

Wurm tapped his sharp nose with his fingers, licked his fingers with his rubaceous tongue.

"Hoo-HOOM! The game is afoot my lovelies!"

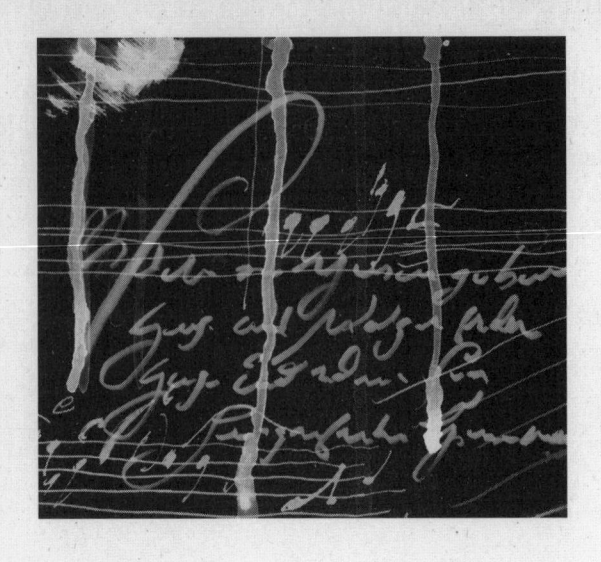

Interlude: Disjecta Membra

SUMMERWIRE & SON
HABERDASHERS AND PASSAMENTIERS TO THE GENTRY,
BOND STREET, LONDON

* **BILL OF CHARGE**, RENDERED WITH RESPECT THIS
second day after St. Adelsina
TO THE ESTEEMED
Mr. Barnabas McDoon, merchant   OF   Mincing Lane
PAYABLE WITHIN THIRTY DAYS OF RECEIPT,
FOR THE FOLLOWING ITEMS *delivered to Mr. McDoon*

One man's waistcoat, tailored, in fine lightweight Highland wool, with sherbasse silk facing, said in pale blue with a yellow floral pattern.

Idem, with a nankin silk facing, said in scarlet with a pale yellow brindille twig pattern.

Idem, with a calicosh pattern.

Idem, fawn brown in the style called acabellado.

One gentlewoman's head-scarf, watered silk, indigo, with white and black cross-hatching and mascles.

Upon St. Vanne's Recognition Day

Dear Lizzie:
Thank you for your letter of the 12th instant, which I have read multiple times. How much I long to see you and tell you what I can of all that has transpired over the past years. How much, dear Lizzie, I wish to hear all about your glorious new state, id est, your marriage (!) to this Mr. Darcy and your removal from Longbourne to his seat at Pemberley. I have heard much from your aunt and uncle, our old friends the Gardiners here in the City, but yearn to hear more and from your own lips.

Speaking of the Gardiners, they recommend that I speak with you also about a commercial project that involves them and the house of McDoon, and that they (or, as I should say, we) feel might be advantageous to you and your husband as well. I know that it is not normally considered an appropriate, let alone a decorous, thing for those of our sex to discuss, at least openly, matters of money and business, but—dear Lizzie—we know each other too well to adhere wholly or even in most part to such protocols. Say rather, that we might even delight explicitly in discussing such matters, since I am proud of being a merchant's niece and grown up in the trade and I know you have never been one to truckle to the opinions of others, especially in matters of pride and prejudice. At least that is how I recall your character, which I should be astonished (and dismayed) to find much changed since last we met and since your recent marriage—no matter how elevated your status may now be. Am I right in this?

The Gardiners mentioned that you might be in town in a fortnight's time, accompanied by your new sister-in-law (who sounds lovely—I am anxious to make her acquaintance, if that suits). If so, I insist that you visit with us, and for more than just a cup of tea! Let us regain our former familiarity and revel in confidences shared between us.

With much affection,
Your Sally

P.S. I may have cause—as part of this business I refer to above—to visit the West Country. It involves the procurement of "china clay," about which I can tell you more in person. I know that you—and your husband—may have reason to visit Bath from time to time;—if so, I could easily contrive to pass through that city in either direction, with the sole purpose of stopping to see you.

To Sir John Barrow, Second Secretary of the Admiralty,
to be delivered in person by Lt. Thracemorton
7th inst.

Sir, with respect and in utmost confidence:

Kidlington remains as glib and effusive as he was when first your man brought him to me, but under his pasquinades and fooleries runs a river of cankerous thought that bodes badly (in my opinion). If he be your tool, then be alert to which edge he applies towards you and your objectives, my lord.

Howsomever that might be, today I write primarily to confirm my letter of the 29th *ultimo*, *viz*. my concerns about possible attentions that Kidlington's activities may have attracted from dubious and insalubrious persons.

I will entrust some of my report directly and in unwritten form to Lieutenant Thracemorton (who has been exceeding competent in the discharge of his duties). For now, allow me only to say that:

a) Kidlington's old creditors, notwithstanding the full extinguishment and surcheance of all his debts (as you recall, we even had writs of decerniture issued in Edinburgh under Scottish law), clearly retain some interest in his affairs. Quilp, Merdle and others dog his steps, and Tulkinghorn has asked me also about Kidlington, which cannot augur well.

b) Yet odder names are also bandied about, many of them of foreign provenance—some of which those with long memories in London's commerce will recall with unease, *e.g.*, Coppelius, Prinn & Goethals (Widow).

Otherwise, on that other (but—I am confident—related) matter, the McDoons are taking many and concrete steps to launch, further and realize the Project, the general outline of which I described to you earlier. As I am their firm's and family's lawyer I fear I may soon come upon a severe conflict of interest, insofar as the Project is a private commercial matter, the details of which I could not in good faith reveal unless His Majesty's Government were to issue a decree so authorizing me to disclose such details, specifically commanding me in fact to do so, and waiving any and all liabilities I might incur or damages I might suffer and holding me harmless from any claims brought against me as a result of said disclosure.

I will write again as soon as fresh news comes to hand. Until then, I am your most obedient servant,

—Mr. Sedgewick, Esq.

From Sir John Barrow to Lord Melville,
First Secretary of the Navy

Memorial in greatest confidence,
on the first day after the Shad Moon.

My lord:
I recommend the Admiralty authorize an investment of ten thousand pounds sterling in the Project that is described fully in Special File 16, and that said investment be made through the Honourable East India Company, *i.e.*, in such a manner that the Admiralty's involvement is indiscernible by outsiders, as this is a matter of National Security.

Treasury will assuredly seek to deny the funding and quash this request, but can be overridden, as well you know. Enlist Lord Bathurst at the Colonial Office to ensure this—I know his Lordship often quarrels with you on issues of policy, especially when it relates to money, but in this instance I think there is common cause to be made against the parsimony of Treasury. Sir Tarleton can help you, if help you require.

My recommendation comes upon the reasoned review of trustworthy evidence brought forth by the Admiralty office responsible for Special File 16. The Admiralty's interest—financial, commercial and political—will be well safeguarded by said office. In turn, they have placed individuals under their control around the Project itself, so that we can be certain of timely, accurate and actionable intelligence.

I shall come to your chambers tomorrow afternoon with the requisite paperwork, on the assumption that you will be amenable to this request, based on our discussion in person yesterday and this morning.

Your estimable servant,
Sir John Barrow

DANIEL A. RABUZZI

[Excerpt from the Articles of Incorporation, Association Agreement, and Heads of Understanding and Consent, relating to the Ship <u>Indigo Pheasant</u>, to be built at Blackwall Yards, and owned by several parties as herein defined, as drawn up by Mr. Sedgewick, Esq. on behalf of McDoon & Co., acting as general partner, lead venturer and ship's husband]

Article 10. *Covenants Running with the Ship.*

All provisions of the Association Documents which are annexed hereto and made a part hereof, including, without limitation, the provisions of this Article, shall to the extent applicable and unless otherwise expressly herein or therein provided to the contrary, be perpetual and be construed to be covenants running with the Ship.

[... . . . .]

Article 17. *Partial or Preliminary Payment for Shares.*

A Partner may pay only a portion of his share in the Ship in cash money upon signing of the Articles of Incorporation and Association Documents, provided that the Partner pay at least one-half of his investment in cash money at that time. The balance of the Partnership investment to be made shall be made upon a series of events described and enumerated in Article 18 below, including the Laying Down of the Ship's Keel, the Final Equipage and Outfitting of the Ship, and the Launch of the Ship. The other Partners, in accordance with the governance and control protocols laid out in Article 8, shall also have the right (upon a majority vote) to demand accelerated and/or immediate payment of some or all of the outstanding Partnership investment balance unpaid.

[... . . . .]

Article 26. *Rights of Offerings and First Refusals.*

It is hereby agreed that each of the associating Partners (including, but not limited to, the General Partner), in the event that he wishes to sell any part of his share in the Ship (up to and including his full share), must first tender and offer his share to the remaining Partners, at a price that reflects prevailing market conditions, and that only in the event that (within sixty days) no market-prevalent price is forthcoming may the Partner desirous of selling offer his share in whole or in part to another party, that is, a party not already a Partner. Conversely, any Partner obtaining thirty-three and one-third pro centum of the entire outstanding ownership shares in the Ship will have the right to buy out the remaining Partners at a price consistent with the market for such ship shares as it currently exists at the time of so bidding.

[*Advertisement in the London Argus/ Commercial News and Price-Courant, during the Week of Meditrinalia, 1816*]

BE IT KNOWN TO ALL MEN, THAT THE *MATABRUNIAN CONGREGATION* HAS JOINED WITH THEIR SISTERS AND BROTHERS AMONG *LADY HUNTINGDON'S CONNECTION* TO EMBRACE THE PREACHER KNOWN AS *BILLY SEA-HEN* INTO THEIR MIDST, ALL THIS WEEK AT THEIR MEETINGHOUSES AT RESPECTIVELY THE *MULBERRY* IN *WAPPING*, NEAR THE *FINCH-HOUSE MEWS*, AND THE *THREE CRANES* IN *SHOREDITCH*, HARD BY *HOXTON SQUARE*. ALL ARE WELCOME. *NO* ADMISSION IS CHARGED.

Dear Family McDoon:
We bring you greetings from the Cape and the Last Cozy House, sent this 14th day of _____ aboard the East Indiaman *Lady Balcarras*.

[... . . . .]

We come now to the strangest news. Three Chinese persons are staying at the Cozy House, remarkable even for us. They are an emissary from the Emperor himself with two young wards (a girl and a young man). The emissary met Staunton and Barrow in '95 on the MacCartney expedition.

We cannot commit all we know about our Chinese guests to paper, for fear that Others might intercept this intelligence, but we want you to know that the Chinese know about Y. and seem to know something of the Project (at least the older gentlemen who leads them).

We think they are somehow important to the success of the Project. The girl is the key. She is a singer. A Singer, *comprenez-vous*? Please hear us when we say that you should include this girl as part of the Project. Sally will understand this best of all.

All of them enlighten and astonish us with their knowledge of mathematics and water-science and astronomy. They tell us that the Chinese have an encyclopedia beyond any our Diderot or Panckoucke have ever conceived, being 745 (!) volumes, called—as best we can write it in a European tongue—the "Goojin tooshoo zeechang." They say it contains references to Y!

The girl and her companions seem inclined to stay with us at the Cape for now, but we suggest they come to you in London in the next good sailing season, it being the kentering time now and so unsafe for the Indiamen on the London-bound voyage.

Send us word soonest, while the winds favour the outbound voyage to the Cape from London.

Until then, we are yours in amity,
—The Termuydens

[*Excerpt of a letter, on the Shad Moon, from Matchett in London to Frew doing business for the firm in Paris*]

Barnabas McD. was in rare form last night at the coffeehouse, had the company in good humour with his tales of the Cape. Sanford his usual laconic self. Something fishy in this, but all in good time, I reckon, and then we will learn the truth from the McD's or discover it for ourselves.

Curious news: do you recall the affair of the cunning man in Marylebone, back during the Peace of Amiens in '02 (the vicious Moriarty, how he pressed us)? More to the point, his confederates—the Leipzig firm of Coppelius, Prinn & Goethals the Widow? With peace again after Nap's fall, it would appear that Coppelius et al. have returned to London. They have opened a comptoir at Austin Friars near Blakensides.

I am more convinced than ever that this Prinn is a grand-nephew of the Ludwig P. who wrote *De vermis mysteriis*.

In nuco: hasten our business in Paris to its end, and return as soon as you may. We have work to do here.

As always, your...

On the Vigil of the Recrement,
by the morning post,
from Mrs. Sedgewick to the Miss Sarah:

My dearest Sally,
Words can barely express my pleasure at re-uniting with you since your return—seeing you these past weeks has raised my spirit beyond measure.

Speaking with you has piqued my curiosity as well, since you tell such amusing and marvelous stories of your time abroad, and yet I sense that you hold much back. Why withhold details from one of your closest friends, one who can guide and support you?

I have shared with you some of my premonitions and dreams, and I thank you for the courtesy you have paid in listening to me with sympathy—which is more than I ever get from Mr. Sedgewick, though I shouldn't complain.

Speaking of Mr. Sedgewick, and on a more convivial topic, I have persuaded His Old Badger-ness to hold a small rout, an *assemblée* (doesn't that sound more elegant in French!), on Thursday next to honour the McDoons upon your homecoming.

You will have discovered already my main goal, which is of course to bring you to the attention of select and attractive young men, with whom you *might*—if the flint reveals its spark!—form a liaison that *might* in due course blossom into something more lasting.

Don't blush or protest! You left us a girl and you have returned a young woman, and must needs be brought into society as best we can—despite all the drawbacks of your temperament (you have too much spirit!) and your education (you have far too much for any one of our sex!). Since you will have to attend such routs and ridottos regardless, where your temperament will be judged wanting and your education will be either dismissed or bevelled down, then you might as well attend one at the instigation and in the embrace of your closest friends—where we who love you can protect and steer you at least some little bit.

Besides, Sally dear, the best cover for your scholarly pursuits is that of an accommodating husband.

Also, to speak directly, I do not understand the dalliance you seem to have established with this Mr. Bammary whom you met on your travels. I do not dispute his impeccable manners and his learning—how could I, given his degree from Oxford? All in all, he is a pleasant enough fellow, almost a gentleman. Yet—and please do not think me forward here, I only think of your welfare, Sally, and what others might say against your reputation—he has the look of an Egyptian or a Hindoo and in the end he is no more an Englishman than you are an Indian. We must respect each other, of course, but the darker races can never be united with ours through the most intimate of relations, if you take my meaning. Think on it, Sally, and do not create in Mr. Bammary—or leastwise your self—hopes that can only be dashed here in London.

Returning to the party: who shall we have there? Your friends the Gardiners would make a suitable addition to the gathering, as well as those lively fellows from our mutual friends at Matchett & Frew—with their droll tales and maggots to match your own.

Also, through my sister's relation and Mr. Sedgewick's connections there, we shall have many naval officers and admiralty officials present.

Two in particular spring to mind, but I will not tell you their names, so as to tease you and arouse in you the intellectual curiosity for which you are best known, thus to lure you out of your books and to the party. One is a lieutenant who fought in Wellington's Army of the Peninsula; frankly, he is a bit on the morose side, but could—I am quite sure—be tempted out of his lugubrious ways under steady feminine influence.

The other is a most peculiar yet wholly charming individual, recently returned from Australia (of all places!), who is clerking for Mr. Sedgewick. He—the young man, not Mr. S.—is trim and well-made, cutting a fine figure and clever in his speech. Mr. S. tells me that there is more to this young man than meets the eye, a mystery of unbalanced ballast beneath his painted sails—

if Mr. S. means to warn me off then his words have had the opposite effect.

So, there is my plot revealed—mischief I am crafting to benefit my young friend, meaning you, Sally.

Please accept this invitation, which I shall follow up tomorrow with a formal letter to your uncle and the rest of your household.

I had a quote to share with you from a poem by the newcomer, Mr. Keats, but now it has gone straight out of my head, and they will collect the morning post at any second, so I must postpone our Keatsian conversation until later.

In haste, your ever affectionate
—Shawdelia Sedgewick

P.S. We have gotten a real pianoforte since you left. I will teach you all the new airs and melodies—it won't do for you still to be singing "Lillibullero" and "Stepney Cakes and Ales" etc. from the last century! And the latest dances, though I know you dislike dancing, still you must do so if only to avoid the censure of a chattering public.

P.P.S. Hoping the weight of your brother's absence is not too heavy to bear. Will remember to honour him with a toast at our *soirée*. Post here, must go.

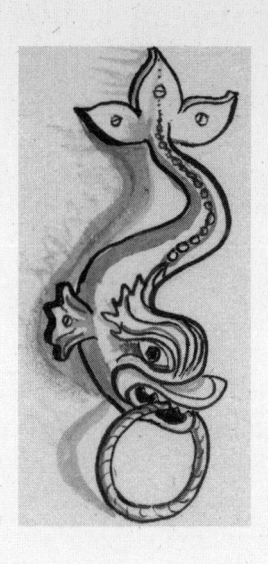

Chapter 2: Many Meetings, or, A Long, Exact, and Serious Comedy

"O charming Noons! and Nights divine!
Or when I sup, or when I dine,
My Friends above, my Folks below,
Chatting and laughing all-a-row,
The Beans and Bacon set before 'em,
The Grace-cup serv'd with all decorum:
Each willing to be pleas'd and please,
And even the very Dogs at ease!"
—**Alexander Pope**, *An Imitation of the Sixth Satire of the Second Book of Horace*, lines 133-140 (1737)

"A man shall . . . sin, by which, contrary to all the workings of humanity, he shall ruin for ever the deluded partner of his guilt;—rob her of her best dowry; and not only cover her own head with dishonour,—but involve a whole virtuous family in shame and sorrow for her sake."
—**Laurence Sterne**, *The Life and Opinions of Tristam Shandy, Gentleman*, vol. II, chap. xvii (1760)

"Insensate doth the dreamer drift
Upon dark Lethe's course,
While song immense from angel-choirs
Whelms vast-flung night, rings swift oblivion's source."
—**Charles Oldmixon**,
The Caliper'd Heart, lines 121-124 (1774)

"Figs and fiddles! Sedgewick and wife have outdone themselves this evening, I must say!" Barnabas said to himself, as he surveyed for the third—or was it, fourth?—time the spread of food before him.

"A knuckle of veal, a ham the size of a house (what a prodigious pig that must have been!), pies full of larks and woodcocks and other wingy little birds," he chuckled. "Eels and burbots, pikelets, tench and trouts! Turtle soup, oh my, oh my. A forced hare. More kinds of beef and mutton than I can name, though 'tis a damnable shame to drown honest English roasts under so many sauces. What is this one?"

He bent down to read the calligraphied card, folded like a miniature tent, set before the dish. Mrs. Sedgewick had missed no detail in preparing her rout to celebrate the return of the McDoons.

"*Les cotelettes d'agneau glacées à la Toulouse*. Well, I'll call it a lamb-chop in onion-butter, I will, and will make short work of it no matter what it calls itself!"

As he ate, he thought, "I wonder that we won the war at all, since everything has become so very French. Once upon a time we called a duck a "duck," but now we must call it a "moularde." And whatever happened to the green bean—poor fellow, now he must answer to "haricot vert." Truly, you'd think that old Nappy was at St. James, and not King George!"

Barnabas turned his attentions now to the desserts.

"I love Yount," he thought. "But I must confess I have so dearly missed sweets. A singular lack, that, in Yount, there being no sugar, just the odd dab of honey. Oh my, figs and farthings, what have we here?"

He stood transfixed before heaps of oiled almonds, peels of candied lemon, golden currants, slabs of marchpain, creamy dariendoles, a great syrupy pulpatoon, a *croque-en-bouche aux pistaches*, pralines, glazed biscuits, an enormous Nesselrode Pudding topped with a froth of whipped cream, . . . all gleaming and glistening in the gas-light (the Sedgewicks being among the first to adopt the new form of illumination), beckoning, alluring with a seeming life of their own.

His satisfaction was complete, nay, overwhelmed and utterly unbayed, when he came upon the selection of port, sherry, Madeira, claret and wine surrounding a most estimable punch bowl.

"Oh Sedgewick, you have sailed clear beyond the Pillars of Hercules this night!" he said. "A most noble punch-bowl. Why, 'tis large enough to launch a ship in; indeed, I believe I detect a tide! Now, then, what about these bottles? No thin, washy stuff here, oh ho! Why here is, no it cannot be? It *is*! A bottle of Cahors, you remembered my old favourite."

Cradling the Cahors (near impossible to secure in England during the Napoleonic blockade), its contents the thick, deep red of bull's blood, Barnabas considered the rest of the crowd.

"Matchett looks very well," he thought. "Nice brandy-coloured stockings, I must ask where he got them. And Gardiner, whose niece just married that Pemberley lord in Derbyshire, also nicely turned out—isabelline and vinegar rose, I'd call it, that cravat of his."

Barnabas turned so that his bretticoed vest in pale blue silk could be seen to best effect in the gas-light.

"I must ask Sanford tomorrow how soon we can get the gas installed," he thought. "Wonderful how it shows the colours!"

Young and old, men and women filled the rooms at the Sedgewicks: bankers, lawyers, clerks, 'prentices, chandlers, naval officers, excise-men;—in the words of the song, "travellers, tapsters, merchants, and upstart gentlemen." Gaiety prevailed. Banished by common if unspoken consent were all thoughts of the recent riots about the Corn Laws, the furor over Catholic

Emancipation and the Irish Question, corsairs along the coasts of Barbary and Tremissa, or the volcanic eruptions in the Water Indies that had played such havoc with shipping between China and India. No one spoke of politics or war, of want or weather (so unseasonably cold and wet). Instead all and everyone talked of fashion and romance, of the new lotteries (especially the big one just established by the Confraternity for Saints Vanne & Hydulphe), of the Crown Prince's latest indiscretions and his wronged wife the Queen-in-Waiting Caroline, of the latest adventures of Dr. Syntax on his doughty horse, the most recent plays at Covent Garden, the likelihood of ripe strawberries from Kent before St. Macrina's Day, and a thousand other frivolities.

When they tired of talk, they sang songs of fair maidens and coxcombs, of drunken livery-men and pert chambermaids, of Tibbert the Cat, of children shantled off by the fairies, of saucy wives and their husbands who stayed too long in the tavern, of Robin Goodfellow and the jealous moon, the King's arms and Britannia, of the fall of Napoleon and the exploits of Sharpe in Spain and Lucky Jack Aubrey on the Main. When they tired of singing, they danced the "Orange-Blossom Water" and the "Ranelagh Trifle" and so many others that Barnabas quite lost count.

"Tum tum de dum!" half-sang Barnabas, as he enjoyed the Cahors. "I like that one: 'Bate me an ace, Morrison old jack, bate me an ace!'"

His already mountainous love for all mankind now elevated to Olympian heights by the meat and the many desserts and, above all, by the punch and the Cahors, Barnabas sought among the convivial fellowship for his family.

"Where has Sanford gotten himself off to?" he said. "Ah, there he is, solemn as ever, talking with Sedgewick in a corner. Looks suspiciously like business. I must upbraid them both. Later."

Spying an unusual figure in the throng, carrying dishes back to the kitchen, Barnabas thought, "That must be the new servant the Sedgewicks have employed, the young black woman. Not much the normal thing anymore, having a black servant, I wonder that they do so, though Mrs. Sedgewick has never been one for the proprieties. Sedgewick himself, now, what is it he said about this young woman? Something strange about her, I think."

Before he could remember what Sedgewick had said about the girl, Barnabas heard—or sensed, rather—a commotion from the entrance-hall, like the dull roar of a wave striking shore.

"Merry as grigs are we, dum de dum de dum," he said. "But where might Sally be? And her Reglum?"

He made his way to the entrance-hall, greeting along the way a naval bureaucrat he vaguely knew ("one of the Tarletons who married into Mrs. Sedgewick's side," he thought) and also a Turkey-merchant he recognized from the coffee-houses.

Pushing his way into the entrance-hall, Barnabas said, "Figs and . . . oh!"

James Kidlington stood in front of the door.

Sally was leaning against Reglum, her mouth working but producing no words, her eyes two lakes of despair streaked with hope. Reglum had one arm around her shoulders. He shifted his gaze from Sally to Kidlington and back again.

Mrs. Sedgewick stood between and a little to the side of the two and the one.

"I, I, this is . . . ," she said. "This is the surprise, Sally, the one I told you I would . . . oh my, oh dear, a surprise it surely is, but not of the kind I wanted!"

"Allow me," said Kidlington, "to rescue this unforeseen moment, if I may. Sally, we must thank our mutual benefactress, Mrs. Sedgewick, for her hospitality. She invited, I accepted, and here I am."

He stepped forward and took one of Sally's nerveless hands, raised it to his lips and left the faintest of kisses before releasing it.

"At your service," he said.

Still Sally said no word. A wave coursed through her entire body, starting with the impression of Kidlington's lips on her hand.

Reglum felt that tremor. Tightening his grip on her shoulders, he half-stepped forward, extended his free hand to Kidlington and said,

"I am Reglum Bammary."

Kidlington took Bammary's hand, shook it once, twice, and then released.

"James Kidlington, your humble servant, sir," said Kidlington, raising one eyebrow. "Mrs. Sedgewick has spoken of you. A member of our Anglo-Indian elite I gather, a scion of the John Company."

Reglum neither nodded nor spoke.

"Buttons and beeswax!" broke in Barnabas. "James! James Kidlington, here in London, free and knotless. Well, boy, out with it, tell us your story! Wait, ho, Sanford . . . someone get Sanford, he must hear this as well!"

Kidlington told them a version of events, abridging it severely. He did not mention the angular gentlemen at the Admiralty at all.

Sally heard none of it.

"James," she thought. "I hate you. Hate. Leave. Leave now. Why? Oh James. Not you, James. A wind. Wind in my heart, a storm. Oh Goddess, I love this man. Please, make him leave. Now. Make him. . . . Oh James, what did they do to you? In that place. Australia! As bad as the. . . . Jambres would understand. He has been in such chambers as you. No, no. Reglum! (—) Help me. Reglum (—), dear sweet Reglum. By my side. Always steady. We read Akenside together, we do. 'Inspire attentive fancy,' you like that line, my Reglum. 'the lark cheers warbling,' oh, 'whose daring thoughts range the full orb of being, . . . the radiant visions,' . . . I cannot remember more . . . 'the radiant visions where they rise' . . . something, 'through the gates of morn, to lead the train of Phoebus' . . . But no more. . . . James (—) is back from the dead . . . a revenant. Flee him, flee him. . . Mother, mother, Saints Macrina, Adelsina . . . help me: I need James . . . but he will devour me. . . . Saint Morgaine . . . And there's Reglum . . . who fought with us in Yount. . . . He loves Tom and Afsana. . . .

THE INDIGO PHEASANT *Volume Two of Longing for Yount*

He.... Oh, the Fraulein:... Reglum tried to help.... And with Dorentius too.... I.... Tom! You know me best of all.... What do I do?... Are you alive or dead, yourself? What of Afsana?... Death, death, death.... Dear Uncle... and best of Sanfords.... You know... you know me from my acornage.... Save me.... Now I am ruined, my love all unfenced.... Fly, fly, all of us, from..."

"... doom," finished Kidlington. "An escape from doom, but perhaps God and the Devil conspired to bring me to this pass... A colossal jest, I just wonder who gets to laugh in the end?"

The circle of listeners had grown, including now many who had no deep connection to the McDoons. Kidlington's tale being as dashing and improbable as any of the adventures they had sung earlier in the evening, and his manner of telling it so bold yet self-deprecating, the audience was moved to clap and cheer at the story's conclusion.

"Why, Sally, you cry," said Mrs. Sedgewick. "I hope you are moved by something other than melancholy? Oh dear, oh dear, I thought... from how you spoke in your letters from the Cape... about... Please, I did not mean to startle you with Mr. Kidlington, only to, oh foolish me, appeal to your finer sentiments...."

Mrs. Sedgewick petered out. Her husband's smile was thin ("dearest dove, look what your cogibundity has resulted in now," he thought). Sanford studied Kidlington carefully.

"Uncle," said Sally. "I fear it is late... Please take me home. Reglum, Mr. Sanford."

Kidlington, without even the shadow of a smile on his face, addressed himself to Sally.

"Miss Sarah," he said, his voice low and, if one were standing very close to hear, chafed as if with a surge of emotion barely restrained. "I—and you must know this, Sally—I truly did not mean to alarm you. My way back here has been strenuous, unanticipated, wholly in the hands of a capricious deity.... My pardon, Mr. Bammary, I do not mean to intrude.... Clearly my presence is not pleasant to you, so I will withdraw and not trouble you further. Good evening, and also to you Mr. McDoon, Mr. Sanford . . . and to you, Mr. Bammary."

The party continued its vivacious course, all the more so for the many who believed the episode with Mr. Kidlington to be just another of the eccentric entertainments planned by Mrs. Sedgewick, but a tumultuous pall had settled upon the McDoons, who made to leave just minutes after James's departure.

"Sally, sweet friend, I miscalculated and I am heartily sorry for that," whispered Mrs. Sedgewick.

"You could not know," said Sally. "At least, not in full."

The McDoons left. No one—not the McDoon party, not the Sedgewicks—noticed that, silent on the periphery of the audience in the entrance hall, Maggie had stood listening to every word of the exchange with Kidlington. Late into the night, as she washed dishes in the kitchen long after all the guests had left and the Sedgewicks retired to bed, Maggie mulled the tale told by Kidlington. Mostly she considered what she felt was missing in what she had heard.

"*Chi di*," she murmured to herself, all alone except for the battery of pans and utensils. "Kidlington is a puzzle—there's a much larger story just below the surface of his fine words. I sense the mark of the Owl on him, and also something else. The McDoon woman, she too is full of mystery—I know her, I think. She is the white one who sings."

The lone gas-light sputtered. Maggie looked at her face, distorted and blurred, in the depths of a copper pot.

"Tonight were many meetings, not all of them acknowledged by those who met, *selah*," she yawned. "Bammary is no Indian, that I would wager. Mrs. Sedgewick all out of words—a rare thing, never saw that before. Her husband, the little . . ."

Maggie jabbed at the bottom of the pot.

". . . the *fat* little *weasel*, oh yes, he sees much more than he says, or says much but never about the things he wants to hide."

Dawn was not far off when Maggie finished. The four hours of sleep she would be allowed were all the more precious for being so few.

"Sally is the girl, the one with the cat, the golden cat in the window," she said just before sleep came. "One of the six I need, the engine needs—with me, that's seven. 'For who hath despised the day of small things? for they shall rejoice, and shall see the plummet in the hand of Zerubbabel with those seven; they are the eyes of the Lord, which run to and fro through the whole earth.' Oh Mama, the Book speaks truth exactly. And we women, we must be as strong as elephants."

"Buttons and beeswax," said Barnabas. "That was a right ra-tat-too last night, meeting Kidlington like that! I don't think I could take two such blows in a lifetime."

Barnabas sat with Sanford in the partners' room in the house on Mincing Lane, taking tea on the afternoon after the party at the Sedgewicks. Everyone had slept late. No one had seen Sally yet, though the Cook had been up to the attic room and left a tray of tea and buttered buns.

"Is Sally going to be alright, do you think?" said Barnabas.

"She will withstand the initial shock," said Sanford. "More lasting effects, of that we cannot yet say."

"Hmmm, I fear you are correct, old friend," said Barnabas, helping himself to another cone of sugar for his tea.

The two sat for a while in the wonted silence of partners, punctuated by the clinks of spoons on teacups and the impartial ticking of the clock on the mantlepiece. Barnabas savoured the smell of the sandalwood box, and let his sight roam over the prints of Rodney defeating the French and of Diana pursuing Actaeon. Sanford looked at the prints of the East Indiamen submerging, reassuring himself that no such shipwreck was imminent for McDoon & Co. Yikes—ageless hound, who seemingly had not moved in all the days and months of their absence—slept by the fireplace, snoring slightly. (Chock the parrot had died while the McDoons had been in Yount). All was as it should be in the house with the blue door and dolphin-knocker on Mincing Lane.

The clock chimed four, echoed at various distances by church bells around the City.

"I say, Sanford, that is four o'clock just gone, and no Sedgewick," said Barnabas. "You said he was coming at four, I distinctly heard you say that, though I won't hold it against him, not after that splendid tarra-ma-do last night, and particularly the bottle of Cahors."

At that moment, the maid opened the door and announced Mr. Sedgewick.

"Gentlemen, as scheduled, as promised," said the lawyer. "Speaking of Cahors, dear Barnabas, I have brought you a second bottle—a little something to accompany your supper this evening!"

"Most esteemed of colleagues and most capital of men," said Barnabas. "All forgiven, or rather, nothing to forgive you for! Now, sit, and let us talk more about the Project. For one thing, we have finally named it, the ship that is. We shall call her *The Indigo Pheasant*. Was Sally who hit upon it, clever girl. So, anyway, you can insert the name into the Articles of Association and all the other legal papers. What, is there something wrong with that name?"

Sedgewick had begun to shake his head about halfway through Barnabas's statement.

"No, no, that's not it," said Sedgewick. "*Indigo Pheasant* is a perfectly good name. I rather like it in fact, has a cavalier ring. Certainly unusual, without lacking respectability. Strong yet unassuming. I will duly record the name wherever it needs recording. No, nothing to do with the name of the ship."

"Well, what then? I know that shake of the head and those pursed lips, you have something difficult to divulge. Come on then, after the eye-opener with Kidlington yesterday, I do not believe there is much you could tell us that could surprise us further."

Sedgewick coughed, the polite sort of cough lawyers use just before they deliver portentous and usually unpleasant news. Sanford made a burring noise in his throat at the same time.

"Ah, figs and feathers, I knew it, you are unmasked the both of you," said Barnabas. "I saw you two up to some sort of commercial conversation at the rout yesterday, I did—'a conspiracy,' that's what I called it, and now I am proven right. Come on then, out with it."

"Kidlington's news—that is, the news that *is* Kidlington, his resurrection and return and perambulations amongst us—is most definitely an eye-opener," said Sedgewick. "But you must brace yourself for an even greater revelation than that, friend Barnabas."

Sedgewick pushed aside his tea cup, opened the satchel sitting between his feet, and brought forth a pile of tawny, flecked and dog-eared papers.

"Barnabas, what I told Sanford last night, is that I need to talk to you today about something other than the Project. Something even more important—yes—and assuredly more needful of prudential action, the discretion of Caesar's wife, the caution of the most cautious enterpriser in murky waters."

Barnabas sat back, mystified.

"Pray proceed," he said.

"Did you happen to notice our new serving girl last night, the black one?" said Sedgewick.

Nothing Sedgewick could say could have nonplussed Barnabas more. In fact, had Sedgewick inquired as to the likelihood of parrots standing for parliament or asserted that the Man on the Moon was coming down for dinner that very evening, Barnabas would have been no more flummoxed.

"I, well, yes," he said. "But what on earth does that have to do with anything, with anything at all?"

"A great deal, I am afraid," said Sedgewick. "There being no nice way to express this, I will come simply to the facts. I believe my Africk serving girl is your first cousin once removed, Barnabas, which thus makes her second cousin to Sally and Tom."

"I . . ." said Barnabas, stroking his vest (snuff-coloured, with dashes of Zoffany red). "Beans and *bacon* . . ."

"Start at the beginning, Mr. Sedgewick," said Sanford.

"While you were away, I had some adventures of my own, if I may call them that," said Sedgewick, closing his eyes. "Nothing as brash or brawny as what I presume you endured, *certes*, but nevertheless picaresque enough to disturb the equilibrium of my small, lawyerly world. Among other things, a bailiff of Edinburgh's courts delivered to me the last will and testament of—be staunch again, Barnabas, here comes another shock—of your mother, Belladonna McDoon, born Brownlee."

Barnabas stood up, so great was his excitement, nearly overturning his tea cup and the slops-bowl.

"Yes, yes, I know," said Sedgewick, opening his eyes. "I should have told you earlier but it has been ridiculously hard, even for me, to bring myself to the point. Three times I wrote letters to you on the subject, and thrice I tore them up as being inadequate to the task. I deemed it best to reveal all this in person—and of that judgment I remain convinced, especially now that I see your reaction. Sanford, it was, who cemented my resolve, in the brief conversation you observed us conducting at yestereve's assembly."

Sanford poured more tea for Barnabas and said, "To the point now, Sedgewick, to the most acute point you can make of it."

"Indeed," said the lawyer. "I will leave for you both the will itself and all the other papers I received; it will take you a while to encompass their entire meaning. But this afternoon, allow me to guide us through the most strange and brocaded of their contents, namely, the events Belladonna relates about her sister."

"My aunt?" said Barnabas. "The Old McDoon never, ever talked about her, his wife, who died long ago. Some sort of scandal, all hushed up, but my uncle was harsh on absolutely everyone . . ."

"Eusebianna McDoon," said Sedgewick. "Born Brownlee. Two sisters who married two brothers. Less common now than it was then, but still no seldom thing. Two Brownlees becoming two McDoons."

THE INDIGO PHEASANT *Volume Two of Longing for Yount*

Sanford stood, walked to the window with teacup in hand, watching the traffic on Mincing Lane as Sedgewick unreeled the story.

"The two sisters were very close to one another, and united it seems in the odd rumours that swirled about them. Barnabas, I will not yield to superstition, but the statements contained in these papers defy my most reasoned approach. What is clear is that the good burghers of Edinburgh saw the Brownlee sisters as witches, hard as that is to countenance or explain."

"I have heard something about that, but not while I was a boy," murmured Barnabas.

"Yes, well, allegations of witchcraft and intercourse with the fairies have never done women any good, not even in this enlightened age. Yet that amounts to no more than relics of a bygone time, a curiosity for the antiquarians. There the matter would rest and have no further concern for you, Barnabas, and the House of McDoon such as it is today, were it not for another matter altogether—assuming the two are not somehow linked in ways obscure."

Sedgewick pulled out a paper.

"This is a long essay, or memorial, written by your mother, dated not long before she died," he said. "Listen well:

'I come now to <u>delicate and disturbing matters</u> that I must commit to paper, as I am the only one who knows the unadorned truth. I write this to honour the memory, and above all the actions, of my beloved sister Eusebianna, and I do so knowing that few will believe what I tell, and those who believe will repudiate the tale and call me liar and worse.

I have absolutely not the least doubt that her husband will deny every word I write and will seek to have my words exposed to the most horrid forms of obloquy, if he can not have them obliterated altogether by the Court or other means that may come to his disposal. I beg the Court not to allow this to happen, i.e., to ensure instead that my statement be entered into the judicial record. In the end, all we have is our <u>honour</u> and the <u>trust of those who love us</u>; so says the

Psalmist and likewise Seneca, Marcus Aurelius and many other of the Ancients.

Sibby—for so I called her all her life, as she called me Belle—travelled with her husband, the merchant Anthony Macarius McDoon, to what was then the colony of Maryland in America, in the last years before the rebellion that created the United States. My brother-in-law had business interests there, relating to his import of tobacco, and centred on his quarter-share in the Blair Plantation at the confluence of the Choptank River and the Chesapeake Bay, in the area the colonials called 'the Eastern Shore.'

The two, having married only months before they sailed from Scotland, settled in rooms within the plantation house (the McDoons being related on their mother's side to the Blairs). Sibby wrote me eight letters during the initial part of their time there, which I have preserved as being my property (and clearly my sister's intent was that they should be and remain so in perpetuity, no matter what my brother-in-law has alleged and attempted via this Court);—I attach all eight as adjuncts to this memorial.

What Sibby described in her eight letters veers between her extreme pleasure at the landskip, the bird-life, and the beauty of the foliage and flowers (which are apparently of a lushness and richness unknown to us in Scotland), and her equally advanced displeasure at what she called the 'debilitating nature of human relations' that she witnessed on the plantation. 'Slavery written about by its apologists or commented upon by merchants, jurists and political men, disconnected and at a distance from the reality of the situation, bears no resemblance to the degradation, the inimical bonds placed upon human beings, that I saw with my own eyes' is what Sibby wrote to me; she then proceeded to document all she could in her ensuing missives.

She disagreed openly and violently with her husband about this state of affairs, and sought to have him sell his share in the plantation and withdraw entirely from the tobacco trade. He was furious with his new wife for her temerity, not least in front of his friends and colleagues, who belittled and tarrowed him without cease about his ill-tempered and illogical spouse. He forbade her to talk about such things in any public place, and he commanded her to discontinue her conversation with the slaves, which was widely remarked upon in the neighbourhood as unfitting for any white woman and especially for the wife of one of the owners.

Sibby, of course, obeyed her husband in neither of these respects (for, if she had, there would never have been a tale to tell, much less the many court proceedings), and their marriage was clearly in a deeply troubled way already, when she took the step that ultimately proved fatal to her reputation and so much more.

In her second letter already she mentioned for the first time meeting an extraordinary slave, someone unlike any other on the plantation or any other person—free or slave—of Sibby's acquaintance. He was what they on the plantation called a 'house slave,' which meant he was employed in the capacity we in Great Britain would recognize as that of a butler or head-servant. Most unusually for a slave (but we shall come to this soon) he could both read and write. He was only a few years older than Sibby and his name was Abubaker Ba—I have spelled it as Sibby did, though I do not believe there is any standard or required way to do so, at least in English.

Mr. Ba (and I will honour him with the title) was born in Africa, of the Fulbay, also known as the Fulani, people;—he was a Mahomettan. In these two aspects, he was highly distinct from the other Africans on the plantation, since they were all Eboes, a people near the coast, who are not followers of Mahomet. Not only was he a Mahomettan, he was one of their great teachers, having been a tutor (to use the closest proximation in our tongue) at what he called the University of Sankor in the city of Timbuktoo, which he said is near a great river in the desert very far from the coast.

My sister believed him, and I see no reason to doubt her faith in Mr. Ba. I know that no white person has seen Timbuktoo and that many believe it to be legendary, like the caves of Serendib or the gardens of Prester-John. Yet the fact that *we* have not seen it is not *prima facie* proof that *it* does not in fact exist; I would rather say that Mr. Ba's voluminous and very detailed account to my sister—which she in turn wrote down assiduously in her letters to me—is deserving of far more acceptance as proof and evidence than otherwise.

Mr. Ba told Sibby that he had been captured in a war with a rival kingdom, called Bambara, and sent down the great river to Calabar, from whence he was added to a cargo of Eboes being shipped to Maryland. When she met him he had been in Maryland for six years, long enough to have mastered the English language, which Sibby said he spoke with great ease and grace, using turns of phrase that most speakers born to the tongue do not conceive or use.

Her final letters to me suggested an increasingly close form of intercourse with Mr. Ba. Sibby spent more and more time with Mr. Ba, as much as they could find in a small place where eyes and ears were at all times primed for transgressions of any sort, especially when it came to relations between the whites and the blacks, the free and the slave.

According to Sibby, they spoke of many things: the stars and the planets, the possibility of other worlds, the likelihood that laws might be universal for all men. He was a mathematician and an astronomer. The two would slip away at night to watch the stars, along the banks of the Chesapeake.

No letters came from Sibby after her eighth; I became very anxious and sent many letters to her and to my brother-in-law to ascertain her well-being. Almost a year passed before I received any news, which was only a short note from my brother-in-law that they were sailing for Edinburgh and to make ready.

Sibby was changed out of all features when she arrived, disjacketed, despondent, *déboîtée*. I scarce recognized her for the gay sister whom I once knew so well. My brother-in-law allowed us only the briefest of reunions and thereafter he had as little to do with me as possible. As the Court knows, Sibby died within two years of her return; of grief and anguish I say.

Just before she died, she wrested from her husband several hours of time to be alone with me privately. In those few, precious hours, as she neared her end, she told me all that had happened, which I now relate.

She and Mr. Ba had become <u>lovers</u>—there is no other way to say it. She knew and I know that such behaviour (the pastors have many words for it, 'adultery' being the least of those) is contrary to all our moral and legal codes. It was the same for Mr. Ba, whose Mahomettan faith likewise prohibits such congress between individuals who are not married to one another. Yet, no matter how keenly the two felt remorse for their sin, they felt much more keenly <u>the purity of their love</u> for one another, a love born from the felicitous intertwinement of their minds as they naturally conversed about matters of mutual interest. I say they loved each other, as men and women have loved one another since the Beginning. If that is a wrong thing, then they will each suffer judgement and penalty as they stand before their <u>Creator</u>; let no other than the Creator be their judge.

Alas, their Creator was not their sole judge. Sibby became with child and when she could no longer hide this state, her husband realized it could not be his (he not having had carnal relations with his wife recently enough) and became devoured of an evil anger, 'his brow dark with hot climates.' Rumour enough there was to lead her husband to Mr. Ba.

My brother-in-law had his vengeance <u>in full</u>. He had Mr. Ba gelded and otherwise mutilated in front of an audience (all within his rights according to the laws of Maryland), before having Mr. Ba put to death.

Sibby most forcefully insisted that I promise to note this next, to convey the full depth and gravity of her husband's conduct, that—as is customary in the American plantations—all members of the community were required to attend the torments in audience. Even at the Gallowlee near Calton Hill or at London's Tyburn, those attending come of their own accord; none are <u>compelled</u> as Sibby was to watch the rending death of a beloved.

Sibby also wanted it known that—again as is commonplace on the American plantations—the deceased's teeth were extracted from his head and used to make dentures, in this case for the merchant McDoon himself.

When the baby was born, my brother-in-law had it taken immediately from Sibby's arms, not five minutes old, and given to the slave-women in the rude dwellings behind the main plantation house. As soon as Sibby was recovered enough to travel, my brother-in-law took her and returned to Scotland. Sibby, of course, <u>never saw her baby again</u> and I have been blocked in all my efforts to gain any further intelligence of the child, whether she be alive or dead, etc.

Here the story stops; I have no more to say, but am relieved and enheartened to have it writ down so that <u>the Truth</u> be aired and now archived.

<u>In final conclusion</u>, I confirm what I have made explicit in my fully executed last will and testament, namely, that I—Belladonna Eulalia McDoon, born Brownlee—do recognize the existence of my niece, the only daughter of my sister Eusebianna Eudelma McDoon, born Brownlee, by whatever appellation this daughter may have received or currently bear, and wheresoever my niece may be, and in whatever situation she may find herself. Furthermore, *in absentia* but having the full force of our law, I declare, recognize and embrace my niece, and any children or grandchildren she may have or will have, to be among my heirs, and I morever direct, instruct and require that my already indicated heirs, being my son and my daughter, to likewise recognize and embrace my niece and any children and grandchildren she may have, as being co-heirs with all rights attached thereto.'"

Sedgewick handed the paper to Barnabas.

"Sanford," said Barnabas. "This explains so much. . . ."

"Yes, as I listened I saw your uncle the day he refused your suit for Rehana," said Sanford.

"And then he flung you out of the house, honest Sanford, for your support of my declaration," said Barnabas.

"You are not your uncle," said Sanford, putting his hand lightly on Barnabas's shoulder.

"Thank you, old friend, but now to you Sedgewick: a painful if important piece of McDoon family lore, but I see as yet no connection to your serving maid."

Sanford broke in before the lawyer could respond, "Wait, wait. Let us use the girl's name? How is she called?"

"Maggie Collins," said Sedgewick. "And with her name our tale continues. I did not start to wonder about her provenance only when the Belladonna's papers came to me. No, I felt something was amiss with her, Maggie, when my wife brought her to us. Perhaps the story rightly begins with her, with my wife that is, *ma petite calebasse*, whose whims I am long resigned to, and so I had no more than desultory quibbles when she announced the arrival of the dark-skinned Maggie."

Sedgewick stood up, his belly caparisoned in a carpish-yellow waist-coat, his neck looped with a glaucous green cloth. He went to inspect the porcelain figurines on the mantlepiece.

"Gentlemen, I was convinced this whole thing was a tale of a tub, a wobbly nonsense," Sedgewick said, his back to Barnabas and Sanford. "But there is an uncanny element to that girl, a set of abilities she exhibits *sub rosa* that I have seen myself and—am forced I tell you, not to my liking!—to own are real. Maggie possesses an extremely developed faculty for mathematics. Hard as it is to credit, she is capable of the calculus, beyond what I can achieve myself or in fact what most anyone outside of Woodhouse and Babbage could aspire to. That makes her a freak, but a potentially useful freak."

"Yes, I can see how that might upset you," said Barnabas, leaning over to pet Yikes. "I sometimes feel that way about Sally and she is my own niece!"

"How does Maggie's mathematical skill tie her to the McDoons?" said Sanford, pouring more tea.

"Ah, you are right, I divagate," said the lawyer, turning from the fireplace to face the other two. "Her obvious intelligence, coupled with her obstinate and porpentine nature, prompted me to wonder as to her origins. So, as a diversion from my daily rounds of legal lucubrations, I inquired at the place from whence Mrs. Sedgewick hailed her, that is, at the Saint Macrina's School. A greasy little person there informed me that Maggie and her mother arrived on a ship from New York, and that it appeared they had taken their surname from that of the ship's captain. I thought that interesting, in an idle sort of way, but there I let the matter dangle . . . until I received the Belladonna papers."

Barnabas said, "A hunch, then?"

"Yes," said Sedgewick. "A hunch, a presentiment, *suspicio tenuissima*. No clear and evident connection, but the more I read of the Scottish court papers, the more I felt there might be some link. Reading about the African mathematician kept reminding me of Maggie. In any case, I found Captain Collins, now retired in Rotherhithe, who easily recalled Maggie and her mother. He had seen a fair few black sailors in his day, of course, but not many black females aboard ship, especially as paying passengers. That led me to the port-records in the Pool of London, where I discovered that their passage had been paid in part by a person named Weatherby and his confreres in the Free Abyssinian Church in New York."

"Bit between the teeth, old boy, bit between the teeth," said Barnabas.

"No denying it," said Sedgewick. "I used connections at Thomas Wilson & Co. to track down 'Weatherby' and the church in New York, which was soon done. Church members told Wilson's agent that Maggie and her mother had come as fugitive slaves, together with Maggie's father, from Maryland. Someone said the words that set all the pieces in place: 'Blair Plantation.'"

"Beans and bacon," said Barnabas.

"I paid Wilson's man to go to Blair on the Choptank (marvelous names they have in the New World!). Under various pretenses, he gleaned the outlines of the story that Eusebianna told Belladonna. One of his informants said the capstone word: 'McDoon.' The dates and ages all work out. There can be no doubt. Maggie's maternal grandfather was an African savant, from Timbuktu no less; her maternal grandmother was your aunt, Sibby McDoon. Q.E.D."

"Does she know?" said Sanford.

"No, but I think she suspects something—she is unholy sharp-witted, has what I should call 'forward-looking peripheral vision.' The real question before us is the legal one. Certain rights of *evantage*, combined with the doctrines of *tresayle* and *cy-pres*, most probably apply and govern here, which would likely prove strong defenses against claims for estoppel based on abatement, annulment, non-recognition, disownment and *repudiatio*."

"In clear text, sir," said Sanford.

"*Ad rem*, Maggie may be one of your heirs, Barnabas, and thus have a claim on the company's equity."

"Wheat and whiskey!" said Barnabas. "First Afsana and now Maggie!"

"In an eggshell," said Sanford.

"What do we do, Sanford?" said Barnabas.

"What does your heart tell you to do? This is—meaning no offense, Mr. Sedgewick—not foremost a legal matter, though the law will certainly tell us what we can *not* do. No, this we must decide as our consciences direct us."

The clock ticked in the room that smelled faintly but always of sandalwood. Rodney forever pursued the French, the many souls perpetually drowned as the East Indiamen went down. Barnabas looked suddenly at Sally's favourite picture on the wall, the one showing the black man saving the white boy from the sleek grey shark. He stared at it for a dozen ticks of the clock, then wheeled with Barnabasian alacrity, his hand arabesqued in his 'clarifying' mode.

Sanford smiled, short but deep, knowing what Barnabas would say and agreeing wholeheartedly in advance.

"We invite Maggie to tea," said Barnabas. "Beans and biscuits, by God, we invite her to a family tea!"

"Dextrous thief of my affections," said Sally, staring out her attic window towards Dunster Court on the afternoon after the Sedgewick's party. "What is the height of your character?"

She had slept no more than an hour or so since returning to Mincing Lane.

The bells of the City, and beyond, tolled four o'clock. She heard the maid admitting Mr. Sedgewick and the thump of the door to the partners' room. She heard dimly that Cook was preparing their dinner, while mardling in the kitchen with Mr. Harris and Mr. Fletcher—familiar and comfortable sounds that came as if from a sidereal distance, providing no comfort at all.

Papers were pinned and tacked up on every wall in the room, in an order known only to Sally, containing spidery sketches, calculations, annotations in a cryptic language (or so it might seem to an outside observer), reefs of mathematical symbols (often crossed out, re-done, written over), lop-sided geometrical processions, more scribblings, here profusely hinched together, there languidly curving over the page—a *rubato* of the mind. The papers engulfed the maps and prints already on the wall. In one place Sally had continued to write onto the wall; if she removed that paper, her equation would start mid-tempo.

A napping Isaak yawned and rolled over on the floor, making a new indentation in the shoals of books and pamphlets, nestling herself between *The Visible World Pictured* by Comenius and Busching's *Description of the Earth*.

"Fly back to regions far from my heart, beyond the steeps of India and the hayles of China," Sally said. "Go walk some other path, with the stars beneath the horizon. For you will not have me, not again."

Sally saw the figures passing by in Mincing Lane below her window, but only as a blurred martingale of movement, darts and spangles of colour in a shimmering shadow.

"Sankt Jacobi," she whispered, "Sankt Nicolai. All the foundations of the earth are out of course. Selah. Hatred is too noble an emotion to spend on him. No, I cherish my hatred, I glut on it. *No, no*, I do not mean that! I would harbour your love forever. Here I stand shorn of all defenses, my mind unroofed, my heart unlaced. This is a source of my most infinite regret but no human foresight could guard against it. Guard against it? *Ha ha*, no fence against a flail. But now, at last, I cast off childish things, the rattles and cobs, taws and tottums of my youth ... Tom! Do you remember how we played at chuck-farthings as children, here in this house? Tom, Tom, is that you?"

Isaak came to Sally, nozzled about her shins.

"Oh, my little golden one, you at least are constant, blessed *tes muddry*."

Sally kicked aside books, knocking Barbauld's *Hymns in Prose for Children* to the one side and Smith's *Minor Morals* to another, upending Wakefield's *Juvenile Anecdotes*, making a scree of sermons by Spener, Thomasius, Tillotson, and Tyndale.

"What use are any of these? Wagonish ideas: big, boxy, creaking-noisy and ... empty!"

Rooks cried outside. Bells tolled again: the deep clamour of St. Margaret Patten around the corner on Little Tower Street, the higher chime of St. Dionis Backchurch across Fenchurch, the claudicant banging of St. Birinus with its imbalanced carillon.

"Ring away, ring away! All you voices of the *pia munera* ... you succour me not."

Sally sat with Isaak in her lap, staring out of the window as the foresummer sun began to set.

"*Quatsch*. No, I shall not speak so. Fraulein would not have me do so. *Notbricht Eisen*."

The upper skies turned pickerel-grey, flecked with gleaming streaks of the colour one sees on ripening sickle-pears. The line of the rooftops across the street dissolved slowly, slowly, into the sky, limned by a murky vinaceous red.

"'O that false fire which in his cheek so glowed;
O that forced thunder from his heart did fly ...'"

Delinquent streaks of sun slanted into the room, now the grey of opals, now the grey of a pigeon's breast with hints of cream in the underfeathers, now the grey of slates.

"'He came on tiger's feet, with borrowed emotion seeming owned. He would yet again betray the fore-betrayed, and corrupt anew a now-repentant maid.'"

Luminescent shadows piled—oozed—into Sally's attic-room. Grey dimmed to the rust- and umber-mottled colours of the cricket's carapace, with an under-tint of jade, forming and reforming in the corners of the chamber.

Isaak jumped down from Sally's lap, lambent in the mantling dusk.

"I shall cut a window in the night. I shall cast there this malign desire."

"No, no, I cannot."

"You must, you must."

In the corners the greys arrayed themselves, the greys known as mignonette and massicot, as gunpowder and grume, as deepest umber and most finely metalled grace, a series of silhouettes in soft plumbago.

"'Felled by a prompture of the blood—upright now with the compress of reason.'"

Motes arose in the circulating greys, a dull white that fascined all other colours, subordinating them to its will.

Sally peered into a corner and said, "Now balefire, come you to mock me in my luckless time?"

A voice congealed in the corner, or so it seemed to Sally. It said:

"Feeling like Dido abandoned, still wanting her false Aeneas even as she burned on the pyre she kindled with her own hand?"

Sally said nothing. The voice continued.

"Indulge in private compline, a parvity of a song for your service. Extinguish the candles at your own Tenebrae, if you will; no aid, no solace, no 'suagement will come of it."

Sally reached for Isaak. The white form (forms?) swirled slowly within grey veilings.

"Mutinous imagination, all debrided, plies her dangerous arts. You think this man a deceiver, yet what is it you now consider in your own place? Will you not deceive in your turn, betray the man from Yount who loves and trusts you wholly?"

Sally sprang up and ran half-blind towards the corner. The white figure laughed and moved to another corner.

"Monster, leave this place!" Sally cried, slipping to one knee on the books strewn across the floor. Isaak leaped forward, knowing an enemy but unsure where the foe found himself.

From the whiteness issued bony sounds.

Sally picked up a book and flung it at the corner. The white dispersed, the greys swallowed the book, which fell harmlessly to the floor.

"James . . ." said Sally, just before she fell to the floor herself. "Reglum."

Isaak ran to Sally's side.

"James," said Sally, just before exhaustion overwhelmed her.

"Where's Tom, that's what I want to know," said Cook. She was holding court in the kitchen, with the maid, Mr. Harris and Mr. Fletcher attending.

"I mean, the whole point of their skipping and skimbering off to quince-pot places was to fetch back Master Tom," she continued. "Yet here they have come back . . . without him! Inadmissible, I call it, and meaning no disrespect to Mr. McDoon and Mr. Sanford."

She finished barding the chicken for the evening supper and set it in the oven.

"It *does* appear to be a confusion," said Mr. Harris (who, as 'clerk' to the Naxes at the Piebald Swan, knew precisely where Tom was). "Plowing with dogs even, but I think we must trust the McDoons to know their business."

"Agreed," said Mr. Fletcher (equally in the know). "The McDoons say Tom is safe and soon to return by separate means. So, no reason for us to fret on their account."

Cook shook her head and waved her serving fork, saying, "And there is the poor Miss Reimer, taken by the plague, dead and all in foreign parts. She did not reckon with that, I suppose. God rest her soul."

All four in the kitchen crossed themselves.

"Still," said Mr. Harris in his broad West Country accent. "Even that may have had some part in the great plan of things, don't you think?"

Cook looked at him severely.

"No," she said. "I'll be coked and slagged, if I do. I don't hold with 'great plans' that regular folks have no say in, and mostly mean the misfortunate ends of people. There, I said it!"

The maid looked mildly shocked, peering about her as if expecting a curate to pop out of a cupboard to excommunicate her aunt.

"Strike the deacon, the devil is in the hemp," laughed Mr. Harris, joined loudly by Mr. Fletcher.

"I mean no blasphemy," said Cook. "It is just that something remains deeply askew and ahoy about this whole affair, if you ask me. I feel that in these old bones of mine."

"There, you are right about that," said Mr. Harris, growing serious. "The game is still afoot, though it is not clear to me what the game is. For instance, the Miss Sally is acting even stranger now than before she left. . ."

". . . And that is saying a mouthful," half-whispered Mr. Fletcher.

"Don't you be speaking ill of Miss Sally," said Cook, swiping at Mr. Fletcher with her dish-towel. "Or you will have me to account with!"

Mr. Fletcher nodded his apologies, while looking to the maid for support.

Mr. Harris continued: "For instance, just yesterday Miss Sally asked me to accompany her to the West, . . . all the way to Devon, no less, . . . in search of something she calls 'china clay.'"

"Chinese clay?" said the maid. "In Devon?"

"It's a sort of coal, I think," said Mr. Fletcher, ever eager to show off, especially to the maid. "No idea why they call it 'china,' but it is a stuff you pull out of a mine."

THE INDIGO PHEASANT *Volume Two of Longing for Yount*

"What's it used for?"

"No idea."

"There," said Mr. Harris, shrugging. "That's what I mean. I am happy to oblige, of course, not least because I can call in on my brother and his family in Somerset on the way, but I cannot say I understand the purpose of the trip."

Cook put a pan of carrots and onions in the oven beside the roasting chicken, and then said, "One good thing though: while they were away in wild countries, we had no more visits from that . . . galder-fenny, the crafty man."

All four crossed themselves again, especially as the dark was growing, making the candlelight seem smaller, feebler.

"Brrrr, wicked as Bishop Hatto, that one," said the maid. "I hope he gets eaten by rats too."

"Will take more than rats to end that one," said the Cook. "At least so I hazard."

"While you are escorting Miss Sally to the West Country," said Mr. Fletcher to Mr. Harris. "I will be doing the same for Mr. McDoon, who travels again soon, only this time no further than to Edinburgh."

"What's his errand, Mr. Fletcher?"

"I do not rightly know, but—as he is Scots originally—it seems perfectly reasonable that he might want to go there. Me, I have never been farther north than Luton, so I confess to some excitement."

"But there you are," said Cook. "Barely home from years away, and already fitcheting off again. Edinburgh, my soul! He should be staying home, here on Mincing Lane, for a spell, get back to regular ways with regular people, rather than heading straight up to the far North."

Talk turned to other topics—the high cost of wheat, the riots in the East End, the scandalous Prince of Wales—as the dinner cooked and night came on.

Taking the chicken out of the oven, moist under its bacon-wrappings, Cook said, "Oh, then I must say something about this Billy Sea-Hen who has come back with the McDoons. No Tom, but a Billy Sea-Hen instead! More London even than you, Mr. Fletcher. But that's not the problem. Londoners are fine. No, it's his preaching I wonder about. I have not been to his meetings, but I hear folks talking of it. The Bible, yes, but a whole lot more is how I hear it described. Makes that Southcott woman and the Muggletonians sound correct as Cocker, from what I hear. What's this Billy got to do with the McDoons?"

No one having an answer, Cook fried on.

"No Tom come back, and the German miss dead (and she will be much missed!), but we get a preachin' sea-hen and two Indian gentlemen instead. Very polite and all, most in particular the Indians, I have no complaints, always praise my cooking, most respectful of this house. Feel sorry for the Mr. Bunce, him with just one leg now, reminds me of Nelson at Trafalgar. And then Mr. Bammary, the most politest man I think I ever met. Attends very carefully on Miss Sally, so I can only think well of him."

As she spoke, she took out the vegetables. She paused. When she spoke again, she emphasized each point she made by shaking the vegetable spoon; droplets of melted butter sprinkled her listeners.

"Lieutenant Bammary loves Sally, that much is plain as the eyes on my face. Like a great beagle, he is, lump lump lump after her, would fight all the wolves of Tartary to protect her, he would. I dare say he deserves our respect for that."

The other three nodded their heads.

"But, not that it is any of our business, but one cannot help but care and wonder . . . does Miss Sally return the favour? Outwardly yes, no doubt. But I know our little smee. . . . She is wrestling inside over something. . . . Even now, has not eaten all day, shut up in her attic. . . . Well, no use speculating and, like I said, not our business to be speculating about."

She emphasized this last point with a very sharp glance at her niece.

"One more thing, before I take 'em their dinner. The Mr. Sedgewick, who is here now with 'em. . . . He is a schemer, poking his lawyer nose into all sorts of sense and nonsense. His wife is even stranger! I hear mumblings from some of the Sedgewick servants."

Seeing no demurral from her companions, Cook ended the conversation and took the chicken, carrots, and onions out to the partners' room.

"Clever that lawyer is, no doubt," she said, over her shoulder as she headed out of the kitchen. "He always finds a way to be here with Mr. McDoon and Mr. Sanford right around dinner time!"

"Take that as a compliment to your cooking," said Mr. Harris as the door shut behind Cook.

"Huummpphh" could be heard clearly through the door.

Two days later, Maggie sat in the partners' room in the house on Mincing Lane. She looked across a table—specially set with a blue-and-white porcelain tea service—at two men of middle age and a young woman (who clutched a large, golden cat on her lap), who sat beside Mr. and Mrs. Sedgewick.

"Oh Mama," thought Maggie. "You told me that Tortoise says 'always travel with your musical instruments because you never know when you will meet other musicians.' Well, *chi di*, I think I just met the oddest musicians of all: the very ones who must sing with me."

". . . so, to conclude: Maggie, that is, the Miss Collins, is a cousin, *omnibus rebus consideratus*," said Mr. Sedgewick. "Mag . . . Miss Collins, the McDoons are willing to accept you as such."

"Rat," thought Maggie. "Chubby little rat, clever *okelekwu*, mouth chattering while mind runs unseen elsewhere."

"Well, ah, thank you Mr. Sedgewick," said Barnabas, waving his hands about, sloshing tea from his cup and very nearly upsetting the cup from Sally's hand entirely. "So then, Miss Collins. . . . That is, ha ha ha, . . . what I mean to say, . . . oh, *Quatsch*, here, try these pastries, the ones with the powdery sugar on top, Cook got them special. . . ."

"Mr. McDoon," thought Maggie. "Roundish in the corners,

but not soft. Strong I think under that bubbly-skittery front. Misplaces words but not their meanings. Bit of a popinjay! Mama, you would like the needlework on this man's clothes."

Everyone sipped their tea and nibbled on the pastries, searching for what to say.

Maggie scanned the room, slowly exploring it in her mind. She noted the porcelain figurines on the mantlepiece—the Four Continents, seemingly conversing, but what sort of conversation might Africa be having with Europe?—and the ornate clock, steadily marking the seconds, the minutes, the hours. She looked at each print framed on the wall, ran with Diana hunting Actaeon, sailed up the Trave to Luebeck and unloaded cargo on the quay at Riga, swam with the survivors of a shipwreck, hoisted a white boy out of the water and away from a shark's jaws.

"What Mr. McDoon is trying to say, is 'welcome,' Miss Collins," said Sanford.

"Not met anyone quite like you before, Mr. Sanford," thought Maggie. "You guard your thoughts well. A ribbon of very deep spirit I sense, coiled and tucked in a weathered case, a burning coal kept in a cold chalice."

"Thank you," said Maggie. "This is the strangest turn of events . . ."

"Indeed, indeed," interrupted Barnabas. "But, well, here it is: you are family, so unexpected, like . . . like something out of all those romances, where the heir turns up all unexpected and everyone is reunited. . . ."

"Yes," thought Maggie. "But I wonder how many of those books have someone looking like me showing up in the parlour for tea. All the sugar in *this* bowl is white."

Maggie spooned sugar into her tea and helped herself to more milk.

Mrs. Sedgewick gave a little half-gasp. Everyone turned towards her.

"My tarictic dove," said Mr. Sedgewick. "Whatever is the matter?"

Mrs. Sedgewick dabbed at her eyes with an embroidered handkerchief and said, "Oh, nothing, it's just that I am so overcome with sentiment at this miraculous event, tears being the sword of the Angel King, and, you Maggie, suddenly revealed as a McDoon, it is all too much. . . ."

"Ah, my mentor," thought Maggie. "*Ndo*, the pigeon in the shade. . . . No, more the *nnekwu ocha*, the white hen. You quote Blake now (misquote actually, dear mistress) and send me his sunflower poem as a condolence on the death of my mother, yet can you stoop—madam—to the labour he prophesizes? You fancy yourself a Daughter of Beulah, but do you understand—mistress—what Blake means when he speaks of rebuilding Jerusalem? Do you hear, as he does, 'the cry of the Poor Man, his Cloud over London in volume terrific low bended in anger?' Do you know what the Wine-Press of Los represents and the Human Harvest? 'Bring me my bow of burning Gold, my Arrows of Desire'—like the Huntress in the print on the wall over there!—I think I shall like this house very well."

Several minutes passed before Mrs. Sedgewick's tears subsided. One member of the company, at least, could not wait for Mrs. Sedgewick to compose herself; Isaak jumped down from Sally's lap, marched over to Maggie and began nudging Maggie's left leg.

"That's Isaak," said Sally. "Come to inspect you, I'm afraid. She's the real owner of the house."

Isaak sniffed at Maggie's shoes. Isaak hopped up on an arm of the chair and looked at Maggie's face.

"Here is a hunter, fearless like a leopard, small-sized *nanwulu*," thought Maggie. "*Her* I will call cousin, if she will admit the connection."

"I apologize, Miss Collins," said Sally. "Isaak knows no boundaries, and my scolding her does no good at all."

"And here is . . . what?" thought Maggie. "The white girl who sings, with her cat. Breathing in front of me as I saw her so often during my mind's voyages. A hunter who is herself hunted. Came back—from where exactly?—looking for me, only I found her first. Doesn't look like she has slept in a week, eyes sunk into the mask of a face. I need her voice, together we can sing down the Owl and drive the ship, selah, but I fear to depend too much on her. Strong but brittle, I deem her. And I wonder if she will follow my instruction."

Isaak jumped down and went back to Sally, her tail a golden frond above the table top, sailing past the tea service, the pastries, the sandalwood box.

"So," said Barnabas. "We'd like to invite you, Maggie—may I call you that? If we are to be family, then hardly seems right to keep saying 'Miss Collins' but we can do whatever you like, and please call me 'Uncle' because if you call me 'Mr. McDoon' I shall feel as if I am at the Exchange and not in my very own home, and now, beans and bacon, where was I?"

"Inviting Maggie to come live with us," said Sanford.

"Precisely," said Barnabas. "Thank you Sanford, that's where I was heading. What say you Maggie? Would you come to us here at Mincing Lane?"

Maggie put her teacup down. Before she could respond to Barnabas, she was diverted by the pattern on the teapot: a blue pheasant advancing through a lacework of blue branches, twigs, leaves, on a gleaming white field.

"I know this," Maggie thought, suddenly drawn into the picture. "A quail . . . no, that is not quite right. It's—Mama, what is the word you used? The *ogazi*! The game-fowl, the . . . pheasant, that's the word in English. A blue *okuku*. Steps lightly, sees with a sharp eye."

"Maggie?" said Barnabas.

"The *ogazi*," Maggie continued to muse, not hearing Barnabas, "Traveller between worlds, very hard to capture."

"Miss Collins, Maggie?" said Sanford.

"The pattern the pheasant bestrides," said Maggie to herself. "The tractix, the evolute of the catenary, the harmony of the *nsibidi*. Where I will pilot-sing the choral-boat!"

Maggie looked up from the porcelain.

"A thousand apologies," she said, shaking her head slightly as if she had just stepped from moonlight into a bright dawn. "I too am overcome from sentiment at this moment."

The McDoons and the Sedgewicks regarded Maggie with anticipation, uncertainty, suspicion, hope, and a dozen other emotions besides. Only Isaak seemed confirmed in full acceptance.

"Oh Mama, these are our—your and my—relatives, our kin," thought Maggie. "You were right! Your mother *was* a white woman. That woman is one of our *ndichie*, one of the ancestors—and she was green eyes from Scotland, this man's aunt!"

All eyes were on Maggie. All sounds faded away.

"Here is part of the choir for the *abu oma*, our great psalm of healing, our *abu mmeli* of victory," Maggie thought.

Maggie nodded her head.

"Yes," she said. "Thank you . . . Uncle."

"Hurrah," said Barnabas, jumping up, his vest a mesh of Tiepolo pink and Wedgwood cream. He rounded the table and embraced a startled Maggie.

"Welcome home," said Barnabas. "May the Old McDoon know of this and repent!"

Sanford smiled a fleeting cutlass-smile. Maggie noticed that over Barnabas's shoulder; she smiled a similar smile back.

"Praise to *Chineke*," she whispered. "God's will be done."

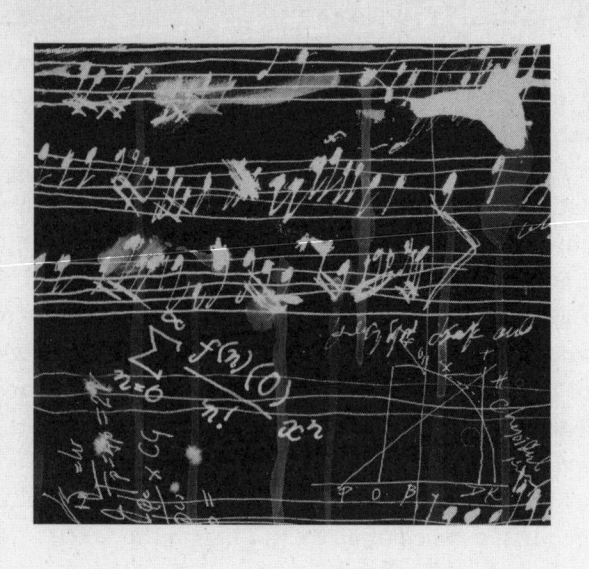

Interlude: Videnda

[An extract from <u>Thetford's Monthly Mirror, Reflecting Men and Manners</u>, vol. XXXI, nr. 10]

A correspondent from Islington reports the following:

Last Thursday sennight a most remarkable, large and vivacious meeting—third in a series—took place in the Spa Fields near Finsbury and Clerkenwell, led by an itinerant preacher of no established denomination but mixing the words of many together in a palette of his own devising, who goes by the extraordinary and uncouth name of Billy Sea-Hen.

This Sea-Hen is, to judge by his accent and local knowledge, a Londoner by birth, though he has not been seen here until very recently, whereupon suddenly he is to be heard from and about on nearly every side. (Where might he have been until his recent eruption into our scope of vision?) He speaks of salvation and redemption in the usual ways but, by adding many unique flourishes and making a multitude of obscure references, he has caused a great stir. Indeed, it is fair to say, as Virgil has it in the Eclogues, he has put 'the whole countryside in a state of turmoil.'

Most notable are the crowds he draws to himself. The Spa Fields meeting was said on good authority to be upwards of three thousand souls. The week before, he spoke to at least as many on the lawns of Dame Annis le Clare in Old Street, and to perhaps only a few hundreds less the week before that, at Black Mary Well on the Farringdon Road. Prevalent in the gathering are a great many of the meanest poor, including many Irish and not a few sons and daughters of Africa (it is startling to see how many of these latter have made their way to Albion's fair shores!). Here are to be found labourers in our breweries, brickyards and barge-shoots, dockers, porters, draymen, carters, coal-heavers, and— among the girls and women whose numbers are not inconsiderable at the Sea-Hen meetings—maids and other servants of the lesser sort. All are esurient for the meal he provides, and clamour for more as soon as he is done.

Most alarming are their actions upon hearing Sea-Hen speak of righteous causes. The crowd, as it disperses back to the warrens and rookeries of greater London, has been seen to make rude gestures and to loudly interrupt the pastimes of gentlemen and ladies taking tea at Bagnigge Wells and similar locales in the more fashionable parts of the city. Sea-Hen must bear responsibility—in the same manner as the Wedderburns and Spences of the world—for any crimes against property and persons that he may incite amongst his auditors.

[Letter from Sanford in London to Barnabas in Edinburgh]

Dear B.:

I hope your efforts to raise funds in Edinburgh have been more fruitful than mine at home.

Sad to report that the Project remains under-subscribed.

Praeds and Rogers are in, but only for small capital, which is—to speak most candidly—a disappointment given our firm's long relationship with each of those houses.

Matchett & Frew have invested to the full limit of their capacity, for which we must be grateful. The Gardiners likewise.

A firm new to my acquaintance—Coppelius, Prinn & Goethals (Widow)—has shown interest. They are originally from Leipzig and have established an office here now that regular commerce between Great Britain and the Continent has resumed. They appear quite solid and respectable, but of course I will investigate further. Matchett & Frew have suggested that something may not be quite as it seems about Coppelius, Prinn & Goethals (Widow), but could not give more detail.

The Landemanns are—as expected—in close correspondence with our mutual friends in the Northern and Baltic trades. By my next writing I may have news to share from Hamburg, Luebeck, Gothenburg, Danzig, Koeningsburg, and Riga.

Most devastating though is the total lack of funds coming from the larger City houses. Barings and the other acceptance houses won't have anything to do with our Project, to the extent of neither Sedgewick nor I gaining so much as a conversation with them. (!)

The pending loan to the Kingdom of Prussia preoccupies many of our other friends—it is for the sum of no less than five million Pounds Sterling, which surely must reduce the stock potentially available to us. I had never seriously entertained hopes that the Rothschilds would back us, but it is frustrating to see the Prussia business absorbing all the focus of Isaac Solly & Son and of Haldimand.

I also thought that the East India Company's investment

would signify and attract Reid, Irving and Hurst, Robinson, yet so far we make no headway with those firms.

Another blow this morning: though they wish us well and will speak kindly on our behalf, Thomas Wilson & Co. is too busy with its new Brazil business to enter ours.

I am beginning to feel apprehensive and look forward to putting our minds together immediately upon your return. McDoon & Co. is now completely invested in the Project, our credit fully extended.

Since we cannot disclose the ultimate nature of the venture, we have had to offer a guarantee of 12% profit as a sort of blind trust—Sedgewick has arranged the legalities and confirms (we must be completely secure in this legal structure) that we are fulfilling our fiduciary responsibilities in this manner. How we are—as a business matter—to make good on that guarantee depends greatly on the outcome of your inquiries in Edinburgh and that of the Landesmanns among our northern connections.

In the meantime, our cash outlays as we embark on the Project are not small. The shipyard has agreed to extend us some credit, but not nearly enough to avoid sizeable payments to the mechanics and machinists, not to speak of the architects and draftsmen.

Not wanting to alarm you, but only to be sure you are in full possession of the relevant facts, I wish you Godspeed old friend.
—S

P.S. Something seems to work against us in this matter, more than just the normal vagaries of the market. I hear many reasons and excuses, e.g., the financial panics in the United States distract some, and the strife between the Greeks and Turks affect others, but there is more to it than that. We are not welcomed in places where formerly we were given freedom at least to propose our ventures; we receive odd and even stony glances from others, among whom we once numbered as friends. I will save more for your return, but think that our designs are being countered by those who sought to thwart us on our recent prolonged journey. More I will not put to paper.

[Letter from Mr. Sedgewick to Sir John Barrow, Second Secretary of the Admiralty, hand-delivered by Lt. Thracemorton, on the feast day of The Lady Gilthoniel, the Prayer-Incarnate]

Sir,

I beg leave to redouble my concerns for the nature and outcome of the matters to which you have entrusted me—my causes for alarm are well beyond my (and quite possibly any one man's) control, as I believe you shall see from what I recount below.

Kidlington has done what you asked and re-attached himself to the McDoons, most particularly to the girl, in whom he clearly has a romantic interest (I assume my lord was aware of this when formulating your plan at the outset?). Not to tell you your business, but it is my considered opinion that an amatory thread in this tapestry may mar the whole pattern.

I do not know what Kidlington has reported to you, for he speaks nothing to me about whatever he is charged to discover. I will, of course, relay to you all that I might learn from him.

However, I do know—and I understand the excellent Lt. Thracemorton knows—that Kidlington has been approached again by those others of whom we earlier spoke, namely, his old creditors, though they no longer have any legal claim upon him. Or it may be that Kidlington has approached them, which would be more suspect still. *Fallaces sunt rerum species*, in the words of Seneca.

Pro tanto, I have not yet been able to connect with certainty these persons with the firm Coppelius, Prinn & Goethals (Widow) but I believe strongly that some such connection exists, and—more important—I believe C, P & G has aims at odds with those of the Admiralty. I recommend that I meet directly with you soon to discuss further, as I will not have all that I suspect captured on paper.

This firm is now negotiating with the McDoons for a share in the Project. Even if the McDoons shared my apprehensions, they are in no position to refuse the possible involvement of

Coppelius, Prinn & Goethals (Widow), since—as I know you are aware—the Project is not yet fully underwritten and the McDoons are beginning to feel financial pressures.

One final item that may—or may not—be relevant to these affairs: the McDoons have acquired a new member, in the most astonishing and circuitous of ways, and in the form of a most extraordinary person. A long-sundered heir has appeared whose claim I have myself probed and found valid; the McDoons have taken her in and accepted her as one of their own. Her given name is Margaret Collins. Be aware, sir, that this Miss Collins is of African origin and that she is something of a mathematical savant (which I have myself witnessed and can attest to). I feel compelled to mention this, as her fame or notoriety has begun to spread, at least here in the City, though perhaps not yet in Westminster, St. James, or Belgravia.

    Awaiting your further instructions,
    and as always your most humble servant,
    —Sedgewick, Esq.

P.S. I debated whether or not to include a final item but do so, in the interest of full disclosure and for the sake of good order. The Miss Collins, now acknowledged as a cousin of the McDoons and living with them, was most recently employed as a servant in my very own household. The coincidences that created this situation being too vast and concatenated to compass here, I beg your indulgence to discuss them with you when we meet in person, should such a discussion interest you.

[From Sir John Barrow to Lord Melville, First Secretary of the Admiralty, sent in strictest confidence, on the Day of the Most Sacred Mundation]

My lord:
The Project outlined in Special File 16, in which the Admiralty now has an interest totalling ten thousand Pounds Sterling, continues to be a source of some concern.

The commercial under-takers have not yet been able to raise the remaining capital, at the same time as the costs of the Project continue to increase. I labour under no illusions that the Exchequer is unaware of or indifferent to this matter; I will have financial statements prepared for your review within the fortnight.

Our agents work strenuously to effect and assure the Project's success, but detect counter-impulses from (to the best of our knowledge) those Others about whom you and I have had occasion to discuss.

More salubrious is the news that the Project is impelling the creation of and deployment of novel technologies and *sapientia*, which will benefit the realm immeasurably in years to come.

Ex mea sententia, my lord: you may wish to discuss the Project—and potentially certain other matters covered within Special File 16, at your discretion—with the Master-General of the Ordnance, and the President of the Board of Control. Their support of Admiralty's position would be most welcome, particularly in the face of certain opposition from the Chancellor of the Exchequer. Gather your junto of all the talents now, my lord.

Your most obedient servant,
—Sir John Barrow

[Excerpts from the contract between the engineering firm of Henry Maudslay, in the Westminster Road (Lambeth) and the ship's venture led and managed by the firm of McDoon & Co., in Mincing Lane, The City of London]:

Clause I., General Premises and Heads of Agreement as between the Parties hereto.

[. . .] Furthermore, the firm of Maudslay agrees to work diligently, closely and amicably with any and all other firms and individual professionals that the firm of McDoon may name or direct them to collaborate with, the object being to make the Deliverables described in Clause III below essentially part and parcel of the total Project, namely, the ship The Indigo Pheasant being built for the McDoon-led consortium at the Blackwall Yards in Rotherhithe. As of the date of this Contract, said firms or individuals include (but may not in future be limited to) the clockmaking firm Gravell & Co. (continuing the firm of Eardley Norton), located at 49 St. John Street in Clerkenwell, and Mr. Joseph Michael Gandy, architect and draftsman, located at The Adelphi Buildings by the Strand, besides ipso facto the Blackwall Yards and all their affiliated workmen, mechanics and engineers.
[. . .]

Clause III., Goods & Services Deliverable by the firm of Maudslay, as hereby specified and enumerated.

[Consideration for and compensation due the firm of Maudslay from the firm of McDoon is specified in Clause IV below]

a. One propulsive engine, to be charged and driven by steam, to the dimensions, specifications, capacity and tolerances laid out in Exhibit I attached hereto, adhering to the design known generally as a double—and direct-acting, with the further specification that it entail oscillation of the piston rods, to generate the maximum force and thrust within the smallest space possible and with the lowest weight of machinery possible; thus, the rods must connect directly to the crankshaft, using mobile cylinders secured by trunnions.

b. A series of valves and connections for the engine, as specified in Exhibit II attached.

c. Specified precision milling, lathing, threading and gearing, to the fineness of one-ten/thousandth of an inch, on materials to be described in an Addendum to be supplied no later than six months from the signing of this Contract.

[Extract of internal correspondence, the firm Gravell & Co., continuing the firm of Eardley Norton, located at 49 St. John Street, Clerkenwell]

On the Physick Moon,
in the month _____ . . . year _____ . . .

Dear brother:

I rejoice to inform you that our firm has acquired a most interesting new client, the merchants McDoon & Co. (Mincing Lane), who wish us to provide the highest quality horological instrumentation for a vessel, *The Indigo Pheasant*, they are having built at Blackwalls. About the McDoons, I have ascertained this. . . .

[. . . . . .]

Now, dear brother, I come to the most novel element of this project, namely, the nature of the requested instrumentation, which bids fair to surpass anything we—or any of our colleagues in The Clockmakers' Company—have ever achieved in terms of precision and delicacy of operation. I eagerly anticipate reviewing with you, upon your return, the preliminary drawings rendered for the client by their draftsman, Mr. Gandy—"horological" only captures part of what is envisioned, if I understand this aright.

Our challenges include the need to maintain as low a friction as possible in the escapement and a reliability never yet attained—we must innovate using the Tompion/Graham deadbeat escapement as our base, or so I will recommend. And, of course, the client demands the most stringent accuracy as a result.

[Extract of a letter from Mary Fairfax Somerville, later translator of Laplace's The Mechanism of the Heavens, to Sir Joseph Banks, President of the Royal Society]

My dear Sir Joseph:
Knowing that your health troubles you, especially in these winter months, and hoping my note finds you well in that and all other regards, I will not meander in my news.

I write foremost to alert you to a possible new mathematical prodigy in our midst, and that of a most unusual origin and demeanour. Her name is Margaret Collins; through twists and turns too bizarre to elaborate here, she has recently reunited with her family—a respectable merchant named McDoon (a Scotsman like me!), resident in The City. I came to hear of her, and then met her in person, through the offices of my friend, Mrs. Shawdelia Sedgewick (whose sister married one of the 'Admiralty' Tarletons, whom I know are friendly with you).

How should I describe her? Strange as it is to relate, she is an African (!) born in the United States but having been raised in London. She possesses a natural born hauteur that would befit a princess; she does not suffer fools gladly. A rare combination, given her lowly origins—already her neighbours refer to her as the 'Hottentot Scholar' and other similar designations, which can only be harmful to her dignity, or perhaps instead such taunts and unkindnesses serve merely to sharpen her already keen and acerbic nature.

She is—and she must be—very self-assured in her skills and knowledge, which I am pleased to tell you are real and demonstrable, Sir Joseph. I quizzed her for almost two hours— which she did not take kindly to, I must confess, and perhaps I was heavy-handed, yet I feel I did no wrong, since I needed to know if she had substance before I could, in good conscience, bring her to your or any other's learned attention—she shows a very clear and unfeigned understanding of Laplace's work, and the most recent of Gauss, besides Monge and others. I am sure you will agree that such an understanding is rare enough among the educated classes; to find it so well developed in one of little formal training beyond a charity school is difficult to comprehend. My friend, Mrs. Sedgewick, who knows her well, says that Miss Collins is the most sedulous reader she has ever seen—the girl apparently has taught herself!

I ask only that you be willing to meet with her, should I be able to arrange such a thing. It does no good for a talent as remarkable as hers to asphyxiate, which it will surely do unless brought closer to the felicitous atmospheres provided by the Royal Society. She has a real contribution to make in the area of the diophantine equations, Sir Joseph, and I modestly suggest that the Royal Society might want to assist the Miss Collins in her endeavours.

With all best wishes,
as always your affectionate friend,
—Mrs. Somerville

[Excerpt of a dispatch from special envoy Tang Guozhi, temporarily resident at Cape Town, South Africa, to the Imperial Second Chancellor in Peking; translation from the Chinese is general and may contain ambiguities]:

In the 21st year of the reign of His Celestial Majesty, the Jiaquing Emperor, in the Year of the Rat, under the Sign of Fire:

[. . . . . .]

Please also inform His Imperial Highness that our plan proceeds, albeit with some delay, primarily caused by the bad weather that has disrupted sailing times and the patterns of the winds, which we understand from the many merchants and ship-captains in this place afflicts the entire Indian Ocean and the Great Sea of China, and is now also turning against us the currents of the Atlantic Ocean as well (many here speculate that the terrible volcanic eruption last year in the Water Indies, at the place called Tamboro, might be the cause of the disturbed oceanic regime).

Thus, we have not yet been able to continue on to London, but hope to very soon, as soon as the sailing season returns.

My two charges are restless here. Xie Mei-Hua in particular suffers from *[ideogram here can mean several things, including 'distress,' 'melancholy visions,' 'poetic inspiration'; a literal translation might be 'a wind-that-stirs-the-mind']*.

[. . . . . .]

I am more convinced than ever that our hosts are fully aware of the Place Beyond that our philosophers and astrologers have divined exists. Equally clear to me is that the English government *[the character is multivalenced, could be translated as 'believes but questions' or 'disputes with intent to prove']* in this same matter.

If we are to counter the aggressive actions of the English—and other European powers, besides the upstart Americans—we must and will prosecute our plan with full strength.

[. . . . . .]

Dear Reglum:

I write from the inn at Slough, as I—accompanied by the redoubtable Mr. Harris, who exhibits great good cheer at the idea of visiting his native West Country—journey out to Devon for our first review of the china clay deposits there. As you know better than anyone, the use of china clay in compounds to glaze and coat certain joints and connections in the Project will enormously increase the efficacy of the Project's performance—I am optimistic that our little westward expedition will be a success.

Thank you for the evening out the day before I left. The lecture at the Society of Dilettanti was diverting, and how can one ever say no to the pastries at Mrs. Wolstaltham's?

I must end now or else I will miss getting this into the mailbag on the London-bound stage.

My best to Dorentius, and Mr. Nax, and of course to all my family.
—Your affectionate Sally

[Fragment of a note scrawled in pencil that appears to be from Sally to James; it is beyond dispute that the handwriting is Sally's]

... James, dearest. I hesitate to say more at this time. *[illegible]* Mr. Harris suspects nothing, and I will not have him made a fool of, so *[illegible]* ... the inn at Slough. We will have only two hours at most, but ...

Chapter 3: Many Perils, or, The Profoundest Dangers of Air and Time

"Or where afar, the ship-lights faintly shine
Like wandering fairy fires, that oft on land
Mislead the pilgrim; such the dubious ray
That wavering reason lends, in life's
    Long darkling way."
—**Charlotte Smith**, "Sonnet" (1798)

"The sleep of Reason produces monsters."
—**Francisco de Goya** (1799)

"We were surrounded by an empty sky without wind or birds in flight, a forest of bare trees without sound or motion;—the only noise at all was the crunch of frozen grass under our feet. Ellenore said: 'Everything is becalmed; Nature herself bows in resignation to the season. Our hearts must learn to be so resigned as well.' She . . . fell to her knees and held her bowed head in her hands. I heard her whisper a prayer . . ."
—**Benjamin Constant**, *Adolphe* (1816; translated from the French by William Copperthwaite, 1818)

Summer passed in 1816, the "year without a summer," inordinately cold, cloudy, and wet.

Barnabas—the weather chafing his lungs—replenished his supply of Bateman's pectoral drops and other pharmaceutical necessaries. Throat wrapped in a scarf, he puttered in his garden, but the chill and endless rain quashed all hopes of getting the smilax to take.

"*Quatsch*," he said with a cough on countless occasions. The only plant that appeared undaunted by the weather was the hardy little bixwort, the blue flower of repentance.

Maggie moved into the house on Mincing Lane, taking Tom's old room. At first she had trouble sleeping because the bed was so soft and the space so quiet. "I have a room of my own," she thought. "Mama, you should see this: my very own door!"

Sally did not sleep well either, partly because Maggie had moved in and partly because the temptation of James continued to haunt her even as she spent her days in the company of Reglum. "So the African girl found me before I could find her—and is believed to be our cousin—and is sleeping now under our very roof, in Tom's room!" she said to Isaak.

Tom—and Afsana—were on Sanford's mind as well. He proposed staging a play—a revival of an Oldmixon piece perhaps, or a novelty like the recent translation of *The Stranger* by Kotzebue, maybe even Buskirk again—something to remind them of their kin and friends in Yount, but no one had the heart for it (despite the ceaseless rain keeping everyone indoors most of the time) so the idea died a quiet death.

Reglum and Dorentius were frequent visitors to Mincing Lane but often noted how distant and even strained the atmosphere felt.

"Homecoming is often sweeter in the anticipation than in the actuality," said Reglum.

"Perhaps it is just this infernal weather that is preying on everyone's temper," said Dorentius, who ached from the cold even in the emptiness where his amputated leg used to be.

James found ways to encounter Sally and the other McDoons:

twice when Sally had tea with Mrs. Sedgewick at the house on Archer Street by Pineapple Court (somehow Maggie was never invited to these appointments), once "by chance" at Lackington's book emporium on Finsbury Circus, once also "by coincidence" outside the theatre at Covent Garden. No one ever noticed the figure who watched over him, on the street in the distance, . . . much less the figure who watched over the watcher.

As summer waned, Barnabas—accompanied by Mr. Fletcher—travelled to Edinburgh to seek funds for *The Indigo Pheasant*. Sally left the same week—escorted by Mr. Harris—for Cornwall and Devon, to investigate and secure for the building of the *Indigo Pheasant*'s Fulginator a mass of china clay of a quality unobtainable from the few London merchants who even stocked the mineral.

"Well, their being away lowers our grocery bill, and that's no bad thing, I suppose," said the Cook to her niece on the day Sally left. "But makes this house much too quiet for my taste, especially with the Miss Maggie still not at rights here, poor thing, how lonely she must be, I need to take her more tea, I do. Of course, is worth markin' that Isaak is staying with Miss Maggie while our little smee smee is in the West Country—that cat is company for three, she is, so I doubt Maggie will be entirely lonesome. I don't think Sally much likes that, if I am very honest in my opinion, but there is no helpin' it since Mr. Harris was clear that the post coach is no place for a cat—though I wonder at that, since Isaak travelled all the way to India with the master, or to Africa, wherever it was, some place close to where the sun rises, we do get such funny answers about that when we ask, so we don't ask anymore. Niece, quit your dranting about, help me here, I cannot find the flour. Oh, now, on the subject of dranting and drunning about: what will the polite Mr. Bammary do without Sally here—or you, niece, without the gallant Mr. Fletcher? Quit your blushin' and hand me that spoon, and where is an onion when you need one? Oh by St. Morgaine I swear trying to set order upon this kitchen is like making clothes for fishes. Anyway, at least Mr. Sanford has not gone off all a-fike, though he is not at home himself most days alike, nor evenings neither, with all the business affairs he is attending to, and looking none too pleased for his effort, if my eye does not deceive me. No, in fact, I do conject both he and the tidy little Miss Maggie need some cheer, so let's make 'em a blanche-bread pudding with rum and raisins, to sweeten up their tea-time!" Sally and Mr. Harris took the post coach west, stopping for two days at Slough (Sally claimed that she felt too ill from the weather and the jouncing coach to leave immediately), before moving on to Reading and Swindon, and then swerving southwest on the turnpike into Somerset. Mr. Harris's brother met them with a chaise at the market town of Shepton Mallet, and drove them the few miles west to Mr. Harris's home village, St. Unys-by-Croscombe.

"How strange to see someone you know only from his life in the city, suddenly transformed back to his native self," thought Sally. "I wish Cook could see Mr. Harris now!"

They spent three days with Mr. Harris's brother. The early fall weather was very crisp and the dew was heavy every morning but it did not rain. Relatives and friends visited by the dozens; Mr. Harris had not been home in a long time, and was treated as a prince returning to his patrimony. Sally marvelled at the Somerset accents, rich enough to eat, she thought ("like one of the puddings Cook makes"), almost as hard to understand as Yountish. One day, they all went on an excursion to Wells to show Sally the famous cathedral. Everyone drank cider and ate cheese, with a great deal of bacon—though talk turned often enough to the terrible weather and what that boded for a poor harvest.

Sally was sad to leave Mr. Harris's warm, boisterous relations—but happy to know that they would stop by again on their way back to London in a fortnight's time or so. On they travelled, on roads that got smaller and less maintained, until they arrived at St. Austell in Cornwall, where the accent was yet more difficult for Sally to understand. St. Austell was the centre of Great Britain's china clay excavations; Sally and Mr. Harris spent over a week visiting the pits in the neighbouring hills, at Hensbarrow Moor, Merracuddle Hill, Wheal Martyn. Sally "clarified" and negotiated her way to several excellent contracts, and received samples sufficient to fill the large trunk that Mr. Harris had brought with them.

"That's the lot of it, Miss Sally," said Mr. Harris. "All stowed as you directed."

"Thank you, Mr. Harris," replied Sally. "None of that rusty-coloured stuff, none with the pinkish hue that is inferior in quality. No, Mr. Harris, what we have gotten—at a fair price, I might add—is the very purest material, and some of it with the rarest tint of all, the bluish that I showed you."

"You are your uncle's niece, that's for sure, Miss."

Settling into the post coach at St. Austell to begin the journey back to London, Sally and Mr. Harris were joined in the compartment by a lively person named Mrs. Hamilton. Mrs. Hamilton was a mine-owner's widow of means from Truro, on her way to London to visit relatives, whose personal post-chaise was under repair thus requiring her to take the public stagecoach. She was one of those people who, though thrown together with others on the road at random, quickly becomes everyone's boon companion, by virtue of her infectious good humour and her interest in the well-being of her fellow travellers. She had jet-black hair framing smooth skin, full lips, and a pair of eyes the colour of jade. She dressed smartly in shades of hazel, deep green, gun-metal. Her smile was cloudless, her courtesy invincible as she conjured conversation from even the grumpiest of their travelling companions.

"You spin light from even the dullest of days, Mrs. Hamilton," said Sally on their shared journey's third day. "I hardly feel the ruts and the rattlings and the chill of the air. Liskeard is past, and also Plymouth, now Exeter. Honiton approaches. I am sorry that we will be stopping at Shepton Mallet thereafter and that our way will part there with yours."

"Miss Sally, genial spirit, you are too kind," said Mrs. Hamilton. "May I suggest that we dine together this evening at the Honiton inn, to celebrate our fresh acquaintanceship and wish each other well? Shall we say seven o'clock?"

Sally readily agreed, and awaited Mrs. Hamilton in the inn's dining room at the appointed time. When the clock struck a quarter past the hour, and Mrs. Hamilton was still not present, Sally went upstairs to inquire at Mrs. Hamilton's room. Passing her own room on the way, Sally heard from within a muffled thump. Sally stopped, paused, heard the thumping again, reached for her key to open the door to her room, found the door already unlocked, pushed it open and walked inside.

"Oh my dear, most unfortunate," said Mrs. Hamilton, with her smile as unmarred as always. She stood at the far end of the room, looking down at the large trunk that contained the china clay samples. Holding the handles at either end of the trunk were two small men, homunculi no more than three feet tall, naked, hairless, and entirely bottle-green. They were wrestling the heavy trunk, "walking" it forward, towards the door.

"Mr. Harris! MR. HARRIS!" called Sally. Mr. Harris had the room next door.

"Really, my dear, that is another mistake," said Mrs. Hamilton. She waggled her sleeves, out of which came a pair of staves or wands, perhaps fifteen or sixteen inches long apiece and each topped with a hand the colour of verdigris.

"My conjure-hands," said the woman dressed in green, gripping the wands.

Mr. Harris rushed through the door and stopped in full puzzlement.

"Boys, kill him," said Mrs. Hamilton, as calmly as if she were ordering tea in Bath or at Ranelagh Gardens.

The two tiny men put down the chest and swarmed Mr. Harris like grasshoppers or like tumblers at the fair. One jumped on the shoulders of the other and then launched himself at Mr. Harris's throat. The other punched Mr. Harris in the groin.

Mr. Harris roared, kicking the one attacker aside, and whirling in an attempt to dislodge the other. He looked like a bear beset by mastiffs. The remaining bottle-green man swung wildly about but held a titanic grip around Mr. Harris's throat.

Sally erupted into song, without plan or conscious decision.

Her song gave birth to a pair of fiery blue falcons, chased with carmine, which flew from her mouth towards the attacking homunculi. Mrs. Hamilton waved the conjure-hands, chanted forth a series of slowly spinning green circles that advanced on Sally.

The blue falcons disengaged with the attacking men and battled instead with the green circles. Mr. Harris fought furiously but began to stumble, lacking air. The second man rejoined the fray, leaping to punch Mr. Harris in the chest. The grip on Mr. Harris's throat was intractable; he could not breathe.

The falcons destroyed the circles. Sally sang the falcons back to help Mr. Harris. The falcons drove the two green men away, strafing their eyes, ripping off hunks of their flesh—flesh that disappeared with a jade flash when it hit the floor. The two little men ran back to Mrs. Hamilton, who hiked her skirts; they scampered under her dress, which she then dropped back to cover them.

But it was too late for Mr. Harris. He lay on the floor, windpipe crushed, writhing feebly, then not moving at all.

Mrs. Hamilton, still smiling, said, "We must needs postpone our dinner."

She clapped her conjure-hands three times and disappeared in a wet-sounding, green explosion that shredded the blue falcons and threw Sally with great force into the wall.

She struggled to stand up. Blood trickled from a gash in her scalp and from her injured mouth. The hostelry was in an uproar. The Justice of the Peace arrived but no one—least of all Sally—could give proper account of how Mr. Harris had come to be strangled, Sally assaulted, Sally's room ransacked, and Mrs. Hamilton absconded with. Murder was a seldom occurrence in Honiton. Suspicion swiftly fell on the green-eyed woman whose whereabouts were unknown and who had disappeared without paying for her room—especially when swift inquiries revealed that no such person, rich widow or otherwise, existed in Truro. Representatives of Praed's Bank in Bath vouched meanwhile for Sally and the McDoons.

Three days later, with his body carefully preserved in ice and sawdust, Mr. Harris returned home for the last time to St. Unys-by-Croscombe.

Sanford and Reglum came themselves to the village for the wake, and to escort Sally home.

When they returned to Mincing Lane, Sally spent much time sharing tears with Cook. Cook baked a small apple tart, laced with cider and topped with cheddar, in honour of Mr. Harris, and ate it with Sally and the maid one evening, in the kitchen by candlelight.

"A very good man was he," Cook said, unable to say more.

On the evening of the day that Sanford and Reglum left London for the West Country, Salmius Nalmius Nax and Noreous Minicate had an errand at the Piebald Swan. As they approached the Yountish pied-a-terre in Wapping, two figures appeared in the dusk before them—slouchy, rangy persons, spiderish-limber with snouty faces and elongated teeth, dressed in long grey coats and fashionable hats.

"Make way there, good fellows, we have no meeting with you," said Salmius. He could see the Piebald Swan over the heads of the two in front of him.

"Actually, you do," said one of the men. "That is, if your names are Salmius Nalmius Nax and Noreous Minicate."

Salmius felt a shiver; no one in London knew him by that name, except the McDoons. Here he was the merchant Oliveira de Sousa.

"If we in fact answered to such names, what appointment would you have with us?" said Salmius.

"Our master insists that the coffeehouse you run here be closed," one of the strangers indicated the Piebald Swan with a jerk of a thumb over his shoulder.

Salmius and Noreous reached for the pistols they carried under their coats.

Their interceptors smiled toothily in the gloom.

"Two pursers caught in a purse," said one.

Noreous said, "*Kaskas selwish pishpaweem*, dear Mother protect us."

Salmius said, "Amen, and remember the *Lanner*."

The Yountians fought as ferociously as lanners, and inflicted great harm upon their attackers but their weapons and their strength could not match those of said attackers, who were spirits from elsewhere.

Salmius and Noreous, rent in a dozen places, fell side by side.

Snarling, staunching their own copious outflow of blood, the two attackers put torch to the Piebald Swan and slid off into the night.

Neighbours and the watch arrived shortly thereafter, responding to the shots of the Yountian pistols and the geysers of flame consuming the coffeehouse.

Examining the corpses and pools of blood, and the charred destruction that had been the Piebald Swan, many were confused because they could not recall a coffeehouse being at that place. No one had ever been inside the house, yet here was indubitable proof of its existence, at least in the form of ashes and blackened timbers. Many crossed themselves and attributed the uncanniness to the eldritch weather, which must surely draw forth both hidden places and stealthy hunters in the dark.

The merchant de Sousa had been widely known and beloved, so his funeral was very well-attended. The burial for Noreous was very small, since he had only a handful of connections in London, but it was no less emotional for that.

Dorentius and Reglum said little but held fire in their eyes. Sanford sent word to Barnabas in Edinburgh, urging him to come home straight away.

Cook sat with her niece in the kitchen. Maggie was with them, and Sally too, together with Isaak.

"Girls, this is a wicked, ettry time," said Cook. "The awlrawnies are about again, paddin' 'round us, snuffing out lives, lookin' for a way in to us. As we used to say when I was a girl, back in Norfolk, we must tine up the hedge, make it tight, and put the gaffles on the heels of the fighting cock, make ready to defend ourselves."

Sally and Maggie nodded at the same time in response, and—without realizing it—drew closer together. Isaak arched her back and displayed her own "gaffles."

"That's the spirit, little tiger," said Cook.

Two nights after the were-molures murdered Salmius and Noreous, Mrs. Sedgewick fell into a trance in her bedroom.

The Owl walked through her window, ushered in by a wind that roared only in Mrs. Sedgewick's head. He floated in his man-form a foot or so over the floor, staring at her with his infinite eyes.

"Shawdelia Sedgewick," he hoomed so only she could hear.

Mrs. Sedgewick could not move, could not speak.

"You know who I am," said the Wurm. "You've seen me in your dreams before. I was not really interested in you then—but now I am. I come to find out from you all you know about two women, you know who I mean: the Maggie and the Sally, the Sally and the Maggie."

Mrs. Sedgewick tried to shake her head but his gaze pinioned her.

The Owl paused. He felt the Mother Goddess stir in her moon-fathomed sleep, stretch out a tendril of her drowsy thought towards him, one tine on her vast harrow. He shuddered, rolled his shoulders.

The moment passed. The Mother continued her slumbers.

The Owl pressed forward.

"All you know, do you understand?" he said, floating towards her but otherwise motionless. "All. Now."

Mrs. Sedgewick had no defenses for an onslaught such as this. Mrs. Sedgewick was not a Singer, nor was she protected in the house of a Singer.

The Wurm penetrated and stripped her mind, like an owl piercing and eviscerating a rabbit.

The next morning, the maid fled screaming from the room, bringing Mr. Sedgewick on the run, his rotund self flying up the stairs, his slippers flying off in his haste.

"Shawdelia! Shawdelia!" he cried, rushing to her crumpled form.

Mrs. Sedgewick lay curled up like a baby in the corner by her bed. She had urinated on herself. Her nightgown was half off. Her lip was bruised from a self-inflicted bite.

Mr. Sedgewick embraced his wife, as carefully as one cradles an egg yet as fiercely as one grips an anchor (hauling it up from the mud). He covered her nakedness. He cleaned off the blood, dabbing it away with an edge of his nightshirt. He dabbed also at the urine-soaked hem of Mrs. Sedgewick's gown.

She looked at him with blank eyes, but she held on to him like a drowning person grasping a bit of flotsam providentially sent her way.

Rocking her steadily, he cried out once—"Dear wife, dear wife!"—and said no more until the maids cautiously approached and offered help.

In the days to come, Mrs. Sedgewick lay in bed, barely eating, eyes shut. She said nothing, no matter how much her husband tried to coax her, except three words, which she repeated over and over again.

"Strix," she said. "Strix, Maggie, Strix, Sally, Strix, Strix, Strix."

Mr. Sedgewick would never forget that word: "Strix." He turned his formidable intellect to understanding what it might mean. When Barnabas—just returned with all speed from Edinburgh—called him to a special meeting at Mincing Lane, Sedgewick came with equal speed.

"Strix," he said. "Maggie. Sally."

"We are under siege," said Barnabas, on a rainy fall afternoon the week following the attacks on the Yountians and Mrs. Sedgewick. "Consider this a council of war."

The partners' room at Mincing Lane was packed. Sally sat next to Maggie, with Isaak commuting between them. Sanford, Dorentius and Reglum were there, as well as Billy Sea-Hen and the three other remaining Minders (Brasser, Tat'head, and Old Lobster), plus Mr. Fletcher. Present too were Mr. Sedgewick, the two principals of Matchett & Frew, and . . . James Kidlington.

(The Cook and her niece were not invited—primarily to spare them a burden of knowledge—but Barnabas half-acknowledged that they would be eavesdropping.)

Even Yikes sensed the importance of the meeting. He actually sat up for a few minutes at its start, before (presumably having reassured himself that destruction and death were not imminent, at least not before dinner time) resuming his usual posture by the fire-fender. He could be seen to open one eye from time to time, whenever the discussion rose to periodic heights, or perhaps just when a particularly large and agile spark landed on his back.

"Most of you know what I will be talking about," continued Barnabas. "As for those of you who are not yet fully aware: Sanford and I invited you here because you are already in danger without knowing it. You have a right to know what this danger is and then decide for yourselves whether or not to persist with us in our efforts."

Sanford added, "Much of what we tell you will be hard to credit, as flying in the face of reason and sobriety, yet we speculate—on pretty firm grounds—that you already know much of this story, even if it has not been fully detailed for you before."

Barnabas stood very straight, stroked his vest (a deep-blue picotte design with checks of vermilion), put his hand up in his "clarifying" stance, and said, "To start at a beginning: there is a place called Yount, and there is a being called Strix . . ."

Before he could finish, Sedgewick, Maggie and James began

talking at once, and Matchett & Frew broke out laughing ("we knew it, we knew it," the latter exclaimed).

Maggie's voice cut across the rest until she was the only one speaking.

"I know this," she said. "I know the Owl, I have sung a wall against him, and aim to sing the fight to him, if you know what I mean."

"I do," said Barnabas, "Beans and bacon, I do."

"I have a plan for us," said Maggie, who then outlined her work and calculations to date.

Sally gasped, "Why, that is *my* concept! That's the Project we are already engaged in!"

Maggie said, "*Mine* has been long in the devising. I lack only the resources to perfect it."

To his own surprise, as much as Maggie's, Sedgewick said, "I can vouchsafe this. I have seen this girl's work myself—it is a potent thing, a metaphysical engine, buttressed by mathematics."

"So is mine, so is mine," cried Sally. Sally described *her* design for the Great Fulginator.

"Your schema lacks the coordinates to entrain the rhythm, and specifically you miss Euler's "i" in your extraction of roots," said Maggie.

"Not so, not so," countered Sally. Isaak darted under the table.

Discussion became debate, lasting some time. Dorentius and Reglum contributed many comments, now siding with Sally, now with Maggie.

"The steam-driven engine will be the determinant of success," declared Dorentius. "Without it, we cannot amplify the effects of the Fulginator to a volume necessary to accomplish the task . . . of moving an entire world."

"True enough," said Sally. "Which is why *my* plan includes a juncture for the steam to impress upon the lusitropic substrates . . ."

"Yes, but, in *my* treatment you can clearly see how the virgulic escapements will channel the steam's force most effectively . . ." said Maggie.

In the end, all the men agreed that Sally and Maggie needed to pool their ideas. Maggie and Sally looked less certain, but—eying each other warily—consented to their newfound partnership.

"Well, figs and footrails, I am glad we have *that* settled now," said Barnabas, shaking his head. "And all that commotion just describes the work on the Fulginator alone, mind you. More slowly still proceeds the work on the design for the ship itself, *The Indigo Pheasant*."

"Sally, Maggie, we need you not only to combine your drafts for the Fulginator," intoned Sanford. "But we need you to collaborate with Mr. Gandy, the master-designer and architect for the vessel."

"A very rum sort, that Mr. Gandy," said Barnabas.

"The hoop calls the ball round," stage-whispered Matchett to Frew.

". . . and with the craftsmen at Blackwall's yard; time is—as Sedgewick will tell us in his lawyer's way—of the essence," said Sanford.

"My vision requires resources," said Maggie.

"*Our* vision," murmured Sally.

"Ah, beyond doubt," said Barnabas. "There's challenges to be surmounted there."

Barnabas and Sanford explained the poor state of the fundraising. Many financial schemes, suggestions, stratagems and ploys were debated, as Cook brought in tea for all.

"The firm of Coppelius, Prinn & Goethals (Widow) looks ever more the saviour, given their strong interest and the correspondingly weak responses from just about every other quarter . . . present company excluded, of course, dear Matchett & Frew," said Barnabas.

"Thank you, Barnabas, we are ever friends of your house, you know that," said Matchett. "And it may astonish you to discover that we have long half-known of Yount and the Owl Strix and surmised that your recent escapades had something to do with that land of fable and its fearsome warden."

"Always knew you two kept strange company," said Sanford. "Now we do too."

"Which brings us back to Coppelius and company," said Frew. "If there is no other way, then we must take them on as partners in the *Indigo Pheasant*, but we hear odd noises—under the cover of night, as it were—about this firm."

"As do I," said Sedgewick.

More discussion ensued, over rounds of tea and scones.

"Like it or not then," concluded Barnabas. "We have no other way if we are to fund the *Pheasant*; we must invite the firm Coppelius to participate. Agreed?"

Without enthusiasm, all relevant heads nodded "yes."

"We might also pursue more and further assistance from His Majesty's Government," said Sedgewick. "The investment by the East India Company surely indicates an interest in the Project beyond simply that of a commercial nature."

Cook brought in meat-pies, a compote of harvest fruits, a bowl of boiled potatoes in cream sauce, and a cold joint of ham, plus bottles of claret and sherry.

"Reglum, Dorentius . . . any reason why we should *not* move forward on the Queen's desire to announce Farther Yount to the British government?" asked Barnabas.

"Our Queen expressly authorized us—and you—to do just that, even if it means the end of the Hullitate dynasty," said Reglum. "The Arch-Bishop and his faction can be no more an enemy than they already are."

"Forge ahead, with all energy," nodded Dorentius, who added, "When Oxonians and Cantabrigians agree on something this swiftly and thoroughly, then the proposed course of action must be resoundingly the right one!"

Sally laughed, followed by everyone in the entire room.

"Thank you Dorentius," said Barnabas. "Between your remark and the effect of this most satisfactory claret, I am beginning to feel a little bit more at ease about the likelihood of our success!"

Sedgewick said, "I can be of particular assistance here, knowing the Admiralty as well as I do."

"Can you get us an audience with Sir John Barrow?" said Barnabas.

"I believe I can," said Sedgewick. At this, Kidlington stirred but said nothing.

"The King's ministers may be particularly attentive to our approach when we tell them that a special envoy from the Chinese Emperor is somehow mixed up in the matter," said Barnabas. He told—to the amazement of the audience—of the letters from the Termuydens, indicating that the Chinese delegation was due to arrive on an East Indiaman in the spring and that the Termuydens believed the young woman in the delegation might be a Singer.

Cook brought out a blond pudding, dense with suet, full of apricots and apples. Flourishing the bottle, she doused the pudding with brandy and set the confection alight, to general approbation.

"One of Tom's favourites," said Sally, between bites.

Barnabas said, "He would have liked the ham this evening too."

"Any sense of Tom's well-being?" said Sanford. "Afsana's? Any news from Yount whatsoever by whatever means?"

Sally shook her head.

"They might all be dead, for aught we know," said Dorentius, rubbing his knee.

"But we mustn't think that way," said Reglum, gently.

"Indeed not," said Barnabas, rising from his chair. "Keep our faith! More than that, 'tis time to counter-attack, run right at 'em, like Rodney against the French once more!"

"Hear, hear, our governor!" said Billy Sea-Hen, standing up as well. Neither he nor any of the other Minders had spoken yet. "We are with you, Mr. McDoon, blood and bone. And with your good nephew, sir, Tommy Two-Fingers, right lads? 'Deep calleth unto deep at the noise of thy waterspouts: all thy waves and thy billows are gone over me.' No hosannas lie dawd-idlin' on our tongues. We have roused the multitudes, who will stand guard over this house and will be sanctified pickets 'round the shipyard. Let the Owl beware how he flies now!"

The others broke into applause.

"Oh, one more thing," said Billy. "Thank you to you and to your Cook for this most fine meal. Me and the boys here ain't et so well in a long time. This be four stout chapters on lean times, as it were."

Everyone raised a glass to Cook, who was loitering in the doorway. She flushed, curtsied and returned to the kitchen.

"To the *Indigo Pheasant*, to Yount," said Barnabas. Everyone toasted again, and then the gathering began to disperse.

James Kidlington and Sedgewick were the last to leave. Sanford and Barnabas spoke with them in the hallway.

"Mr. Kidlington, we weighed long whether or not to invite you to this parley," said Sanford. "Mr. Sedgewick's vote in your favour was the decisive one. You owe him your gratitude."

"Thank you, sirs," said Kidlington, his face yielding no purchase for interpretation.

"Yet you said nothing here today," said Sanford. "Tell us your thoughts in private, please."

"I have little enough to add to what has already been said," replied Kidlington. "I appreciate learning the whole story, having had . . . ample time to mull and marinate the snippets and snappets of information I previously possessed."

"You agree with our plans?" said Barnabas.

Kidlington played with his gloves before replying.

"More than you could know, sir," he said. "I know the enemies haunting us, I know them much too well. As for Yount . . . it could hardly be stranger than some of the places on this Earth that I have visited."

Sanford opened the door. Just before Kidlington passed through, Barnabas said, "Sally, what are your inclinations towards Sally?"

Kidlington halted, turned to face his questioner.

"I will not disturb Sally, nor will I ever allow any harm come to her, if that is what you mean, sir," he replied. "More than that does not bear discussing."

"Another has a strong claim on her affections," said Barnabas.

Kidlington strode down the steps of the house on Mincing Lane. He turned at the bottom of the stairs and said, "Yet she has a will of her own."

Before either Barnabas or Sanford could respond, Kidlington was gone.

Sedgewick was the very last to depart.

"Is he to be trusted?" asked Sanford of the lawyer.

"So far and so long as it coincides with his own plans," said Sedgewick. "But, then again, is that not the best any of us can say, or expect of any other?"

Sanford put his hand on Sedgewick's shoulder, and said, "How is your wife?"

"Poorly," said Sedgewick. "But thank you for asking."

Sedgewick walked into the darkness beyond the lamp by the blue door of the house on Mincing Lane.

"Not a single Latin word from him all evening," said Barnabas. "Old Sedgewick is in a bad way."

"The Owl has much to answer for," said Sanford, shutting the door.

The Cook was meaning the very same thing, down in the kitchen.

"Not just a brewery of eggshells this time, or a hanging up of witch-bottles," she said. "Just as I said, everything is all a-swickle. Well, if the Devil wants a fight, he will get one from me! I will make him swallow a fork, I will. Gather your feet now, niece, and get ready. Where's my knife for heweling, the really big one?"

A week later, at supper time, Sally called on the Gardiners in Gracechurch Street. She excused her escort, Mr. Fletcher, saying she would come straight back on her own by hackney.

But she did not come straight back, instructing the hackney instead to deliver her to an address just off Fenchurch Street.

As the coach clattered through the lane-fractured City, Sally argued with herself.

"One foot over the stile now, must go either forward or back."

She reached up to rap on the ceiling, instructed the driver to turn around and head to Mincing Lane . . .

She felt the trickle—turning into a rushet—of the blood, flowing from the contusions on her heart: the imperious pressure of a thwarted humour in its most jussive mood, insistent, undeniable, scoring the pericardium of her emotions, gouging still deeper the endless channel into which desire flows without regard for equity or equipoise, indifferent to rectitude or retribution.

. . . She lowered her hand before she knocked on the ceiling. The coach rolled on towards the address off Fenchurch Street.

She glimpsed in her mind the Berosiana, the Book of Rue and Repentance, saw inscribed there many words in a fiery script on pages patined in gold. She reached her hand up again . . .

She felt the siking of desire, widening into an ocean that grew but had no shore, a tempest-straked, illimitable ocean, its surface japanned with seductions and spooning eddies, a heaving, froth-scurled surface over plumbless depths.

. . . Again she retracted her arm.

The carriage stopped and Sally got out.

A door opened. James stood in the lamplight, extending his hand.

Sally took his hand. The door closed behind the two of them.

On the morning two days after Sally's tryst with James at his lodgings near Fenchurch Street, Maggie accompanied the Cook to Sally's room in the attic. Sally had not been out of her room since returning late the evening before last. Cook had on a tray for Sally warm milk with honey, a fat jenneting cut into quarters, a sliver of slipcote cheese from Sussex, and two fine wheat buns still warm from the bakery just off Dunster Court.

"Come along, my love," said Cook. "Whatever the matter is, it won't get any better if you don't eat. Ewe's-milk cheese, Sally, with a rosey-greeney pear, just the thing to help you cast off your blue spectacles."

Sally opened the door a few moments later. She took the tray from Cook. Seeing Maggie behind Cook, Sally said, "Oh, it's you."

Cook stepped back, thinking, "Two queen bees in one hive will never do. So alike, yet so different. A black Sally and a white Maggie. But that Maggie is no little smee ducking around in the bulrushes. She's a game cock, got 'er gaffles on for fightin'. Or a shrike, with a bill for tearing. They might ought to name that ship of theirs the *Shrike-Pheasant*, though no one's asking me."

Cook left the two young women facing each other at Sally's door.

"May I come in?" said Maggie.

"If you must," said Sally, shrugging and turning away.

"A galled back it is that breaks easily," said Maggie.

"A hog oversat is cause of its own bane," said Sally.

Maggie shook her head and entered Sally's room.

"*Chi di*," said Maggie. "How do you live like this? How do you find anything when you need it?"

Sally put the tray down so hard the milk slopped over the glass and one of the buns rolled onto the floor (which Isaak then chased and batted into a paper-choked corner).

"*You*, how dare you?" said Sally, her hair uncombed, her feet bare.

"Cousin, cousin, please, I meant no harm. . . ."

"Don't 'cousin' *me* . . . You're the interloper, Maggie Collins, not me, make no mistake."

"Oh, *ma chi kwe*, will you calm yourself . . . please? We've work to do, you and I; whether we hold hands doing so is beside the point, don't you think?"

Sally turned her back, sat down, ate and drank a bit before replying.

"Maggie, . . . I am sorry. It's just that . . . you are so new here, and we McDoons have already carried ourselves through so much, our plans are so advanced, I would hardly know where to start in developing your state of knowledge."

Maggie looked around the room, contained her anger (barely). She acknowledged the many intriguing calculations and drawings pinned on the walls and she was eager to delve into many of the books she saw piled on the floor and leaning one on the other in the bookcases.

"But there is no cohesion, no system," Maggie thought. "As Cook would say, this is a regular scrimble-scramble, higgles and piggles. Over there I spy a fragment of a fugue, and there the origins of a cantata, but the instrumentation is incomplete and there is no overall composition. Sally, you think too small: we are in search of an oratorio, a Singing on a very grand scale."

All she said aloud was, "I have been through trials of my own, Sally, and would be in my turn uncertain to know how to convey their effect to you. Let us postpone such discourses. Instead we must prepare for our visitor, or have you forgotten? Mr. Gandy arrives in an hour, and we need to show him our designs, together downstairs in the partners' office."

Mr. Gandy arrived right on time. The first Sally and Maggie saw of him was a pair of energetic, well-trousered legs and worn but nicely brushed shoes below an enormous birdcage carried by two ink-stained hands. In the cage was a thrush-sized bird, glossy black with a single sharply tranched white bar on each wing and an equally well-demarcated white belly. Its tail was long and black with white edges. It sang prodigiously, filling the house with tumbling, soaring, darting notes, small eruptions, a rill of effervescence.

Yikes sat up and stared. Isaak circled the cage, which Mr. Gandy set down on a chair.

"I work best this way," he said, without any other introduction. "Hope you do too. Song, melody, makes my mind dance, draws forth all the best propositions. Beauty isn't he? I have no name yet for him, only bought him yesterday you see, at the bird market by White Lion Street, on Great St. Andrew's, so I pray you, help me name him, will you?"

"What is he?" said Sally. "Looks like a wagtail waxed overlarge, or a nightingale dressed as a domino."

"He is a Dial-Grackle from Bengal, a Magpie-Robin, but I like best what the Indians call him: asaulary."

"I name him Charicules," said Maggie without hesitation, pronouncing it to rhyme with "Hercules". "Like the heroine from the *Aethiopica*, he's half-black, half-white. If he is to inspire our work, then he—like Chariclea in the romance—must be ready for every sort of adventure and peril, including the possibility of sacrifice to Heaven."

"Well and finely expressed. Charicules it is," said Mr. Gandy. "Further apt by chance or foreknowledge (it does not matter which) because saularies fight as well as they sing. The Bengalis and Burmese pit them against one another, just as we do gamecocks. Perfect little pugilists, these birds!"

Yikes went back to sleep (the bird might be a herald but not of lunch, so what was the point in staying awake?); Isaak stared at Charicules; the bird ignored the cat and spooled out a leaping line of melody; the three humans spent the rest of the morning, and all afternoon until tea, engrossed in the Great Plan.

Mr. Gandy had a bulimic approach, swallowing information of every possible kind (no matter how obscure or ill-defined) and in every variety of configuration (no matter how contorted, complex or conspiratorial), then sluicing most of it back out again, in new and unexpected patterns. He half-sang his thoughts, in a multi-contrapuntal conversation with Charicules the saulary and with Sally the smee and Maggie the shrike, with dormant Yikes and Isaak the restless, with the clock on the mantlepiece, with the clink and swankle of Cook in the kitchen below, and the swish and rustle of the maid here and there throughout the house, with the voices of wheels, winches, cogs and pintles from the street.

"Oh, here you startle the spirit of geometry . . .

. . . unlike anything I have ever seen . . .

. . . with steam to breathe large the melody . . .

. . . sleek and shimmery as greylings under a physic moon . . .

. . . my query is only percontative, you understand . . .

. . . the shipwrights will need a helping hand . . .

". . . to attain an agreeable motion and fervent attitude . . .

. . . needs here modillions, and there postiques . . .

. . . zealous fermatas will suspend time, and the delicate hemiola . . .

. . . pour passion into the vasty hollow breves . . .

. . . the basso continuo steps with grace up nautiloid casings . . ."

"But can we get this built, Mr. Gandy?" asked Maggie.

Mr. Gandy scratched his head, his eyes very bright, smiled, and said, "Yes, with much time, money and devotion, but the more consuming question is: *what* is it that you are having built, and why?"

Maggie said, "Are you willing, sir, to put a final answer aside—for now—and accept an answer deliberately elliptical?"

Mr. Gandy pulled up his chair and nodded, "So long as the tale is a good one in the telling."

"Oh, it is," said Maggie. "Do you know about imaginary numbers?"

"Of course, the square root of less than nothing, but—as an architect and draftsman—I find them of no interest except as objects of eccentric contemplation when I have finished a good bottle or two of sherry, late at night, when my birds have quieted themselves in their cages and my mind roams over the chimney-pots."

Maggie and Sally laughed.

Maggie continued, "Yet what we propose is to use a mechanics and an architecture as real as the bricks of this building to drive a ship along a road defined by . . . imaginary numbers!"

Sally added, "Expressed musically, and swelled through the application of steam power!"

Mr. Gandy looked to the birdcage and said, "Hello Charicules, here's a fairy tale of grotesque proportions! Bring us our seven-league boots and our flying carpets! Set sail for Laputa and Brobdingnag!"

The women laughed again.

"You must meet Mr. Bunce soon," said Sally. "He can explain

this in mathematical terms that may overcome the opposition of your logic."

"Which *I* can also do, at least in outline before Cook brings us our tea," said Maggie.

For the next hour, Maggie (with only occasional interjections from Sally) spoke of four-square unity as demonstrated by Euler and Gauss, of construing this unity into planar space as Lagrange theorized, of thus rotating one's self into spaces on the "other side of the axis," of finding congruency between the spaces there and here. She expounded on the budget of paradoxes, the method of fluxions, and the doctrine of chances, relating these to what she called "the trigonometry of voiced rhythm" and "an oratorio of brachistochrones." She emphasized the central role of indeterminancy, of multiple interpretations and improvised solutions, the role of porisms and the skewed metre, the note held and bent and elongated into new space, the chord liberated, the harmony released. She covered a dozen sheets of paper with secants, catenaries, tangents, axes, musical notation sprawling into four planes, sprays of curving lines, florettes of co-sines, numbers becoming a new array of stars.

Mr. Gandy sat mostly silent throughout the lecture, only now and then asking a short question about a shape or a form, a vector, arc or trajectory. When Maggie finished, he sat up very straight, looked at Charicules and hum/whistled for a full minute along with the bird, which began to respond, matching notes in new variations.

"You are mad, the both of you," said Mr. Gandy, suddenly stopping his duet with Charicules. "Mad as moonrakers, as the men from Gotham in their tub, the dropsy knight asleep in his cockle-boat. Trying to catch the wind in a net, making ropes from sand!"

Gandy paused, for full effect, and finished in a laughing rush, his words somersaulting from his mouth: "Therefore and thusly: I am wholly yours, all in, enthralled, bewitched, ready to believe whatever you whistle up. These ideas—mapping a terrain that exists only in our minds yet is as real as Westminster—I do not even know what that means but it captures me. All in, my young women, all in. Miss Maggie, I dub thee now 'Lady Improvisatrice' and 'Dame Calculus.' What did you call it? 'A rhapsody of the equations'?"

Sally looked out the window.

"You—we—will be roundly ridiculed, possibly condemned, about this work, even without observers understanding its true purpose," said Mr. Gandy, his laughter gone. "Having the East India Company as an investor may actually worsen the matter, as it will attract much more public scrutiny than if this were an entirely private matter. Worse, given the public's low regard for John Company. How shall we call this chimera, this star-crossed hybrid?"

"It's 'incertae sedis,'" said Sally in a tight voice. "'Of uncertain placement.' We are outside all natural taxonomy."

"'Indigo Pheasant' fits well then, a creature of fable, wit and passion," said the architect. "Certainly not a bird seen in the market on Great Saint Andrew Street!"

"Anger, Mr. Gandy," said Maggie. "Do not overlook 'anger' as one of its chief virtues, and a prime element in its creation. Our construction will be a pianoforte—nay, a pipe organ—filled with wrath. A selah-machine."

Bemused, Mr. Gandy could only say, "You have given me a long explanation of the *what*, but only very oblique glimpses of the *why*. Yet, as I begin to grasp your hopes—while freely admitting my confusion about the ultimate ends to be achieved—I feel I can content myself with your descriptions. For now, at least."

He paused to bend over and rub Isaak between the ears. Standing upright again, he said, "I have never met anyone like you, Miss Collins. You articulate your thoughts with force and facility beyond what anyone could anticipate from someone of your . . . original situation, meaning no disrespect. Your acquirements strike me and will surely strike others, should there be a way to bring your facility to their attention."

Neither Maggie nor Sally responded, the former because she

disliked the back-handed nature of the compliment, the latter because she had not been complimented at all.

Mr. Gandy seemed oblivious to the emotions he had inspired, but—like Charicules—he brabbled happily on.

"Speaking of attention and scrutiny," he said. "Have you thought of protecting your invention, getting a patent? Not sure how you would disallow claims of prior art, the *Indigo Pheasant* and all its accoutrements being such a welter of differing ideas all incorporated as one. There may be more than one patent here, for that matter, though it would require much stamina and very adroit composition to describe what you have invented. Not an insuperable task though, I imagine."

Departing, he left Charicules for the household, as a token of friendship, a promise of his return in the near-future, and—as he put it with a grin in his voice—to keep a spy under the McDoon roof, an agent who could uncover more of what the *Indigo Pheasant*'s ultimate purpose might be.

"Rum fellow, I told you so," said Barnabas when he came home for dinner and found a black-and-white magpie-robin filling his house with liquid notes that swivelled around corners and stretched themselves into the eaves. "Left us a what? A saulary, did you call it? Well, whatever it is, it chirps a sight better than old parrot did; plus, this one never sings the same note twice!"

Interlude: Qualia

[Extract from a report by Lieutenant Thracemorton to his superiors at the Admiralty]

Mr. Kidlington continues to seek money from me, which I constantly refuse, and to complain of the short budget he feels your Honours have forced him to abide with. To this end, he has also sought the resources provided by money-lenders and pawnbrokers. In particular, he has visited one Mr. Smallweed, an invalid of vicious nature (in my estimation, this individual is reprehensible in all his parts and behavior), who appears to have extended to Mr. K. a loan of one hundred pounds. I was unable to determine the tenure or terms of the loan, but as this Smallweed operates on the margins of propriety, I can only surmise that Mr. K. has received this money on conditions not fully favourable to himself.

I believe Smallweed is known to the lawyer Tulkinghorne, whom Mr. Sedgewick, Esq., has warned us about.

[Letter from Charles Babbage to Sally]

Upon the Interdiction of the Maculate Angels,
at the waning of the Mercury Moon,
5 Devonshire Street, Portland Place, London

Dear Miss MacLeish:

It gives me great joy to respond to your letter of last Thursday; I am particularly delighted to learn that your colleague, Mr. Dorentius Bunce, knows my esteemed tutor, Robert Woodhouse, from their time together at Caius College; and moreover, that you yourself have been in correspondence with my friends the Herschels (if ever a family was more devoted to the study of the stars, then I have not heard of it).

In direct response to your query, allow me to note the following:

The best use of hypothesis is not confined to those cases in which they have subsequently received confirmation—it may be as great or greater where the hypothesis has defeated the expectations of its author. I go so far as to say—in support of what I understand your own inquiries to rest upon—that a hypothesis possessing a sufficient degree of plausibility to include various facts at the outset will help us arrange those facts in correct order and will suggest to us experiments to confirm or refute the hypothesis.

I recommend to you the work of Laplace, and—among the earlier students of mathematics—de Moivre, Bombelli, and Bachet. Given your questions to me, I stress to you Argand's *Essai sur une manière de représenter les quantités imaginaires dans les constructions géométriques*, a copy of which I could supply you with. Argand is, like you, a gifted amateur—proof that a tenth Muse exists, inspiring us to follow the path of Mathematics!

My wife Georgiana and I will welcome you to tea or dinner in our home, should you wish to visit. The younger Herschel dines frequently with us, also from time to time George Peacock, Olinthus Gregory, and other men whose investigations of mathematical phenomena would—I am sure of it—excite your interest.

Your most esteemed servant,
—Chas. Babbage

[Letter from Friedrich Wilhelm Bessel, Director of the Prussian Royal Observatory at Koenigsberg, to Sally; translated from the original German]:

To the most genteel Miss Sarah MacLeish:

Thank you for your letter of the 12th of last month, which arrived via our mutual friends, the firm of Kulenkamp in Bremen.

Your query astonishes me—I had no conception that anyone else, let alone a young Englishwoman otherwise unknown to me (and one who writes in flawless German to boot!), could possibly be interested in such things.

Permit me to tell you that my soul is thrilled to know I am not the only person pursuing this line of exploration. I enclose some of my equations, to advise you of the current state of my own knowledge, and to ask how far these may corroborate your own work.

My goal is to demonstrate how measurements of the aberrations in the Earth's nutation, precession, and rotation may be used to calculate distances of fixed stars and other objects within the deepest Aether. I am most interested in stars within the constellations we here call the "Globus Aerostaticus" and the "Coma Berenices," which can be said to balance one another in their respective hemispheres. As you intimate, mapping through the seasons the relative positions of Horvendile's Toe, the Great May Star, The Crossing Star, and The Ark Star may also repay the effort.

My best thinking at present is to use parallax calculations and the scalar range of the perpendicular in obliquity as the most effective means to derive the distances. Would that concur with your own thoughts?

                        With felicitations and friendly greetings,
                                      —F. W. Bessel

[From *Poor Robin's Almanac for London Families for the Year 1817, Being a Florilegium of The Good, The Useful and the Entertaining for All Ages*]

[... . . . .]

Concerning the weather (inclusive also of the behaviours, activities and sentiments it brings forth), we may only hope that 1817 is better than the *annus horribilis* of 1816.

As must be known to all, it rained in 1816 on St. Swithin's Day (July 15th)—which by popular understanding provides reliable foresight about the weather for the following forty days—and in fact the rest of summer and the entire fall saw an almost unbroken, cold downpour. One goodwife of our acquaintance in Southwark claims that her house-cat has learned to swim, and we receive reports from farmers across the country that their plough-horses are indistinguishable from those of their neighbours, all such creatures being one colour only: namely, that of mud.

Other reports are more ominous. The red sunsets witnessed everywhere have no natural explanation, nor the thick chilled fumes and fogs that seem to arise at every hand, reducing sight and sound for even the hardiest traveller.

London has been especially plagued by these atmospheric tumults. The Thames and all the other London rivers (the Effra chief among them) have threatened to leave their banks.

Cause for even greater dismay is what the great deluge and its attendant mists may portend. Many (in all of London's many and varied parts, from Mayfair and Belgravia to Wapping and Rotherhithe) have reported seeing—or quarter-seeing, to be more accurate—strange forms and figures in the rain, giving rise to a multitude of odd stories that would seem to belong more to Fairyland than to our modern metropolis.

What sort of stories, a gentle reader might ask? Poor Robin has done his best to separate the oats from the ewendrie, and winnow out the quack-nonsense and tales of steeple-climbing pigs; he will not indulge or incite idle fancies, but he has no doubt as to the veracity of much that is related to him. Here he displays a mere handful of the great many verifiable anecdotes sent his way.

— One of our most reputable clockmakers, on St. John Street in Clerkenwell, has described unwanted attentions from three mysterious tall men in tall hats with long grey coats, who speak in antique accents and are not known in the neighbourhood; these men have appeared twice on the premises, emerging from the cellar without first having come through the door opening onto the street, both times in heavy rains at dusk; all the clocks in the workshop stopped at the very moment of the strangers' appearance and could only be restarted with much labour by the apprentices; the three men made strange gestures and chanted what some said sounded like The Lord's Prayer backwards and then vanished.

— One of our leading shipyards has been the scene of repeated affronts and affrays between its workers and various unsavoury individuals, some of whom are said to perform what can only be described as rituals out of a pagan past, with the likely object of frustrating the building of a ship whose keel was laid just this most recent

St. Nicholas Day; one such individual is credibly described as having ears resembling those of a serpent, another was—upon close inspection—seen to have her left foot facing backwards, while yet another had no mouth visible though he was heard to sing (in a language no one present could identify).

—— A laughing, raven-haired woman—dressed in shades of green—has haunted an eminent maker of pianofortes, on Wigmore Street very near to Cavendish Square in the West End; on several occasions the proprietor and his workers, arriving at the locked premises just before dawn, have heard one of their fine instruments being played; they unfailingly describe the music as rough, discordant, of the broken sort the Italians call "arpeggiare," that awakens the blood; upon unlocking and entering the workplace, the piano-makers found this woman (no acquaintance of theirs) playing one of their finished instruments with a wild twitching of her arms and limbs, and having no earthly explanation for how she gained access to the place; most perturbing and least explainable, her arms were several feet longer than they had a right to be, and ended in stiff, small, coppery fingers that travelled too swiftly over the keyboard; when confronted, this person laughed, fled into the back of the shop and then seemingly disappeared; whichever pianoforte she touched went badly out of tune, and several even had to be destroyed.

[... . . .]

THE INDIGO PHEASANT *Volume Two of Longing for Yount*

[A farthing broadside, very popular in the winter of 1816-1817 throughout the South Bank and the East End. At the top of the sheet is a rough woodcut of a man wrestling a horned, two-headed dragon, with the Hand of God suspended in heaven above and between them, the hand pointing from its cloud in the direction of the man; various cherubim and winged fish adorn the skies, while the arena in which the two combatants battle is littered with fallen lambs, broken eggs, grinning skulls and scattered flowers; in the left-hand corner of the picture is a crowing cock atop a sheaf of wheat, in the right-hand corner a glowering owl, holding what appears to be a rabbit in its claws; the image appears to be recycled from the religious controversies of the 17th century. Scrawled on the verso side of the archived example are the words "December at Bell & Burbot, Bethnall Green—'Thou art a priest forever after the order of Melchizedek'—burnt offerings at Gilgal—the sign of the baker's peel, a key to the new Salem—anointure by trumpet?"]

PATRIOTS,
BELIEVERS,
FELLOW WAYFARERS!

You have been a good ear to me in the past!

☞ **READ NOW** ☜

the latest news in our struggle to climb the path to salvation, to bring the peace of Shiloh and advance the Jubilee so none will remain slaves.

YOU WILL KNOW OF THE ONE STYLING HIMSELF

BILLY SEA-HEN

and his preachments on the holy path and the steps necessary to hight true to this road.

I was one of his first allies in his program, and instructed many of you to join me in this alliance.

~ YET, ever the Devil ~ is an unwearied tempter!

We see now that *Billy Sea-Hen* has spewed falsehoods in his campaign to enroll marchers on the sacred way.

He is Unmasked at last—*We* are undeceived.

Come *HEAR ME* speak to his perfidy on *Sunday next* in *the field by the ropewalk* on the *Basin Road, Millwall*.

My sisters and brothers, you oastlers of lime and scutchers of flax, heavers of coal and workers of cloth with your needles by rush-light: You will not be disappointed as I recount the many knavish tricks of this deceiver, and enumerate all his trumperies.

FRIENDS,

come see me *CUT OFF THE HEAD* of this *HEN*, and do so using his own words as compared to those in *HOLY SCRIPTURE!*

'And Saul said unto his uncle, He told us plainly that the asses were found. But of the matter of the kingdom, whereof Samuel spake, he told him not.'
(1 Samuel 10: 16)

—The most humble John Matthew Peasestraw

Chapter 4: More Perils, or, A Thousand Strokes of Mean Invention

"A Merchant Ship ought:
1. To be able to carry a great lading in proportion to its size.
2. To sail well by the wind, in order to beat easily off a coast, where it may be embayed, and also to come about well in a hollow sea.
3. To work with a crew small in number in proportion to its cargo.
4. To be able to sail with a small quantity of ballast.
[... . . .]
. . . We can conclude nothing concerning the length, breadth, and depth of ships, since different qualities require conditions diametrically opposite to each other. We may succeed in uniting two of these advantages by a certain form and by certain proportions given to ships, but it is impossible to combine all four in an eminent degree. It is not possible to gain on one side without losing another."

—**Fredrik Henrik af Chapman**,
Architectura Navalis Mercatoria (Stockholm, 1768; translated by James Inman, 1820, ppg. 79-80)

"Porism: A proposition affirming the possibility of finding such conditions as will render a certain problem indeterminate or capable of innumerable solutions.
—**John Playfair**,
in *The Transactions of the Royal Society in Edinburgh*,
vol. iii (1794)

"Her madness hath the oddest frame of sense, such a dependency of thing on thing, as e'er I heard in madness."
—**William Shakespeare**,
Measure for Measure, Act V, Scene 1 (1604/1623)

The gloomy fall of 1816 calved an even more lugubrious winter. The sun, already half-forgotten through a rainy summer and fall, abandoned London and the rest of Great Britain altogether. Rain, mist and clouds muted everything, casting the world in the dull bronze-grey shades of bell-metal and the soft sheen of vermeil and pewter. When the sun did appear it shone with an eerie, oily, reddish glow, as if blood were seeping through the gauze of heaven. No one was happy except the makers of umbrellas and those who supplied them with oiled silk and baleen ribs.

The McDoon household was very unhappy that fall; the rain, though irksome, was the smallest source of their melancholy. Most of their distress and frustration ran like rivulets just below the surface, near enough at all times to keep everyone's feet wet without completely drowning anyone. The only members of the house on Mincing Lane—the house with the dolphin-shaped doorknocker—who kept up their cheer were Yikes (for whom the ceaseless rain was simply an excuse to stay napping by the fire) and Charicules (who sang in time to the raindrops on the windowpanes and in counterpoint to the wind rattling the sashes).

The Project crept ahead, fitfully, with erratic eighth-steps.

By Martinmas in early November, the McDoons had raised

THE INDIGO PHEASANT *Volume Two of Longing for Yount*

only half the necessary capital but decided to proceed any way ("what choice do we have?" said Barnabas). Despite the lack of full financing but against various forms of additional surety and further rights in collateral, Blackwall's agreed to lay the keel for *The Indigo Pheasant*. The McDoons felt strongly that laying the keel for a choir-boat should best happen on November 22nd, the day of Cecilia—patron saint of music—to capture and bind into the vessel "in broken air, trembling, the wild Musick, . . . in a dying, dying Fall" (as Pope had written a century earlier). Yet their fortune was ill-annexed: the momentous occasion was delayed until Saint Nicholas's Day on December 6th, due to last-minute contractual controversies and to difficulties maneuvering the length of elm for the keel into the yard. An irritable fate continued to dog the McDoons: at the keel-laying ceremony, a windy tongue of rain washed off the rowan branch that Sally had tied onto the bow-end of the keel. Some of the shipwrights, carpenters and blocksmen muttered under their sodden hats that the ship might be cursed or at least resolutely wayward if it would not accept the rowan's warding and guiding powers. The McDoons pretended not to hear such talk.

Yuletide brought no respite. During the ember week of Advent, Blackwall's caused further delays by disputing the proposed dimensions of the ship—not its total scantlings, but the degree of beam required for the housing of the mysterious device (still being designed by Maggie, Sally, Mr. Gandy, and Dorentius, with Reglum's help) and its revolutionary steam-engine. Barnabas and Sanford did not finish "clarifying" with the shipyard until late in the afternoon of Christmas Eve.

"*Quatsch*, so much for the spirit of fraternity and putting to rest all discord during this wondrous season," sighed Barnabas, as they rode in a hired carriage on December 24th back to Mincing Lane from Rotherhithe. He looked forward to a long river of wassail-punch, a small mountain of goose topped with rosemaried sausages, and a larger mountain ("no, better yet: an entire mountain *range*!") of desserts, afters and delicacies.

"Men make much of a season when it meets their needs,

less so when it would force them to more charitable conduct," said Sanford.

"Takes a good eighteen months from laying the keel to launching the ship," said Barnabas as the City's rapidly darkening maze of streets, chares, alleys and snuggeries fled past their coach window (the driver was thinking of his own rendezvous with Christmas dinner, and did not spare the whip). "That means a midsummer delivery in 1818, at the earliest."

"Given our unauspicious start, I would not stake more than a dod's worth on even that early a date," said Sanford. "The more so since the ship itself is not the main part of our worries—we have the Fulginator and its steam engine to think of too."

"The heroes in all the stories never had to wait so long," said Barnabas. "Buttons and butterflies! Add in the sailing time, slooping right out into the Somewhither and assuming no miswandering like the last time, that means we might arrive back in Yount sometime spring or summer 1819 by our clock-time here."

"Just more proof that we are *not* in a one of those stories," said Sanford. "No seven-league boots for us, no magic carpet, no hippogriff to whisk us like Orlando hither and yon. We can wish all we want for the winged chariot that flew Palmerin and Fiona to the End of the World in the blink of an eye, or for the enchanted wagon that took Silvander to Davinella his beloved in the *Nonamerone* . . ."

"Hard work being fairy tale heroes when we aren't in a fairy tale."

"I fear our task will get harder still, old friend."

"You chastise my ambition! No more such bleak cheer from you, Sanford; it's Christmas, after all!"

Yet, despite his admonitions to be earnestly cheerful, Barnabas thought with increasing despondency that evening of Tom and Afsana, Nexius and the Queen, the little Malchen and even the Cretched Man. Arriving almost three years' hence might mean utter defeat for them, death, or worse.

"To Tom and Afsana," he raised a glass, but by then

everyone else had gone to bed. "For all we know, they might be dead already."

The arrival of New Year's Day ushered in no relief. The weather turned harsher than the almanacs' most dour predictions: the Thames froze almost as far downriver as Westminster, halting the erection of the Strand Bridge. Sleet laced the rain. Ice buckled gutters. Everything stank of brown coal. The sun—already on short rations—starved itself and all those who depended on it.

Everyone got sick, for weeks on end, with half-drowned lungs, distempers of the throat, agues of the head. The cold sneaked into even the best-heated rooms, lodging itself in knees and necks and the roots of teeth. It was so cold that the napping Isaak slumped herself against the bulk of the ever-dormant Yikes; no one could remember such a thing.

Charicules alone defied the dark and the cold, singing for hours, starting before what little dawn there was, with soft experiments and gentle matins to wake the house. Isaak was usually first to greet the saulary, coming down to the partners' room while the only other sound was the maid cleaning out the fireplaces and Cook beginning the breakfast in the kitchen. Maggie was rarely far behind; Cook often found the three—bird, cat, and woman—alone together in the partners' room, composing their own little antiphonies. Without realizing it, Cook sometimes hummed or even whistled a clumsy counterpoint when she left the room, and continued to do so intermittently throughout the day.

Legato lark, rhythm-bender, tactician of the fugue: Charicules recked not the cold and the wet. He sang ostinatos into the collied sky, building his themes upon the repetition. Maggie sang with him, providing the basso continuo, shaping motets and passacailles that would become part of the Great Song. They sang in and around the ticking of the clock, now fleeing the tempo, now meeting it gleefully. They poured out their own *stabat mater speciosa* to celebrate the joys of the blessed Mother, and plucked down grace notes to inflect the under-meles service in mid-afternoon. They seethed vespers with the hymn to the

Alma Mater, layering hope-notes and chroma onto the steadily offered waves of thanksgiving.

Charicules gave the McDoons courage to continue, necessary since their business fortunes declined in the winter of early 1817. The funds from Coppelius, Prinn & Goethals (Widow) helped, of course, but as fast as money flowed in, the faster it flowed out again. The workers at Blackwalls, complaining of spectral disturbances and a spate of "unnatural" accidents, insisted on higher wages. For similar reasons, both Gravell—the watchmakers on St. John Street—and Wornum—the makers of pianofortes on Wigmore Street, by Cavendish Square—respectfully (but firmly) requested additional payment.

"Cost overruns, a goblin's picnic of cost overruns!" said Barnabas, on Candlemas Eve. The saulary burbled quietly away in its corner of the partners' room. Cook had thoughtfully brought up some Burgundy wine, as it was late afternoon and—more important—Barnabas was suffering from a very raw throat.

Sanford nodded without looking up from the latest pile of bills and invoices.

"Beans and bacon, most of these demands make little sense to me," growled Barnabas, after a long sip of the Burgundy. "Bills from a maker of pianofortes—and now we are to engage the services of an organ-maker as well. What next? Makers of drums and flutes?"

"Maggie says the Fulginator needs elements of both these arts or it will not work properly," said Sanford, still scratching with his pen at the sums before him.

"Well, yes, but at such an expense? *Quatsch*. And then there's all the special wood she wants to house the blasted thing in. Sabicu, teak, macassar ebony . . . oh what else?"

"Bubinga, palisander, antiara, it is all specified quite clearly here, and here, and here," said Sanford without looking up. "I like the cost even less than you do, but we must put our faith in Maggie. She says each of these woods will play its assigned role, some kinds for durability, some for their flexible nature, some because they most effectively withstand damp and salt, and so on. The list extends—as I suppose it must— to 'sacassite bearings,' 'blue bolcotar oil,' 'indrademous stone for fittings,' something called 'terential colianasthium.'"

Charicules followed the rhythm of the names of the exotica, making a sonatina of

"sabicu, bolcotar,

bubinga, sacassite,

antiar', colianasthium."

Sanford glanced at the bird, recognition flitting across his Norfolk features.

"And very specialized, *very* expensive cabinet-makers," said Barnabas, the Burgundy soothing his throat without smoothing his temper. "Morgan & Sanders in the Strand with something called a 'metamorphic chair,' and the fellows, what's-their-names, in Soho with their fancywork and scroll-detailing and I don't know what else. *Quatsch*."

"Maggie says the housing and cradle for the Fulginator need the most profoundly precise assemblage, all the dovetails truer than true, the joints without flaw," said Sanford. "I share your discomfort, but her arguments convince me that to spend less here is a false economy."

"What does Sally say about all this? And how much will all that china clay of hers empty our pockets? The clay, I am so sorry to say, that cost Mr. Harris his life."

Sanford put down his pen and paused before answering.

"*That*," he said. "Bears thinking about in much deeper detail. What, in point of fact, *is* Sally's opinion on this . . . or any of our related business, for that matter? She has not been with us enough lately to give us the benefit of her thoughts."

Barnabas winced, and drank more of the Burgundy. In the house with the dolphin door-knocker, restless secrets ganged under the roof-beam and unacknowledged truths tip-toed up and down the staircases.

Sally was frequently absent. Ending her room-bound reveries and crises, Sally had swung into frenetic action—away from the house on Mincing Lane. While Barnabas and Sanford had all they could do with the raising of the capital and the constant shipyard negotiations, Sally took it upon herself to represent McDoon & Co. with the Project's myriad other contractors. When Barnabas asked her about her sudden spate of errands, she said simply, "Tom's not here, so I will be Tom." Barnabas did not contest her right to act—after all, she had attained her majority and had full rights of procuration in the company— but meant only to show his concern for her safety, as she was so often in distant corners of the city. She retorted that Mr. Fletcher usually escorted her, but that she possessed a power more likely of use protecting Mr. Fletcher than the other way around (Barnabas thought better of mentioning the late Mr. Harris in this regard). Sally added that, far from questioning her, the rest of the house should be thanking her for taking on tasks that others either could not or would not handle. Barnabas retreated in a hurry.

Many evenings Sally also spurned Mincing Lane, visiting and calling on friends and establishing new connections. She called many afternoons on Mrs. Sedgewick, sharing long hours with her recovering friend, who absolutely refused to visit the house on Mincing Lane so long as Maggie was living there. Lizzie Darcy and her remote husband were in town for the season, at their house just off Grosvenor Square; Sally was a frequent guest there, and at their friends the Bingleys, and many others in that set. Sometimes Sally dined with the Babbages in Devonshire Street, sometimes with Mary Somerville in Hanover Square, sometimes she went to the lectures at the Royal Institution on Albemarle Street in Mayfair.

Above all, Sally received the great honour of an invitation to breakfast with Sir Joseph Banks, First Baronet, President of the Royal Society since 1778, confidante of the King, a Trustee of the British Museum; *the* Banks, who had documented the Great Auk off Labrador, and who had sailed with Cook on the HMS *Endeavor* to Tahiti, New Zealand and Australia, observing— among so many other things—the Transit of Venus; *the* Banks, who had played a role in Lord Macartney's embassy to China and Sir Staunton's publications about the embassy.

Sally did breakfast with Sir Banks and his wife at their famous house on Soho Square, the epicentre of British science, the crossroads where natural history, exploration, politics and state power all conversed. She did call on Mrs. Sedgewick, the Babbages, the Darcys, the Somervilles. She did visit offices and workshops to "clarify" on behalf of *The Indigo Pheasant*. One day she harangued the timber-merchants by the Greenland Docks and at the Floating Mead in Lambeth, another day it was the turn of the cabinetmakers on Wardour Street and Gerrard Street in Soho, on the third day she browbeat the specialists at the Java Wharf in Bermondsey, on the fourth she was bedeviling the engineers at Henry Maudslay's. She saved her most refined pressures for the representative of the china clay producers. The pianoforte manufacturer near Cavendish Square learned to dread her approach almost as much as he feared the appearance of the Green Lady (which was unfair, but he could not know that), as did his counterparts at Flight & Robson, the organ-makers on St. Martin's Lane near Leicester Square.

But there was more to the story. Sally was away from the house on Mincing Lane far longer than even her expansive itinerary required. Four hours became six, and six became twelve, as Nicobella said in the well-known story. In the thin of the night, Sally sang up a glamour to dull and confuse the minds of the others in the McDoon house about her comings and goings, a cloak for her whereabouts. She even (reluctantly) cast her spell over Isaak.

Sally was going to James on every chance and pretext she could seize.

The Wurm leaned back in a chair in his sharded house half hidden in Hoxton Square. He laughed and hugged himself.

"Hooo, hooo, hooom! You sing small songs, to hide your

crepuscular creepings. Please, Sally, abuse your power, betray the trust your family places in you. I encourage you, *ma petite papelarde*."

He rocked himself, rasping his teeth with his tongue.

"Oh hoo, yes, my little larroon, sing your tawdries—a pilfering from the Great Song you and yours are trying to compose—divert the melody from the commonwealth towards your own selfish ends."

He stood up and slowly raised out his long, long arms.

"Sing on, Sally, mortgage yourself with a narrow song, a song that runs out into sand."

Cook was pottering late in the kitchen, two days after Candlemas. Maggie had just left her after a good "mardle."

"No Sally tonight either," said the Cook. "Tain't right. Change in the breast of the little smee. But I don't see things clearly with her the way I used to. Glakes and glamours in my eyes."

She finished putting the pans in order, ready for the next day's round of meals.

"Poor Mr. Reglum. A real gentleman, he is. In his stead, most other men would be throwin' daggers right about now. Sally not actin' the lady—much as it pains me to say so."

She placed her leaching knife beside the others, all lined up like soldiers on parade with the heweling knife as the general at their head.

"What was I just thinking? Something. . . . I cannot make it out. Maybe it will come to me, but now I am off to bed."

Cook wiped her hands, gave the kitchen one last look, and—taking her candle—went out to her quarters behind the house.

The dike began to give way just after Easter, which in 1817 fell on April 6th.

THE INDIGO PHEASANT *Volume Two of Longing for Yount*

The shipyard announced on St. Gilthoniel's Day that the McDoons had two weeks to make good on all arrears, or work on *The Indigo Pheasant* would cease, and the yard would consider proceedings to realize their claims *in rem*.

The day after that, the firm of Henry Maudslay—also citing late payment—said they would not continue working on the steam engine.

In mid-April, the first ships of the spring season arrived from over the North Sea, bearing ill tidings for the McDoons. The merchant house in Riga that was to supply the fir for the masts insisted on full payment in advance before shipping in the summer; the McDoons' Hamburg bankers wanted an additional fee for issuing their bill. The Landemanns confirmed that McDoon credit was sliding—and that Coppelius Prinn & Goethals (Widow) was the only firm actively seeking to buy McDoon notes, albeit at a very steep discount.

Matchett & Frew shared news that Coppelius Prinn & Goethals (Widow) were everywhere present in London as well, scooping business from others at ridiculously low prices, "depriving us of our profits." Matchett half-joked about the wits and gossipmongers in the coffeehouses who claimed Coppelius & Co. had an enchanted mill producing gold sovereigns in the cellar of their counting house, or that Prinn was an alchemist whose familiars were trustees of the Bank of England.

The Gardiners—stalwarts of Gracechurch Street, Elizabeth Darcy's relations who had invested in *The Indigo Pheasant*—suffered a calamitous loss in April. An entire ship load of lemons and oranges from Malaga had gone rotten, from bright and aromatic to murrained and sulpy in the course of one night, between the vessel's tying up at the wharf and its unloading the next morning. No one had ever seen the like. The wharfinger mumbled tales about voluminous hissings and rustlings emanating from the ship's hold that night. Others spoke of seeing weevils the size of human babies scrambling about the ship just before dawn, "beetles, cenchers, scalavotes, scorpions." Whatever the cause, since no one had ever heard of an entire cargo rotting overnight, the Gardiners had not insured the lading for more than half its worth.

Mr. Gandy's tale was just as strange. The droll architect, never fortunate with money, claimed that a "Damosel O' The Green"—who had befriended him the previous autumn—had cozened him out of all his wealth (such as it was), to the extent that the bailiffs sought to arrest him for his own unpaid debts. The McDoons bought Charicules and the birdcage from Mr. Gandy, in an attempt to add a few coppers to his meagre pot, but the architect was forced to withdraw from the Project as he fended off the poorhouse.

On April 29th, most appropriately the Day Marking St. Adelsina's Dismission from the Flesh, Coppelius Prinn & Goethals (Widow) sent notice that—under the terms of Article 8 and 17 (on governance and control among the associates, and partial payment for shares) of the Association Agreement relating to *The Indigo Pheasant*—they were calling on McDoon & Co. as general partner to pay in the remaining unpaid capital, and further that—under the terms of Article 26 (on rights of offerings and first refusals)—if McDoon & Co. were unwilling or unable to pay in, then Coppelius Prinn & Goethals (Widow), having over the required 33.3% share of the entire project required to tender for all shares, would exercise its right to buy out all partners including McDoon & Co.

"We'll fight 'em!" said Barnabas. "We'll fight 'em all. We will not be 'all broken implements of a ruined house.' We will see ourselves in Hell first!"

"We are in the Devil's forecourt already," said Sanford, looking perversely happy, as if a battle he had long feared was now upon them and he discovered he was ready after all.

"We must get Sedgewick, he will know the legal ins and outs," said Barnabas.

Sanford looked at the prints of the foundering East Indiamen, then dashed off a note to Sedgewick.

But Sedgewick would not come.

"Conflict of interest?" said Barnabas that evening, when

Sanford had read Sedgewick's reply aloud for the third time. "What in the world can he mean by that? He drew up all the contracts for *The Indigo Pheasant*. Figs and fishwater, he has been lawyer to the McDoons for years!"

"Be that as it may, Sedgewick writes that he cannot help us directly as it could be construed (notice how carefully he puts that) as a conflict of interest," said Sanford. "I dare say this has something to do with our other partners, the East India Company. I smell the Admiralty behind this. After all, where is our promised meeting with Sir John Barrow? Sedgewick made very large cakes of that, his capacity to get us with Sir John. It has been months now, and still not so much as a whisper from the Admiralty about us. Why *is* that?"

Charicules warbled a very low series of notes, challenging the clock on the mantlepiece (or was that ticking the sound of an elf-mill in the wall?).

"There is more to this than just business," said Barnabas. "Sedgewick has not been right since the attack on his poor wife. He hardly comes by anymore, not even to sample Cook's meals. And Mrs. Sedgewick, who used to come by so frequently. . . ."

"Mrs. Sedgewick declines our hospitality for other reasons, you know that Barnabas. She is a vehement study on the subject right now."

Barnabas ignored this last. He thought of Maggie, and of Afsana. He saw a ghostly army of foes approaching Mincing Lane. One hand gripping his vest (an especially resplendent corded silk and sagathy in the pattern called "The Rising Lark") and the other waving his invisible saber, Barnabas exclaimed:

"Tighten our belts, declare emergency, we've thrown and must now stand the hazard of the die," he said. "We'll fly right at 'em, by God we will Sanford!"

In an unmarked room within the Admiralty building, still as dust except for the ticking of a clock held by hippocamps, two black-clad acuminate gentlemen traded notes.

"Mr. I., the affair of *The Indigo Pheasant* goes less well than planned," said one. "The general partners appear to have overextended themselves; I begin to fear the ship shall never get built, which would mean even more—possibly much more—than the loss of ten thousand pounds sterling to His Majesty's Government."

"Yet Kidlington and Sedgewick report interesting developments that might mean—with our careful husbanding and oversight, Mr. Z.—a very attractive outcome for the Crown and for the Empire."

"I think we wait until we have more clarity before we have Sir John meet with the ship's principals. Agreed, Mr. I.?"

"Agreed. No reason to be over-hasty: Sir John is more than busy as it is, with the Navy's new ports at Mauritius and at Simon's Town in South Africa, besides new acquisitions on Madagascar and in Malta."

"Not to mention at Trincomalee."

"Do not forget the coming fight with the Marathas."

"Nor should we overlook young Raffles and his grand ideas about Sumatra, or Beaufort in the Hydrography Office agitating for more funds."

"All hands are applauding Lord Exmouth's marvelous victory at Algiers last summer, little time for distractions relating to a ship that is yet unbuilt and a land that may or may not exist."

"In short, the plan's virtues still lie buried too deeply to be immediately perceived (except by ourselves, of course)."

"Thus, we will let the natural agency of time promote the airing of the plan, and only then speed it to its beneficial conclusion. Sir John can wait—at least until the Chinese arrive, which we hear may happen this summer, the winds from Cape Town allowing."

"Yes, Mr. I. The Chinese will pique Sir John's interest."

"In the meanwhile, Mr. Z., let's keep Thracemorton, and most of all, Shufflebottom, tight to their tasks—especially as wards against the Others."

"Without doubt, Mr. I. Now, moving to our next file, in the matter of . . ."

"Mr. Sanford says we are to be more 'economical,' as he calls it, and so we shall be," said Cook to the maid, Mr. Fletcher, and Maggie, on an evening the week after The Glorious First of May. "I can tighten a belt as well—no, better!—than anybody, just you wait and see. Can work a wonder with eke-meats, tripes, stale hare. They sell broke-bellied fish at Billingsgate for half the price of the whole ones, and taste is no different, if I dress 'em right!"

Her audience, marveling at Cook's genius with a menu but dreading its manifestation under the emaciated new regime, nodded with less than full vigour.

"Come on now, you lot," said Cook. "The house needs us—one and all, come cut, crop or long tail—to pull up and push forward."

"I, for one, am no stranger to going light and bony," said Maggie, shrugging.

"That's the spirit, my girl," said Cook.

"I suppose ropy vittles is better than none," said Mr. Fletcher.

"Oh, there you sound like Mr. Harris," said Cook, going quiet for a minute. She made a little fuss of pouring milk into a bowl for Isaak, who had come downstairs with Maggie.

The maid and Mr. Fletcher left for even more intimate surroundings.

"Sit and mardle a piece with me, Miss Maggie?"

The two talked for a time, while Isaak lapped at her milk.

"I don't suppose Miss Sally is upstairs, is she?" asked Cook.

"No. She is out again this evening."

"You know, it may not be my place to say so, but I think this house would feel better in its bones and kidneys if you and Miss Sally were on better terms. Meaning no disrespect there, of course."

"I try, I really do, *chi di*," said Maggie, reaching out to help Cook polish the forks. "But Sally won't have me. Surely you see that, you who know her best."

"Hey-along there, Miss Maggie," said Cook, with a smile but gently pushing away Maggie's offer of help. "You have no need to do that. My place to clean the forks and all the rest of this."

Maggie smiled in reply.

"On the matter of Miss Sally," said Cook, returning to the topic. "My head has hattled long on her, and on you, these past months. Here is what I reckon: she thinks you will take her place."

Maggie rose in protest, saying, "But I barely feel a part of this house, as it is! *Me*, take over *her* place?"

They talked a long while. As Maggie made to leave, the Cook said, "When we sift and shred it, the fact is: Miss Sally *fears* you are taking her place. She thinks you are trying to steal something from her."

"By Macrina, I don't want to steal *anything* from *anybody*," said Maggie, loudly. "Why would she think that? Except maybe because . . . why do so many white folks think blacks are thieves?"

The Cook looked uncomfortable. Just before Maggie left the kitchen, Cook blurted out: "I thought so too, when you first came here! I took to countin' the spoons and such."

A hole opened in the air between the two. Maggie stood so still that Isaak might have been forgiven for thinking her a statue.

"What would you have me say?" said Maggie, crossing her arms.

"By Morgaine, I am so ashamed," said the Cook. "I don't even think about counting spoons or any such things now. Can you forgive me?"

Maggie did not answer right away. At length she said, wearily, "Yes, I can . . . but not straight off, not at this moment. In my own time."

Cook looked simultaneously miserable and relieved, saying, "I understand, I do. My confession tastes yarrish in my mouth."

THE INDIGO PHEASANT *Volume Two of Longing for Yount*

"Not half so bitter as it does in mine upon hearing you," said Maggie. Then—stately as a queen, with astringent grace—she walked out of the kitchen.

Two nights after the Cook's sad, embarrassed confession, Maggie took the battle to the Owl. On tiger's feet, she strode through the long-case clock in the shrouded house on Hoxton Square.

The Owl was shocked. No one, in all his endless memory, had ever walked through that gate without his invitation or else being under his orders. Despite himself, he admired her bravery and wondered at her skill. How had Maggie sung herself through the mazy gate, over the wickets and hurdles, past the wide-awake guardians? What song had she sung to unlock the locks, unbolt the bolts?

He bowed. His black-red lips stretched very wide in a sardonic smile, he said that her audacity was out of all proportion to her frame, and that her impudence was matched only by what he called "the finitude of her strength."

Maggie did not bow in turn. Putting her hands on her hips, she surveyed the interior of the Owl's earthly demesne. Completely against her will, she found herself admiring his taste in furnishings: the subtly carved oak armoire (dolorous faces, their tongues sticking out; a phoenix wreathed in ivy); snakes and frowning dolphins twining the candelabra, gleaming in the candlelight; dark grey draperies patterned with chevrons the sweet, deathly red of bryony; a hanging in pale slate bordered with symmetrical rust-coloured pilcrows; the ceiling painted, a great oval, slightly cupped, with a procession of robed figures bearing books, staffs, carpenter's tools, sextants and musical instruments, led by a man dressed in sheeny satin white, with on his head a red mitre, carrying before him in both hands a monstrance, the ensemble surrounded by solemn putti; another wall covered almost entirely by a map of the world, delicate black and umber inkings on sepia, a multitude of seahorses and spouting physeters in the seas, elephants with impossibly long trunks, insouciant smooth-legged camels and shaggy lions disporting themselves in the corners; engravings of fleeing nymphs being transformed into trees and birds, centaurs being shot with arrows, other forms of martyrdom ancient and modern, Saint Anthony in the desert, comets over cities with conical towers, annunciations, Saint Fulgentius at his labours. She let her gaze linger on the many, overflowing bookcases.

Swinging out his right arm in an elegant arc, the Owl said, "A universe of knowledge, all yours for the taking, if you just accept a few words of recommendation from me."

Maggie said, "I can take whatever knowledge I want, without your recommendations, without conforming in any fashion to your will."

The Strix regarded her. He rubbed his long lean white hands (a meticulous silken twist of his fingers), shifted slowly from foot to foot. He wondered—and was amazed to be so wondering—what she had come to do: interrogate him, warn him, command him, *threaten* him? He thrilled to the novel feeling that the game had turned to confront its pursuer.

Maggie hummed a small theme, that uncurled around the room as if inspecting the engravings, the map, the putti on the ceiling.

"You cannot win," said the Owl, hooting in the back of his throat. "You are all alone in this foolish quest."

Words, faint, indistinguishable, entered Maggie's hum. The Owl blinked twice, brinched his globular head sidewise.

"Your so-called family," continued Wurm. "Do you really think the white people trust you? Respect you? Let alone love you? Hoom, you are no more than a ragged shadow that has somehow come attached to them."

Maggie paused, her song dwindling back to a hardly audible hum.

"Yes, you see that, don't you?" said Wurm. "Mrs. Sedgewick, as one example very close to home, so solicitous when you were naught but her plaything: does she visit you now; does she invite you into her own drawing room?"

Maggie said, "I myself am not so friendly towards Mrs. Sedgwick, I cannot refute that, but what you did was cruel, exceeding so. She did not deserve such."

The Owl laughed and said, "'Deserve' has nothing to do with it. Do you deserve *her* antipathy, her scorn? She blames *you* for what befell her. Someone else breaks the window, but she blames you for the glass that shattered into her eye."

Maggie started her song again, wisps of melody that barely escaped the Owl's swiping hands.

"Sally mocks you," hoomed the Wurm. "She writes and receives letters in German, knowing you cannot read the language. She never includes you on her calls, in her meetings—she is credited with all your invention, all the fruits of your genius. No one has heard of you, except in a backhanded, bored way; they view you (to the extent they see you at all) as a freak, a 'Calibanna' who has learned a few tricks for the parlour. No one will ever believe your claims to original thought. Where is your invitation to breakfast with the great Sir Joseph Banks? Do you sit with Sally when she visits the Royal Institution?"

The Owl crushed with his long, adroit fingers Maggie's incipient motet. He made a tremendous gulping sound, and his chest hove up.

Maggie staggered back. She remembered her lone visit to the Royal Institution, a month earlier. She could hardly sleep the night before. Sanford had escorted her. An excitable young man—an acolyte of Davy—had lectured on advances in chemistry, especially the recent discoveries of barium, iodine, magnesium, potassium, and (her two favourites) niobium and colianasthium (which the speaker advocated calling "terentium"). What she most recalled, however, was not the content of the lecture, but the fact of her being the only dark face in the audience. White heads turned constantly to stare at her, dozens of viscounts, bishops, bannerets and banneresses, pointing, snickering, sending her (and Sanford) a thousand darts of icy, margravine pettiness.

Dear old Sanford. Maggie realized she was very fond of him. Perhaps 'fond' was too emollient a word; she would need to think of one more fitting. Sitting by her side, the two of them isolated in the back of the Institution hall, Sanford had pointedly ignored all the gaping, all the whispers. Sanford, she decided, was like an old medlar-fruit: tough and acerbic on the outside but, with time and mellowing ("bretting" is what Cook called it), his inner core turned soft and sweet.

Sally had ostentatiously decided not to attend the Institution that evening, despite being somewhat familiar with the speaker. Maggie remembered that too.

"Do not pretend to deny it," said the Wurm. "You are condemned otherwise to suffer the delusions of Hope's lacquered mime."

The Owl advanced on her, arms outstretched, slowly swooping, his mouth a slit to swallow her.

Maggie stumbled backwards. The long-case clock, tunking and tinking to the rhythm of a distant place, pressed against her back and would not admit her.

Then, faint but sure, she heard Charicules singing—a nightingale far off, his assuasive tune unabridged and never ending. Small harlequin herald of the Great Mother, sing on! Farther off still, the Mother sighed and smiled in her long dream.

The Owl hesitated, veered away. Maggie pushed herself off the tall case of the huge clock, and stood so erect that she cast no shadow by the candlelight.

"Hollow-throated dragon-owl," she sang. "See how you by the wick of your tongue bring up venom to scorch me, and how it does me no harm! Hear you how the Mother anoints me even as she sleeps? Oh yes, you feel that, I know you do. Who is deluded now, spiry worm?"

The Strix took a small step backwards, eyes blazing. He closed his mouth.

"I am beyond you, Old One," sang Maggie, a deep, rapid trill that gained strength in the singing. "For all your grey-wether wisdom, you do not understand me. I re-fortune brass with my singing, annealing it with melody so smooth that one's fingers are cut by the air when they leave the surface of the metal. I read a sundial by moonlight, etching with my madrigal the mathematics I derive there. I sing now the *abu oma*, a psalm of steam flowing through the whorled chamber and of the cylinder turning, of the wheels so finely made they define for us anew the word 'circle.' Nay, Old Nightmare, I am a student of new things, while you have passed your meridian—your philosophy vinewed, your insights decayed."

The Owl retreated no further, but neither did he move towards her. In the deepest part of his mind, he experienced for the second time within an hour an emotion he had not felt for eons. First astonishment, now fear—the faintest flutterings of fear.

"Hoom, hoom, human," he boomed. "I am a Dominion in the hierarchy that precedes the creation of your world. My time is always and forever."

Maggie's song beat down upon the Owl's shoulders and head.

"I sing now of your sin—which was indecision and cowardice," sang Maggie. "You sided in your heart with the rebellious ones, but you did not dare to declare yourself openly. Oh no, both sides derided you in the cataclysmic struggle, did they not? And still do, since that struggle is not ended. Lucifer will ever be remembered, proudly pent in his hell, but you—half-fallen, vicious but timid—you are just quaint mummery. Yours will only be a cenotaph, an empty tomb with its name effaced. I, on the other hand, *I* am very decisive. I will sing myself and all of my people free."

The Owl surged forward, with such wells of malevolence in his round eyes that the clock stopped ticking.

Maggie sang even louder, with notes pure and true.

The Owl grappled with the air around her, but could not seize his prey.

Maggie smiled as she sang. The clock, starting up again, yielded this time to her, as she stepped backwards without taking her eyes off the Owl.

"Old Owl," she sang. "*Chi di*, your day is coming very soon now."

She stepped back through the clock. The Owl was rebuffed, could not follow her.

That night, residents in and around Hoxton Square trembled in their beds, as anguished groans and cries of rage filled the air.

Interlude: Fontes

May 20th, 1817.
Fezziwig & Co.,
St. Macaire Passage,
Aldgate, London

My dear esteemed friend Mr McDoon:

Per your instructions received on the 15th inst., I hereby—but most sadly—cancel your order for three new waistcoats.

May I say that it grieves me sorely to learn of your recently straitened circumstances and that I pray for the swift restoration of your natural state.

As a token of my true concern, and sincerest demonstration of my unquenchable friendship for you and your house, I offer you one waistcoat—a quinette whose background is mulberry, with ebony flashings and the most delicate pale yellow border-stitchings—at half my usual asking. I recall that the quinette is a favourite of yours, and also well-liked by your niece.

Your most humble servant,
—Alexander Edward Fezziwig

[Letter from Reglum to Dorentius, May 27th, 1817; translated from the Yountish]

Dear Dorentius:
Your letter of May 24th pleased me no end. I am so happy that your visit to Cambridge goes so well, especially the reunion with your old Caius College friend, Mr. Woodhouse.

You know I do not comprehend the outer, more abstruse elements of the mathematics required by the Fulginator, but I certainly appreciate their importance;—hence, my excitement at learning that Mr. Woodhouse has been able to illuminate for you those isoperimetrical equations which have eluded you and Miss Collins these past months.

I hereby remind you—as you requested upon your departure last week—to take up with Mr. Woodhouse his ideas on the method for best solving what you and Miss Collins call 'the problem of necessary abaxility.'

Miss Collins sends her regards. She misses her discussions with you; I think her work on the Fulginator suffers in your absence, to the detriment of us all. Without her, we would have no chance (in my estimation) of making the Great Fulginator a reality. Miss Collins is a talent of the highest water, 'the osprey who uses an astrolabe to calculate the patterns of its flight' *[English has no exact equivalent for this Yountish expression, so the phrase is literally translated here]*. It pains me to see her so shunned by so many; she has done nothing to deserve the spite and calumny that finds its way to her door. As you and I have discussed, she might be better off in Yount than here, though that would have to be a decision of her own making, not ours.

Most painful of all to me is the continuing carriage and attitude of Sally towards her family, and towards me. The change that has come over Sally is shocking and sad to perceive. I will not belabour the issue here, as you and I have spoken of this many times, but I beg you listen to my complaints just a little longer, dear friend.

As you know, Sally has long held my heart in fee simple *[this legalistic term best conveys the sense of the Yountish original]*, yet—as she apparently has offered her own to another, without clearly relinquishing her claim on mine—I am now utterly confounded. Worse, I suffer from a saturation of violet-purple thoughts, which begin to threaten my sense of life.

I cannot bear much more of her indifferent veto and disregard. I am tempted to 'sew buttons on the kraken's jacket' *[a Yountish saying that implies an action of well-deliberated but futile heroism, not to be mistaken with bravado or impulsive acts]*. I confide this to you, Dorentius, because we are not only two Yountian exiles, we are friends . . . and *batmoril*.

Please forgive the depressing raiment of this letter; do not give up on its author. I look forward to your return in a fortnight's time. Write again soon, with more news about Cambridge—which, though it is not Oxford, is I am sure a worthy approximation.

Yours in friendship always,
—Reglum

[*The following is translated from the Chinese*]

To His Most Excellent Scholarship,
the Third Chancellor for Foreign Relations,
at the Court of His Celestial Majesty,
the Jiaquing Emperor,

From his humblest servant, Tang Guozhi.

I write this from the ship that is bringing us from Cape Town to London; we have crossed the southern Atlantic and are now refreshing our stores at Recife in Brazil. I will post this letter back to you on one of the East Indiamen just arrived from London here at Recife, bound for China.

The captain of our vessel says we shall sail the day after tomorrow, winds and tide permitting of course; with a fair weather and no mishaps, we can expect to arrive in London medio August.

I have little to add to the many reports I sent from Cape Town, but will emphasize that the British clearly intend to find Yount with the purpose of acquiring that legendary land for their ever-growing empire. Given their rapacity and their recent great victory over the French, and especially their endless wars in India, the British must be considered a significant threat; I know that many at the Celestial Court do not share this evaluation, indeed they seem barely aware of the British challenge, but I will continue to issue my warnings in the hopes that it is not too late to counter their encroachments.

While in Cape Town, I heard much of British ambitions in Sumatra and other parts of the Long Archipelago, their having returned those lands to the Dutch notwithstanding; also, they clearly intend to swallow all of India, and appear to be contemplating war with the Kingdom of Burma, which would put the British on our Chinese doorstep.

Consider too their methodical acquisition of ports across and around the Indian Ocean, an unequivocal indication of their strategic design: the new harbour at Simon's Town in South Africa, freshly gained anchorage rights at Diego Suarez and Tamatave on the island of Madagascar, the taking in the last decade from the French of Mauritius, Diego Garcia, and the Chagos Islands (situated as these are at the heart of the Indian Ocean), the plans to build out the deep-water harbour at Trincomalee on Ceylon, their ceaseless work on the harbours at Bombay, Madras, Calcutta, and a dozen smaller places along the Malabar and Coromandel coasts. We learn that they are surveying the western coast of Australia, that they exert pressure on the Persian port of Comrow (that is also called Bandar Abbas), they meddle in the affairs of Aden, and court favour with the Sultan of Zanzibar.

What can all this mean but a very well-contemplated plan by Great Britain to encircle and control the gateways to Yount? The very portals which our illustrious Admiral Cheng Ho discovered on his mighty voyages fully four centuries ago and which many of His Imperial Worship's philosophers and analysts have verified and studied since, are these to be surrendered without so much as a protest? Our Chinese claims and right to priority can hardly be disputed, and yet the British are utterly disrespectful of our rights, shunting them aside with a breathtaking arrogance—must we bear such indignities?

I beg leave to conclude this missive, but will send you word immediately upon our arrival in London. I urge you to continue your excellent work of influence upon members of the Court who may not fully grasp the severity of the situation and the potential for loss if we do not act, swiftly and decisively, on behalf of the Emperor.

With my most humble obediencies,
—Tang Guozhi,
Special Emissary

DANIEL A. RABUZZI

[A notice from <u>Grandison's Weekly Record</u>, issue 32, August 1817]

Bethnall Green, Limehouse and Wapping have once again been visited by scenes of tumult and disputation these past two weeks, in the form of loud and vocal contests between various religious factions of the Dissenting and Ranting varieties. Reports are mixed and obscure, but the main division appears to be between those known as 'Hennites' or 'Hen's Men' (though many of the so-called men are actually females, which is a scandal in its own right) and those who follow the preaching of one Peasestraw. The origins of the disagreement are— as is so often the case in matters religious and especially among the fissiparous sects of individual fanaticism—but dimly to be understood, if they can be understood at all. What is understood is that the public order has frequently been breached, with outcries, taunts, jeers, old fruit and vegetables thrown as missiles at opponents, etc.. It should also be understood that all good subjects of the King and parishioners of the various afflicted localities need call upon the warring parties to cease their unconscionable actions towards one another, towards bystanders who are in no fashion involved and towards property.

[From the chapbook, Cries and Crudities of London, as Commonly Heard and Collected in the Year 1817, by an Amateur]

Who is scared of Jenny with the Green Teeth?

Not I, not I. *(I am, I am.)*

Who is scared of Aunt Peg Tantrum and Old Yallery Brown?

Not I, not I. *(I am, I am.)*

Who is scared of Blue Annis Lady and the Gallow's Man?

Not I, not I. *(I am, I am.)*

[An encrypted report from Captain Shufflebottom of the Admiralty's Special Branch to his superiors, the two gentlemen known only as Mr. I. and Mr. Z.; some elements of what follow are speculative, given the difficulties of deciphering the Admiralty's code]

August 10th, 1817

Sirs,

Little additional to relay on the matter of Kidlington, who is easily enough marked by Lt. Thracemorton, not least because Kidlington is very frequently at his lodgings (as he often entertains there the Miss Sarah MacLeish). I assume Lt. Thracemorton's reports to you confirm what I say here.

Freed partly from the duty tracking Lt. Thracemorton, which is to say minding Kidlington, I have taken liberties to increase my vigilance vis-à-vis the Others, whose numbers and activities expand almost daily.

Their particular attention is definitely the Blackwall shipyard, for reasons that are all too logical. The Power or Faculty that protects the shipyard is too strong for the prowling Minions to breach, but they never let slip an opportunity to gain entrance and do harm when and where they can. They are busily relentless in their efforts, walking by night (and now sometimes even by day) around the perimeter of the shipyard like wolves around a sheep-fold.

They are equally industrious in their initiatives elsewhere, and—since these places are less well picketed—more easily persuaded to cause mischief at, say, the Maudslay works in Lambeth, the Gravell clockmaking premises in Clerkenwell, the Wornum pianoforte factory on Wigmore Street.

I shot one of the Others two nights ago, on the stairs near Calloway Close in Limehouse, a small being with a very sanguineous and speckled complexion, a mouth that worked more like a pike's or a salmon's than that of a human person's, and a ruff of bristly, stiff hair like that of a heron or a crake. I used bullets sheathed in regulus of antimony, which were most effective. Unfortunately, the corpse dissolved before I could arrange for it to be transported to the Experimentarium for further examination, excepting only its teeth, some of its vertebrae and random other bones.

The creature I shot two weeks ago—the large one with the nuchal gills, near the Greenland Docks at Gascoigne's Chare—did not decompose so rapidly;—he needed an entire, obese carboy for the pickling, but it was worth the expense and effort, as our Experimenters tell me they have learned much from the dissection of this one's anatomy.

For the benefit of my brethren in the Corps Venatical, I add the following notes for inclusion in our archives:

• Dr. Dee's Glyph remains the most potent sign available to us; only the most incautious or passionate Others will ignore this symbol.

• Only slightly less useful are Fludd's Mundane Music, Lambsbrinck's Fifth Figure, and the Corascene Dog, especially when combined in each case with the Prayer of St. Macrina.

• Sir Isaac Newton's calculations on the sacred geometry of Solomon's Temple, and in particular those pertaining to the golden ratios, provide excellent graphing for the laying of ambuscades and enfilades against the Others; I will leave it to my more mathematically inclined colleagues to understand why this might be so, but I have seen how practical Sir Isaac's work is in this quarter.

• Among the chemical compounds, besides the regulus of antimony, I find most beneficial: orpiment and the other arsenical bases, Homburg's phosphorus, and cennus of Saturn (but be sure it is calcined very well). On the other hand, *luna cornea* and its derivatives have but feeble impact.

• I cannot recommend the Egg of Ostanes, as it too often fails to ignite. Also, the relics of Saint Praxedes had no signal effect on any of the Others.

• Using the *tabellae defixiones* and other necromantic items might seem counter-productive, blasphemous or both, but I have tried them—using a flame to fight a flame, as it were—and will attest to their efficacy.

Until my next report, scheduled in two week's time,
>
> I am your most humble servant,
> —Captain Shufflebottom

P.S. Please have the Librarian retrieve the Ezekiel Foxcroft testimonial from 1670, the one in which he outlines how best to 'hunt the Green Lion.' I will explain to my lords on my next visit why Foxcroft's investigation may be helpful to us.

P.P.S. Still no sign of the one called The Cretched Man. Very odd, and beyond my ability to explain. But the one we managed to capture and question last month—the female with the purple eyes, whose back was hollow like a breadpan under her beautiful dress (she being the one who lured Richard Morgan to his death)—told us that she and all the Others consider The Cretched Man the worst of all traitors and would have nothing to do with him, except to hunt him down themselves. What the nature of his betrayal was she would not say, and I cannot imagine;—these creatures have a different morality than ours. Before she died, the prisoner added that some other Being has come to London, to replace The Cretched Man, someone with greater powers and a strict adherence to mission. She only laughed when we tried to find out more from her. Whoever this new authority or leader may be among the Others, he appears to be mighty indeed, which is cause for concern.

Chapter 5: A Delayed Beginning, or, Brisk Entanglements of Wisdom and Folly

"These speculations may appear wild, and it may seem improbable that they will ever be realised, to persons who have not extended their views of what is practicable by closely watching science in its course onward; but there are many mysterious powers, many irresistible agents with the existence and with some of the phenomena of which all are acquainted."

—**Percy Bysshe Shelley**,
quoted by Thos. Jefferson Hogg in "Shelley at Oxford," in
the *New Monthly Magazine*, 1832
(Shelley and Hogg were close friends at Oxford in 1810)

"There is some Angel that within me can
Both talk and move,
And walk and fly and see and love,
A man on earth, a man
Above."

—**Thomas Montague Traherne**,
"An Hymn Upon St. Bartholomew's Day" (c. 1665)

"He sat in his grotto, tormented in his breast by longing [*Sehnsucht*], hot tears on his cheek, wishing that a star in heaven might enlighten his shadowed path, when suddenly a beautiful woman emerged from the woods surrounding the grotto, the fullest rays of the sun falling upon her angelic face. 'The holy St. Emerentia!,' he cried out. 'No, no, even more than her;—my highest Ideal!'"

—E.T.A. **Hoffmann**,
"The Church of the Jesuits in G.," (in *Night-Pieces*, 1817, translated by Dorothy Elisabeth Ridgeon, 1820)

Jambres sat alone in his house in Sanctuary, in the room that overlooked the enclosed garden, the path to the beach, and the bay beyond. Early morning sounds filled his ears through the open window: the ascending trills of larks, the songs of chaffinches and wheatears, the gustling of pheasants in the fields behind the house, the steady pulse of the surf in front. In the garden the summer flowers—the glossy yellow St. John's-wort, the pale white campion, the brash orange hawkweed—were retreating in favour of the fall flowers—the bunched purple of the aster, the tall, feathered golden of the solidago. The first fox-grapes—rusty sheened, heavy—had appeared the day before in the hedges, while the last of the hawthorn fruits had fallen.

Jambres sat secluded in his thoughts, buoyed by the sounds and smells. He heard the day's first stirrings of the sailors and soldiers bivouacked further down the shore, the freedmen and refugees from Yount who continued the fight against Orn. He smelled their breakfast cook-fires, heard their banter and complaints. Someone played a few runs on a mouth-organ. A baby cried out for its mother.

Jambres heard Tom, already issuing orders. He heard Afsana say something to one of the armourers. "The Crippled Queenlet," they called her. The bullet on the quay had shattered her right hip, the night the last tough-ship had sailed bearing

Sally, Barnabas, Sanford, Reglum, Dorentius and the others back to Earth. Afsana had almost perished, first from the bleeding, then from the infections. But she refused death, pulling back from the threshold time and again, using the pain as her ladder back to life. ("And Tom," she said. "I could not leave the poor man to fend for himself, so here I am.") Tom had fashioned for her a brace; supported by her brace and using a cane made of strongest oak, Afsana returned to lead the Yountian troops.

The Crippled Queenlet and Tommy Two-Fingers . . . the Yountians would follow these two anywhere at any time, to whatever end. Their world reduced itself to the war, a war that the Ornish were winning. As Nexius Dexius had predicted, the Ornish had taken Yount Great-Port and overrun almost all of Farther Yount. The Arch-Bishop held several small Yountish islands with his Sacerdotal Guards and troops from Optimate houses siding with the Learned Doctors and the Gremium. Separately, Nexius led the resistance in the name of Queen Zinnamoussea, the Queen Who Is, and Afsana, the Queen Who Will Be, a resistance consisting of the remnants of the Royal Navy, those Optimate houses loyal to the Hullitate dynasty, and the freedmen of Sanctuary. Based in Sanctuary, the Hullitate forces conducted hit-and-run raids on the Ornish, harried Ornish shipping, supported sabotage and covert actions in Yount Great-Port and other cities of Farther Yount. The forces of the Arch-Bishop and those commanded by Nexius rarely communicated, and never coordinated their attacks. The Ornish consolidated their conquest and—if they could not eradicate the threat posed by the Arch-Bishop and that of Queen Zinnamoussea—they had little to fear militarily; the Ornish lion disliked the thorns that pricked its paws, but was otherwise unfazed.

Jambres picked out the low growl of Dexius. The Yountian general was conferring with Tom and Afsana and their gathered lieutenants, preparing for another sortie against the Ornish, another foray in what promised to be a war without end. Dexius barked an order; Tom did the same, the troops huzzahed in a quiet, determined way that was infinitely more chilling than the parade-ground bravado of untested recruits. Every man and every woman on the detail had been under fire, seen friends and family killed, had taken life. Sails billowed, ropes were thrown, the squadron was made ready as the soldiers waded out to the ships.

The Cretched Man recalled recent conversations with Tom, Afsana and Nexius—each of whom wondered what news Jambres might be able to give about the return of the other McDoons, preferably with a reinforcing army. Afsana was quick to doubt, prone to criticize. Having only just gotten to know a father who did not know of her existence until very recently, not wholly convinced that he would not ignore or evade her again, Afsana voiced her distrust with increasing vehemence.

"And Sally, dear as she may be to me, yet for all her talk of—what do you call it in German, Tom?—*Sehnsucht*, is it?, right, *Sehnsucht*—and the glorification of longing, homecoming, a grand re-arrival, where is she? I feel as if Yount barely figures in her thinking anymore, maybe not in any of their thinking. We are become an after-thought, at best. What is that saying about 'out of my sight, out of my mind'? Is that the saying in English, Tom? Yes, well, then that is what it feels like to me, that they have left us to our fate, abandoned us."

Jambres—sending the raiders a blessing—turned to look into the ansible-telescope, as he did twice a day every day. He searched long with the device, seeking to pierce the veils of the Interrugal Lands, to discover news about Sally and the other McDoons. He searched fruitlessly; the ansible showed no clear images, sent no clear messages, but provided only a stream of blurred and enigmatic signs, penny-pictures of saints and beatas, a tarot-reading of half-visible portraits.

"The Owl flares his wings, clouding all," murmured Jambres. "Wreathes the Earth in white-winds and sounds of death, blinding me—barring me from the gates and streets back to London or any other place on Earth."

Jambres saw distant flashes in the night-time of his mind, like lightning or cannon-fire just below the horizon. He heard hollow mutterings, a shailing, shooking sound as of nuts being shaken in their shells, and the creaking of stairs under clandestine weight. He sensed doorknobs being tested, cries muffled by uncaring hands, and weeping in deserted places.

"He's called in a multitude, nurselings of foreign climes. The desiccated ones. The half-fallen, the horse-saints, the illicines and alcharates."

Jambres peered for hours into the ansible, but got no news of the McDoons. He felt Sally's anguish and her fall into betrayal but received none of the details. He sensed the distress of Barnabas and Sanford but discerned nothing of why.

"Billy, my precious Sea-Hen. Your preachments cast vibrations even this far, well done my fighting deodandus, but I cannot hear them directly. Yet I sense that you, too, are frustrated and uneasy. What is it, Billy, what troubles you?"

Jambres sat long into the day, feeling for the signs. He mused on Afsana's characterization of an absent father, and felt much the same way himself about the Great Mother's consort ("an empty throne, abandoned in favour of some other universe more congenial than this one?"). He saw heaven's bureaucracy continuing to grind away at its tasks even in the absence of the Father, even as the Mother slumbered: companies of angelic clerks and under-secretaries making entries into the *Liber Berosianus Superioris,* the Great Book of Repentance and Rue; seraphic tabellions and notaries summing, erasing, reckoning. Once even—to his great and lasting surprise—he spied a House he had not seen before (let alone visited), a House of Gentle Februation overseen by a Dominion of Patience, a House of Mercy in the garden of which sat the archangel Gabriel guiding the hand of St. Luke as the latter painted the Great Mother, on the flower-strewn lawns of which the infant-saint Sambandar laughed and sang in perfect harmony with the stars even as he was born and re-born over and over again.

With such fleeting, slender visions did Jambres keep his own hopes alive, buttressed more closely at hand by the singing he heard among his charges.

"I would tell you, Sally, Barnabas, Billy, about our youngest singer, the little Malchen, how she is growing, how her voice is maturing. She will be ready, selah."

The Cretched Man scratched at his face, the skin of which—the white, white skin of which—had been itching him exceedingly for days. He peeled off a layer, shed it like a snake, a long translucent sheet that he sent floating out the window into the evening and across the beach. He marvelled at this.

He thought above all about the mysterious singer in London.

"I see you in glimpses, I do, young brown-eyed princess, child of Africa as I am (once long ago). As it stands in *Lamentations*: 'What thing shall I take to witness for thee? what thing shall I liken to thee, O daughter of Jerusalem? what shall I equal to thee, that I may comfort thee, O virgin daughter of Zion?' The Owl stands between us."

Jambres had felt the Owl shudder and he felt the Mother swim-singing towards wakefulness.

"Is this your doing, beautiful dark singer? Who else, if not you? You challenge the Owl—no one has done this before, at least not on our world. You are nigh to waking the Mater Magna. Unheard of! Such deeds as these are boastworthy; I would meet you just to honour you."

Jambres smiled to think of the Owl's discomfiture.

"You advert it not, dread Wurm, but I feel your fear from afar. How does it feel, your half-holiness?"

He picked at a shred of skin on his left cheek, pushed unbidden thoughts of the Tailors and the House of Decortication out of his mind, focused instead on the McDoons.

"One more piece of news I would desperately share: Afsana is pregnant. She and Tom will have a little girl (I have not told them but they will know the child's sex soon enough). In the midst of our losses and the threat of the Owl, new life! New life, a new little song, a new voice for the Great Song, selah!"

The Wurm-Owl sat in his house in (but not of) Hoxton Square. His chieftains sat across the table.

Coppelius could have passed for a vicar or alderman. He had to coach himself to blink and swallow regularly.

Prinn fiddled with his glasses. His fingers strolled across his face, tarrying over his features.

The Widow Goethals was resplendent in a dark-green dress, with roan piping and a subdued black floral pattern. She smiled, shaking her long, black hair.

"No more frivolities," said the Owl. "We strike hard now. Understood?"

Coppelius, Prinn & Goethals (Widow) nodded.

The long-case clock ticked a commemoration of their enfleshment.

Talk turned to stratagems, especially relating to the legal and financial occupation of the *Indigo Pheasant* by the firm. They then discussed the matter of Maggie.

"For her impudence, she will offer us hecatombs of hearts, drained and rendered," said the Owl.

The clock tocked an alien rhythm.

"*Quatsch*, and more than *Quatsch*," said Barnabas, rubbing his well-worn vest (an old favourite in times of stress, a champakali design picked out in chalk blues and sharp reds). "How do we handle 'em, Sanford?"

Sanford shook his head. No one could read a balance sheet better than Sanford; he knew a conspiracy of debits threatening to overwhelm the credits of McDoon when he saw one.

McDoon & Co. was beset on all sides, and everywhere the firm of Coppelius, Prinn & Goethals (Widow) cropped up.

Charles Matthew Winstanley—their new lawyer, a young man with the face of a whippet, and the habit of being the first through every door—cleared his throat and produced a mass of papers from within a satchel that could easily have housed several changes of clothes and possibly a small tea-service. He beckoned Barnabas and Sanford to sit. Young as he was, Winstanley came highly recommended by Matchett & Frew, and had already secured himself a seat in the Lowtonian Society and other leading legal associations.

"Mr. McDoon, Mr. Sanford," he began, rapidly fanning papers out on the table, long rows of remittances, *factura*, bills of exchange, bills of lading, invoices, claims and counter-claims on insurance and salvage, letters of hypothecation, bottomry bonds and respondentia, exemptions for demurrage, waivers on edulia and other duties, writs of cassation, reclamations for Danish Sound Tolls paid, connoissements, *contrati de arrendamiento financiero*, rescriptions, subrogations, documents relating to virement, supervenience, cession and assignment, certificates of contingent remaindership, licenses for disjunctive distribution and for non-abatement, *lettres pour l'aiguillage et le gaspillage*, shares in tontines, deeds of title, lien and encumbrance, records of *dadny* advances to merchants in Surat, Calicut, Cannanore and Oddeway Torre, *cowl-namah* agreements with traders in Tranquebar.

The three passed a long afternoon planning the McDoon position and counter-attack. Winstanley darted quickly to cases. He recommended, in short declarative sentences inviting little argument, that McDoon & Co. sell immediately its shares in a wide range of miscellaneous assets: the one-sixteenth part of a timber, flax, and hemp warehouse in Riga, the sixteenths and eighths held in brigantines, galleases and other ships home-harboured in Hamburg, Luebeck, Stockholm and Danzig, the two dozen wine-barriques held by a correspondent firm in Porto, the consignment of salt from Setubal, the raze of ginger jointly held with the Muirs out of Bombay, and so on. He advised delaying payment on this bill of exchange, refuting the usance on that one, calling for a moratorium on this debt due, disputing the traheration of the other.

Barnabas was fascinated. Winstanley's angular phrasing formed a complete contrast to the oleaginous rondure of

Sedgewick's words. Charicules noticed as well, singing softly and without sidebars at an *andante* pace to counterpoise Winstanley's clipped *allegro*.

Sanford experienced something in the neighbourhood of joy, despite the grim situation. If every cloud has a silver lining, then this was a most stormy cloud and Winstanley appeared to be most refined silver.

Sanford had argued for years that McDoon & Co. needed to sell its many idiosyncratic, small, and random holdings ("fleas," he called them), to consolidate and focus on its core business. But Barnabas consistently objected, in each case with a different but equally strongly held rationale, at core based on immoveable loyalties to kin, swelling convictions about the goodness of humanity and the utility of trade, a boundless bent towards the curious and the assymetrical.

Thus, whenever a fellow Scot wrote to implore or induce, Barnabas would invest as a matter of nationalistic pride and faith in Scottish character. As Sanford observed, Barnabas's Caledonian loyalties resulted in McDoon & Co. owning five shares in The Company for the Dredging of Harbours in the Baltic (sponsored by Scots located in Stettin, Koenigsberg, Memel and Libau), ten shares in the Gothenburg Arctic Whaling Company (founded by a Murray, a Cameron and two Gordons), a claim in the bankruptcy estate of Tulloh, Ramsay & Halyburton in Madras, and—Sanford's favourite—one ticket in the New Lottery of The Argentine (purchased from a Mackay in Glasgow, whose brother-in-law was an organizer of the lottery in Buenos Aires; one of Barnabas's great-grandmothers had been a Mackay out of Glasgow).

Likewise, Barnabas felt compelled to show support for any project promoted by the Landesmanns and Brandts in northern Germany—our *"cousins-germaines"* as he would pun. Which placement of trust led McDoon & Co. to possess—among other curiosities—a handful of shares in a sugar refinery in Altona, in a tileworks in Flensberg, and in the Diskonto und Kurant Bank of Hamburg.

But the amount of cash that might be raised through sales of assets held far and wide, from the realization of long submerged, half-forgotten, ill-defined and phantasmal profits, from the accelerated ravening of debtors and from delayed or halted payments would still not be enough to meet the ever-mounting demands of the Blackwall shipyard, the Maudslay engineering firm and all the other contractors and vendors on the Project. Nor was it enough to meet the capital call precipitated by Coppelius & Co.

Winstanley, looking like a stage-magician as he swiftly put some papers back into his valise while pulling others from out of the bag, said that he could find legal ways to stall Coppelius but that the ultimate call and claim were based very solidly on the *Indigo Pheasant*'s articles of association.

"So, beans and butter," said Barnabas. "We could actually lose the ship, if we don't find additional capital."

"Yes," said Winstanley.

Sanford said (stressing in his broadest Norfolk accent all the adjectives and adverbs, emphasizing how seldom he used either part of speech), "We need that meeting with Sir John Barrow at Admiralty. Also with our erstwhile silent partners at the Honorable East India Company. I suspect there is little difference in this case between Admiralty and the John Company. Whoever precisely is on whose lead-strings, they are our last, best hope to keep control of the *Pheasant*."

Winstanley—nose up, fingers tapping more quickly than the clock ticking on the mantlepiece—said, "Yes, yes, and yes. I believe we can expect some resistance to such a meeting now from my predecessor in this position, but I also have faith that I can effect such a meeting through means and connections of my own."

Barnabas, looking at the engraving of Rodney damaging the French fleet, hopped to his feet, threw one hand in the air and said, "Let's go . . . now!"

Mr. Winstanley declined the offer to dine with Barnabas and Sanford, taking his leave with a statement that he had much to do on their behalf and would start at once that very evening. As he left, Reglum and Dorentius arrived as scheduled to join the McDoons for dinner.

Over a plain roast of mutton (with just the merest hint of mint-jelly, as Cook strove for economy, much to Barnabas's chagrin), Reglum announced that he was removing himself to Woolwich.

"Figs and farthings, Woolwich? Whatever for?"

Reglum reminded them that he was a military man and that Woolwich was an ideal placement; he was joining the staff of the Royal Military Academy at Woolwich, which was next to the Royal Arsenal and the Royal Artillery Barracks.

"While you build the *Indigo Pheasant*," said Reglum. "And Maggie and Dorentius here create and have installed the Great Fulginator, we must also look to the ship's defenses. I will get us supplied with the latest in gunnery and ordnance—so necessary, as you know, if we are to traverse the Interrugal Lands successfully."

"All the more important with the Owl taking a direct and personal interest in our little adventure," added Dorentius.

"Precisely, thank you Dorentius. And then there's the Ornish waiting for us on the other side, with their rapid-fire cannons. I want to learn what might best be applied to the *Pheasant* in terms of bombardment geometry, range-finding, that sort of thing. Also, we will need gunners onboard or will need at the very least to train to professional standards some of the volunteers Billy Sea-Hen is recruiting. No place better than Woolwich for that. Oh, and I will also have a secondary appointment at our sister college, the Addiscombe Military Seminary in Croydon."

"Where the East India Company trains gunners and engineers for its army," said Dorentius, in his most helpful voice.

"Spot on again, Dorentius, thank you."

Cook entered with a plate of four small boiled sweets, one for each of the men at table. She looked apologetically at Barnabas (whose face had fallen when he saw the dessert) and indicated with her eyes that the fault lay entirely with Sanford; Sanford saw their exchange, and said nothing, maintaining a face of resolute determination.

"Well, bells and butterflies, that is all very stimulating news, Mr. Bammary," said Barnabas while he nibbled on his sweet in a vain attempt to make it last. "We shall of course miss you being near us in the City, but neither Woolwich nor Croydon are more than an hour or so by chaise or by the Thames ferry for the one, so you will not have gone so very far. Jolly good thinking that, about the cannons and all—we'll need as many of 'em as we can get, to handle whatever the Owl and the dismal roads may put in our path!"

The four men toasted to Reglum's new position in Woolwich, and to the success of the *Indigo Pheasant*.

"Also, ahem, I do not mean to intrude where I am not welcome," said Barnabas. "But Mr. Bammary, besides the guns and geometry, might there be any other reason for your decision to remove to Woolwich?"

Reglum shook his head and did not reply.

"Ah, well, I see then, and I apologize if I am too forward."

Dorentius shifted the topic in the next moment by announcing that the Chancery Court had probated the will of the merchant "de Sousa" and had that very day accepted him and Reglum as the sole heirs.

"The money was, of course, never Salmius Nalmius's in his own right," said Dorentius. "Nor will it be ours as private persons. It was and is property of the Yountish people, held in trust by the Queen and her duly appointed representatives."

"How much?" asked Sanford.

"Just over three thousand pounds sterling, net of all charges, fees, and etcetera," said Dorentius. "We will deploy the majority of that amount towards equipping the *Indigo Pheasant*—as we are sure the Queen and the Chancellor would approve."

"How soon?"

"I think you have a better grasp of your English judicial pace than we do, Mr. Sanford, but we are told by the Chancery solicitors that we can expect the first installments within the next few months, subject of course to how fast the assets can be liquidated, and etcetera."

All four men toasted anew. Barnabas asked if that news did not also call for more sweets but Sanford rejected the motion.

As Reglum and Dorentius made ready to leave, the maid admitted a messenger in at the front door.

"Begging your pardons, sirs, I came as instructed, which is to say, as quick as rain and lightning, by St. Adelsina, I did."

"Out with it, man," said Sanford.

"Yes sir, here it is: I am ordered to tell you that your Chinese visitors will arrive within the next few days, sir, wind permitting. They are in an East Indiaman that has anchored in the Kentish roads just off Ramsgate, awaiting a turn in the wind to allow them to beat up the Thames. I came chip-chap straight up the Watling Street from Ramsgate to tell you, wore out three horses on the way. They will be staying in Devereux Court off the Strand, next to the Outer Temple and the other Inns of Court."

After Barnabas tipped the messenger and sent him on his way, Reglum said, "'The osprey pulls a fox from the ocean!' So long as the fish-hawk stays aloft on his way back to shore!"

"We will, we will," said Barnabas.

"We must," said Sanford.

Sir John Barrow, Second Secretary of the Admiralty, was a man of vast and varied experience. He had visited China and lived for a while at the Cape in South Africa. He had seen and heard many strange things. Yet now his face was a picture of perplexed indignation, as if he had been told that the giants had walked down off the Guildhall Clock or that a temerity of dragons was soaring around the dome of St. Paul's.

"Allow me to understand you completely," he said. "Behind this entire project is a young woman of dark complexion, a child of Africa, who you are telling me is a gifted mathematician, some sort of black, female Newton?"

It was the second Tuesday after the day Winstanley had met with Barnabas and Sanford; as good as his word, and—confirming initial impressions—supremely well connected, Winstanley had gotten the meeting with Sir John. Besides Sanford, Barnabas, and Winstanley, five other individuals sat in the Admiralty chamber with Sir John: the two black-clad men known only as Mr. I. and Mr. Z.; James Cumming, the head of the Revenue & Judicial Department for the East India Company's Board of Control; Lieutenant-Colonel James Salmond, head of the Examiner's Department at the E.I.C., and William M'Culloch, Assistant Secretary for Revenue, also of the E.I.C.'s Examiner's Department. Conspicuously absent was any representative from the Treasury.

"Very well," continued Sir John. "I see from your faces and the scraping of your feet that this is exactly what you would have me understand. Gentlemen, I trust you understand in turn the gravity of the circumstances, to wit, that our government has invested a full ten thousand pounds sterling—and is presumably being asked now to invest further sums—on the basis of this girl's alleged and purported capabilities. A girl born enslaved on a tobacco plantation in Maryland, a pauper's daughter educated at the whim of charity, until very recently a servant!"

No one spoke.

"Within the confines of this room, we may acknowledge that our sovereign is mad, and our prince-regent a wastrel," Sir John plowed ahead. "Yet their government is neither. We will not be played for fools or spendthrifts. We did not beat Napoleon being either. We are not building the greatest empire since the Romans, based on projects of dubious outcome. Do I make myself clear?"

The meeting lasted exactly one hour. Sir John asked all the questions and issued all the orders.

"The Chinese have not declared themselves to His Majesty's Government," he intoned. "But they are here in London and we must view them as a *de facto* embassy. Lt.-Col. Salmond, please have the E.I.C. extend all courtesies and receive the Chinese as soon as can be arranged, with all due protocol and circumstance.

THE INDIGO PHEASANT *Volume Two of Longing for Yount*

In the meantime, what is their purpose in being here? They have come a very great distance at great expense—the Emperor of China does not send us even his semi-official ambassadors on any regular basis; in fact, he has never sent us any ambassadors at all. Do they know aught of Lord Amherst's embassy to Peking?"

He looked directly at Sanford and Barnabas, and said, "How very strange a coincidence—if coincidence it be—that both you and these Chinese are connected with that funny Dutch couple at the Cape."

"The Termuydens," ventured Barnabas.

"Yes, yes. I knew them rather well, actually, when I lived at the Cape. Rum pair, the both of them. Marvellously sociable, to be sure, quick with the most comical and far-fetched stories, but I always felt that there was a secret or two lurking behind that gay façade of theirs. Now I am very certain they have been hiding something. I think you know what that something is, and my two associates here indicate the same."

Mr. I. and Mr. Z. bowed slightly.

"Of McDoon & Co. we know a fair amount," continued Sir John. "Respectable house—no, do not bow, I simply state facts—long tied to the India trade, especially on the Malabar coast, and to the North and East Seas in Europe, Hamburg and all that. Known for wise dealing, honourable and, above all, profitable. Yet now, the house of McDoon is—again, I simply state facts—on the verge of ruin, having overextended itself trying to build a ship called the *Indigo Pheasant*. So, I ask myself, what has caused this sudden and unforeseen reversal in fortune? Standing before me, neither of you appears to have lost your wits or qualities since you returned from your long stint abroad, so what might be the reason for such a downturn, . . . unless something happened on that sojourn overseas that could possibly be the threat or challenge, hmmm?"

Sir John proceeded in his shrewd way. As the clock rang the three-quarter hour, he said: "The ineluctable conclusion thus far is that McDoon & Co. will lose the *Indigo Pheasant*, see it acquired in whole by the firm of Coppelius, Prinn & Goethals

(Widow), in the very near future unless you receive a significant infusion of fresh capital. Capital, which equally inescapable, can only at this juncture come from His Majesty's Government in one form or guise or the other. Is that how you read this at Cannery Row?"

Mr. Cummings nodded in agreement.

"And at Leadenhall?"

The lieutenant-colonel and Mr. M'Culloch said "yes" in unison.

"Most unfortunately, the government can not snap its fingers and produce funds willy-nilly. In fact, the hounds from Treasury are already barking hard about the initial investment. What funds His Majesty's Government do possess are claimed by the Foreign Office and the Office of War for various initiatives necessary to protect the Crown and expand the Empire—I am certain that you have read in the papers about some of those undertakings, yes? Nevertheless, the affair of the *Indigo Pheasant* seems bound up in our imperial policies, like as not. The Prime Minister himself has taken an interest. Your little ship and whatever project is additionally linked to it have become matters of some importance at Whitehall and at St. James."

Barnabas and Sanford shook their heads, half in relief, half in disbelief.

With five minutes left on the clock, Sir John said: "Finally, we come to the most peculiar piece to this entire peculiar business. Are you aware that several of your associates, including a member of your own family, have applied for patents relating to the equipment to be installed on the *Indigo Pheasant*?"

Barnabas and Sanford were stunned.

"Oh my, I see this comes entirely as news, and not happy news either. Yes, last month the lawyer Sedgewick—very well known to you, and also to us—applied for six patents at the Six Clerks Office at the Court of Chancery, all done in good and proper order."

"Sedgewick?!"

"Yes, on behalf of one James Kidlington, also well known

to us, and—I hesitate to say it—the Miss Sarah McLeish. Your niece, Mr. McDoon."

"Kidlington! But he has nothing to do with making the technology aboard the *Pheasant*! Sally? *Sally*?!"

"Yes, she is presented as the chief author on all six patents. What most intrigues us is the nature of the devices and technologies for which patents are sought."

Mr. I. handed Sir John a paper dense with writing in a fine hand.

"'Intent to apply for an engine, partly powered by steam, to be known hereafter as a Fulginator,'" read Sir John. "The preliminary specification is—mildly put—cloudy, vague, a taunt to real comprehension. We flatter ourselves at Admiralty in being very well-informed on most matters, particularly as they relate to novel technologies, yet we have never heard of a science called 'fulgination.' Trust me when I say that we have burrowed through our extensive library and archive this past month searching for so much as the whisper of a suggestion as to what 'fulgination' might be, and have found . . . absolutely nothing. But I see from your faces—do not deny it!—that the art is not unknown to you."

The clock chimed the top of the hour. Sir John handed the paper back to Mr. I., and stood up.

"Another group of people sits two rooms away awaiting my presence," he said. "Involving the bold young Raffles and his plans to create a city he calls Singapore on the Straits of Malacca. There, some advance notice on a trading opportunity, I presume—perhaps a chance for McDoon & Co. to earn some of the capital it needs for its *Pheasant*. In the meantime, we will continue to monitor your difficult and—for the Crown—potentially unfortunate set of circumstances. Mr. McDoon, Mr. Sanford: you will hear from us again soon."

With that, Sir John strode out of the room, followed by all the E.I.C. and Admiralty officials, leaving Sanford and Barnabas to find their own way out.

"Oh, beans and bacon, Sanford, I don't know what to say!"

Sanford said nothing, but he left thinking many thoughts, each thought possessing the clarity of very cold, still water, and the sharpness of air breathed at a mountain-top.

At the very moment that Barnabas and Sanford were leaving the Admiralty, Sally was drinking tea with James Kidlington at Hatchards on Piccadilly. Hatchards was one of their favourite rendez-vous spots, a decorous haven to which they repaired two and even three times a week. One of London's leading bookshops, Hatchards had instituted the practice of serving tea in their private reading room (Hatchards deftly met all the proprieties: its white-gloved stewards brought out the tea to customers, but respectfully understood that the ladies must be allowed to pour and offer the tea themselves). Delicate society widely regarded Hatchards as one of the few places a single young lady could, without danger to her respectability, venture on her own; being seen there with a gentleman was likewise accepted, or at least did not start too many tongues into the courseways of gossip.

The reading room had been refreshed after the wars ended, setting the tone for shops and places of restoration throughout the West End (the bookshops at Paternoster Row and elsewhere in the City, once frequented by an eager Sally, remained dour, strictly mercantile places). The wallpaper was broad stripes, a crimsony claret bordered by pale gold alternating with *bleue celeste*. The wainscoting was made of a mellow rufous mahogany, with steadily darkening undertones. Hatchards had just put in gaslights, casting a gentle glow from brass sconces, making diffused shadows across the wallpaper and along the dado, seeping down into the mahogany below. On one wall was an elegantly understated black clock with a white face and gold numbers and hands. It announced each hour with a low, lingering, deep-bellied note, reminding visitors that time was in fact passing but reinforcing in them the complacent conviction that here in Hatchards they were insulated from the pressure of that passage.

On a large table upfront, the kind with massive lion's paws carved as the feet, lay neatly arranged all the day's serious newspapers and all the important journals and reviews. Just beyond was the main room, its walls lined floor to ceiling with books. Patrons conversed in a hushed mood of reverence, votaries at the temple. The noise of Piccadilly and the streets beyond receded to a swash of muted sound, as if those fortunate enough to be on Hatchards' premises were enclosed and protected within an ornate whelk.

Sally needed the refuge of Hatchards especially badly that day. She had had even less sleep than usual; her tossing and fretting had driven Isaak away long before dawn. That bird with the ridiculous name had been the culprit, his endless nocturnal whistling and gurgling the source of her insomnia. It was not right that everyone loved the intruder so, and made such a fuss about it coming with them on the return-journey to Yount. She—Sally—had named the ship. The ship was the *Indigo Pheasant*; it was emphatically not named for a ragged, party-coloured grackle. Why would not the others see that? Because they were enthralled by Maggie, whose chief talents (so it seemed to Sally) were to unearth unhappinesses and to traffic in arrogance and pride, and whose only beliefs were in herself alone and in the unchallenged supremacy of her plans and designs, as opposed to those of anyone else.

Thus she pinned all her hopes for the day on James; seeing James was to be the antidote for her trickling anger and growing frustration. At Hatchards, she could escape the conglomerated contempt for James shown by the rest of the McDoon household. Alone with James, Sally felt free of their criticism, and could see again each day for herself the depth of feeling, the cleverness, the adroit and caring little gestures that James embodied, and that James so quickly and willingly shared with her.

Upon ensconcement in the soothing surround of the Hatchards tea room, and aglow in febrile anticipation of sweetly murmured confidences, Sally was quickly dashed into near-despair. James ignored her special needs of the day. Instead, he launched into a serious discussion of the patents applications. Heedless of the present's demands (specifically those of Sally seated directly across from him), James galloped far into the future: how they would gain their fortune by licensing or selling the patents, the manner in which they would do so (his mind fairly buzzed with plans about this), the importance of her maintaining her claim no matter what blandishments her family might bring to bear, and the equally important concept of ownership of the patents when they were . . . married.

Marriage! James spoke of it frequently, yet had not made any formal proposal, let alone declared himself openly to Barnabas or any other person. He merely assumed their eventual marriage to be a fact as real already as the giants on the Guildhall Clock or the statue of St. Macrina by the East India House on Leadenhall Street. For all his cleverness, James was purblind in regard to Sally's desires for the formalities. Or perhaps it was precisely his cleverness that guided his behavior in this very regard. Sally could not tell which it was. Some days she was convinced James was a rogue trifling with her heart (with aims on those cursed patents? On her dowry otherwise?), other days she was reconciled to his being merely an oblivious gournard, which is what she believed most men were, even the ones whose hearts were true.

James began to notice that Sally's responses were desultory trending towards peevish and soon to become sullen. He realized she was fatigued beyond even her usual weariness, that she was tired of talk about the *Indigo Pheasant* and patents and the rest of it. He moved away from that topic, essayed gentle jokes and *les petits gestes capricants*, but to little avail. He composed himself (the patents could wait), then lapsed into silence.

Sally and James were sharing an amber tea, the *Keemun*, with its tightly rolled black leaves and fruity aroma. They had chosen for their service genuine Meissenware, the cups and saucers, tea pot and waste bowl of which were in a smoothly powdered puce framing gilt-edged panels painted in a wide palette with quay scenes and images of travellers on a river. Their cups had similar scenes within, which disappeared every time they were drowned and which became visible again as the tea was drunk.

Frustrated with James, Sally drifted into reverie, finding herself lost in the scenes on the Meissenware service. The painters had used masterfully delicate strokes and vibrant glazes. Sally would have sworn that the scenes weren't paintings at all, but frozen images of a distant reality, the people and animals, the trees and even the water all merely in a state of suspended animation, ready at any moment to come back to life.

Looking closely, Sally realized the scenes powerfully reminded her of the Last Cozy House, and the idyllic times she and James had spent in the garden at that house. In the pictures on the teapot, she could smell the breeze off scented bushes, could hear the bokmakarie birds and the scarlet-winged lorikeets, could see Isaak and the Termuydens' dog Jantje hunting the baboon through the undergrowth.

The last Edenic afternoons before his fall . . .

She peered at the scene on the interior bottom of her cup: a well-dressed gentleman standing under the arc of a swooning willow tree, doffing his hat to an unseen person. Who was the invisible person (surely not the tea drinker, or was it)? Why was the tree bending at such a precipitous angle? Did it bow to the same person to whom the gentleman paid his respects? Or was it attempting to seize the gentleman? Was that a small dog cavorting at the man's feet, or something else, a less salubrious creature? Were those butterflies flitting around the willow branches, or mice with wings?

Sally pulled back, a moue creasing her face.

She avoided James's puzzled glance. She thrust aside memories of the days in the Last Cozy garden.

Immediately after, she suppressed thoughts of Reglum. She pushed down her emotions about Maggie. She fled from the faces her conscience showed her of her uncle and Mr. Sanford. Tom, Afsana. . . . She rushed away, away.

Exhaustion loomed. The tea had only revived a part of her.

Looking again at the image at the bottom of her tea cup, a picture now skewed under translucent brown dregs in the soft flimmer of gaslight as evening drew on, Sally turned away quickly and begged to be taken home.

She was certain she had seen the gentleman in the cup put his hat back on, but dared not check to confirm that her eyes might have deceived her.

As Sally drank tea with James, and as Barnabas and Sanford made their way back to Mincing Lane, Maggie was visiting Mr. Gandy in the debtor's prison at Giltspur Street Compter.

He sat alone, unshaven and dishevelled, enveloped by and part of the baggy stench of the place. A fresh bruise adorned his left cheek.

"Oh hello, hello, Miss Maggie, so very, so very, *very* good to see you! Oh thank you, you are my only visitor this past sennight, so I am so very obliged. Do you know, I shall be out soon, or so my creditors say, if I may believe them, which I am forced to do, I have no choice, you see. How is Charicules? Singing as always, I hope. No birds in here, how I miss my little fellows, excepting the poor pigeons that find their way through the holes in the roof, can't fly back out. The lads in here trap them, turn them into dinner."

Maggie brought out a basket containing a small roast chicken, a loaf of bread (with whipped butter), and a roast onion, a gift from Cook. To bring it in, Maggie had bribed the jail guard using her own pin money. Gandy's eyes went wide, his nostrils likewise. He inhaled the smell of the chicken and onion, and then let out a sigh crinkled with laughter and tears.

They talked of minor things, the latest sayings from the London streets, novelties of expression, curiosities and quiddities, while Mr. Gandy ate. He tried to be polite but could barely contain himself, sometimes putting a second and even third bite in his mouth before finishing his first. Maggie fully understood the needs of the stomach, and was—truth be told—impressed with his futile attempts at genteel behavior for her sake under such brutal conditions.

When Mr. Gandy finished, having eaten every scrap and ounce, he said, "Now, tell me Miss Maggie, more about those dreams of yours, the ones you began to tell me about on your last visit to my palace here, about the very pale man in his very red coat, he sounds so delicious and divine, the one who flickers, shimmers in your mind."

Maggie and Mr. Gandy talked until evening began to come on. He looked stunted, attenuated, as the shadows lengthened, a dreamer caught in a very wrong dream. The other inmates made lewd comments about Maggie, and from some other room came a muffled moaning.

Just before she left, Maggie handed Mr. Gandy a small, thin empty bottle, with a cork, the sort of bottle apothecaries use for individual sales of powders and solutions. Maggie had gleaned it from a scrap pile on one of her roamings through Clerkenwell and Holborn (despite the improvement in her clothing, passers by did not see her as a lady or any other variety of respectable person; the one advantage in that being the freedom it allowed Maggie to move about on her own and explore some of the queerer parts of London). Maggie grinned as Mr. Gandy pulled the cork and shook the bottle up and down.

"It's Essence of Isaak," she laughed. "I had Isaak breathe into the bottle, then stopped it up. Just for you!"

The two of them laughed until tears came. The other inmates hooted at first but quieted in the face of genuine and unperturbable emotion. Their snickers ("oddster loves blackbird," that sort of thing) petered out.

On her way out, Maggie watched the charity boys lining up in their blue coats at Christ's Hospital across the street from the prison. She scanned their faces—anxious, bold, dulled, alert—and remembered walking not so long ago in her charity jacket at St. Macrina's.

From the debtors prison in Smithfield near Newgate it was

only a short walk to the house with the dolphin door-knocker in Mincing Lane. As always, Maggie marvelled at the proximity of the two worlds, one world really with a top and a bottom tightly if sometimes invisibly wound together, inextricably entangled.

As she walked the short width of the City that evening, Maggie also noticed other things. She caught sight of wizened faces staring down at her from behind chimney-pots, gnarled hands clutching roof-beams. In the crowds were figures that slipped and sidled away when she turned to see straight on what her peripheral vision had glimpsed. In the mouths of alleys were eyes that flashed unnatural colours as she passed by, eyes that receded into the gloom, in the manner of predatory fish pulling back into their grottoes when deciding that the creature before them is too strong to be prey. Behind the normal cries of London at even-tide, beneath the calls of rooks home-bound for steeples, under the tolling of the bells, was a slurred note, and scufflings and scritchings as if centipedes had mated with rats in the walls, and a shobbling as of too many mouths at a trough.

She noticed everywhere—obscured in plain sight—chalkings on walls and pavements, daubs of murky colour, and here and there affixed to grates or hanging from lampposts pieces of carved wood nailed together, leather pouches filled with rattly things and shooks of withered wheat bound with horsehair. She could not read the symbols fluently but she knew them for what they were: trollish calligraphy, etchings by the Owl's folk, wayposts for the half-fallen as they sought to map London onto the hours and liturgy contained in their own looking-glass version of the psalter.

Maggie shivered—not for herself, since she could rout the gathering ones with a few casual notes of her song, but for the innocents of London, walking about their streets, scrapping for their livings, ignorant of the forces marshalling in their midst.

"I've been to set a warning on the Owl, that *akakpo*. 'Tis time to rouse our Mother from her sleep."

Maggie sat long that night mardling in the kitchen with Cook, feeding tidbits to Isaak.

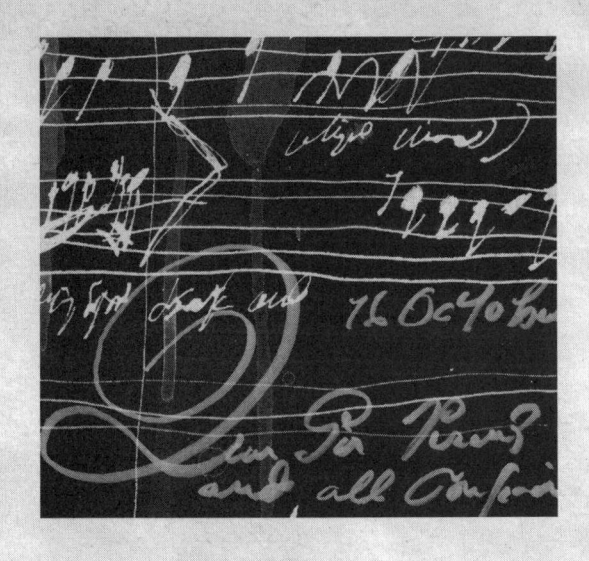

Interlude: Indicia

[Letter in full from Elizabeth Darcy, née Bennet, to Sally]

_____, 1817
(Honouring the Three-Fold Feast of St. Anne)

My dearest Sally:

Our friendship continues to be an importance to me; I will not see it marred or disturbed, though I suspect some of what I write below will test your feelings for me. Please, dear one, know that I write only with your best interests at heart, and would never do anything knowingly to harm you or your family.

I discussed at great length and in utmost seriousness with Mr. Darcy your proposal that we invest a substantial sum in the building of the *Indigo Pheasant* at the Blackwall yard. Alas, we cannot, for many reasons good and solid. As you are a merchant's niece—and, in your commercial perspicacity, practically a merchant in your own right—and because I so value your affection, I spell out here those reasons in greater detail than I would for another correspondent.

* We have lately had to assist my uncle and aunt, the Gardiners of Gracechurch Street, whom you know well are themselves investors in the *Indigo Pheasant*. My uncle lost a not inconsiderable sum—as I believe you have heard—on an entire cargo of oranges and lemons that, defying all rational explanation, went rotten in the course of a single night.

* We must set aside funds for my remaining sisters' dowries. I will hear no end of it from my mother if Kitty and Mary cannot present possible suitors with impressive dowries, while I have it in my means to help them.

* Mr. Darcy's aunt, the Lady de Bourgh, has still not forgiven him for marrying me. As a result (and here I will spare you the details, as it has most to do with a more familial matter, as I am sure you will understand), she has sued us over certain monies, rights and appurtenances—a spiteful action, and one that I do not believe she can prevail in, but nevertheless an affair we at Pemberley must take seriously to the extent of allocating some of our finances towards her suit, as a contingency. (Am I not sounding like a merchant now myself? You have taught me well!)

* Finally, let me say that Mr. Darcy's readily available means are far less than many might surmise, given the wealth over which he does dispose. Most of our wealth is tied up in our rent-rolls. Most of our leases were set before passage of the Corn Law in 1815 which established a minimum price for wheat, etc., which means—as you surely know—that our leases do not reflect the increased value of the land. Our tenant-farmers enjoy long leases; we cannot re-negotiate for years to come in many cases.

Pray do not think ill of me for what I feel compelled to say next. Mr. Darcy also felt disinclined to invest so long as you continue to consort with Mr. Kidlington—he says Mr. Kidlington reminds him far too much of Mr. Wickham. I cannot but agree with my husband on this point—and you know how capable I am of disagreeing with Mr. Darcy on so many other points! Please be the sensible Sally I knew when first we became friends—do not allow this Mr. Kidlington to assume too much influence in your life, as I fear his behaviour is not above conjecture and his brashness may lead you both into errancy.

I know you read these words now with a hotness on your brow and a tart response leaping to your lips. Please, do not allow my words to call down such a rugosity of spirit as to strain our friendship.

Allow me to explain myself more fully, and in person over tea, at your convenience next week when I am in town. Come to me at the Elvaston suites by Grosvenor, or else we can meet at Hatchards.

You can tell me then more about progress (as I know it will be) on the *Indigo Pheasant*, and also about your application for patents (which is most exciting news—I have never heard of a woman doing any such thing). Also, please remind me to tell you about a Mrs. Goethals, a widow who is part of a merchant house recently established here from Germany. She has also been advertising for investment into the *Indigo Pheasant*, which is confusing at the very least, and has in particular been asking me and others in "the Grosvenor set" about you and your family. Though she is perfectly charming and correct in her bearing, there is something unsettling about the manner in which she pursues her questions.

With much love,
your affectionate friend Lizzie

P.S. Thank you for referring me to Wornum the maker of pianofortes. We have ordered two from him: one for Mary at Longbourn and one for Georgianna here at Pemberley.

[Letter in full from Mr. Sedgewick, Esq., to Sally and James]

_____, 1817

Dear Miss McLeish and Mr. Kidlington, acting separately and jointly, in the matter of the application for six patents relating to equipment to be placed on board the ship *The Indigo Pheasant*: We must now be prepared for a long wait, as the Court of Chancery is slow at the best of times, *nolens volens*, and for patents the process includes approvals from no less than seven separate offices—including a review by the Lord Chancellor's Office, an opinion from the Attorney General, and the receipt of the Great Seal.

I am, at least, confident that the Sworn Clerk assigned to our applications is trustworthy, exacting and expeditious. Upon his initial review, he has already notified me of likely challenges, disputes and other problems arising from and pertaining to our applications. Among these, each of which bears our scrutiny and all of which together present a formidable barrier to our success, are:

I. Lack of clarity as to the precise patentable nature of the devices and technologies. He says the Court will need many more renderings and descriptions, especially as to the purpose, before it can evaluate—let alone rule on—our applications (*vide*, Lord Mansfield's opinion in the Liardet case). Otherwise, we are up in the clouds, *in nubibus*.

II. Lack of certainty in the law as to how best to construe and characterize our technologies, insofar as we have stressed less the physical manifestation of said technologies but rather their underlying and supporting principles of thought and design. The Court must view the rents and benefits flowing from these as 'incorporeal hereditaments,' *viz.*, as 'a thing invisible, having only a mental existence.' Case law and rulings are as yet unformed in this area (*vide*, Stat. 53 Geo III c.141; *cf.*, Blackstone, *Commentaries*, Book 2, chap. 3).

Having said that, our Sworn Clerk commended us on meeting with zeal and force the main thresholds for a grant of patent, namely those of novelty and potential utility. He says he has neither heard nor seen anything like our applications, and referred with favour to the cases *Rex v. Arkwright*, *Boulton v. Bull*, and *Morris v. Braunson*, any of which can serve as precedent for our successful petition.

Yet threats abound on every side. I have learned only this morning that we have rival claimants in the form of both the Maudslay engineering works and the Gravell firm of watchmakers, each of whom separately (but, I think, acting in concert) have applied for patents covering some of the themes we outline in our applications. I will not be surprised if Wornum the pianoforte manufacturer and possibly Flight Robinson the organ-makers also file. We may, in these instances, be estopped from pursuing our claims until the Court decides on priority amongst us. A distressing development, but one we can overcome with patience: *ne cede malis*.

Also—and the following is personally vexing—Gravell has sought injunctive relief on the basis that I am acting as agent and have provided you two with the money to cover the two hundred fifty pounds sterling application fee, which they assert is a clear case of champetry and thus in violation of the law. That I may be acting as champeter by lending you the money on terms that include my receiving a set percentage of any earnings derived from the patents is true enough, but that such an action violates any law is untrue, unjust, and unfounded. Allow me to handle this accusation directly and swiftly, as *virtus in medio stat*.

Finally, and it grieves me to note it, we must be prepared for possible counter-action from the firm of McDoon & Co., with whom I worked so closely and so amicably for so many years, and for whom I bear no ill will. I was induced, Miss McLeish, to pursue our present course of action (initially against my sense of judgement and honour, since some possibly might see it as a breach of trust or conflict of interest) by your arguments and declarations that your uncle and Mr. Sanford would not take umbrage at your separate train in this matter. As you have reached your full maturity and as an unmarried woman, a *feme sole*, you have agency in your own right in contractual and other commercial matters, I assume that neither your uncle nor Mr. Sanford will see the logic of contesting your actions—but their hearts may overrule their heads in this case, as you well enough understand.

I was further induced, Miss McLeish, by your declaration that the subject and substance of the technologies etc. described in the patent applications are the product of your intellectual labours, i.e., matters over which you can dispose and command, separately from your uncle and Mr. Sanford (who you assert have had no hand in the devising of the patentable materials). I rely fully upon you, Miss McLeish, to preserve the comity and concord within your family that is central to any success you might wish to have in applying for the *Indigo Pheasant* patents.

With best wishes for a swift and complete accomplishment at the Court of Chancery,

I am your humble servant,
—Sedgewick, Esq.

[Excerpt from a letter to Sally from Mrs. Sedgewick]

By the Palustral Moon,
in Veneration of St. Euthina.

Dearest Sally:
I regain my strength a little piece every day, though I will never regain it all, or so I fear. Among other things, I hear always—at the very lowest level of hearing, but never absent—a feathery wind blowing.

[... ....]

You know how much I support your bold ventures at the Court of Chancery, with the aid of my husband (who is, at bottom, not a bad creature, though he can be trying even when the sun is shining in full). I was pleased to be able to help you by providing the two hundred fifty pounds sterling you and Mr. Kidlington required for the application fees—this is very nearly my entire personal wealth, from the inheritance I brought to my marriage.

You strike a blow, Sally, for the emancipation of woman-kind, with your fearless step here. Why should men lay claim and assert suzerainty over Thought itself, and harvest all the fruits thereof?

[... ....]

I confess to the prickings of conscience where it concerns Maggie. I was perhaps too rash in my turning aside and abridgement of communication, yet at the same time I do not feel, nor have I ever felt, the gratitude and warmth of true affection that I feel she owes me—I who have done so much for her, while receiving so little in return. Her coarse, indelicate and precarious status should compel her to it, yet she owns it not—which is to me insupportable.

[... ....]

[Confidential memorandum from Sir John Barrow to Lord Melville, head of the Admiralty]

Your Lordship:

The following will memorialize the steps you have approved the taking of, in the matter of the *Indigo Pheasant*, and to further acquaint you with the material facts of this affair:

The Admiralty shall invest in the *Indigo Pheasant* project a further twenty two thousand pounds sterling immediately ("Tranche Two") and up to an additional eight thousand pounds sterling ("Tranche Three") as, and if required, under terms and conditions laid out under separate cover, for a grand total in all three tranches of up to forty thousand pounds sterling.

As before, all Admiralty investments shall flow through and under the name of the Honourable East India Company (see agreements between them and us, under separate). The Governor-General of the E.I.C., Lord Rawdon-Hastings (who is grateful for the support you gave him in the recent bestowal upon him of the Marquisate of Hastings) readily agreed, as did Canning in his role as President of the E.I.C. Board of Control— after the revocation of its monopoly rights in 1813, the E.I.C. is keen to shelter under Admiralty's wing.

With the disbursement of Tranche Two, the Admiralty and thereby His Majesty's Government becomes the *de facto* majority owner of the *Indigo Pheasant* and all equipment and technologies belonging thereto (the latter described in full also under separate).

The hitherto lead partner, the private firm McDoon & Co. (London), shall remain as a minority interest, and shall continue as a co-manager of the Project and as co-ship's husband, with the Admiralty—in consultation with the E.I.C.—as equal co-manager and co-husband, with final approval on all actions and statuses pertaining to the Project.

The firm of Coppelius, Prinn & Goethals (Widow)— which has acquired a plurality of shares outstanding in the venture, and which has in accordance with the partnership association agreement called for remaining in-payment and declared their right to buy out the remaining partners—can be expected to contest our actions. We will see to it that they have little grounds upon which to stake their case (reasons of state alone will suffice, if more narrowly defined arguments arising from within the laws of commerce cannot be found), and less likelihood of success in the courts. We may need to guard, however, against their taking extra-judicial measures against the ship and its equipment, as we have reason to believe that they are not a conventional firm of merchants in the normal sense of the designation.

In a separate but related matter, a member of the McDoon household, aided by the lawyer Sedgewick (whom your Lordship may recall has done much work for the Admiralty over the years, and whose patrons include the Tarleton family) has filed an application for six patents connected to devices and instruments to be fitted to and carried by the *Indigo Pheasant*. It is my considered opinion that the Admiralty must control or outright possess any such patents as the Court of Chancery and His Majesty may grant—the patents are of vital interest to the Crown, to the Empire, and to the well-being of our island Nation. I will write further under this heading in the near-future.

Concerning the raising of the necessary funds, which you can expect to be subject of intense scrutiny by the Treasury and against which the Home Secretary and possibly the Prime Minister himself will opine: We have sterilized the impact through re-allocating certain monies by virement from one part of the budget to another, and most satisfactorily through placing the primary burden on those we vanquished: Lord Castlereagh at the Foreign Office has negotiated additional payments from the French for our restoration to them of Pondicherry and Chandernagore in India, from the Dutch likewise for our restoration to them of Pulicat, Tuticorin and Negapatnam, and from the Danish for our forebearance in not seizing Serampore and Balasore and for our returning to them Nancowrie and the Nicobar Islands. Also, Lord Castlereagh has arranged with the Kingdom of Prussia that a portion of the loan it is raising via the

Rothschilds shall be used to pay us for our allowing them use of Heligoland in the North Sea.

Also, the presence of the Chinese alters all our strategic possibilities and forces us to draw under the mantle of *raison d'état* many threads that previously existed separately in our thinking. Ensuring our control of the *Indigo Pheasant*, for the reasons I have told you in strictest confidence, has become a matter of imperial exigency. You can expect the Duke of Wellington and also Lord Bathurst at the Colonial Office to support you in this. Incidentally, as you so astutely supposed, our support for the Regent in his so-very-public and increasingly embittered discussions with his wife about her impending royal prerogatives has also gained the Admiralty his patronage—which can be useful vis-à-vis his faction in the House of Commons, should any of our business be made the target of parliamentary inquiry.

In closing: I recommend to you the lawyer Winstanley, who has been remarkably useful to us in constructing this entire plan. He is connected to me through my wife's family, and can also call the Duke of Wellington a patron.

As always, your servant,
—Sir John

Addendum: I agree with your Lordship that Mr. Kidlington has not been wholly the asset that we had hoped he would be—he is the template for rakish inconstancy. However, neither has he wholly disappointed, and I think he may prove even more useful in future. He has communicated some unique and incisive information—albeit sporadically and with many lacunae—about those Others of whom I have spoken, and the nature of the foreign Land that is their and our focus of interest and that we hope to acquire for the British Empire. Above all, Mr. Kidlington has played an essential and irreplaceable role in precipitating the application for patents by the McLeish girl—upon which so much else hinges in our machination.

Chapter 6: An Awakening, or, The Publication of a Marred Peace

"The tygers of wrath are wiser than the horses of instruction."
—**William Blake**,
The Marriage of Heaven and Hell (1793)

"I ascend into the holy, inexpressible, mysterious Night. Far off lies the Earth, fallen into a deep chasm, desolate and alone. . . . I will intermingle myself with the ashes, fall back and dissolve into the ocean of dew."
—**Novalis**,
Hymn to the Night (1799, translated by Emilia Emeryse Smallwood, 1805)

"There, with malignant patience,
He sat in fell despite,
Till this dracontine cockatrice
Should break its way to light."

—**Robert Southey**,
"The Young Dragon" (1829)

Maggie went looking for the Mother.

"She must wake up," said Maggie to Charicules, perched on her shoulder.

"No more sleeping," Maggie said to Isaak, who trotted along beside her.

At first they had moonlight, but then they walked a long way in a lightless place that became narrower and narrower. The ground beneath them flattened, walls flowed beside them.

At last, they saw ahead a sharp, thin line of light perpendicular to what had become a smooth floor under their feet. Making their way towards it, Maggie knocked a hammer from a shelf on the wall, reflecting the shaft of light for a moment as it fell. Isaak jumped three feet in the air when the hammer banged and hopped along the floor of the tunnel.

The line of light was a gap between two doors. Maggie reached out, pushed the doors, and stumbled blinking into a brightly lighted hallway. Isaak, regaining her poise, stalked gracefully out of the doorway. Her pupils got very small but she did not blink.

They had exited from an enormous armoire made of mahogany. Turning and peering back into the cabinet, they saw rows of hammers, files, rugines, bores, crimps, and many other tools neatly hung or stacked on hooks and shelves, gleaming, dustfree, ranks of implements diminishing into the gloom.

"Ah, there you are, right on time," said someone behind them in the hallway.

Startled, Maggie spun about, dislodging Charicules from her shoulder. Isaak's tail burst up and her claws went wide. A large woman wearing a body-length leather apron over a black muslin dress stood before them. She was consulting a golden pocket watch.

"Well, tick tock, come along then, mustn't keep her waiting," was all the woman said before putting the watch into an apron pocket, spinning on the heels of her sturdy boots and proceeding briskly down the corridor.

Rooms and rooms they passed, each providing a blurred glimpse of women—and men—working at drafting tables, blowing glass, hammering on strips of metal, twisting wire, weaving, cording, painting, colouring, carving stone and wood.

Beneath and around the sound of the work—all the tapping and clinking, the burring, bending and clanking, the sound of voices raised in debate, praise, and exhortation—was a low, steady humming, like a thousand bees at a thousand beeskips, a hum that rose and fell rhythmically. Or maybe the humming was the sum of the sound of the work, not external to the effort, but the quintessence, the very circling, soaring spirit of the effort, rising and falling, opening and shutting, spire and respire, always coming back to its source.

Charicules began to harmonize atop the basso continuo of the humming.

Eventually they came to a very large room, filled with people coming and going. Two hundred yards across and five storeys tall, the room was ringed with balconied gangways on each of the upper storeys. Overflowing bookcases were built into every wall, a seamless expanse of books interrupted only by great louvered windows letting in rivers of light, by framed maps, drawings, paintings and charts celestial and nautical, and by vitrines filled with tools, specimens, maps, maquettes, models, and objects less describable. Four large brass-figured clocks stood on columns one storey high, one at each major point of the compass. Floating at the centre of the roof was a rose-window skylight.

On the floor in the very middle, directly under the skylight far above, was a massive wooden bench, surrounded by dozens of people. On the bench was an incomplete model of a ship, seven feet tall. Blueprints, sketches and maquettes surrounded the large model.

Maggie pushed her way into the crowd around the bench and stared hard at the model, the blueprints, the maquettes. Charicules flew up and perched on one of the ship's spars, singing notes of inquiry. Isaak, after a prodigious leap to the top of the bench, explored the rudder and pintle—purring all the while with suspicion. Murmurs and whispers ran through the crowd, right 'round the bench. Everyone watched her.

The woman who had met Maggie at the tool-case in the hallway disappeared into the throng. A smaller, older woman walked up to Maggie.

"I know you," Maggie said. "Saint Macrina."

"Indeed, well met again," said the older woman. "Be at home here in the House of Design, the workshop of desire and architective joy. But I think you already know your way around this place, though perhaps you do not yet fully remember."

Maggie looked upon Saint Macrina wonderingly, and mused a while. She felt the humming in her ears and mind and heart, a melody she knew but could not quite name. She shook her head at last.

Saint Macrina smiled, took Maggie's hand, and led her out of the great workroom. Charicules flew along side them in the hallways and Isaak trailed, stopping frequently to interrogate the tools in a glass cabinet or to challenge the leather boots of a worker.

They walked for about an hour, through corridors and across other workrooms—none so vast as the one containing the large ship model, but none of them small either—and up many staircases. Isaak was a bounding ball of gold as they ascended.

Opening a blue door, Saint Macrina ushered Maggie, Charicules, and Isaak into a garden encompassing a roof two hundred yards long and one hundred yards wide. Crenellated brick walls five feet tall enclosed the garden, espaliered with rose canes, clematis, small pear, quince and plum trees. Beds of herbs, brambles, shrubs and flowers—most notably the blue bixwort, grace-noted by hedge mustard—constituted the garden proper, traversed by winding brick walkways and dotted with a profusion of fountains. Hundreds of bees worked the flowers, bending down stems under their temporary weight, flying off in minute showers of pollen. Hundreds of butterflies dappled the air just above the blooms: sylvanders, marbled yellows, ecailles, great coppers, tortoise-shells, apollos no larger than a half-penny piece, lucines the size of a horse's hoof.

Charicules and Isaak lost no time losing themselves in the

garden. Maggie followed Saint Macrina more slowly to the centre of the garden, where a white-columned, blue-roofed pavilion sat, raised ten feet up on a dais. A large, white-faced clock, encased in a ruddy metal, crowned the pavillion. The saint left Maggie at the foot of the stairs. Maggie went up the stairs and found there another woman, seated at a table.

"Sit with me," said the woman.

Maggie and the woman sat across from one another, saying not a word for many minutes. They looked out over the garden and beyond, at a city that stretched to the horizon on every side. The garden sat on a roof that was nearly forty storeys high, taller than the top of Saint Paul's Cathedral, the tallest building in London. The upper air was clear, the lower smudged by smoke issuing from many chimneys. The humming took on an even thicker note, an accumulated bass line. The bees in the garden syncopated that line; the butterflies slip-winged and worried it.

"Impressive," said Maggie. "But I am not here to enjoy a view, no matter how glorious. I am seeking the Mother. She must be woken. Can you help me?"

"Of course I can," said the woman. "Yet not so hasty, if you please, dearest. Let us dine first. I have not eaten in a long time, you see, and I am very, very hungry."

Maggie could not recall seeing food or drink on the table when she arrived, but now two pale yellow plates sat there filled with beef tripe-and-eggs on boiled potatoes and two tall glasses of cloudy deep-golden beer topped with a mass of foam.

"Ah, the *Hefeweiss*, I have dreamed of this!" said Maggie's host, before taking a long pull at the glass.

The two ate in silence, the host because she was utterly engrossed in the eating and the drinking, Maggie because she was examining every feature of the woman across the table. The woman resembled Maggie, except for the addition of a decade or perhaps fifteen years (though around the eyes and the corners of the mouth she seemed much older still).

Maggie thought, "Well, Mama, if you could see me now. Your little eagle has flown very high."

Polishing her plate with a last bit of potato, the woman said, "Now then, Miss Maggie, ask me your questions, or else I fear you might burst."

Maggie, pausing before her response, said, "I have come a very long way and will not burst now of a sudden at this final step."

The woman laughed merrily and said, "I felt your spirit come to me on tigerish feet while I dreamed! I see now that your precursor was but a weak outline of your fierce reality, my child."

Maggie said nothing to this, though the woman's tone was disarming and seemed to invite a reply.

"You seemed quicker to speak when I saw you in my dreams, but perhaps that was the element of your character that your shadow-self overweighted," continued the woman, puzzlement creasing her face for a moment. "Howsoever that may be, here you are now. You—not you alone, by the way, please do not presume so highly—have wakened me. Though be warned that I am still very sleepy, and some part of me sleeps still, while yet another part of me yearns to return to my bed. It is hard to rouse oneself in the middle of such a sleep, and a well-deserved one at that."

Maggie said nothing, but narrowed her eyes and shrugged ever so slightly.

"You *are* bold, my Maggie. Most mortals show a bit more deference when first meeting me, those few who find their way to me at all. Perhaps I should appear as a dragon or a sphinx, something to compell awe or fear. Though seeing you now, I do not think even a dragon would cow you."

"I mean not to be impolite," said Maggie, picking up Isaak, who had wandered in from the garden. "It's just that I need you, *we* need you, and it has been a long time since any of us heard from you. And very few of *us* get much sleep either, down where we live."

As if to emphasize the point, Isaak glared at Goddess.

"Ah, I must concede a point fairly if brusquely spoken," said Goddess, furrowing her brow. "Having set the mainspring of self-direction within each of you, I am obligated to abide by the results of how you govern yourselves, . . . no matter how coarse or ill-judged I may find those results."

Charicules perched on the railing nearest Maggie but did not sing.

"Goddess, I am not so foolhardy as to pick a quarrel with you, who are the object of my searchings. I need your help. I can fight the *okakpu* of an owl, but not all his followers too, and at the same time outfit and send a ship into the riddlesome places, *and* haul a world-island back over those same unlucky roads."

Maggie ceased talking when she realized she was being ignored. The Mother was giving her complete attention to a slice of honey-glazed almond cake that now sat on the plate in front of her. No cake or dessert appeared on Maggie's plate. Isaak walked across the table and sat in front of Goddess, who slowed her chewing.

"I do not recall giving the same free will to cats," she said, her mouth half-full. "It seems much has changed since I nodded off and now cats, *some* cats at least, have grown almost to become people."

Maggie feared then she might have stirred the wrath of Goddess, though she did not let her fear show. Isaak sat as still as marble.

Goddess laughed instead. A slice of cake appeared on Maggie's plate.

"Forgive me, children. I am peevish when I wake and easily crossed, mostly because I do not yet understand the state of affairs but hate to admit to my ignorance and my own possible need for assistance. Not befitting divinity, I know, but I must own it."

Isaak returned to Maggie's lap.

The mood having been softened, Maggie and Goddess talked for hours in the synagogic garden, each learning from the other. Goddess spoke of the Original Song that she and God made together, how they sang themselves into existence, two paired notes in self-aware harmony and mutual rhythm who pierced and overwrote forever the precedent silence. She told of how they sang the angels into being, how the universe was sung from nothingness to house them, how they massed the seraphic choirs to shape a near-infinite variety of other beings.

"You know the Song, little Maggie, we all do: it is inscribed in the blood and sinews of every single being past, present, and future across all the multitudes of worlds. You hear its aortic bass line right now, the upbeat and the downbeat, the diastolic and the systolic. I *am* that song, Maggie, and I also hearken to it, both itself and following it at the same time."

Goddess recounted the story of the three great rebellions, born less of wickedness (though this was often a consequence) but more from folly and despair. The first angels to rebel wished to un-make themselves, being unwilling and unable to accept self-awareness, and especially desperate to avoid their own immortality. But Goddess and God could not un-make; notes once sung cannot be un-sung. The first rebels have sought fruitlessly to obliterate themselves since their beginning very near to the Beginning—in their ever more inventive and grotesque attempts at their own un-doing, they have caused and will continue to cause great havoc across the universe. The second cohort of rebels enjoyed their consciousness but rejected its musicality; they could not abide being, hearing, and singing the Song for eternity, and have sought to live purely in prose, only to discover over and over again that there is prosody also in prose, as in all things, and thus no escaping metre and harmony. Forever thwarted in their efforts to denude music of melody and flatten all rhythm into static, the second-wave rebels rage against the universe, laying waste and causing pain (the resulting dirges and lamentations being musical only incites these angels to further rage, propelling the cycle forward endlessly). The third flight of rebels loved music but too well, seeking to commandeer it for their own various purposes, and to impose singular, rigid musical regimes where they could. The inherent flexibility of music precluding the permanency of any such regime, each of the rebellious paladins angrily tries to force compliance through punishment and denial.

"Alas," said Goddess. "One way or the other, each of the poor rebels craves un-knowing, wants nothing more than to unlearn what the music is, what it offers, what it provides. Some do not realize they can never achieve unlearning, any more than they can detach themselves from their own selves. It is as if your little Isaak'en here furiously went to war—a war of extermination, mind you—with her own tail. Cats sometimes do just that, but the result is always the same: a cat exhausted and perhaps badly mauled but still very much itself. Of course, unlike the cat at war with itself, most of the rebellious ones realize that they cannot achieve their goal, which only makes them more proud, more furious, more desperate. It is a terrible thing to witness. There appears to be no cure, though I have searched, experimented and prayed for one through all the eons."

Isaak groomed herself in Maggie's lap. She avoided her tail.

Maggie asked about the half-fallen.

"A sad squadron," said Goddess. "Dawdlers, indecisive, lingering at the threshold of great deeds, gnawing at the tassels of a grand drapery they are both too scared to pull back and thrust through and too afraid to leave undisturbed. They love the Original Song but pretend otherwise, fearing the scorn of those who rebelled, rather than trusting the praise of those who stayed true. They end up singing carceratory tunes of their own making, songs they despise but are too proud to give up. Much of what humans (and their counterparts on the many other worlds) call 'evil' stems from the actions of the half-fallen. Yes, great harm comes from the actions of the various rebels, but a great deal of that is unintentional, damage inflicted unknowingly upon ants by rampaging elephants. The half-fallen, on the other hand, delight in deliberately causing pain to mortals, as a way to make themselves feel important, to divert the effects of their self-loathing onto beings weaker than they are."

Goddess yawned.

"I will be some time waking up in full. Right now, the lovely meal and the foamy yeast-beer are making me especially drowsy—that, and the humming of the bees in the garden. What more can I tell you, young Maggie?"

"Goddess, I came to ask your help. *Chi di.* I can imagine that the woes of my little world may not be much for you to consider, being, I suppose, just a few discordant notes in the universal symphony but they loom large for me and many others. I need to sing a new song, an *oba ema* of sacrifice and repentance."

Goddess yawned again. Eyes half-shut, looking at the garden, Goddess did not answer right away.

"I can only intervene, to the extent I can at all, through you and others like you, Maggie. The music is independent, follows it own course separate from the musician. The composer can revise and abridge, but who is to say that the new version is necessarily better?"

Maggie began to retort, when Goddess started forward, pointed to a corner of the garden and exclaimed, "Selah! Look, there! Do you see it? Just under the oblong-shaped rhododendron near the tallest fountain."

Maggie looked to that spot, shading her eyes. In the shadows under the bush a large bird scratched at the soil. A minute later, it strode out a few feet from the shelter of the shrub, stopped abruptly, raised its crested head and surveyed the garden. Its tail was rapier-like, its plumage dazzling for the moment in the sunshine. Just as suddenly as it had stopped, the pheasant dashed across a bed of portulacas and vanished into the tangle of roots under a viburnum-bush.

"An Indigo Pheasant!" said Maggie, turning her head back towards Goddess.

The Mother did not reply. Like the pheasant, she had disappeared. On the plate in front of Maggie a fresh slice of almond cake lay, wrapped in a linen napkin. On the table beside the plate stretched a freshly killed mouse, still warm.

Isaak ate the mouse. Maggie took the cake. Joined by Charicules, they descended the pavillion steps and walked down one of the brick lanes leading through the garden back to the door through which they had entered. Maggie stopped only once, looking behind her to confirm that the pavillion was empty and to watch the second hand travelling on the clock perched like a planet atop the pavillion's peak. The ticking and the tocking of the clock at the centre of the garden matched the pulse of her heart, an elastic marriage of blood and metal, not in the sterile manner of a metronome but as the organic expression of beats shaped to suit the needs of life.

Saint Macrina greeted them as they entered the hallway.

"No adjectives are strong enough to describe our emotions, daughter," said the saint, as they walked back towards the great workroom. "I have never met the Mother; none of us here has. You are our *nuncia*, our ambassador to Goddess. So, tell me, what is She like?"

Maggie was somewhat at a loss as how best to answer, so spoke in generalities. She described the garden and its clock with as many details as she could recall, but said little about how Goddess seemed to her. Ambassadors carry the expectations of many upon their shoulders, after all.

"And God, did the Great Mother speak of Him?"

Maggie shook her head, able to be completely truthful on that score.

"Mysteries upon mysteries," sighed Saint Macrina. "So many rumours and speculations. Some even say He does not exist."

"What do you think?" asked Maggie.

"If there is a Mother, there is a Father," said Saint Macrina, though in a tone lacking the stern definitiveness with which saints and beatas often express themselves. "I favour most the notion that he is gone on a long journey, seeking a means to repair or remake the Great Song. Or perhaps (as some would have it) He is looking for another universe altogether, believing He hears music not of His or Her making beyond the furthest stars, a muffled melody behind the wainscoting of Heaven. Whatever the case may be, God is not here and He left us no forwarding instructions."

They returned to the large workroom, which overflowed with expectant faces. Maggie said as much as she thought prudent and turned the discussion as quickly and as unobtrusively as she could to the purpose of the activities in the workshop.

"Maggie, we honour you by making a faithful record of your vision," said Saint Macrina, pointing to the large model on the central workbench and the smaller models and all the related schematics, blueprints, maquettes, tables of offsets, and reams of notations scattered around its base. One of the other saints nudged Saint Macrina, whispered in her ear. "I am reminded that, of course, the copy reflects not only your vision, dearest Maggie, but that of Sally. You see, we too have our little factions here, and who could be surprised? Factions have been with us in this universe almost since the Original Song was composed."

Sub-currents of muttering coursed through the lake surrounding Maggie. She weighed making a speech about Sally, about the wish for collaboration and rights of authorship, but quickly decided it was better to avoid the topic of Sally entirely. Her prior impression about the Mother having been tested this very afternoon, Maggie did not relish also calling into question her beliefs about the nature of the saints as well—she'd had enough disillusionment for one day.

Maggie instead examined the large model. Isaak scrambled into the model itself, sniffing around the mock-ups of the Fulginator and the steam engine.

"Ingenious solution to the problem of the steam engine couplings, there where you have inserted what I think must be coxa-trochanteral joints," said Maggie. "I do not think that is Sally's concept, and I know it is not mine or Mr. Gandy's, so who else's thoughts do you capture here? Mr. Bunce's? But no, he is very smart with the mathematics but not so mechanically minded, so who then?"

Saint Macrina and several others in the front turned to look into the crowd, which parted to allow two men to come forward. Shyly, they said they were *chola* bronzesmiths, saints from Tamil-land, and that the joints had been their idea.

"We are not simply copyists and archivists here, Maggie," said Saint Macrina. "We are curators and editors, and makers in our own right. We revise and we amend. We add and we pare away. The final model of the *Indigo Pheasant* shall be the most perfect, most ideal, it can be. See it in your dream-walking, import the improvements into the world below, with our blessings."

Maggie would always recall the next hours as some of the happiest of her life. She swapped craftsman's notes with the assembly, an excited bourse for artisanal ideas. They talked about helicoidal drills, pivot rounders, microtenices, mandrels, dautic fuses, curcurbites, cyclostats and all manner of other specialized tools, some of which they came to realize they would need to invent in order to complete the Selah-Machine. They debated the efficacy of this lathe versus that one and the usefulness of the torquetum to measure eliptics. They reviewed the suites of axes, gimmals and gears ("*les engrenages*," as the saint from the little mill-town near Arras insisted on calling them, to the gentle teasing of the others, who reminded her that they had left their old languages behind). They analyzed the value of using sabicu and mottled purple bubinga wood for the cabinetry, the supple, pale yellow antiara wood for Fulginator casements, macassar ebony for the musical components, wood from the nobiron tree for the heavier Fulginator struts. They talked of china clay and lead marcassite, of niobium and terentium. As only those with direct, hands-on knowledge can, they pondered how to achieve goodness of fit, to attain the greatest precision and fault tolerance, to maintain desired levels of strength, ductility and flexibility in their materials.

The four pillar-clocks, impartial referees, tolled the hour for vespers. As the multitude of labouring saints moved to various chapels for the singing of the divine office, Saint Macrina pulled Maggie aside.

"Leave us now, daughter, to our cantations of melancholy experience. Return to the middle-earth with our good will and your newfound knowledge. Come back to us when you can. Your greatest challenge is very soon upon you. No matter that you have faced down the Owl once—that was so far the one time only, and he was unprepared for the sudden revelation of your strength. Do not underestimate his guile in your final contest with him. He is old and cunning, subtly poisonous in ways you cannot yet have understood."

Isaak arched her back and hissed.

"You too, little lion!" laughed the saint. "Truly you gratify my eye and my soul, the both of you!"

They paused in front of the tool-cabinet that would be Maggie's portal to her room in the house on Mincing Lane.

"Two more advisements, if I may," said the saint. "Sally is crucial for success in this endeavour. Remember that."

Maggie said nothing, only nodding her head.

The saint withdrew a hand-mirror from a pocket on her work-apron and said, "Secondly, you need to find poor Jambres—the Cretched Man. He is frantic to find you and Sally and to help, but he cannot penetrate the defenses set by the Owl. So instead you must go to him, in his place of sanctuary."

She held the mirror up to Maggie's gaze. The mirror was misty and did not reflect Maggie's face. In the mirror, the mist cleared. Maggie could see in the mirror an interior scene, akin to a picture from a book of hours with a figure sitting bent over his books like Saint Jerome in the library.

"He is beautiful!" she gasped.

"Cursedly so," said the saint.

"I do not mean merely his white shrouding," said Maggie, scrutinizing the image in the mirror.

"I did not think you did."

Isaak jumped all the way up to Maggie's shoulder and likewise peered into the mirror. Isaak purred mightily and softly reached out a paw to the surface of the glass.

"Find him. Go to him," said Saint Macrina.

They hugged. Maggie, with Isaak on one shoulder and Charicules on the other, and the linen-wrapped almond cake in one hand, opened the door to the armoire, walked past rows of tools, down the long, swiftly darkening hallway as the saint shut the doors behind them, and eventually found herself in the house with the dolphin door-knocker in the City of London. She ate the cake later that day, but did not find it nearly as delicious as she remembered the first slice being in the garden.

Sally wept alone in her room, in a wandering hour between midnight and dawn.

She clutched at her Saint Morgaine's medallion and she counted the steeples of Hamburg's churches, to no avail. She prayed to the moon, which yielded no indication of listening, let alone answering.

She whispered for Tom, and begged Frau Reimer for succour. She dared not call for Uncle Barnabas, much less Sanford.

Where was Isaak, so often absent of late? Little golden traitor. Into a pillow she sobbed.

"I am come to the ends of spiritual reckoning," she thought, shuddering. "Oh dear Goddess, help me. I know not what to do."

She thought again of Reglum and wept more.

"Sweet man, how I have wronged you. Even now you would help me, I am sure of it, or at least not turn me away. Yet you above all I cannot confide in."

A wind arose, softly fingering the window-panes and sighing over the roof-tiles.

Sally felt James in her mind, always. But no more so than this past week, with its dawning realization, its panicky denials, its sleepless evaluation of every possible course of action . . . and its lack of a viable solution.

Another presence seeped into her thoughts, borne it seemed on the mounting wind.

"Oh no, oh no . . . you are entirely unwelcome!"

"What have we here?" came a voice gliding. "Does Sally sing the compline, buttressing the glory of God with the beautiful strength of her selfless voice? Nay, I hear something more selfish: a most earnest and pathetical contemplation, it would seem, based on the irrefutable proof of the body, yes? The moon is a most punctual herald, wouldn't you say, my dear Sally?"

Sally tried to move and tried to sing, but could do neither. She even thought about calling out to Maggie, only to have her voice falter on her tongue.

Atop a newel-post of her bed a small white owl emerged from the darkness, shining in the darkness, a miniature Strix. It grinned an awful grin and bobbed in a parody of a bow.

"What entry does this fall under in the encylopedia of happiness?" chuckle-rasped the Owl.

Sally managed to moan.

"Perhaps your orchidaceous yet virtuous continent was overwhelmed by an army of brigands, your aromatic coast savaged by a fleet of pirates? Some action to which you did not consent and against which you had no defense?"

The Owl winked out atop the newel-post, to reappear a second later on the mantlepiece.

"Oh no, oh noooo-hooom. That was not it, not at all."

The Owl hopped from one foot to the other, vanished from the mantlepiece and popped up momentarily on the wash-stand.

"Let's see then, the only mystery remaining is who the father is."

The Owl flickered off the wash-stand, snapped into view again on another newel-post.

"No, actually I see no mystery there, and I am very sure others won't either. To learn the identity of that fine fellow no one will need to read the pattern of tossed hemp-seed on All Hallow's Eve or look backlengths into an old mirror."

Sally looked around wildly for an object to throw at the tiny Strix.

"Stay your hand, *Miss* Sally," laughed the owlet. "I have not come merely to mock your hypocrisy, your pretensions or the transgression of your body, though clearly you deserve all the censure you will receive. (Say what you may about me and my kind, yet we uphold the strictest of moral standards, that we do to a fault)."

"What then, hated one?" said Sally, hoarsely.

"A more polite bearing might be called for, given that you are dancing with fettered legs upon ropes. Still, I am the epitome of forebearance this night, so will overlook your rude outburst. Hearken closely now, girl. I have come to make you an offer, one that I will make just this once."

Sally sat still as an urn.

"You cannot lawfully discharge the treadle from the egg. Barring some unforeseen accident, the child within you will quicken and be delivered from you. Much sooner than that (the moon's passage being implacable), very soon indeed, the child will announce its presence to all with the swelling of your belly. What an impression that will make on Lady Somerville and Mr. Babbage and all your other fine new friends."

The Owl flitted to the table-top. His eyes were like flares.

"I can spare you that. I could take the child as it is now in your womb, as yet unformed and nearly invisible, with no harm to yourself, and with no one ever to know."

Sally nearly retched. When she caught her breath, she said, "Even if I consented . . . how loathsome even to say those words. . . ."

"Spare me your piety," snapped the Owl. "You lost that platform when you willingly entered into this state."

"Monster! I did not wish to bear a child. Nor does James wish for paternity. We . . . we love each other, and for our . . . conversations . . . I have no regret. What I bear is an unintended result."

The Owl opened his beak, half-opening his head, revealing a gullet seeming larger than his diminutive body.

"What will James say when he finds out?"

Sally shuddered.

"Ah, hoooo," said the Owl. "You play the Corinthian Maid, painting an idealized portrait of your beloved Endymion while he sleeps. Charming, I am sure, but a wallow on a foundrous road. Your James will want this child, once he learns of it and can confirm it is his. You know that! It is his one sure way to gain the family and the fortune he needs. You will be in no position to deny his suit when the child comes. More important, your uncle and your brother, the uprighteous Sanford, the little queen, Afsana . . . and Maggie, who has supplanted you in the affection of all, . . . none of them will be able to shut him out, either. Such disgrace you will otherwise bring upon your family, a house already struggling under the weight of financial distress and likely ruin."

Sally tried to sing down the Owl, but her voice held no potency and she lost the melody after just a few notes.

"You have forfeited much of your power in this matter," laughed the Owl. "Here is the tender proof of it!"

The Owl capered on the table top, his fork-tail knocking over a bottle of ink.

"I must be off now," he said. "I am not as soft-hearted as Rumpelstiltskin to give you three days to make up your mind, but in my mercy I will allow you twenty-four hours to decide. Look for me tomorrow night at this time. You do not have much choice in the matter, but I will grant you the illusion of free will, as a balm to your pride if nothing else. Hooooo!"

The Owl popped out of view and did not return.

Sally had no more tears to cry. Her insides were cold ash powder, her thoughts sat scattered like scoria in the dry plains of her mind. She slid down into sleep that bordered on death.

Isaak woke her up in mid-morning, walking imperiously on Sally's pillow and butting Sally in the face while purring loudly enough to rouse a graveyard. Cinereous light filled the room. Sally heard a carriage rumble by in the street and the cry of an oyster-man. She thought it might be the Beata Audomara's Day, then vaguely remembered that it was the Week of Lustration and a Tuesday (or was it Wednesday?) so must be the feast-day for either Saint Emerentia or Saint Bavo. Not that any of those things mattered any longer.

Holding Isaak close, Sally lay in bed for an hour. Gradually her thoughts flowed again, the cold within lessening. In her mind, she could see James, laughing, sipping tea with her at Hatchards'. How dashing he looked, especially framed by the bookshop's tasteful wallpaper, his marvellous hands stirring

THE INDIGO PHEASANT *Volume Two of Longing for Yount*

sugar with an elegant spoon. He spoke animatedly about the patents for the Fulginator and the shape of the hull on the *Indigo Pheasant*, of making one's fortune in the world and of sailing to find the nutmeg of one's desire below the horizon. He talked of marriage and family (didn't he?). Of children?

"I have sailed clear out of this world, driven by *Sehnsucht* and the flourish of fallacy," she thought, stroking Isaak. "Cinnamon-trees and cloves receding ever before me, calentures, mirages induced by the mocking waves."

She sat up, felt dizzy, noticed the overturned ink bottle.

"Mute the dulcet string of hope, though desire remains unabated. A wan lustre stands upon my brow, my heart trembles, deaf to the entreaties of my conscience. I sing this grey morning the doom of the first-born world, wherein impiously a woman and a man essayed to scale the battlements of heaven. Yet surely mercy plays some small role in this drama? *'Canticum autem exultatio mentis de aeternis habita,'* as Saint Aquinas says. Do you hear me, God? I quote your scholar-saints to you."

Uncle Barnabas cautiously called up the stairs for her. Dimly she heard the others below, smelled cabbage being stewed (more of Cook's economizing) for their lunch. She made noise sufficient to reassure Barnabas and send him back to the partners' room.

"'*Ich muss im Dunkeln sein.*' Dear Frau Reimer, how I miss you. What would you have me do? Nay, 'tis my decision and mine alone. Were you here, I would not place this burden upon your estimable shoulders, nor sully you with the blood of it. Still, how much I would give to hear your words of consolation."

Sally dressed herself indifferently.

"And you, Owl. Threatening angel, speaking ass, in worm-smooth silk composed. You may think to exploit my sin, you may dance on my decayed virtue, but you shall never possess the child. I know what things you would do to it, you doctor of sarcology, molder of flesh. Implanted in some nurturing filth of your devising, the little life-spirit you would twist into a homunculus, a changeling wholly enslaved to your will, a pseudo-James or a *doppelganger* of me. A torment to me through all my days that creature would be, and I have no doubt you would ensure its propinquity."

Isaak nudged her ankles.

"And Strix not tell anyone? Of course he would. Betrayer, pinnated liar. He would certainly inform James at the earliest opportunity."

Accompanied by Isaak, Sally went down to join the others. She had forgotten: today Mr. Gandy rejoined them after his stint in debtor's prison. Cabbage notwithstanding, the lunch was warm, tasty and reasonably plenteous—in all, fit for a reunion. Though Mr. Gandy was the ostensible object of attention, the McDoons most closely inspected Sally (none more closely than Sanford, though at a distance, with his neck and head retracted like a camel's or an old stork's). Barnabas pattered gaily but walked on the points of his toes around the subject of his niece.

Sally surprised them all—and was herself surprised—at her positive participation in the afternoon's discussion about the status of the *Indigo Pheasant*. She contributed thoughts on the Fulginator's tractices and how the apical pulse might best be amplified. She congratulated Bunce on his use of the Ludolphian number in solving one of the knottier problems in their likely navigation. To surreptitious looks shared around the table, Sally even supported Maggie on the coordination of the septuary brachistochrones—a topic on which all who understood the mathematics knew she had hitherto opposed Maggie's proposal. Maggie herself raised an eyebrow but courteously thanked Sally. Above all, Sally provided masses of detail on her recent mercantile negotiations, and gave Sanford and Barnabas excellent recommendations on several key points.

"Peacocks and peonies," thought Barnabas. "Sally has come back to us. Smart as ever. A little tired looking perhaps, but her head is filled with the best commercial stratagems. How she can handle 'em! Well done in every particular!"

Running his hands over his vest, Barnabas added to himself: "Well taught too, I dare say."

Sanford was not so easily fooled. He watched how Sally

periodically looked at the pictures on the wall and how quickly she averted her gaze from the sea devouring the crews of the East Indiamen and from the boy about to be eaten by the shark. He saw boundless hollow spaces behind her gaze, and the tattered fragility of her mien.

"Something to do with James Kidlington, I warrant, or I am a tambalacoque tree," he thought.

Nor was Maggie deceived. Distracted as she was, she nevertheless felt the forced nature of Sally's afternoon behaviour.

"The Owl has infiltrated," Maggie thought. "I felt him slip through an accidental caesura, a splintered eighth-note quaver. What turpentine has he uncorked into Sally's mind? She fairly seethes with it."

Dinner passed likewise with fruitful discussion and convivial small talk. Cook was gratified to see Sally at table twice in one day, but she observed how little "her little smee" actually ate.

"Not correct as in Cocker," thought the Cook as she helped clear the dishes.

So, the Cook was not as surprised as she might have been when Sally came to the kitchen much later that evening. The rest of the household was already abed, even the maid. The Cook was organizing the cutlery one last time for the day, and making mental notes of the groceries she needed to buy first thing in the morning.

"Sally, whatever is it, my love? You have not visited me in my kitchen for so long that you being here is almost like seeing an owl in the ivy bush."

Sally shivered at the reference. She put her candle next to the hooded lamp on the cutting-board table. The annatto glow from the two candles reflected off the polished chesnut furnishings and copper utensils. The resulting rufuscence made the dark in the corners of the kitchen seem even deeper. The candlelight projecting from below made Cook look like Judy of the Punch & Judy show—Sally did not know whether to laugh or to flee from the apparition.

"I am so sorry, dear Cook," whispered Sally. She had invoked the small gods of the hearth, asking for the strength not to cry, but they had not heard her prayers.

"Oh no, my little smee," said Cook, enveloping Sally in her arms. "Hush, wipe those tears. Come on now, tell me straight and I will help you defeat any bugbears that plague you. You know I will."

Sally left the Cook's embrace, leaned back to rest against a table, and told Cook about James and the pregnancy. She did not say anything about the Owl's intrusion the previous night, let alone mention his offer.

The Cook said nothing while Sally told the tale.

"Well, my dear, this is a real pig's mackle, and make no mistake," said Cook when Sally finished.

Sally nodded.

"The real question is, what do you plan to do?" said the Cook

"I have thought on that question more than any man can ever know, all this week, and with the vigour of Diana all this day," said Sally.

Cook leaned forward, shadows dimpling her Judy-face, making her eyebrows look like brooms.

Sally breathed deeply and said as softly as she could and still be heard, "I cannot deliver this child."

Cook-Judy leaned even closer in. Her eyes reflected candlelight. After her heart beat once, twice, three times, four times, Cook took Sally to her bosom.

"Oh Sally, oh Sally, so be it," she said softly, choking back tears.

In 1803 Parliament had passed an act (43 George III c. 58, to be precise) making abortion a capital felony.

"Tell no one of this," said Cook. "Not James. Not Mr. Barnabas or Mr. Sanford. Not Tom, should he return from wherever he is. Not even your friend Mrs. Sedgewick. None can ever know."

Sally nodded, fully resolved.

"I know a woman, someone we can trust. One of my countrywomen from Norfolk, a barny bishy-bee, lives now in Stepney. She can help. She'll use the old recipe: savin, dittany, mercury-oil, hellebore. I can take you. I am sure she could see us well within the week, a sennight latest."

Sally agreed to go to Stepney with the Cook as soon as could be arranged.

A few hours later, sometime after midnight, Sally refused the Owl's offer to his face. The pygmy owl raged about her room, upsetting books and papers. No one besides Sally could hear him though, his wrath reduced to squeaks by the protective songs woven round the house on Mincing Lane.

Regaining his owlish composure, Strix glared at Sally and said, "Unlike Rumpelstiltskin, I am not rent in two by the stamping of my feet. You and I will most assuredly meet again. I will not be so tranquil at our next encounter."

His sending vanished with a popping sound.

Sally, though shaken, dismissed Strix from her mind. She thought instead about the woman she was going to visit in Stepney.

"What's this?" hissed the Owl. "*Une petite bambochade très amusante*, a most charming and piquant little scene from everyday life."

James Kidlington sat alone in the room rented for him by the Admiralty. He sat at the writing table, a sparse affair badly constructed, its spindly legs uneven.

The Owl had made his way in through a picture on the wall. The landlord was a devout soul who supplied the rooms he let with prints depicting the lives of the saints, hoping thereby to inspire his tenants both to pious reflection and to punctual payment of the rent. The prints he purchased very cheaply from the used-book stalls on Paternoster Row (such prints being so abundant that they were often used to stuff cracks in windows or as kindling to start fires), but he did not simply pin them to the streaky wallpaper—he took pains instead to install them within frames he made himself from strips of cast-off wood, the perfect compromise between respectability and economy. The irregular angles of the home-cobbled frames gave Strix his entry-point, and the presentation of virtuous models to produce commercial behaviour acted as a beacon.

The Owl replaced Saint Alphege in the print of the medieval martyr being stoned by the Danes in Cheapside. Flapping his wings as if to ward off the missiles, the Owl-in-the-picture said to James, "What might we title the pleasant *bambochade* that my eyes bestride?"

James put down his pen, turned, and said, "You do not frighten me, you know. Nor even amuse me. I wish you really would become Saint Alphege—I would gladly pelt you to death just like a Shrovetide cock."

"I esteem your depth of spirit, James, I really dooooo," hooted the Owl. "Fitting indeed for our amourous amiger, the little squire in the lists of love."

James waved his hands in disgust and turned back to his table.

"Let's see," rasped the Owl, reviewing the scattered books open on James's table. "He pens a letter to his Thisbe. What does he use for inspiration, besides the prints on his walls? Oldmixon's *Caliper'd Heart*, yes of course, and Shakespeare's *Sonnets* (nice to see them coming back into style again). Donne. Herrick. Golding's Ovid. Your tastes are a bit old-fashioned for one so young. No wait, here are two sharp newcomers—Keats and Shelley—to demonstrate the modernity of our bold Pyramus in the nineteenth century."

James shook his head. The Owl disappeared from the print of Saint Alphege's martyrdom, reappearing in a print portraying the Roman emperor Valerian frying Saint Lawrence on a gridiron.

"Away with you, ghost-snipe, trouble me not with your mocking wit," said James.

The Owl-Saint Lawrence hopped up and down, as if the iron in the picture really were searing his feet.

"Not before I advise you, as all good nightmares should,"

laughed the Owl. "You are Abelard, she is Heloise: 'crooked eclipses 'gainst his glory fight.' You think to impress Sally with the melody of your worded love. You believe she moulds herself to your design, overcome by the fervour of your expression. Yet what do you know in truth of her heart's untuned nature, of the voices her blood carries to her brain?"

James frowned.

"Nay, James, your desired one harks to others before she gives her loyalty to you."

"What do you mean, you filthy creature? Sally is truer to me than anyone has ever been."

"Is she? Poor James, scratching out love letters to one whose heart is impregnable. Hold now: impregnable though Sally's heart may be, another part of her anatomy is far more receptive to the fertility of your gestures . . ."

"What do you say, what do you mean?" James nearly shouted, half-rising.

The Owl sank back from Saint Lawrence and re-surfaced elsewhere as Saint Praxedes being mauled and devoured by the Hounds of Tindalos.

"You know what I mean, James," said the Owl. "She is pregnant, James. With your child."

James sat down so quickly the chair creaked.

"No," he said. "It cannot be. We were so very careful."

"But it can be and it is," said the Wurm.

"No, no, Sally would have told me," yelled James. "You lie, you lie."

The Owl-Saint Praxedes said, "You want the evidence of research. Ask Sally yourself."

James rose again and strode the short distance to the print of Saint Praxedes.

"I will," said James. "She will tell me the truth. I know it."

"Do you? As a friend of the finer sensibilities, I must gently disagree with you there."

James thought of the garden at the Last Cozy House and of the locket.

"It is I who have lied in the past to Sally," said James, in a low, strangled voice. "Not her to me."

The Owl shook his head, and said, "No, my dear James. She wrongs you twicely. While you at least air your wrong-doings, Sally hoards her misdeeds deep, makes of them an 'unsunned heap.'"

James placed his palms on the worn wallpapering on either side of the Praxedes print.

"What more can there be? Out with it, monster," he said. "Since I have no choice but to listen."

"I aim only to help you in this, James," said the Owl. "On my word, it pains me to think of Sally withholding her truth from you, even as you drink tea with her at Hatchards and enjoy the breakfast rooms together at the Tavistock. You, so blithe and unaware, so good and true; Sally, *la belle sauvage*, hoarding the truth unto herself, within herself, a spirit senseless to the claims you so rightfully have."

"The child is . . ." whispered James. "Mine. I am the father."

"Rightly said," sighed the Owl. "So, here is the second bone of the riddle, the canines of the truth to be extracted from the jawbone of falsehood: Sally will not deliver your child."

James reared back, aghast, uttering no words but half-formed groans. "She goes with the McDoon's cook this very morning to abort the baby growing in her womb," said the Owl, turning his head almost right around and back again, hooming and making tsk'ing sounds. "To wash away the rose before e'er it blooms."

James cried out, "Why?"

The Owl blinked slowly, "Did you really think she would have a child from you? In the end, you are naught to her but a prop for her ambition, an instrument for her vanity. Sally proposes to move a world, the greatest folly since Icarus or Archimedes. You figure in that plan no more than a mole might in the creation of a garden."

James punched the picture, breaking the frame and sending the print fluttering to the floor.

The Owl laughed, "You strike at me who is only the messenger, not the author of this deceit."

"Leave me, leave me," said James. "Sally loves me. She wants to marry me. She could never . . . abbreviate our child's life!"

"Wake up now, blind foolish James! Can you not see the truth of it? Sally is the daughter of a merchant-princeling, a family of wealth and honour and respect in the great City of London, known from Koenigsberg to Serampore. She—they—will never allow one such as you—an upstart magwitch, a chowser, a tattered slick-slack boy—to join them, except in the role of lackey, of servant. Marry you? You, a transported felon? Let you become part of the family? The giants will walk off the Guildhall clock first!"

James hurled a book at the blank spot on the wall, uncertain where to aim his anger.

"Goodbye for now, James. I came only to enlighten. I bear you no chafed feelings for your understandable outburst of emotion, which is emotion well sourced and in need of proper direction."

"For God's sake, leave now!"

"I will," said the Owl. "But I will always return if you call. As your immediate wrath hardens into obduracy, think on my offer of goodwill and avail yourself of it."

The Owl left.

James sat with his head in his hands, elbows on the writing table. He cried silently, while his mind leaped like a monkey through the forests of his grief.

Billy Sea-Hen had begun to visit the Cook some time earlier, initially seeking remedies for his incessant colds and those afflicting Tat'head and the other Minders. He approached her cautiously, not liking what he saw as Cook's imperiousness and her overly structured approach to life. The Cook was equally wary at first, liking neither what little she knew of his past nor what she deemed his insouciant fanaticism. As the visits became more regular, and each visit turned more conversational than strictly transactional, Billy and the Cook began to find common ground.

One drizzly Saturday afternoon late in October, the Cook glanced at the clock on the kitchen wall and found herself wondering if Billy might be stopping in as he usually did around then. Almost as if she had summoned him, Billy Sea-Hen knocked on the kitchen door. Cook moved to the door more quickly than she herself realized, and let Billy in. At a bench in a corner, her niece the maid nudged Mr. Fletcher, both of whom grinned. Cook shot a blasting look at her niece, and at Mr. Fletcher for good measure, prompting more grins.

Cook put the kettle on and soon the kitchen buzzed with the warm conversation of friendly spirits who are glad in one another's company, especially while cold raindrops fell on the window panes outside. Talk turned to more serious topics.

"Just you look at all these bills," said the Cook. "Mr. Seddon the cabinetmaker in Aldergate Street demands back the chairs he sent, owing to non-payment. Here's one from the druggist on Birchin Lane, and one from the garden in Chelsea for greengage cuttings and special food for Mr. McDoon's smilax bushes (not that it has helped them much, poor things), besides more seeds for that little blue flower I never gave much thought to before, the bixwort."

"Lean times," said Billy, wanting to be supportive.

"Lean as a lark's leg," said Cook. "Mr. Sanford commands economy and thrift, and Mr. McDoon agrees in the partners' room, but then—bless him, he can't help himself—he comes 'round after to me, and begs for his Bateman's Pectoral Drops, so what am I to do?"

"He's an original is Mr. McDoon, meaning no disrespect," said Mr. Fletcher. "An 'Old Original, like the Chelsea Bun House.'"

All four nodded and smiled, thinking of the century-old establishment that served royalty and commoners alike with buns no imitator could rival.

"We are jammed into a tight little dog-hole, and no mistake," said Cook, her smile fading. "Soon we will have to buy all our clothes at second-hand on Monmouth Street."

"There's many as are glad to have even that," said Billy quietly.

"True enough, and I shall not complain," said the Cook. "Still, we aren't hardly affording meat any longer—I get us mostly herring from the middle of the barrel, and soon it will be dried habardines to go with our potatoes."

Mr. Fletcher made a face at that.

"Well now," retorted Cook. "As Billy says, that still fills the belly and there's many as can't say even that in these hard times. Hallo you two, you are still young and should not be sitting here mardlin' on such gloomy things with older folks. Be quick as Tibbert's Cat, be off with you."

She pulled a little purse from her apron and pressed some small coins into her niece's hand.

"Really, why not go to *The Dun Cow*, across from Saint John Sacharies?" said Cook. "You know you like their ale and their little mincemeat pie is not so very costly. 'Tis a Satur-eve after all."

"They make a handsome pair," said Billy, after the maid and Mr. Fletcher had departed.

The Cook agreed. She and Billy talked a while about the other two and their prospects for an enduring marriage, which topic gradually, almost imperceptibly, slid into a conversation about themselves.

"Billy," said the Cook. "You have been to the back of the North Wind—back behind the shoulder-blades of God for all I know—but I hear so clearly the voice of a Londoner, yet you never tell us of your upbringing. What do you call home?"

Billy sipped his tea before answering.

"Well," he said. "It is a funny thing you asking me that just now, on account of I have thinking on that very question myself of late. Since I have—as you rightly put it, Mistress Cook—shipped out to some very distant parts."

Cook refilled his cup of tea, and pushed a plate of scones across the bench to him. ("Plain, no currants in 'em, and a day old, but they will have to do," she thought.) Billy took a bite with gratitude.

"I am born a true son of Queenhithe," he started, naming the ward on the Thames that ran uphill almost to St. Paul's Cathedral, slightly upstream from the London Bridge and directly across the river from Southwark. "In the parish of Saint Mary Somerset . . ."

"Hold a moment," exclaimed Cook. "Not the Saint Mary where the communion plate was stolen and never returned, maybe ten year ago?"

"In aught-five, yes, that's right," said Billy.

"Such a wicked deed!"

"Yes," said Billy hastily. "Weren't me, of course, though I own that I might know the chowsers what did it. As you say, hard times then as now, though I agree that is no excuse to make off with churchly silver."

They both crossed themselves.

"I was raised by my blessed mam alone in a chare that has no map-name but those what lived there called it Finger Alley, off Broken Wharf. Had the run of the hithe itself—where the corn hoys land from Kent and Suffolk—and was a duke in the tribe that wandered High Timber Street, Bread Street Hill, Three Cranes in the Vintry."

Billy sighed, glanced at the Cook's face.

"That's a foreign country to me, your Queenhithe," teased the Cook. Queenhithe was less than half a mile from Mincing Lane.

"Oh come," said Billy, rising to the bait. "Surely even you who live near the Tower have heard about the wonders of Queenhithe, as royal as the name makes it! Why, the Black Lion Inn on Saint Thomas Street is as famous for its veal pies as the Chelsea Bun House is for its buns. I had one once, a Black Lion veal pie, have never tasted its like since."

The Cook admitted that she might just have heard of the Black Lion Inn, and then confessed further that she had even been within the confines of the marvellous ward of Queenhithe. One of her Norfolk connections, another barney-bishybee, was in service to a mercer there. Once the Cook had even spent a Saturday afternoon being shown by her friend the glories of the

Painters & Stainers guildhall on Little Trinity Lane, and looking upon Mr. Thornhill's altar-piece mural at Saint Michael's Queenhithe.

"Saint Michael's with the golden ship on its steeple-vane!" said Billy. "That is forever the sign of home, if no other sign exists for me!"

"Well, you have city cunning, that's for sure," said the Cook, paring a dowl of cheese for Billy. "But you seem also to have a goodish share of what I will call country wisdom, and how you come by that, I do not know."

"Ah," said Billy, thoughtfully eating the piece of cheese. "We were country folk on my mother's side. My grandfather was Royal Under-swanherd, at His Majesty's swannery near Staine's Bridge, on the Thames not far from their castle at Windsor. Heard much about that from my mother, though she was herself only a child then, this being I reckon about the time our George came to the throne. A game of swans, and swan-upping, and what have you, and all the joys of a calm river-life, that's what she told me."

"What happened?" said Cook.

"Someone poached three of the royal swans," said Billy. "My grandfather got the blame and was turned out. Like most unfortunates in such circumstances, he came into London, bringing the family. Hard times then, hard times now. He failed at most things here in the city—he died before I could know him, likewise my grandmother. My mother was their only surviving child. Worked hard all her life, some needle-trade though Queenhithe's not really the place for that, then years as a dog's-body in a throwster's shop. A hard life. No man around once my father left for sea and never came back. He served on an East Indiaman, I am told, but I barely remember him."

Billy left a quarter of hour later. As Cook finished preparing the evening meal, she thought about what she had learned. Hearing about Billy's Queenhithe childhood helped anchor him in known territory. His roots in the upper Thames Valley reminded her—with a sad jolt—of Mr. Harris. She disliked the fervour with which Billy talked about "gehennical fire" and "the immarcessible crown of glory," and she remained disturbed at his embrace of the Cretched Man.

"Needs much more explaining and by means unknown to me," she muttered, putting an extra sprig of dill on a very attenuated filet of plaice, in hopes of diverting Mr. McDoon's attention from the scantiness of his supper. "Cavorting with an eel-rawney, a conjure-man—who has in the past attacked this very house. I do not see how Billy can defend that connection!"

She puzzled over this as she dished the boiled potatoes, trying to reconcile what she knew about the McDoon struggle against the Cretched Man with the obvious depths of Billy's devotion to Tom.

"Plain as the dragon on the steeple of Saint Mary-le-Bow, he loves that boy like his own son or nephew," she thought. "He fought for Tom, saved his life sounds like, in the foreign places—against enemies worse than the Cretched Man or even Tipu Sultan. So maybe a crooked stick can hit a straight lick."

Holding a tray with dinner for the two partners, Cook surveyed the kitchen.

"World is topsy-tosticated," she said. "Enemies are friends, and friends may be enemies (what's Mr. Sedgewick playin' at?), and maybe the giants *will* walk down off the clock after all."

Later, alone as she scrubbed dishes, Cook came bit by bit to understand that the intelligence about Billy no longer alarmed or alienated her. The thought that he was sprung from similar origins persuaded her, against her judgment.

"He calls himself an old dumbledore," she said suddenly and out loud, pausing at her task. "And I am a barny-bishybee, which is the same thing said a different way. Hmmmm."

She could hear Mr. Fletcher escorting her niece home, the two younger members of the household kissing goodnight just outside the kitchen door. The Cook blushed to imagine it.

"Fallabarty," she thought, giving the pot she was scrubbing an extra vigourous swipe. "Me at my age and all!"

Interlude: Cartulae

[From <u>The Proceedings of the Asiatick Society</u>, Calcutta, vol. XXII, 1817]

We have recently discovered in our collection a noteworthy painting, by the renowned miniaturist Ustad Mansur, court artist to the Mughal Emperor Jahangir a full two centuries gone; the painting depicts a species of pheasant not previously described for India (viz. Mr. Latham's *General Synopsis of Birds*, and Mr. Pennant's more recent *View of Hindoostan*). Mansur being famous for his extreme fidelity to Nature and graceful delineations of particulars, we are in no doubt that—far from being a product of his imagination—the pheasant he drew from a live, or (at most) preserved specimen. Beyond dispute, the bird portrayed is an Indigo Pheasant, hitherto known from Chinese examples only. Anyone among our correspondents who can shed light on the provenance of Mansur's putative specimen is asked to write to the Society, care of Mr. Nathaniel Wallich, Curator and Superintendent of its Oriental Museum.

DANIEL A. RABUZZI

[From Anders Erikson Sparrman, <u>Notes on a Voyage to China Undertaken in the Years 1765-1767</u> (published in Stockholm, 1771; translated 1785 by Elizabeth Maria Grantham)]

The Author of Nature has endowed even the most reclusive and cautious of birds, namely the partridges and pheasants, with plumage brought down from heaven, brilliantly reflecting the sun-beam in one case and imitating the rubicond lustre of dawn in another.

... While in China I had described to me, on credible authority, a type of pheasant hitherto unknown to Europeans, a bird that despite my many and strenuous efforts I could not observe *in vivo* with my own eyes nor provide ocular evidence of any sort, not even to the extent of procuring a specimen. The Chinese call it, as near as I can tell, the Celestial-Pheasant, both because of its bold blue colouration and because it is of a mild and beneficial disposition when left undisturbed but fierce when provoked, willing to defend itself mightily against those so arrogant or malicious or unsagacious as to attack it.

My hosts were at pains to indicate and emphasize the majority colour of the Celestial-Pheasant (there being also in its plumage many counter-hatchings of ivory and eggshell-white), stressing its importance as a matter of some urgency within their systems of philosophy and cosmology. Apparently our languages do not possess an identical equivalency for this colour, but when shown a sample of what this colour might be—in the form of inks stroked with the most conscientious of brushes—I would assay to describe it as a blue strongly undertinted with purple, and overwashed with the palest grey, approximating most closely that hue we know as 'indigo.'

THE INDIGO PHEASANT *Volume Two of Longing for Yount*

Altogether the effect of this colour was simultaneously entrancing and elusive, being that of white and black balancing in perfect harmony, projecting a species of numinous impulsion, which is to say creating a mutability of shadow and light of the sort that I am told the Italian painters called 'cangiante' and that I would otherwise say supports the evidence of spectral images on the human retina described by Dr. Huyghens and confirmed by Dr. Boerhaave in their recent works.

. . . Allow me here to elaborate some of the many legends associated with this indigo pheasant, as told to me by my Chinese hosts, starting with the one about how the bird spits fire when goaded into defense. . . .

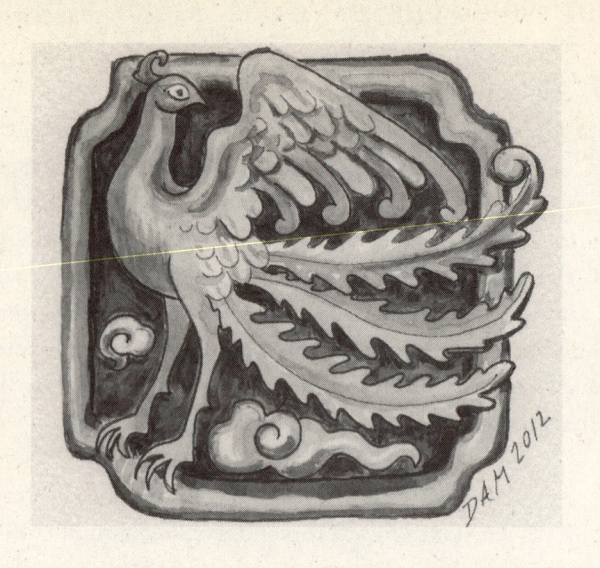

Chapter 7: Battles Big and Small, or, Malicious Affections Roused

"It flies with an easy untroubled flight,
This fearless pheasant . . .
With its martial crest and
Its plumage bright . . ."

—**Anonymous**,
"The Pheasant," in the *Shih Ching*
(*Classic of Poetry*, or, *The Odes*),
c. 800 before the Common Era

"The tall grasses on the river-bank rustle to the breeze,
The tall mast of the boat sways,
Alone in the starlight (that washes the wide flat fields),
Now the water shines too with moonlight . . .
Floating, skimming to the here and there,
I am a bird aloft between earth and deep heaven."

—**Tu Fu**,
"Nocturnal Reflections While Travelling" (c. 765 C.E.)

THE INDIGO PHEASANT *Volume Two of Longing for Yount*

"Termites, fleshy ghosts," thought Mei-Hua, as she, her brother Shaozu, and their guardian, Tang Guozhi, were being given a tour of yet another pagoda in London (the "Great Pagoda" in Kew Gardens; they had already been taken to see the "Pagoda Gardens" in Blackheath). "Building hollow imitations to match their white words."

The three Chinese had been in London for months. They were increasingly frustrated and despondent. No one knew quite what to do with them. As accredited emissaries from the Jiaquing Emperor, they were unique and honoured guests—and were subjected to every kind of official visit, tour, and meeting. The Prince-Regent received them; they were trooped through Westminster Abbey and the Tower. They sat for hours with the faculty at the East India Company's college for its civil servants, newly established at Haileybury just north of London (and based on what little the English knew about the two thousand-year tradition of civil service in China), helping the EIC compile the first-ever Chinese-English dictionary. Society matrons tumbled over themselves to host the strangers at fetes, routs and of course elaborate tea parties—the Chinese were the season's sensation. Lady this and Banneresse that vied with one another to escort the Chinese to the British Museum at Montagu House, and to the Egyptian Hall in Piccadilly. Mei-Hua had been brought to hear the orphans sing at The Foundling Hospital on Great Ormond Street, had been shuttled to see Hogarth's "Pool of Bethesda" at Saint Bartholomew's Hospital, had accompanied a viscountess on a walk of the wards at the new Universal Dispensary for Sick and Indigent Children near Saint Andrew's Hill. And so on, for months.

Yet one old man and his two teenaged charges hardly counted as a full-scale embassy. Mei-Hua knew that—behind their polite facades—the English were angry at what they perceived to be a slight by the Jiaquing Emperor. She knew the English did not trust her and her brother, let alone Tang Guozhi. She reciprocated the mistrust. Above all, she feared the intentions she felt everywhere signalled though by no one stated. The subcutaneous sensations of threat and suspicion neared the surface most forcefully in their interviews with officers at the Admiralty and at the East India Company, who claimed official responsibility for their well-being.

"This one is a blade of sternest steel," thought Mei-Hua, watching Sir John Barrow spar verbally with Tang Guozhi, a duel between two wily, martial veterans (Tang Guozhi was the scion of a mighty Manchu clan, a captain in the Bordered Red Banner, reporting directly to the Grand Council; he had served with the general A-Kuei, victorious in The Ten Great Campaigns in the last century). They had met long ago, in Peking when Lord MacCartney represented King George III at the court of the previous emperor, the first embassy ever from Great Britain to the Middle Kingdom. She admitted that Sir John paid them the compliment of very intelligent questions. His appetite for detail was well informed and seemingly endless.

"So your two wards come from Tsinan Fu in Shantung Province?" said Sir John, pointing at Mei-Hua and Shaozu, who sat as far from the English as they could. Mei-Hua thought happily of her home city, the capital of the province, with its Five Dragon Pool and other natural springs, its plum rains in spring and summer, its markets filled with pears from Laiyang, apples from Yantai, eggplant and chickens from Dezhow. She missed steamed buns. The homesickness flooded in even as she listened to the terrible old men, filled her to bursting, the *suhsiang* that tried to drown her. She made of her face a plaster mold and refused the tears their outlet, while her heart screamed within her. Steamed buns! Sweet winter cabbage braised in vinegar! Hot peanut soup on the coldest days!

Tall, inscrutable men with close-cropped heads (government functionaries without queues running gracefully down their backs—Mei-Hua was astonished) hovered around Sir John, scribbling in notebooks, as he drilled on. He wanted to know everything about their journey: how Tang Guozhi had travelled down the Grand Canal from Peking to the lake by Suquian, where Mei-Hua and Shaozu met him after their own journey from Tsinan; how the three had continued together on the canal, through Pengcheng, Yangchow (Sir John probed specifically about the salt magazines of this city), Soochow, and finally to the port of Hangchow (Sir John wanted to know about the role of the many Muslim traders in this city); how, emboldened by the recent capture of a famous pirate, they had taken the quicker coastal route rather than the traditionally safer inland roads, sailing from Hangchow to Canton (Sir John pressed for details about Canton's Thirteen Factories, the holdings of silver in the banks there, the volume of the opium trade). He seemed to know something of their trip from Canton to Cape Town, and was remarkably well apprised about their stay at the Cape and the final leg of their voyage from there to London.

Mei-Hua was half-amused, half-terrified as Sir John tried to badger Tang Guozhi, who blandly deflected the queries or calmly fabricated responses. She knew Tang Guozhi was furious, she could hear it in his voice even as he spoke in his polished English, and she was equally sure that Sir John knew this too, but neither man (nor anyone else in the room) acknowledged the ire or any other element of discord. Again, Mei-Hua noted the back-handed compliment that Sir John was paying to his guests (prisoners? hostages?) by allowing a smooth surface of tranquil harmony to prevail, even as the deep currents ran to turbulence.

Afterwards, Tang Guozhi was less restrained.

"Barbarians!" he said. "See, children, how they taunt us? While they pump us for information on our commerce and our industry, they share as little as possible with us about their own! They ask me to reveal the size and number of our garrisons on the Grand Canal, and how many troops we have at this city and that city, without the courtesy of telling the same about their own strength. Hah! They seek to borrow a pig from a tiger!"

Mei-Hua could not disagree, but she reminded herself that her guardian was a military officer and a Manchu (not a proper Han like herself, which mattered even after one hundred-seventy five years of Qing rule); his interests were not entirely hers. Her own memories of the journey in China—which seemed part of another life—centred on the well-ordered fields of white-flowering buckwheat and the plantations of dark, shiny, green lamp-oil camellia visible from their boat on the canal, on landings heaped with freshly dug sweet potatoes (steaming slightly in the early morning sun) awaiting transport to market, on azure-winged magpies exploding with loud calls and flashing tails from thickets as the canal-boat swept in too close to their nests. She remembered the Lingering Gardens in Soochow, and Soul's Retreat and King Yue's Temple by the willow-stroked waters of Hangchow's West Lake (English pagoda copies were sad and stiff by comparison). She had thrilled to the close-knit singing and ribaldry of the imperial courier stations dotting the Grand Canal, where hierarchy was loosened and everyone participated in the telling of tales from all over China. The trip had seemed a grand adventure, like the Monkey King's voyage to the West, or Li Po farewelling his friend at Yellow-Crane Tower, the blossomy haze off the river swallowing the distant glint of a sail, until nothing was left on the clear-green horizon "but a river flowing along the ramparts of heaven."

Mei-Hua pulled back from these memories. She focused on her experiences of England, marvelling at how smoothly brazen the English were in refusing to divulge any information of real value to the Chinese delegation, how offhandedly devious their hosts were in delivering half-truths and misdirection, how subtle in the art of intimidation. All of London seemed drenched in a triumphalist vintage, its people tippling the wine of victory. Their hosts took special pains to point out Napoleon's carriage, a trophy in the Egyptian Hall, and the tiger-mouthed brass cannons once belonging to the vanquished Tipu Sultan, now occupying a prominent place in the central courtyard of East India House on Leadenhall Street. They ensured close scrutiny of the large white-marble bas-relief above the fireplace in the entry courtroom of East India House, which depicted Britannia sitting on a globe, looking eastward, one hand lolling on her shield, the other grasping a trident, while a woman representing India bows down to her (offering a chest of jewels), and women portraying China and Africa likewise offer tribute, albeit while still standing. Admiralty officials were solemnly delighted to get the Chinese front-row seats at the reenactments of Trafalgar and the Battle of the Nile, staged in the artificial pond at the Sadler's Wells Theatre. Their minders from the East India Company did the same with the revival at the just-opened Royal Coburg Theatre in Southwark of the comic opera *Ramah Droog*, with its ostensibly realistic staging of pitched battles between the army of the nefarious Indian usurper and the troops of the legitimate nawab (led by the English officers of the EIC), long lines of dancing girls, enormous painted scenes of rajahs on elephants, camel caravans and trains of buffalo. Mei-Hua, Shaozu ,and Tang Guozhi applauded (not unimpressed by the English ability to stage splendidly loud and ravishingly colourful spectacles), and never once missed the underlying point.

No one—neither the British nor the Chinese—mentioned a place called Yount. Mei-Hua guessed that Sir John, at least, knew of Yount, though her premonition had mostly to do with the way he looked at her whenever discussion at the Admiralty sessions came to the Cape and the Termuydens. Just when she thought he might be on the verge of broaching the subject, Sir John seemed to tack away, leaving Yount an unspoken cipher, a restless gap at the centre of the serpentine conversation. Tang Guozhi had forbidden Shaozu and Mei-Hua to raise the topic with the Admiralty or the EIC before they did. For their part, the Admiralty and the EIC contented themselves with making sure their guests saw several men-of-war in the Thames at a distance (but close enough to see all the guns on parade, protruding each from its port-hole)—they did not grant access to any of the shipyards, least of all to the Blackwall yard where construction of the *Indigo Pheasant* proceeded fitfully.

Mei-Hua might have borne well enough the diplomatic maneuvering and negotiation of nearly impenetrable social codes under other circumstances (she was, after all, the daughter of Tsinan Fu's deputy salt tax inspector) but the sheer alienness of London pressed down upon her. Challenged by the cloacal smells, constant cold rain and winter's short, mist-laden days, she felt they had sailed through a hole in the world and landed in the *guiyu shijie*, the domain of ghosts. Everywhere she went, legions of ghosts surrounded her, shockingly white, the colour of mourning. The ghosts stared at her, leered at her, touched her skin and especially her hair—they could not stop their desire to stroke her straight, glossy black hair. The ghosts did not have hair like hers or any Chinese. She feared they might cut it off, possess it. She thought them capable of seizing her spirit, embalming her on a tavern-sign, another trophy, like the images she saw when she passed The Saracen's Head Inn in Aldgate or The Black Boy & Camel on Leadenhall Street.

Mei-Hua knew that her brother and Tang Guozhi suffered as well; she was profoundly grateful to be together with them in facing the wrenching mysteries of life in England. In all of London were no more than perhaps two hundred Chinese—the only others were sailors barracked by the East India Company in Shadwell, besides a rumoured handful of shipjumpers thought to be living clandestinely further east in Pennyfield and Limehouse Causeway. (The EIC allowed no contact with the sailors, who in turn had no idea that their Emperor had sent an embassy to Great Britain.) Mei-Hua and her companions had expected—if not viscerally understood—that England would lack many familiar foods, soaps, and medicines, but had not grasped that the linguistic categories for many of what they considered the most essential domestic items would be incommensurate with or altogether absent from English thinking. For example, they were stymied seeking remedies for stomach distresses and blocked sinuses, for colds and headaches. London's physics and apothecaries, even those employed by the East India Company, could not understand what the Chinese meant by *longgu* (which translated to "dragon bone," serving only to further baffle the English) or *yuyuliang* or *lurong*. Even when the English could translate the elements of the words, the Chinese concepts did not fit English taxonomies. Mei-Hua's sinuses stayed blocked, Shaozu's stomach remained upset, Tang Guozhi's arthritic knee continued to plague him.

THE INDIGO PHEASANT *Volume Two of Longing for Yount*

Mei-Hua suffered uniquely. She was the only Chinese woman in all of Great Britain. While in London that winter, she had her first period. Her brother and her guardian—so valuable as allies in the daily struggle with London's unrelenting foreignness—were useless in this context. This was women's business, not a topic one discussed with men; Mei-Hua was not even sure what words one used for the occasion (let alone what words the English might use). With effort and artifice, she hid her menstruation from Shaozu and Tang Guozhi, and missed her mother and her aunts more than she could say.

The one warm, harmonious note sounding for the Chinese in London emanated from the McDoons. Mei-Hua, Shaozu, and Tang Guozhi were relieved and happy to attach themselves to the McDoons, and soon became (despite sporadic efforts by Sir John to block them) regular visitors to the house on Mincing Lane with the blue trim and the dolphin door-knocker. Here they found at least one place in London where the stove-god held sway.

"Sadness dwells here too," thought Mei-Hua. "Sadness, disappointment, envy. Under the eaves, a tang of bitterness like the taste of oleander that we import from Yunnan." She paused, thinking that Yunnan once seemed as far away to her as the Jade Emperor's mountain.

At the house on Mincing Lane, Mei-Hua found others who understood what she felt, having themselves felt it: *hsiangnien, chuanlien*, which is the home-sickness for a home one has never seen, the hopeful longing for a place that might not exist.

Sally—the sad one, a grey spirit eclipsing unto itself—nodded wearily and said, "Yes, we know that. Forlorn hoping. *Sehnsucht* the Germans (our neighbours across the narrow straits, in case you do not know of them, for they do not send many ships to China) call it."

Mei-Hua said, "'Crows call at early moon-rise by the river-bridge. I hear a far-away bell ringing, as the fishermen light the lamps on their returning boats.' That's how I feel most of the time, like Chang Chi in this poem."

"Hmmm, yes," said Sally, nodding again.

"But now that I have come so far from my own home, I am not sure I really want to keep feeling this," said Mei-Hua. "The sickness for my own home—my own home with my parents in Tsinan Fu, by the Tsi River with its cheerful kingfishers—is enough for me. The awful strangeness of your London, and of Cape Town before that, is more than I can bear."

"We know all about that too," said Sally. "Believe me, the longing tricks you, makes a beggar of all your hopes. Best never to leave. Turn back now while you still can. Don't listen to all the voices in your heart."

Maggie put her tea-cup down so hard the spoon rattled off the saucer onto the table.

"Stop it," she said, loudly enough to startle Yikes by the fire and Charicules perched on the mantlepiece by the clock. "Both of you, now."

Mei-Hua thought, "This one is an osprey-princess. She is the ghost-killer, Zhong Kui, in a woman's body. Her eyes daunt me."

Maggie said, "We are none of us come yet to the jubilee-home, so we stay true to the track until we arrive there. *Chi di*, no choice in the matter for any of us. Of course, Hope mocks us, and perhaps some more than others. As Mr. Sanford likes to say, we are all things out of place and order, and that disorder needs to be repaired. No one else can do the task to which we have all been called. But we are women: we are as strong as elephants. And even if we wanted to just hive off and turn around, stay home, or wherever you might think is safest, there is the Owl, the filthy old *akakpo*, waiting to deny us all and everything."

Mei-Hua listened intently as Maggie, and with much reluctance from Sally talked about the Owl. In response, she told Maggie and Sally about the glimpses of Strix that she had had in dreams. She talked about the demon-owl known as *chi xiao* and the malevolent god-let named the *shashen*, and about the intimations of his coming written in the ancient *Bowu zhi* (that is, the *Annals of Strange Things*), leading his armies of fox-women, crane-wives and famished ghosts.

"One world, many names," said Maggie, pouring more milk into her gunpowder tea. (Mei-Hua had learned not to remark upon the desecration of the tea; some abominations even your friends and allies must be allowed). "One song to defeat him, sung by many voices."

As if on cue, Isaak appeared in the doorway. She approached Mei-Hua slowly, on her stalking feet, inspecting the young Chinese woman.

"Oh, most honoured one!" said Mei-Hua. "I have a cat like you at home, only not so hunterly (can I say that in English?). Your coat is the emperor's colour, which is the most good luck."

Isaak relaxed, started to purr, rubbed Mei-Hua's shins. All three women laughed, even Sally (Sally most of all). Mei-Hua told them about Lu Yu, who in his celebrated *Book of Tea*, dedicated a well-known poem to the cats who protected his library, and about the famous scholar Chang Tuan who had seven beloved cats whose names were legendary throughout China.

"One was called 'White Phoenix,'" said Mei-Hua. "One was 'Pattern of Cloud,' another was 'Silk Sash With Fine Threads of Raised-Up Gold and Silver.' So, in memory of Chang Tuan's seven cats, I give this little hunter a name in Chinese which means 'Emperor's Sharp-edge Flows-like-the-Sun.'"

Mei-Hua wrote the Chinese characters for this on a piece a paper.

"Oh marvelous," said Sally. She later gave the paper to the Cook, who hung it in the kitchen next to a small devotional portait of Saint Morgaine (right by the the rack from which depended the soup and stew ladles).

"What do you think of that, Isaak?" said Sally and Maggie nearly in unison (to each other's amazement). Isaak meowed, dropped and rolled, wriggling her back on the floor, half-exposing her sweep of pale-golden belly fur, while half-extending her claws.

Sally added, "Mei-Hua, your name for Isaak is very much of a piece with the one the Yountians gave her: *tes muddry*, the 'golden claw.' Well done, I should say."

"Yount," whispered Mei-Hua. "Tell me about Yount."

Over the days and weeks that followed, Sally spoke at length about Yount, and Maggie laid out the plans for the return voyage. The three young women spent hours in the partners' room poring over charts and calculations, joined frequently by Dorentius and occasionally by Mr. Gandy. (Mr. Gandy was unsure whether all the talk of fulgination and Yount was just an exceptionally rococo game or madcap hoax, but did not care; he loved the play and elegance of it, had decided he would be unfazed if Yount turned out to be real, and regardless he would do anything for Maggie). Equation by equation, egged on by the songs of Charicules, they solved the fulginatory, chulchoisical and xanthrophicius challenges confronting them, and resolved the nautical, hydrostatic and aerodynamic design issues that otherwise threatened to hobble the *Indigo Pheasant*.

After one long debate about abaxile properties and the need to allow the ship to tralineate without losing its way, Dorentius shifted his amputated leg and whistled, "Point to you, Miss Mei-Hua. Cleverly done, your differentiating the epenthetical from the cissoid curve—never mind the specific words, I will write that down for you and you can compose them in proper Chinese later. Was your thinking here that cleared our vision, or I am a pine tree."

Mei-Hua blushed. Working with Maggie, Sally and Dorentius on equations was like a dance, like the rush of wings moving in unison. She felt like the magpies must have felt when they (every magpie in the world!) made the bridge among the stars on *Qixi*, the "Night of Sevens," uniting for that one night the herdsman Niulang with Zhinu, she who spins the thread, seventh daughter of the Goddess. She told the story—a legend almost universally known the length and breadth of China—to Maggie and Sally, pointing out on a celestial atlas the positions of the stars in the story.

"Your Niulang is our Altair, which we are told means 'the eagle' in the original Arabic," said Sally, reading the notes in the atlas and momentarily forgetting to be depressed as lexicographical fervour gripped her. "Zhinu is Vega, 'the vulture landing,' not very inspiring I fear. I prefer the Chinese there. Your magpie-bridge cruxes at our Deneb . . . which name hails from 'the tail of the hen,' thus also known in Europe as Gallina, the Hen. . . ."

"Close enough to 'pheasant' for me," said Maggie.

"My friend the German astronomer has written me," said Sally, pausing as she flushed and looked away from Maggie. "He says that he believes Deneb may be a blue-white star, based on the latest observations through his new telescope. The Herschels in Slough suggest the same."

Maggie ignored the memories of Sally's correspondence with astronomers on the German Baltic (letters that Maggie could not read and was, in any event, not invited to hear in translation). Maggie also ignored the memories of talks being held at the Royal Society by the King's Astronomer Sir Friedrich Herschel and his sister Caroline (talks to which Maggie was not invited).

Instead Maggie said, "A blue-white pheasant flying across the Milky Way, buoyed by all the magpies in the world, and heralded by a piebald swan (burnt offering whom we will honour forever). The Owl has met his match!"

"Remember the *Lanner*," murmured Sally.

Charicules, as close to a magpie as never mind, raised his soft singing and slung notes around the room.

Mei-Hua said, "My brother Shaozu and I brought something all the way from Tsinan Fu, something that I must give you now. I had a dream before we left. I had a painter paint what I dreamed. I did not know why I had this dream. I did not know why I had to have the dream painted or why I must bring it to the West. I only knew these things when we came to London. Working now with you, Miss Maggie and Miss Sally, I know it is the right time to give our gift to you."

She took out from her bag a parcel wrapped in heavy cloth, about one foot square. She unwrapped it, revealing two identical porcelain tiles. Each depicted a pheasant. The background was white, the pheasant delineated in exquisitely fine and lively black strokes, and painted in a rare bluish shade that seemed to skew now greyish, now green-like under the translucent glaze as Mei-Hua moved the tiles in the sunlight.

"We call it *qingbai* porcelain in China," said Mei-Hua. "No one here or there seems able to translate *qingbai*—*qing* is part blue but not all blue, sometimes green but not fully green. *Qing* is a colour all its own, see? It is not possible to define it. Blue, green and something else. *Qing* is youth, is spring coming to us, is the colour of life. This is a bold pheasant—see how he holds his head, how his tail is like a sword?—painted in *qing* colour."

Sally and Maggie each took one of the tiles. Isaak jumped from one lap to the other, eager to get a better view.

"For the bow," said Sally.

"Yes," said Maggie. "One on each side. Eyes to guide us, a figurehead for the *Indigo Pheasant*."

"I wish I could see the *Indigo Pheasant*," said Mei-Hua.

"You shall," said Maggie. "Soon. I am working on the arrangements."

The lawyer Winstanley was central to all Maggie's arrangements. Sir John had appointed Winstanley as the daily liaison between the Admiralty and the Chinese delegation, aware of course that Winstanley was working closely with the McDoons. Moreover, Winstanley already had an indirect connection with the Chinese: one of his cousins was a partner in the Canton firm that had issued the letter of credit for Tang Guozhi and his proteges, the letter that enabled the Chinese delegation to draw down money on London banks for their local needs. (The credit was large; the English hong relied on guarantees issued to it by a leading *shanxi* remittance bank in China, which based its support on the sizeable amount of imperial silver Tang Guozhi had deposited with the *shanxi*). Winstanley, with a surgeon's dexterity and the implacability of a boxer, steered Sir John towards a more accommodating (if not truly trusting) opinion of Tang Guozhi's aims and goals. More cynically, Winstanley emphasized what a good-will gesture of this sort might buy the English in terms of negotiations with the Chinese (thinking of Lord Amherst's embassy currently in

Peking). Winstanley said a little theatre—showing off the *Indigo Pheasant*, for instance, without displaying the inner working of its steam engines or its other, more rarefied and innovative, equipment—should mollify Tang Guozhi, while denying him anything of real substance.

One day in very late January, Winstanley came to the house on Mincing Lane, to announce Sir John's (grudging) approval for a (limited) visit to the Blackwall Yard.

"But why so glum then?" said Winstanley, taken aback at the subdued reaction from Mei-Hua and Shaozu.

"No, we thank you sir," said Shaozu.

"Something else makes us sad," said Mei-Hua.

"What is it, my friends?"

"The Spring Festival, the *chun jie*, begins very soon home in China," said Mei-Hua. "The New Year on *zheng yue*."

"The biggest, most important time of the year, but here no one knows anything about it, and even your calendars are different," said Shaozu.

England's foreignness was nowhere heavier, more opaque, more knotted than in the reckoning of time and the seasons. The Chinese felt wholly out of place in this regard, unmoored from their own calendar. Bells tolled the hours, but announced feast-days that held no significance whatsoever for them. The seasons differed. New Year's Day had already come as far as the English were concerned, and winter would not end in the English mind for another six weeks. Mei-Hua, Shaozu, and Tang Guozhi had continued to maintain the Chinese calendar privately, marking the passage of each day in a special diary that Tang Guozhi kept, so that they would not forget the proper order of the months and the timing of the festivals they cherished. From the Cape forward, they had laboured over this, reminding one another every day what day and month it was, keeping China in their minds even as their bodies moved through an entirely different world. Mei-Hua sometimes thought she was a shadow sent out from China, that her real self remained at home, cupped and floating within the rhythm she had known all her life.

Winstanley had some inkling of what Mei-Hua, Shaozu and Tang Guozhi must feel. His cousin had written him from Canton about the strain of living in a country where the calendar itself differed. Yet at least his cousin could ignore the strain, surrounded as he was by countrymen and other Westerners in their rigorously separated enclave. Apparently the English carried on their traditions blithely under the Cantonese sun, celebrating New Year's on January 1st, hunting the wren on St. Stephen's Day, carrying the rattle on St. Adelsina's Day, and so forth, quite indifferent to the flow of time outside the walls of the Thirteen Factories. Mei-Hua, Shaozu and Tang Guozhi had no such luxury.

Winstanley went directly to the Admiralty and persuaded Sir John to

". . . pay for a feast, in fact an entire series of feasts, for the Chinese!"

Winstanley said, "Yes, Sir John. You will recoup your investment many times over, I am sure of it. Think about the feelings of warm gratitude you will generate in their hearts, the seeds of benevolence you will plant in their breasts, whose fruits you may harvest when His Majesty's government has need."

"Yes, yes, you with your taffeta phrases. You make very free with the government's money. Clever little quab. Treasury will turn itself in knots over this, will howl for my head when it is known that His Majesty's government is laying out a hundred pounds to indulge in oriental festivities, subsidizing their food and drink. The *Chinese* are the ones with all the silver, not us—there will probably be an inquiry in parliament about all this. Oh no, young Winstanley, I want you right by my side when the bill falls due and Treasury sends its most humourless accountants after me."

"As it is said, Sir John, the daw knows naught of the lyre," said Winstanley.

"All the more reason to have you standing beside me, to face the minions when they come shaking their ledgers and quills. Let us see how unblinking your guile is then, my boy."

So, armed with a hundred-pound draft issued by the East India Company as instructed by the Admiralty, Winstanley set out organizing a Chinese Spring Festival at the house in Mincing Lane. Mei-Hua and Shaozu could not believe their good fortune, throwing themselves into the planning. Tang Guozhi understood what prompted the sudden outpouring but was nevertheless swept up in the congenial mood, his own yearnings for home outdistancing his more clear-headed political deductions. Barnabas was delighted, immersing himself in the details of preparation ("Figs and fiddles! Parties, with red lanterns! And every kind of dumpling!"). Sanford gave his support, once satisfied that the outlay would not impinge upon the straitened McDoon finances. Sally urged herself to better spirits, but thinking how much Tom, Afsana and Nexius Dexius would have enjoyed the gatherings clouded her mood, which led her to dwell on the absence of Frau Reimer and of Mr. Harris . . . and on the loss of Salmius Nalmius and the doughty Noreous Minicate. Then she realized that she could invite neither Reglum nor James, much less the Sedgewicks, and began to bear something of a grudge against the entire proceeding, no matter that she had grown fond of the inquisitive and gifted young Mei-Hua.

Cook was anxious, uncertain about the recipes let alone their execution.

"We do not have such things in all of England, no more than a sheep has wings," said Cook, looking at the list of ingredients (many vaguely worded or in need of far more precise translation) that Mei-Hua had excitedly given her. "Whatever shall we do?"

The Cook, her niece, and Mei-Hua sorted through the great fruit and vegetable market at Spitalfields, and the specialty food shops in Soho and around Covent Garden, to uncover rough equivalents for at least some of the many items a proper Chinese feast required. Winstanley had East India Company officers supply seldom-seen spices from their personal stores. He also procured from the EIC's warehouses the very best, hill-grown, carefully cured and tatched teas: *campoi congou* and the single-culled *lap tay souchong*, fragrant *tien hung hyson* and *khee kee hyson*, the *chulan hyson* so rarely found in Great Britain or anywhere in Europe. Noodles—a necessity for the Spring Festival—were particularly problematic. After much persuasion, Mei-Hua accepted as a plausible substitute the vermicelli used by the Italians who ran the restaurant at La Sablonière in Leicester Square. Likewise, they were forced to borrow bowls and pans for deep-frying from the Hindostanee Coffee House in Portman Square.

So it came to pass that two dozen people sat down together, packed very cozily into the house on Mincing Lane, on Chinese New Year's Eve. Sanford and Tang Guozhi found they had much in common: an interest in strategic budget-making and in military history, a stringent code for living that still allowed for fine dining and feasts. Barnabas wanted to know from Shaozu how and where smilax was grown in China. Mr. Fletcher and Billy Sea-Hen were there (along with male and female members of the variegated Sea-Hen congregation), seated with the Cook and her niece. Dorentius and Mr. Gandy sat next to Sally and Maggie. Winstanley brought his fiancee, a Miss Bascombe from Sussex—who took an instant, and quickly reciprocated, liking to Mei-Hua. Red bunting hung from walls and adorned window-frames. Wine flowed freely. (Tang Guozhi, missing the fiery fortified wines of his homeland, after several rounds of toasts nonetheless pronounced the Burgundies quite good, agreeing with Barnabas's assertion that these were "nourishing, theological, and able to hold death at bay," and soon became just as enamoured of the Cahors as Barnabas was). Everyone praised the inventive, hardy and delicious meal, all the more so for its hybrid origins. Much gaiety ensued over multilateral mistranslations and meanings construed awry. Everyone fed Isaak scraps under the table, and to Yikes by the fireplace. Songs were sung (some accompanied by Charicules), toasts exchanged, ancestors and missing friends remembered (Barnabas broke down in tears when he led a toast for Tom and Afsana, provoking a round of explanations for the Chinese), the concept of Family held up to honour by all.

Mei-Hua felt at home for the first time since arriving in the West. The evening's conviviality appeased momentarily her direction-less yearning. She wanted Maggie to reassure her that the warmth she felt was not illusory or fleeting. She was relieved to see that Sally seemed happy, or at least a little less sad. Yet Mei-Hua too felt sadness gnawing at the edges of her new-found mirth, a snake's venom curdling the sap in the roots of a new-flowered tree.

"This good moment is marred by my knowledge that everyone here must leave all too soon for far-distant lands," Mei-Hua thought, paraphrasing a famous poem by Li Qingzhao, who had also hailed from Tsinan Fu more than seven centuries earlier. "Will the blossoming pear-tree entice us to stay, now that the raspberries have all withered?"

She remembered that Li Qingzhao, bereft of her dear husband and exiled by an invading army, had spent the last decades of her life alone and wandering. With effort, Mei-Hua pushed all melancholy thoughts from her mind and re-joined the feast.

The evening ended well past midnight. Maggie pulled a sleepy Mei-Hua aside as the Chinese made ready to return to Devereux Court. Maggie hugged her.

"Little sister," said Maggie. "Little eagle. I wish you all good fortune, and am glad you have come to us."

Mei-Hua hugged Maggie in return.

"Me too," said Mei-Hua, tears in her eyes.

"Good night then," said Maggie. "Oh, and one final thing before I forget. Your monthly visitor? You know what I mean, yes I see you do. You can always talk to me about that. The Cook and her niece are good ears as well. We will help you with the necessaries for it, 'just never you worry,' as Cook says. Good night again, little one."

Mei-Hua felt at home for the first time since coming to London.

"Would you make a slave of me again?" said Maggie to Sir John on the Tuesday morning two weeks after the feast of the Chinese New Year. Sir John had called her to this meeting, and sent a marine sergeant to Mincing Lane to force her attendance.

They sat in the small conference room (the so-called Green Baize Room) just off the Old Sales Room at East India Company House on Leadenhall Street. On the walls hung colourful prints of the EIC forts at Tellicherry, Bombay and Madras, along with portraits of Clive, Cornwallis and Sir Eyre Coote, besides a random selection of sextants and other nautical instruments. Over the mantlepiece a clock stood on very curious brackets.

Two EIC clerks sat to one side of Sir John, his personal secretary on the other.

"Do not bait me, girl. I stood with Wilberforce and am committed to abolition," said Sir John, in tones laminated with exasperation. "You know yourself to be a subject of His Majesty—no more, no less than I am—and thus no slave, but free."

Maggie crossed her arms, as she sat alone on the other side of the table, and raised one eyebrow. Sir John glared back. He dismissed the two clerks and his secretary.

"As we are alone now, I shall speak as frankly as nature and my spirit can possibly allow," he said. "You are, Miss Collins, the most vexatious, captious, and irritating person I have met in a very long time. You are also the most intriguing, unique, and arresting individual that Fortune has cast into my path. No, do not respond—I do not wish to hear your insights, insinuations, or imprecations just now. You will listen . . ."

He proceeded to tell Maggie that she must and would follow all his instructions regarding the outfitting, governance and command of the *Indigo Pheasant*—now that His Majesty's government effectively owned the ship and fully controlled its mission.

"The Crown has seen fit to preclude and preempt any further claims for extrinsic ownership over either the ship or any part of its equipment and machinery, and has vested all rights unto itself in essence, kind, and usufruct," said Sir John, in a judge's tone. "As a point of commercial and contractual law, the Crown is the majority owner. The Crown has also invoked its ancient allodial rights of purveyance, requisition for the benefit of the commonwealth, and enprisement. One consequence of these actions is that the Lord-Chancellor has refused the petitions for patent put forth by Sarah McLeish. Of course we are not surprised to learn that the lawyer Sedgewick—admittedly once an agent of ours, now becoming a minor irritant—has filed a suit of protest and counter-claim at Chancery. We have no qualms in asserting that this suit will never succeed, going the way of a *Jarndyce* case at best."

Maggie shrugged slightly and blinked. Not having been party to the patent application, she was little inconvenienced or perplexed. She was instead amazed at how quickly and mechanically Sir John could speak when he discussed judicial matters. She wondered if the Law itself had descended from whatever high throne it sat upon and had at that moment made of Sir John an automaton for its pronouncements.

Maggie was relieved when Sir John's voice resumed its more human timbre—but she became alarmed at the content of his speech as it became clear that his next declarations concerned her directly. His voice rose and his eyes shone as he described the power of the steam engine and the sleekness of the hull.

"Forgive me," said Maggie (having to remind herself to add "Sir John"). "I embrace the mission the vessel represents but I cannot share your unbridled enthusiasm for the instrument itself. Ships may be your pride and the King's glory, but they have a rather different meaning for my people. Seeing them arrive off the coast at Whydah or Elmina or the French Goree, well sir, they arouse very different emotions there than the ones you express here."

Sir John saw her for the first time.

"Your candour deserves mine, sir," Maggie continued. "At times I fail to subscribe to the particulars of the mission I myself have helped to instigate and that I will lead. Meaning only that I am pledged to sail thousands of miles—clear into another world (yes, Sir John, let us speak plainly)—to cure an ill that rages still unchecked in this, our own world. Why should I do this, when the evil is unabated in the very land of my birth?"

Sir John had no answer for Maggie.

"Would that His Majesty sent a fleet of *Indigo Pheasants* to Jamaica or to South Carolina," said Maggie.

The clock on its bizarre brackets ticked and tocked in the ensuing silence.

"I cannot disagree with you, Miss Collins," said Sir John at last. "Despite what you may think, and all appearances notwithstanding, my own power in this matter has its limits. I can share your wishes, but lack the influence to effect them. Perhaps the *Indigo Pheasant*'s immediate objective is but the first sally in this much wider struggle. There are deep and abiding interests working against the *Pheasant*, as well you know."

They talked for another hour. They shared what they knew about Yount and the Owl; Sir John stressed that knowledge of these matters was a Secret of State, and commanded her to maintaining the secrecy. Maggie, while understanding the need for the utmost discretion about Yount and Strix (and having neither a history of nor a propensity to casual conversation about such things), resisted most mightily the concept of being commanded to do anything. They each tried to bend the other to his or her will, neither able to secure the advantage. If the clock had been able to, it could have written an epic based on the battle between Sir John and Maggie Collins: Apollo versus Diana, hoary Jupiter trying to out-debate Minerva, the old tortoise versus the yam-queen.

"You tax me out of all countenance, Miss Collins," said Sir John. "Cannot you see that I am under the very injunction that I place upon you, that the canopy of constraint covers us both for mutual benefit?"

Eventually, the two declared a truce of sorts. Sir John tried to impress upon Maggie the importance of the United Kingdom acquiring Yount as a protectate or trusteeship, if not an outright colony, to eradicate the very evil she spoke of and to protect the Yountians from further encroachments upon their liberty. Maggie remained unconvinced, saying that she would not be party to such machinations and that her willingness to continue depended on Sir John guaranteeing Yountians their own voice in deciding their future. Sir John agreed, while hedging his agreement in a thicket of conditions and caveats.

They spoke of the strategems necessary to defeat the Owl, their common enemy. Sir John listened with ever-expanding interest to the intricacies of the mathematics involved in fulgination, requesting (he was careful not to command) a memorandum on that topic. He wanted to know whatever Maggie could tell him about Dorentius Bunce, and especially about Xie Mei-Hua. Maggie said a little about Dorentius and protected Mei-Hua from Sir John's investigation. Sir John skirted the issue of the McDoons' near-bankruptcy and told Maggie nothing about the Admiralty's dealings with James Kidlington and the lawyer Sedgewick.

Another hour passed.

"What can you tell me about the itinerant preacher who associates with the McDoons, this Billy Sea-Hen who has stirred up so much controversy?" asked Sir John.

"Not much," said Maggie, instantly wary. "And, if I could, I doubt that you would expect me to spy for you."

"No, no," said Sir John, repressing a snort of anger. "I only mean that I get the strangest reports about the Sea-Henners or whatever this canaille calls itself. Tied up with the Yount business, I am sure of it."

"This much I will say," replied Maggie. "Billy Sea-Hen is as staunch a foe of the Owl and the Others as any man alive. You can have no concern in that quarter."

"Perhaps," said Sir John. "But he is affiliated in our files with a most peculiar person who once resided in London, now seemingly vanished. A sort of mountebank they called The Cretched Man. Who in turn had some sort of ties to the Owl itself, though our records are scanty on these points."

Another half-hour passed. Sir John's secretary knocked on the door and, in response to a barked "enter," timidly said that they were already late for another meeting at the Admiralty.

"Before you go, Sir John, I must ask you: are you a musical man?" said Maggie.

Sir John said, "Beruthiel's cats, that is the most eccentric question you have asked in a conversation filled with eccentric themes. Not that it can have much bearing on anything we have discussed but, yes, as it happens, I have some modest talent in the musical way. A little scraping on the viola da gamba: Telemann, Lully, though the youngsters find them old-fashioned and silly these days. Why, I even played once with Lucky Jack and Stephen Maturin, in Portsmouth."

Sir John actually looked wistful.

"Ah, so you know about the conventions of tuning," said Maggie, preempting any possibility of further reminiscence, and honing down to her point.

Sir John murmured a nonplussed "yes."

"Tuning, or rather deliberate cross-tuning, is the route to success for the *Indigo Pheasant*," said Maggie. "The mathematics is clear on this, beyond all doubt. Translated into musical terms, we must alter the pitch on the Fulginator. What the Italians call *scordatura*, tuning so that one surprises not just the listener but the notes themselves! We will augment the sixth chord, 'the Italian sixth.' Will capture the comman of Archytas, worry the line, *chi di*, will dance a passacaglia along a septimal harmony based on the prime numbers."

"I don't really see . . ." began Sir John.

Maggie waved him aside, saying, "We will sing a song not just powerful but intelligent, alive, one that bends the scales and the chroma, that is not just a key to unlock a door but a compass to find a new door—a door without keys or locks at all."

Sir John began to understand.

"An utterly new form of harmony, of intonation and temperament," said Maggie, transported by her own vision. "The Great Song, the New Song: . . . that is the purpose of the

THE INDIGO PHEASANT *Volume Two of Longing for Yount*

Indigo Pheasant and our mission, Sir John, not the politics of which you speak, not the policies you would prefer."

As he sat in his carriage on the Strand heading back to the Admiralty, Sir John thought, "She makes me uneasy, this woman. Black woman. Unheard of! And yet, and yet: her mind is a radiant wonder that I do not think anyone can contain. She is the baby griffin singing within its ivory shell—the notes have breached the egg, the cracks are become fissures."

He mulled Maggie's words, her entire disposition, her character. It disturbed him to think that Maggie had done the same about his words and presumably his own character.

"Unstoppably presumptuous. She will sing forth a new world," he thought, as the Admiralty Building hove into view. "On her own terms. Impossible, but she will—I suspect that she will. A sublime horror."

He stepped into his office, shut the door, and looked at the map of the world on the wall.

"Be that as it may," he thought, with finality. "The Empire must have Yount, one way or the other. Miss Collins can help us there, whether she will or no."

Propelled by anger at the way Sir John had treated her, but exhilarated by the knowledge that she alone could ensure the success of the *Indigo Pheasant*'s voyage, Maggie strode that night out onto the xanthrophicius roads.

Some time later, she fell through the eyepiece of the ansible-telescope in a funny little house in a place called Sanctuary. She lay stunned and exhausted on the floor.

The Cretched Man stooped over Maggie, cradled her carefully in his cold arms.

"At last," he said. "I thought you might never come."

When Maggie woke up, she talked for hours with Jambres. She met Tom and Afsana, sang a little song with Malchen. She spoke with Nexius Dexius and Queen Zinnamoussea.

"We are almost ready to sail," she told them. "A Fulginator to lever a world, on a ship that can sail unmolested through the worst storms. Or so I believe."

She felt drained.

"The cost of coming here was very high," Maggie said. "The Owl has gated this place against outsiders, the road was stark and ragged, *ebe Uzuzu nete egwu*, 'where dust dances to the drums.'"

Afsana hugged Maggie, and said, "God be with you, sister."

Maggie slipped back out through the ansible-telescope and hurtled towards Earth.

As she tumbled and swam through the Interrugal Lands, she thought, "So that is Jambres, the Cretched Man."

She wondered that, by the time she left, his alabaster skin had become faintly translucent. Visible below the surface, hidden as if by glacial ice, brushed briefly free of snow, was pale brown.

James Kidlington—dressed in a crisp, grey herringbone suit, with a sulfur-yellow foulard (the latest fashion)—sat in Hatchards' bookshop, drinking tea and reading a copy of D'Israeli's *Curiosities of Literature* (the third volume, published two years prior) while he awaited the arrival of his lover. He might appear to all the world like a man engrossed only in his own leisure, concerned with nothing more than the savouring of his tea, the enjoyment of D'Israeli's witty disquisition, and the anticipation of sweet, idle conversation with his mistress.

Nothing could be more distant from his reality. His internal conversation ran in totally different avenues from his outward projection.

"Sally, Sally, . . . you felt yourself barbarously used when I confronted you about your wicked deed . . . but *you* it was who insulted *my* heart and savaged *my* pride! . . . cruel and monstrous, you called me, but what course did your actions leave me other than to sever our relationship completely, supremely and immediately? . . . You would have perjured yourself, told me a story about miscarriage or never told me at all that you carried my child. . . . Disgusting to know that the Owl—*the Owl*!—it was who bequeathed this confidence upon me, and not you, whom I love— . . . whom I loved— . . . and who I thought loved me."

An especially perspicacious observer might have noticed that Kidlington's hand shook just a little, and that he had been reading the same page for almost half an hour.

"You gave me no choice, *belle dame sans pitié*! You stung and goaded me to this pass. Do you think me unanguished, hurtless in my sleep? (Sleep, hah, what is that?) No, your betrayal was beautifully sized to wound me to the blade-bone. You wailed at me, eyes like liquid rubies with all your tears, but I guess your recovery is speedy and complete: your divinity and majesty always comes reinstated, fair gorgon, mistress of your grand house. In any case, I do not see you subjecting yourself to the obloquy you deserve, or issuing any form of apology, private or otherwise."

A young woman entered the room. James looked up from his book, but it was not she for whom he waited.

"The pain is all the greater for the nectareous times we had before. Such unspeakable pleasure. Did you feel that too, Sally—or was it even then a play-acting, a sham, merely a way to injure your family? Was I but a means to those cursed patents?"

The server offered Kidlington more tea.

"Oh, Sally, how it grieves me to consider you a mere swindler, a common thimble-rigger. Can you truly reproach me for this conception? Rest at ease then to know that I will study to preserve our time together as a happy time—even at the risk of rendering thus more galling the fetters I cannot sunder."

James let his tea get cold.

"Bloody patents, . . . bloody ship: . . . I hope it sinks. No, no, James, you don't mean that—the ship is nearly all the hope you have left. Bloody Crown thinks it can just steal a man's property, does it? Not so quick, you chowsers. I know what the Crown's ownership means, felt it on my backside in Australia. Poor Sedgewick! Quite beside himself, poor chap. I told him it was just a bigger beast devouring a smaller beast, taking our skin with a load of learned, latinate words. Good old Sedgewick then, with his back-talk of 'rights in fee simple' and *ne cede malis*,' and the law working *'per saltum.'* Fight on, courageous fool! I know they will never let us win, but—if we can scissor off a toe here, a finger there—then I say, 'why not?' They've left me with little enough, nothing really, but I still have my *cheval d'orgueil*. Hope Sedgewick can withstand the stagnant rigors of Chancery. Brittle he was when I saw him last, pale and brittle as a St. Katherine's cake. He'd broken his pounce-box, had grey cuttlefish-bone powder all over his waistcoat; he didn't even notice until his wife came in and had to clean him up. Crumpled, that's what I would call him, crumpled and all dried up."

James sipped his tea, not noticing that it had gone cold.

"Ha ha, the devils at Admiralty unhappy—*very* unhappy—with me! Good, may they choke on their own scorched tongues. No more use to them now that I am no longer with Sally. *Persona non grata* at the McDoons, so expelled like sour thokes by His Majesty's dogfish. I thought Sir John was going to throttle me himself. Have no doubt he has instructed the loyal Lieutenant Thracemorton to do just that, given even a half-possible pretext. Well, mop and mow, boys, mop and mow. Thracemorton, I know you shadow me still."

James shrugged.

"Cut me off with ruffian blasts and arrowy lightnings, very dramatic show in that hidden Whitehall office. 'Not one shilling more, by Juno!' Missed their truest calling, could have been the main attraction at the Lyceum or Sadler's Wells. So where was poor James to go then, hey? Kicked out of his fine lodgings in the City, he could only find a mean little room in Whitechapel... with that horrid monkey Smallweed for my landlord, ghastly invalid with his demanding, yellow teeth... 'so we meet again, hope you are properly grateful for my generosity here,' said Smallweed... a room whose main accoutrement is a broken clock (no doubt stolen) sitting on a mantlepiece riddled with wood-lice . . . over a fireplace that allows no fire . . ."

James etched patterns with the teaspoon into the fine linen tablecloth.

"Fortune has a queasy-making sense of humour, she does, and loves to bestow rough caresses on the undeserving James. But she will reward me in the end—she owes me. Sent me an angel on brasiliated wings, not five days after the rupture with Sally. A fine woman, a merchant's widow, rich, seemed to know precisely where to find me and exactly how to ease my suffering. Let me borrow money right off, enough to re-pay Smallweed for his advance on the rent, though not quite so much as to allow me to move. Says she will arrange for me to move to rooms on twice-gilded Audley Street, near Grosvenor Square, to be near her, if I can just grant her a boon or two. 'Of course,' says the ever-helpful James."

James fidgeted with his foulard, caught himself.

"She's not ashamed to be seen with me. Here, at Hatchards. At the cocoa rooms in Piccadilly, on the Great Piazza in Covent Garden. Her kindness is a minister to her depth of feeling, her winning sedulities coax from me a passion I scarce can gainsay. Bought me this suit, didn't she? (No, James, she lets you borrow it, but being a dress lodger is better than having no suit at all, and you have worn far worse, haven't you?). She smells like jasmine and cassia, holds me in a gentle glamour, washing away all my sins and errors."

James pushed the book aside, checking the clock.

"She is on my side. 'We've been wronged by the same people, you and I,' she says. 'Let us help each other regain what is rightfully ours?' She's Aristotle and Tully all rolled into one with that logic, impeccable and irrestible. Just an errand or two, says she, and our future together is assured. Ah . . ."

A woman entered the room, stopped just beyond the doorway so that all could admire her and bestowed upon James a smile that was the envy of all other males in the room. She was magnificent, turned out in a crimson-collared, dark-green dress of immaculate tailoring, with her lustrous, raven-black hair perfectly coiffed under her black-trimmed kingfisher-green bonnet. She wore a silver brooch at her neck.

James stood, held her chair, kissed her hand.

"Oh, a most glorious afternoon to my merry widow," he said. "Mrs. Goethals."

Sanford had come after supper to the kitchen (Maggie, Mei-Hua and Sally were engrossed in the partners' room) to review the household accounts with the Cook.

"Well done," he said, his finger ticking off debits and credits on sheets of grey-green, lined paper. "You've stretched a pea into a pie. Thank you."

"Made old soup bones young again, made three meals out of one small potato," said Cook. "As my mother used to say, if women ran the government, there'd be none of this national debt we read about in the papers, nor the fuss over e-cono-mizin' so as to pay back our creditors."

"I remember your mother well. Formidable woman. I dare say she might have been right."

Sanford's family and the cook's family had been connected for several generations, beginning with service in Norwich.

"Mr. Sanford, sir, before you go, I need to ask you your opinion on the status of this house, if I may. Speakin' more broadly than just about the money and the accounts."

Sanford paused and considered before responding. In the garden a chaffinch sang in the spring. The first bixwort flowers had appeared, and the vetch was blossoming as it sent out creepers up the wall.

"Of course you may," said Sanford. "In fact, I am glad you asked. I have been meaning to get your ear for some time—so many wretched, pressing things get in the way of a good meeting."

Cook nodded and made tea (a really fine *lap tay souchong*, the last of the left-overs from the Chinese Spring Festival).

"Well, I worry about Mr. Barnabas," said the Cook. "How stands it with him, in truth, beneath all of his jollity and jump-up-and-strike-the-roses?"

"I worry too, dear Cook," said Sanford, sipping his tea. "He calls forth his best Gaelic temperament, but is pretending to more levity than he feels. Tom is a constant weight upon his mind. And the daughter he never knew he had, the lovely fierce Afsana whom you have not met (but will I hope)."

A linnet joined the chaffinch singing outside. From the partners' room, Charicules answered.

"She sounds lovely, from all you and Mr. Barnabas have told me," said Cook. "Bless me, I would not have believed it except that now there is a Miss Maggie too. Not a daughter, of course, but close enough. The house of McDoon has many rooms, it seems."

"Yes, it has. Tell me: what is your impression of Miss Maggie?"

"Nothing but the best, Mr. Sanford, nothing but the best. She has the spirit of ten lions. Impatient, doesn't suffer fools gladly, but why should she? And you, sir, how does she impress you?"

"In the same way. She thinks like a razor, and acts like one too. Providence sent her to us in the barest slice of time. We have great need of her as the storm bears down upon us."

Cook jutted out her chin and said, "Storm is comin', and that's a fact, Mr. Sanford. My niece and me—Billy Sea-Hen and Mr. Fletcher—we all feel it, we do. That great galder-fenny is flyin' all around us, with his Orkney skolds and Lapland witches. We see his grizzle-merchants in the streets, and hear Rat-a-tosk the Squirrel skitterin' up on the roof-beam."

"Yes, but fear not. We are no easy prey," said Sanford. "Especially now that the massy swift choir boat is nearly complete at last. We will go on the attack soon."

"Good. I'll stick 'em with my largest knife, if I can. Time to avenge our losses: the brave Miss Reimer, our dear quiet Mr. Harris with his muddy boots. Your friends with the funny names, Mr. Salmius and Mr. Noricate."

Sanford and the cook said no more for a while.

"And Miss Sally," said the Cook. "Part of her has gone missing too. Poor little smee. I do not think she will ever be the same."

"No, nor I. But come, you and I: we are Norfolk born and bred, strong and sensible. We must continue to be a foundation for this house. Sturdy as our Norfolk clay, right? And we must be wise as Wisdom herself, who 'hath builded her house,' who 'hath hewn out her seven pillars' and 'killed her beasts.'"

"Wisdom 'mingled her wine,'" nodded Cook. "What's that other part, the bit about 'furnishing her table'? I like that."

"Yes, you would. This is my favourite part: 'She hath sent forth her maidens.'"

The Cook nodded, touched the portrait of St. Morgaine, and bade Sanford a good evening. Just before going to bed, she poured a little milk in a bowl for Isaak. Watching Isaak drink the milk (with a dainty tongue that could as easily down blood), the Cook murmured, "'She hath sent forth her maidens.'"

"The Battle of Blackwall" is typically considered—when it is considered at all by modern scholars—as at best a prelude to the infamous Peterloo Massacre that took place a month later in Manchester and that galvanized the entire nation. This tendentious judgment—that the Battle was a minor incident almost immediately overshadowed by much more important events—was cemented early and has seldom, if ever, been challenged since. For instance, Macaulay, in his *History of England*, dismissed the Battle of Blackwall as "religiously inspired thuggery, without the political import of either the Spa Fields Riots of 1816 or Wedderburn's agitations of 1818, let alone Peterloo." Lord Acton, in his *Historical Essays*, relegated Blackwall to a single footnote in his study of Chartism's precursors. To the present day, the Cambridge University Press's authoritative *Companion to Nineteenth-Century British History* contains not one reference to the Battle.

To which, the Cook would have said, "Fallabarty!"

THE INDIGO PHEASANT *Volume Two of Longing for Yount*

The Battle began innocently enough, as a summertime meeting advertised by Billy Sea-Hen to be held in the fields straddling the Blackwall Causeway and Poplar High Street, where the latter ended at Naval Row by the East India Dock, abutting the Blackwall Shipyard. The Hen's-Men organized coaches and ferries to bring the anticipated thousands from across the East End and the South Bank. Starting at the noon-time ending of working hours on that July Saturday, hundreds of coaches began their runs from Goodman's Fields in Whitechapel, St. Anne's Limehouse, Dawson's Gardens on Commercial Road and St. George's-in-the-East (familiar to all with its "pepperpot towers"), while dozens of ferries stopped at Wapping Old Stairs, Shadwell Dock Stairs, The Pageantry, Millwall Quay on their way around the Isle of Dogs to Blackwall.

So they came, in their tens of thousands—women, men, boys, girls, with dogs barking by their sides, cats carried in baskets, canaries and bright-eyed rooks in cages,—some landing at the Blackwall Stairs and pouring up the Causeway (no few stopping for refreshment at the many alehouses there), others arriving by coach and wain at the East India Dock Tavern, still others walking a mile or two from whatever court, lane, chare, yard or alley they called home in the eastern warrens of London. By late afternoon, under warm clear skies, a great sea of humanity (*Bell's Monthly* estimated sixty thousand, *The Morning Chronicle* thought as many as eighty thousand) had formed all around the Blackwall Yards: the "lambs of Limehouse and tribulations of Tower Hill," coal-heavers, brickmakers, mechanists, "Whitechapel doves and Rotherhithe wrens," sempsters half-blind from working by candlelight, washerwomen, junior officers and clerks minor on half-pay, "abandoned men and dissolute women, insolent people harboured in noisome and disorderly houses," porters, fishwives, serving maids.

So vast and cosmopolitan had London become, so powerful and transcendent the call of Billy Sea-Hen, that its centripetal impulsion drew to Blackwall that day representatives from five continents and many dozen lands. We know this in part because

William and Catherine Blake joined the throng, and William described (in a letter to Coleridge, rarely cited by scholars, perhaps because it is seen as too fantastical even for Blake) encountering "pilgrims, sages, and mystics of every stripe, disembogued upon our shores—viz., a gnossienne from the Vaucluse; sailors from Tamil-land carrying small bronze statues of their saints; marabouts from West Africa; a Mohock of the Howdenosawnee, who had shipped out from New York and elected to remain in London when his vessel sailed back; a tobacco-processionary from Bahia, with a tray of braided feitissos, as he termed them; bearded Hebraic saddiks, dressed in long, black coats despite the heat; alumbrados from Castile, bearing portraits of their beatas held high (very colourful)." Coleridge's reply, if he sent one, is lost to us—but one can imagine his chagrin at not himself being present in Blackwall that day.

Any multitude in London—especially one gathered on a Saturday afternoon and evening with fine summer weather—attracted platoons of entrepreneurial souls, selling everything from sweets to gin, votive offerings to souvenir trinkets. Political opportunists, petty demagogues, haranguests passing out broadsides and pamphlets, all these and other members of the chattering tribes swarmed to Blackwall, joined by jugglers, tarot-card readers, stilt-walkers, puppeteers, fire-eaters, and professional writers of love-letters. And, of course, thieves, pickpockets, slick-slack men, and chowsers answering every description in the complex catalogue of London's underworld.

Falling into a category all his own—or fitting simultaneously into several categories, depending on an observer's prejudices—was James Kidlington. James had joined the cavalcade at the Sun Tavern Fields, arriving at Blackwall in late afternoon. He had eaten a small mince-pie and had drunk a small pot of ale. He had laughed heartily at the antics of Punch and Judy, and listened courteously to the prelusive elements on the program. Anyone watching him—had anyone wanted to keep track of one fish in that colossal shoal—would have thought him content, possibly happy, willing to succumb to the festive embrace of the crowds.

THE INDIGO PHEASANT   *Volume Two of Longing for Yount*

By all reports, the crowds *were* in a festive mood at the start. They sang hymns, carols and ballads in various English dialects and several other tongues, chanted Matabrunian marching-anthems, roared out the latest burlettas and stage-songs by Mr. Dibdin and Mrs. West. They raised impromptu maypoles, festooned with bixwort-wreaths, strands of yellow thyme, dog-rose, vinaceous sanicle and celandine. They danced to the beat of drums and bodhrans, to the elegiac slide of the penny-whistle, drawing forth emotions broad and emotions narrow, "fat as the bullock's thigh, more slender than the quill of a crow." Kites flew. Flags and banners caught the breeze: "London Cabinet Makers Trade & Benefit Society," "Amicable Assembly of Saint Macrina's Charity School," "Sons & Daughters of the New Shiloh," and hundreds of the like.

Looming over the masses were the three masts, bare rigging, bowsprit and lone steam-funnel of the *Indigo Pheasant*, the rest of the great ship obscured behind the revetements of the shipyard— embodiment of their hopes, nave for the oratorio of lustration and deliverance, a visible reminder of their purpose for gathering.

In the slanting rays of the high summer evening, with gossamer motes gleaming in the hazy air, the circumambient smell of sweat, wood-smoke, dung, tobacco, tar, and beer lush in everyone's nostrils, after his lieutenants had laced the atmosphere with vatic pronouncements and intimations of marvels to come, Billy Sea-Hen took to the platform.

"Cousins, friends, roadsmiths, diminished franklins and fallen friars, fellow AMATEURS and SEEKERS of the FIERY HEART," he began, and the crowd surged forward, those in front repeating quickly to those behind what Billy said, so that his words coalesced in a rippling wave back through the throngs.

He preached them to the mountain-top and he preached them through the valley. He warned them of the Great Enemy, whose malice was no flaccid, carious conceit but a force ceaselessly exercised and promoted.

"He is a serpent, sleek and sinewy, swift and slithery," hissed

Billy. "A winged serpent, a many-footed serpent, whose shanks are made of stained and sharded steel."

The crowd recoiled, with an "ohhhh" sweeping from their lips.

"He breathes a resinous gall, a cloud of antimony. He opens a mouth full of teeth: angry-yellow, scorching teeth, teeth longer than your fore-arm! He rises, rises, rises on veiny wings to swallow your sweet children!" boomed Billy. "The ancient snake will have you stretched out on the scalding wike, helpless, naked to his claws! Is that what you want? Tell me, is that what you WANT?"

"NO," the crowd roared, pushing towards the stage again. "We are with YOU, Billy Sea-Hen, we are with YOU!"

The crowd preached his words back to him, half-repeated, phrases murmurating, ramifying. He spoke of the massive choir boat sitting nearly finished just there, fifty yards from the platform on the other side of the Blackwall Shipyard palisade. He reminded them of its imminent voyage, and the Great Song to be sung, into whose notes all their voices would be woven. Unasked, members of the crowd passed forward to the platform objects to be placed on the ship of hope: talismans, deodands, mementoes, placards, twists of bright, hand-woven cloth, lustral carvings and figurines; pictures and statues of a hundred saints, of holy men and women, of sacred animals; and scraps of paper covered in names, prayer and numerical symbols.

"Thank you, thank you, dear visitants," shouted Billy. "This ark will be gilt with your gifts and etrennes, a thousand splendid shillings and high-sheltering arms."

The many thousands shouted back their approbation.

"Selah!" said Billy, and the many thousands quieted. Over the tidal rush of the nearby Thames, Billy half-sang the words of the angel Uriel to Noah:

"Now hast thou Noah
Heard the whisperings of baleful Beezlebub,
Crowned in his writhen shadow,
His tongue a smoldering arrow.

THE INDIGO PHEASANT *Volume Two of Longing for Yount*

As you measure your vessel,
Span its keel and masts,
A glistering ship, many cabin'd,
You might yet construct.
So, son of Eve, Enoch's offspring,
What chuse thou?—:
Earth's blandishments, seeming safe, or
The long-road of brine, a storm-wrought way?"

The makeshift congregation on its eucharistic parade-ground responded:

"The sea, the sea, we take to the briny roads!"

Later, when those present tried to disentangle what Blake called "a delicious frenzy" and the Cook "a most perfect hattled scrimble-scramble," the McDoons agreed that this was the juncture at which the mood began to change. Adherents of the rival preacher, Mr. Peasestraw, being numerous in the acre nearest the houses on Naval Row off the Poplar High Street, and seeming to coordinate their actions, started heckling Billy. Billy's (far more numerous) supporters attempted to silence the Peasestraw faction. Scuffles broke out. As dusk seeped into darkness, and a thousand lamps and torches were lighted, and Billy's sermon reached its climax, the contest became more intense. Pitched battles with clubs and knives erupted in corners of the fields, still on the fringes of the main body of the crowd but ominous, like the forerunners of a slowly but inexorably unmoating thundercloud.

In the flickering play of torchlight and shadow, under the sway of fervid rhetoric and themselves praying for the opening of the visionary's way, crowd members began to sense the presence of the very force that Billy had warned them about. Above their heads in the molasses air, some saw in glints the slow swirling of sliverous beings, others the jagged, jinxy flight of slick, scaly cherubim.

"Goddess save us," some in the crowd cried. "Saint Macrina protect us."

Panicky sounds welled up in their throats.

Some thought they saw man-shaped figures with blurry faces on the edges of lamplight, coarse bonelets wandering in the lanes leading off the Blackwall Causeway and in the ropemaker's fields by the Shipyard.

Many in the crowd instinctively sought shelter closest to Billy and the speakers' platform, closest to the sacred ship. Billy looked out at the waves of his followers pressing ever closer against the hoardings of the dais. He smelled the tang of passion and inchoate fear. He knew the meeting was turning out of his—or anyone's—control. He could no longer be heard above the mounting roar of the crowd. People pushed and jostled the platform. In the crazy torchlight, Billy thought for a moment that he saw James Kidlington move past the dais, towards the walls of the shipyard.

At the nape of midnight, someone slammed with the dolphin knocker on the door of the house in Mincing Lane, and called urgently for Barnabas and Sanford.

"Wheat and whiskey! Winstanley?" said a sleepy Barnabas. "At this wicked hour?"

"I'm afraid so, and no time to lose," said Winstanley. "Sir John sent me himself, with dispatch—the *Indigo Pheasant* is under attack!"

"No, oh no!" said Barnabas, electrically awake. "Come on, we can handle 'em!"

Barnabas—dressed only in his satin night-gown (a pale grey with vermillion florettes; very stylish, if now rather worn)—ran straight past Winstanley and into the street, waving an invisible cutlass and brandishing an imaginary pistol.

Sanford collected Barnabas, sent him upstairs to get properly dressed.

As Winstanley waited in the partners' room, someone else clacked away on the door with the dolphin knocker.

"*Quatsch*," yelled Barnabas down the stairs. "Who is it now?"

The Cook let in Mr. Fletcher, accompanied by a scarlet-jacketed marine.

"A thousand apologies, my lords," said Mr. Fletcher. "But, chip chap chunter, Mr. Bammary sent this good sergeant to me, with a vital message for you."

Sally and Maggie followed Barnabas into the partners' room. The Cook's niece brushed sleep from her eyes, followed Mr. Fletcher's every move as she bustled with coats and hats in the hallway.

"Billy Sea-Hen," started Winstanley.

"Billy what?" said the Cook, putting down a plate of shop-bought wheat biscuits and a jar of ginger jam (the best she could provide on such unusually short notice, but no one was going into battle on an empty stomach if she could help it). "Oh, my pardon, I . . . its just . . ."

"No, all understood," said Barnabas, slathering jam on a biscuit and already eying a second one. "Now, pigs and ponies, what's all the hey-hulloo?"

"Billy's camp meeting has gone sideways," said Winstanley. "Not at all clear what caused the disturbance but the Admiralty received word an hour ago that there's a near riot out there, at Blackwall. Huge crowds, by the way, fifty or sixty thousand by some reckonings. Men, women, children, whole families."

"That's what Mr. Bammary said," added Mr. Fletcher. "At least according to the good sergeant here. 'The Royal Artillery ordered from Woolwich Arsenal barracks to make with all haste to Blackwall Shipyard,' that's the message in a thimble. Using all available boats to cross the river. Isn't that right, sergeant?"

The Marine nodded.

"Exactly," said Winstanley. "Serious fights, with damage both to limb and property, all hard by the shipyards and the East India Docks. Officers at Naval Row sent the first messages already at sunset. More came in shortly thereafter from the guards at the Docks, and at the shipyards."

"But who is fighting whom?" said Sanford. "And why?"

"Dimly known, hardly grasped," said Winstanley. "Reports

most unclear on all points. Some of Billy's—shall we say spiritual—opponents appear to have taken issue with one or two of his dogmatical points. Some of them are just excitable young men, full of ale and gin, looking for a bang-up, always a risk in such gatherings. But there is more to it, if I understand Sir John's mind. He thinks that there is some sort of concerted attack on the ship, using the incidental fighting as a cover. By a vicious cabal indifferent to the sermon or any wider theological speculation."

"Then we must go," said Maggie. "Now."

Winstanley nodded, "Those are Sir John's instructions, his requests even. Miss Collins, he very explicitly told me to tell you that those are *not* commands. He hopes you will see the need for you to go, regardless of anything he can say to you."

"I do, I do," said Maggie, smiling despite the nature of the news. "By the *ndichie*, time is very short. We must be off now."

"I must go as well then," said Sally. Barnabas asked her to stay at Mincing Lane; Sally refused and—under gentle but firm pressure from his niece—Barnabas aquiesced.

"I have sent a detachment to Devereux Court, to make secure our Chinese guests," said Winstanley. "Another half-dozen marines on their way here, and a guard for Mr. Bunce at his quarters too."

The Cook and her niece looked relieved.

"Mr. Fletcher . . . ?" said the maid.

"I must go to the shipyard," he said to her, in his softest voice. "But, why, you know me—a slyer cove has never existed, I will slip by every dart the devil might toss at me, never you fear! Will be back in time for breakfast, my darling, so put the kettle on!"

He kissed the maid on the cheek and left for one of the two carriages waiting outside, joined by the sergeant.

Maggie and Sally each hugged Isaak, left the cat with the Cook and let Winstanley escort them to the second carriage. Sanford and Barnabas joined them.

In the carriage, Winstanley said, "The constabulary is completely overwhelmed, and who can blame them? The magistrate has called on the Home Office for reinforcements.

THE INDIGO PHEASANT *Volume Two of Longing for Yount*

The artillery cadets from Woolwich are only the half of it. Be prepared to see more troops in our London streets."

True enough, in Commercial Road they passed a line of hussars on enormous horses, trotting towards Poplar and Blackwall.

"Home Secretary is anxious enough already, sees Jacobins under every bed, especially after that business at Spa Fields, the attack on the Crown Prince, and the noises made by the likes of Hunt and Wedderburn," said Winstanley. "Suspension of habeas corpus possible—just like in '17, 'prudent action to forestall seditious calamity,' Home Secretary will claim. But don't fret on that account—Admiralty has already asserted its rights, will not let any true harm come to Billy and his confederates."

As they approached Poplar, a thickening crowd began streaming past them away from Blackwall, back to London proper. Hanging out the carriage windows, the McDoons and Winstanley gathered scraps of garbled news, hasty sketches and incoherent reports. Some of those fleeing past the carriage implied that the world was coming to an end by dawn. It was impossible to tell whether the phantoms they described were real or products of impassioned imaginations over-stimulated by Billy's words, the lighting, the music, the alcohol. Other pedestrians paused long enough to say they had not seen any fighting or much of anything else, but simply felt it wise to leave, given the rumours of violence. The overall impression was one of confusion.

By the time they reached Poplar High Street, their carriage was blocked by walkers leaving the meeting fields farther east. They left the carriage by the Poplar chapel-of-ease at Hale Street, and continued east against the stream, until they reached Naval Row across from the southwest gate of the East India Docks. Winstanley recognized several marine officers there. Joined by these men, the McDoons and Winstanley pushed south through the mob, along the Blackwall Causeway towards Billy's platform and the shipyard. An eerie silence now prevailed, as tired meeting-goers shuffled past, whispering, mumbling, shushing children—punctuated by one or two gun-shots and sporadic, indistinct shouts in the direction of the shipyard. The darkness was nearly complete, except for an orange-brown scumble of torchlight off towards the shipyard. Passing as quickly as they could the small houses of New Row (some with windows broken, all with gardens trampled) and St. Nicholas Church, then the Old Dock and the Ropewalk, the party finally reached the open gates of the Blackwall Shipyard. They could see the *Indigo Pheasant* beyond. Billy Sea-Hen stood at the gate with a knot of men, all of them holding pistols.

"Billy!" said Barnabas. "What's the news?"

"Mr. Barnabas, sir," said Billy, looking neither rattled nor alarmed, only fixed in his purpose. "Not good, to be sure, but far less bad than it might have been. Come, take a look."

They toured the shipyard. Smoke curled up from the masthouse and from the sailmaker's sheds.

"They came over the walls on the north and nor'east sides, from the direction of the East India Dock Road," said Billy. "While most folks were busy over to the west and the sou'west of the yards, where we preached our words. Some few—of the creatures and half-folk, that is—slipped in at the tweenlight, and then the main crew of 'em rushed over around midnight. Over there."

The McDoons could see fallen bodies in the torchlight, strewn around the yard, clustered along the northern wall as Billy described.

"They tried to set the tar and pitch stores alight, of course they did, the Moabites," said Billy. "That would have been the end of things, by Saint Macrina, that would have burned the *Pheasant* and everything on it to a cinder, made a furnace like Hell itself and killed many, a great many. So that's where the battle was hardest fought, to keep the Owl's folk from getting to the tar-houses. The real honour of winning victory there goes to Mr. Bammary and his young artillery cadets. Over there he is."

Reglum turned at the sound of his name, caught sight of the McDoons, came rushing up. His hat was gone, his clothes covered in soot. He held a sword in one hand.

Sally's mind contained rivers that flowed several ways at once, thundering, clashing, spuming into the furthest recesses. She could not withstand the look in Reglum's eyes. She looked away.

"We only just arrived in the nick of time," Reglum said. "Our good fortune, really: Woolwich is downstream from here; we had to pull hard to cross the river. Tide at least was with us, or else I fear we would have come too late."

"How many men lost, if I may ask, Mr. Bammary?" said Sanford.

"Eight of ours, all good men," said Reglum. "Very young, but very brave."

They went onboard the *Indigo Pheasant*. Here matters were far less bloody, but the damage far greater.

"I believe you know Lieutenant Thracemorton," said Winstanley. "He works a special detail for the Admiralty, reports to Sir John if I am not mistaken. How stand things here, Lieutenant?"

"The Others did not make it onto the ship itself with the exception of some few who clambered up onto the bow, got into the rigging on the foremast. My men vanquished them speedily. It felt—and please pardon what you may find hard to credit, or perhaps not—as if the ship was defending itself. The creatures could find little purchase on the ship, for all their ferocious attempts. The *Indigo Pheasant*, she just shrugged them off. Hard to explain, but you ask any of us, and we will tell you the same."

The McDoons and Billy had no problem believing that.

"Thank you, Lieutenant Thracemorton," said Maggie. "The *Indigo Pheasant* has a proud, vivacious song in her. Her very walls are an incantation."

"I believe it, miss," said Thracemorton. "But something did get through, or someone. Let me show you, aft and down below."

Several small but utterly crucial elements of the steam-engine and of the Fulginator were missing.

"Oh, *onye'ala*! This is bad," exclaimed Maggie. "The bascule is gone, and the abaxilic gear-box. Likewise the clairon and diapason that modulate the tones. And the cransal joint. Without these, the steam-engine cannot transfer sufficient pressure to the Fulginator to amplify the Song. Without these, the *Pheasant* cannot sulquivagate properly."

"Cannot find its way through the Interrugal Lands," said Sally by way of explanation. "It will drift a-wandering without these parts of its machinery."

"We can, of course, have them re-made and re-fitted," said Maggie. "But that will mean several more months delay, heaped onto the long delay we already suffer. We would most likely be unable to replace these parts before winter sets in."

"Which means missing yet another sailing season," said Sanford.

Maggie nodded.

They surveyed the theft.

"The *Pheasant*'s in-sung defenses would not suffer any of the Owl's people to pass," said Maggie.

"No," said Sally, an uneasy recognition blossoming within her.

"The *Pheasant* would only allow someone into its most vital places whom it knows and trusts," said Maggie.

"Someone who, in turn, knows the inner workings of the *Pheasant*," said Sally. "Intimately."

The small group standing in the Fulgination Room said no more but shared looks told each person that the others were thinking the same thing. The name of one person, and one person alone, had formed and crystallized in their minds.

"Not you . . ." Sally thought.

That person's name never entered the accounts of the Battle, cursory as they were. The Home Office started an investigation but dropped it when the Peterloo Massacre a month later in Manchester superseded the Battle in the minds of the public. (The Admiralty Lord had a quiet word with the Home Secretary and with the Lord-Chancellor, just to be sure the affair was forgotten). The important inquiries were conducted by those much closer to the events.

"Here then, Billy," said the cook the following week, handing Billy a copy of *Clarke's Weekly Observer & Miscellany*. "Did you really say what is reported here? Something about 'a worm with great veiny wings and teeth like hot pokers,' coming to eat up small children?"

"Well, somewhat like that," began Billy.

"Well, by Saint Morgaine, I never," interrupted the Cook. "No wonder you stirred up such a fuss, Billy Sea-Hen! You cannot go around scaring your parishioners, you know, with sermons like that!"

"No, I mean . . ." said Billy. "You know it wasn't me. It was that scoundrel Peasestraw at the start, and then the awl-rawny took advantage of the confusion to send in his monster-folk. I never meant any of that mess to happen, especially not the deaths of those brave lads. You know that. You know that, right?"

The Cook put her ample arms around his neck, looked him square in the eye, and said, "Billy Sea-Hen, prince of Queenhithe, as I live and breathe! Of course, I know that, of course I do."

She kissed him on the lips. Billy blushed.

"Wondrous day, an old dumbledore can still learn a new trick!" he said, and then returned the kiss.

The one report that deeply interested Sir John was a very confidential memo prepared by Captain Shufflebottom on the remains of the creatures that had attacked the *Indigo Pheasant*. Most of the fallen Others had dissolved in the first dawn's tweenlight, leaving little more than scattered teeth and bones, streaks, smears, and olivaceous sludge on the ground to attest to their having been present at all. Dr. Murray at Guy's & St. Thomas's Hospital examined the bones, declaring little about them to be human ("e.g., lacking diaphyseal trabeculae, possessing dual rather than singular linea aspera, tibia and fibula fused in several cases, a sacrum with three—not the requisite five—fused vertebrae"). More interesting still was the discovery of tunnels bored into the embankments all around the western flanks of the East India Docks and the northern aspects of the Blackwall Shipyard, tunnels containing digging and cutting tools made of alloys that no one at the time could identify, bits of parchment (covered with pnakotic script), glaucous bottles filled with dried herbs, nettles and the bones of small animals, and miniature lead coffins.

(Shufflebottom's report is marked "highly confidential" to the present day. An addendum was written in 1893, when the boring of the Blackwall Tunnel at the south side of the East India Dock Road, uncovered various, still-unnamed items that caused the tunnel-labourers to threaten strike. The Home Office called upon Sherlock Holmes to analyze what was found; his notes are allegedly affixed to the expanded report. A small section of the parchment unearthed is on view in an obscure corner of the British Museum, listed only as "Putatively attributed to the Pnakotic civilization, provenance unknown.")

Shufflebottom himself held his own counsel. No one had marked him in the hold of the *Indigo Pheasant* on the night of the Battle. He had tracked his quarry through the entire melee, right up until the assault on the tar-house. Forced to join that desperate affray, he had—so uncharacteristically—lost the one he followed.

"Well, well, well," he had thought while leaving the shipyard unobserved in the dawn's first light. "Slipped by me this time. Only because I was detained elsewhere. Your very prime fortune. Not the next time. I know you have taken items of essential value, without which the *Indigo Pheasant* cannot fly. But fly she will, mark my words, or my name's not Shufflebottom."

He smiled, and adjusted his smoked-glass spectacles. He was Captain Shufflebottom of the Corps Venatical. He knew where his quarry would go, sooner or later.

"I have seen you with the Widow," Shufflebottom said to himself. "Sooner or later, that's who you will visit . . . or she will visit you . . . and then I will have you."

Even as Captain Shufflebottom spoke those words—at dawn on the Sunday morning after the Battle of Blackwall—James Kidlington was in a post-coach on the way out of London. He was wearing the smart grey herringbone suit, with the foulard sportily knotted. He held a large valise on his lap. He was heading to the coaching inn at Slough.

"I am James Kidlington," he thought. "I have the keys to

paradise in my bag here. I have what they all want, and I will make them bargain for it. Bargain hard. The coin I demand will come with an influx of respect, while I collate all the sins and misdemeanours they have committed against me. I will show them all. Every one of them. Teach them they cannot command me as if I were their pet monkey. No, no, am much too clever for them. I diverted Thracemorton, I did. To the devil with the Admiralty. I wish I could see the look on Sir John's face when he hears this news, oh truly I do."

London's western suburbs rolled by.

"The Widow thinks she owns me—'get the items we agreed to, and come straight away back to me, my darling boy, and I will reward you richly.' Yes, indeed you will, dearest widow. I know you for what you are. Richly indeed!"

The coach rolled past Gunnersbury and Kew on its way to Slough.

"Slough," thought James. "Oh Sally. I will call for you here. I cannot live much longer this way. Could your love for me still loiter in your heart? I will call for you."

The coach passed Hounslow. James patted the valise, could feel the outlines of the items he had gathered off the *Indigo Pheasant*, as well as a pair of pistols.

"We can negotiate with these toys," he thought. "What will your family care, if they must ransom these back to help you regain your true happiness? I will beg your forgiveness, as you will beg mine—we can start anew. I promise."

The coach arrived at Slough, to change horses for the journey on to Bath. James descended from the coach and entered the inn. With almost the very last of his pocket money, he rented a room for a week.

"Here, boy," he said to the ostler's lad. "Do you see to it that this letter I give you is posted back directly to London. To this address, on Mincing Lane, do you hear?"

James smiled, clutching the valise with its precious cargo.

"I will show you Sally. I will show them all," he thought.

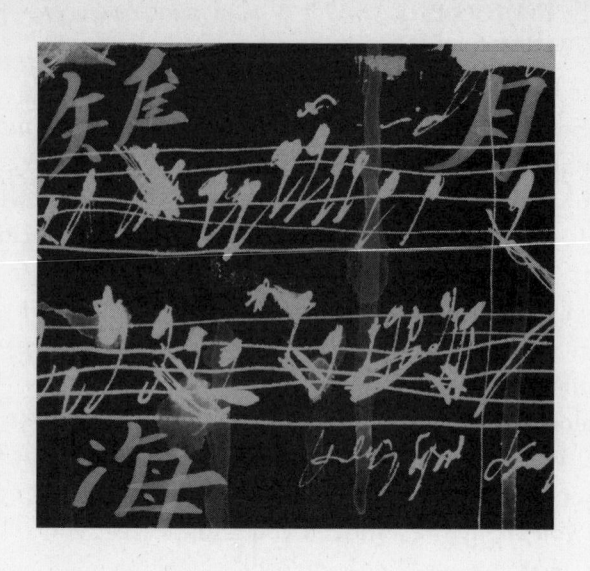

Interlude: *Vestigia*

[From the preamble of <u>A Modest Treatise on the Art of Fulgination</u>, by Dorentius Bunce, B.A. Cam., with Notes by Margaret Collins, original draft held in the Admiralty archives, c. 1820]

Though Fulgination is assuredly based upon the most highly defined and sophisticated terms of mathematics and natural mechanics, it is ultimately expressed through the language of music, so that it is truly more an aesthetic endeavour than an abstracted action of logic and rational philosophy. Its finest practitioners understand that the success of their Fulgination depends in the last instance on their ability to conjure forth a sentiment, a sensation of the Sublime, that will cause the dissimilar points of the compass and the unlike elements of the human heart to coalesce into a Unity that delivers the Fulginator and his or her vessel and its contents (along with his or her companions on the journey) to the desired and calculated destination. Fulgination proceeds from general principles, building thereafter upon a wide range of minute experimentations, aleatory probes and bold tatonnement. Put another way, we can also say it is a kind of mapping of empathetic impulses, allowing us to re-order and re-create the Space and Time originally laid down by the Divine, enabling a faithful translation or even re-translation of the World, or a part thereof. The ablest Fulginators will agree that the art uses rhythm and harmony to unite the Outer Corpus and the Inner Essence of a thing, thereby capturing the two-in-one in song, which song is then re-sung in a new space, leaving only empty silence behind.

[From <u>Notes on Various Styles of Music</u>, by Muzio Clementi, 1815— a copy of which had many comments written by Sally, and later Maggie]

The realization of any significant piece of music must . . . be free from fault in the execution but not at the expense of feeling and character, be supple and lively without being merely ornamental, be sublime without overwhelming or offending the ear and in every respect ingenious without being superficial.

DANIEL A. RABUZZI

[From Stoddard's Cyclopedia of the Arts & Sciences *(London, 1783; second edition, 1805), volumes X and XIV]*

Indigo (from the Latin "*indicum*," derived from the Greek "*indikon*," meaning "dye," highlighting the origins of said colouring agents in India during ancient times): A colour, familiarly deemed to be a sort of blue, but more formally a separate hue, as Newton demonstrated in his *Opticks*—the seventh universally fundamental colour, completing but not entirely subservient to the spectrum, and distinct from the cerulean or cyaneous that is "blue." Newton connected indigo thus to the seventh note in the Ionian scale of music, the key to augmented unison in harmony, and also to the polynomials of cubic planes in the calculus. As the seventh colour, indigo enjoys notoriety for its eccentricity and idiosyncratic ways. Indigo is the colour uniting but also differentiating the other six in the trichomatic scheme devised by Th. Young; we might say it is akin to the universal solvent among chemical elements or perhaps to the Sabbath as Queen of the Week. The poets consider indigo a fugitive, liminal, well nigh magical species of colour, "a vagrant cool flame/ whose orbit eclipses both sense and sensibility" as Oldmixon has it in *The Caliper'd Heart*. Our divines, influenced in part by Jakob Boehme on the seven days of the Creation, associate indigo with Our Lady, with the intercession of St. Adelsina and with the effulgence of the Beata Carolina. Shewing yet again the universality of revealed wisdom, we learn recently in the translations by Wilkins and Anquetil-Duperron of ancient philosophical texts by the Indians that indigo is the colour of what the Hindoos call "The Third Eye," which we might call the "divine inspiration." Likewise the Jesuits have recorded that indigo is the colour the

THE INDIGO PHEASANT *Volume Two of Longing for Yount*

Chinese philosophers reserve for "the most subtle of understandings, those that translineate worlds and find meaning in oblique spaces between other, more commonplace destinations" (to quote Staunton in his newest work).

Pheasant (from the Old French, "*faisan*", derived from Greek "*phasianos*" via Latin "*phasianus*", possibly from the same root as "*phase*," meaning "to appear, to make visible, to shine," primarily used in reference to the moon; compare also "phantasm," from the same root): A bird of the gallinaceous sort, characterized by bright and splendid plumage (typically variegated, with lunules and reticulated patterns), a bristly retractile crest, a long stiff graduated tail, and sharp unciate tarsal spurs with which it defends itself against all foes. Sometimes called "the Egypt Bird," for its pharaonic appearance. The origins of the pheasant are mysterious. Buffon believes that the pheasant is the source for the tale of the phoenix in Pliny. Cuvier supposes that the Argonauts brought the pheasant to Europe from Colchis in Asia Minor. Alain of Lille writes in *The Complaint of Nature*: "The pheasant, after it had endured the confinement of its natal island, flew into our worlds . . ." Chaucer, in *The Parliament of Fowls*, his revision of Scipio's Dream, attributes strange powers to the pheasant. Hemmelincx in *Seven Spheres* refers to the pheasant's mutability and even hermaphroditic qualities, as suggested by its secondary designation of "tiercel-hen." All authors agree on the pheasant's hardy, robust nature, its wary shrewdness, and its unerring ability to navigate hidden paths, mussets and small-ways amongst brambles, hedgerows and the like.

Chapter 8: A Great Singing, or, The Fluid Signature of Joy

"Our cage
We make a choir, as doth the prison'd bird
And sing our bondage freely."

—**William Shakespeare**,
Cymbeline, III:iii, 42-44 (c. 1611)

". . . The sound
Symphonious of ten thousand harps, that tun'd
Angelic harmonies."

—**John Milton**,
Paradise Lost, VII: 558-559 (1667)

"Or, on thy instrument, with touching grace,
Awaken all the witcheries of sound . . ."

—**Matilda Betham**,
"To Miss Rouse Boughton . . ." (1808)

"Tell me, moon, thou pale and grey
Pilgrim of heaven's homeless way,
In what depths of night or day
Seekest thou repose now?"

—**Percy Bysshe Shelley**,
"The World's Wanderers" (1820)

"In an age far-off and yet to come, Ocean will unbind the chains, revealing thereby a great land; Tiphys will unveil broad new worlds, and Thule will no more be the Ultimate."

—**Seneca**,
Medea, 369-374 (60)

James had a splendid Sunday. He was exhausted but his mind strode over such physical concerns, emulating the stilts-men at Billy Sea-Hen's camp meeting. James could not rest while awaiting Sally's response—and then possibly Sally herself.

He walked all around the village of Slough, reliving the gay escapades and intimate moments from the time he and Sally had purloined from the magazines of propriety. The July sun was out, the sky an eggshell blue. He peeked at the Herschel Observatory, recalling how he and Sally had done the same, marveling at the huge telescope set on the lawn. He wondered if Sir Herschel or his sister might be at home, but—even in his febrile state—thought the better of intruding on the astronomers.

He strolled south to the Thames, a dark glittering thread this far upstream. He looked across at the playing fields of the Eton School, and beyond to the dense oak of Windsor Forest. He doffed his hat and bowed in the direction of Windsor Castle.

"Your most faithful servant, Your Majesty, back from enjoying your fine hospitality in Australia," James said, putting his hat back on at a slight angle to his forehead. "You shall hear of me, as well, if I have anything to say about it."

At supper, he received Sally's response.

"She is coming!" he said to himself, wanting to shout the

news to the innkeeper and all the many guests taking their Sunday meal in the public room. "She is coming. 'Dearest James' . . . it starts. 'Dearest,' she writes. 'Dearest James, I will come by the first coach out Monday morning. Expect me then. Do not leave The Red Lion. Yearning for your embrace once more, yours forever, Sally.'"

James could hardly eat. Elated and dizzy, he surveyed the bustling room. He watched people stream in and out, the door with the inn's name painted in festive curlicues on a pane of frosted glass swinging open and shut: Red Lion . . . noiL deR . . . Red Lion . . . noiL deR.

"Come join me, dearest, in our land of Noilder," he thought. "Where all will be well again. Together, we will spy out all the nells and heals of our little empire, you the Queen and I your most loyal King. Banners of tarragon, chervil and rushwort will flutter over our castle. Tamarind ropes shall lift the drawbridge. The roof we'll coat with nutmeg-paste."

Looking out the window, James thought the air itself was alive, so incised and bright were the colours, so defined the shadows that stirred in the high-summer evening. It seemed his eyes and ears, all his senses, had been touched by Robin Goodfellow. He heard greenbottles buzzing against the panes on upstairs windows, horses champing on their mash in the stables, the creak of the pump-handle in the back-yard, the hiss of beef-fat dripping from the joint on the spit in the kitchen.

He re-read Sally's note for the tenth time, then carefully folded it and put it in his breast-pocket.

"Sally: your kindness is a minister to your deeds, your mercies supple and strong," he murmured. "Come, enter this kingdom with me. Nay, it shall be a queendom, where the elves dance on the green in your honour."

James was Jack o'the Green, Sir Thomas under the hill, Titania's consort. The cider at the Red Lion was the best he had ever tasted. The bacon, cheese and pickles came from Cockaigne.

"I hear the larks ascending from the hay-stubble, singing to greet the eventide, I witness the preminent auburn sunset," he thought. "I am as the pilgrim in Miss Stillingfleet's poem—Sally, you will remember it, we read it as we sat on the banks of the Thames not a half-mile from here!—the 'pilgrim lonely,' who 'in a chaos weary of disarray waits for the moon to climb, waits and stays his wrath, waits for a love sublime.' I am that patient pilgrim, Sally, I am."

James barely slept that night. He was up before dawn, anxiously awaiting the first coaches from London. Several arrived, bearing the morning newspapers, but none carrying Sally.

Reassuring himself that Sally would arrive no later than the noontime coaches, James tried to distract himself with the newspapers as he sat by the window in the Red Lion's public room. He scarcely grasped what he read about the campaigns in India or the sailing of His Majesty's men-of-war from Ceylon. News of corn prices and canal companies slid away from his eyes. The only items that caught his attention were those relating to the events at Blackwall the day and night before.

"'The preacher, the one with the bizarre appellation of Sea-Hen, came with the sidling thunder of a modern-day Wycliffe to his peroration, having sufficiently aroused the passions of his multitudinous listeners, agitating them into a temper that over-toppled all reason, when—as a natural consequence of such Lollardy—the crowd stormed the sermonical stage and caused all manner of pandemonium to ensue,'" read James.

"To put it mildly," he chuckled.

Morning drew on. The July sun beat down on Slough. James dozed at his table, at all times cradling the valise in his lap. He grew increasingly worried. He thought he heard a kingfisher diving into the Thames from the branch of an alder tree. He was certain he heard hares carefully insinuating themselves through the hedgerows, and the stealthy padding of stoats behind them. He was convinced of these and a thousand other sights and sounds, each pellucid, the tinking and tacking of elven smiths at their forges deep within his mind.

Shouts from the courtyard roused him. The first of the

noontime coaches had arrived. He sat straight up, looked out the window.

Sally stepped out of the coach.

James looked to the door of the inn. A few moments later it opened (nioL deR became Red Lion and then nioL deR restored itself). Sally stood there, searching for James, found him. She smiled at him over the heads of the intervening lunchtime crowd.

The world was in perfect equilibrium for that moment. The hares in the hedges, the greenbottles at the windows, the kingfisher hovering above the river . . . all paused, poised in a perfect balance.

"Everything is just right," thought James.

And then it wasn't.

James noticed that Sally's head shook a little: a warning, a stifled sob, a surge of fear? He saw that she had tears on her cheeks.

He turned to look out the window. Sally had not come alone, as promised. From the coach issued Sally's uncle Barnabas, and his partner Sanford, followed by the slender black woman, Maggie, and then Mr. Fletcher, Billy Sea-Hen, and Lieutenant Thracemorton.

His motions slowed as if he were swimming in sun-thickened honey; James turned back to Sally—who, immobile at the door, shook her head more forcefully. She appeared to be speaking, but James could not hear over the hubbub in the inn.

James had once seen a hawk take a pigeon in Piccadilly, strip and eat its prey on a roof all unobserved by the throngs below, a pantomime of violence no more than twenty feet over the heads of hundreds. The hungry, busy, news-seeking people in the coaching inn ate and bustled and talked all around James, unaware of the drama unfolding in their midst.

Another coach clattered into the yard. James, keeping track of Mr. Fletcher and Lieutenant Thracemorton as they appeared to be heading around the building, paid little heed to the second coach until he noticed the passenger who stepped down: the Widow Goethals in her dark green dress. She wore a small hat with one long metallic blue heron's feather trailing from it, the better to highlight her waves of bold black hair.

"Well," thought James. "That settles matters."

He pushed back his chair, put on his hat and picked up the valise. He put a small coin on the table for his lunch ("Some want to believe otherwise, but James Kidlington is no thief," he said to himself). Seeming casual and unhurried, he made his way towards the kitchen.

"James!"

He turned and looked at Sally, seeing only her face across the crowded room.

"My Goddess," he thought. "You are a beauty—even in your despair."

Still mired in the honeyed air, James slowly waved his free hand. Sally waved back, tentative at first and then with increasing fierceness.

"James!" she cried.

Suddenly released from the layers of heavy, occluding atmosphere, James spun around and darted into the kitchen. He nearly bowled over startled kitchen maids and pot boys, losing his hat as he rushed out the back door.

He sprinted south down the Windsor Road : "See! 'From the brake the whirring pheasant springs; And mounts exulting on triumphant wings.'"

Behind him he heard a general outcry, pierced by a horse neighing.

Gasping for breath, he risked a look over his shoulder. A horse and rider were rounding the inn and entering the Windsor Road. The rider wore dark glasses ("like the ones the overseers wore in the Australian camps," he thought, momentarily surprised).

The valise hampered him but he would not drop it unless he were dead, and maybe not even then. On he ran, out of the village. Tall hedges lined the road, with a fringe of larkspur, convolvulus, daisies, and masses of pink and purple Sweet William. Through occasional gaps in the hedges, he caught ragged glimpses of long-stalked red poppies waving on the margins of the fields.

With each hot breath, he inhaled the deeply satisfying smell of the tedded hay as it dried in the sun.

He heard behind him the nearing sounds of a fast horse. Another sound overrode the beat of hooves. Looking back, James saw the Widow Goethals racing along the tops of the hedgerows, laughing, her brilliant white teeth flashing in the sunlight. Green dress billowing behind her, her black tresses whipping the air, the witch-widow whirled and skimmed, "a-whistlin' and a-wheeplin' o'er the haws."

James cursed and leaped forward. He heard another noise, even closer, from just the other side of the hedgerow to his left. Out of the corner of his eye when he raced past one of the openings in the hedge, James caught a glimpse of two small men loping like apes over the hay-strewn fields. Green-hued men. Naked green men.

A little over a quarter mile down the Windsor Road, desperate to elude his various pursuers, James shanked left onto the road to Upton Court Farm. He had to go to ground. He knew that the only chance of refuge now was Saint Stephen's Church, some six hundred yards further on.

His lungs burned, his legs bent under the pressure of his speed. He slowed for a second to shift the valise from one hand to another, and to check on his pursuit. The rider had pulled even with the widow. Over the hedges and down upon the rider leaped the two green men. The rider adroitly maneuvered his horse to avoid the onslaught. As the two men rebounded off the surface of the road and reached for the reins, the rider fired a pistol at immediate range. One of the grappling men collapsed backwards.

James had no more time to watch the battle. The widow was nearly upon him, dancing like a beautiful spider on the leaves and spines of the hedgerow above him. She laughed as she held out long, stiff fingers to grab him. James sprinted again.

The final dash into the church was a rust-and-brown-tinged blur. James had no more energy but his will drove him on, his will and the great fear at his heels. He stumbled through the churchyard gate, urged himself past the elms and yews, made for the massive, ivy-mantled Norman tower.

"Why run, my darling?" said the Widow, at his neck, her voice silvery, melodious. She might have been asking him if he wanted more tea at Hatchards, so calm and entrancing was her tone.

James almost slowed despite himself. Instead, he threw himself in one final spasm towards the church door . . . and prayed it would be open on a Monday at noon.

It was. The day was Saint Morgaine's, the patron of bakers, the leavener of dough and protector of the hearth. On this day, churches opened their doors for the poor, who might receive at the altar a free loaf of bread.

James crashed through the door, into the nearly derelict Saint Stephen's Church. The Widow Goethals followed.

James felt the Widow's long nails on his shoulders, as he ran down the nave. He knocked over the worm-riddled rood-screen as he scrambled into the apse. He hurtled onto the altar, scattering half a dozen loaves of bread as he slid across it. He dropped onto the floor on the other side. With nowhere further to run—the sacristy wall blocking his way forward—James turned at bay to face the Widow.

"Honestly, James," she sighed, gentle as a zephyr, her green eyes sparkling, with the stone altar between them. "You should know better. You cannot escape me, though I applaud your heroic efforts. Impressive. But, my sweetheart, I would not harm you, if I could."

James, panting, with sweat-slicked hands, struggled to open his valise.

"*Méchant, mon chère, pas sage,*" she shook her head, the smell of her locks filling the apse with a sweet perfume.

James pulled out one of the pistols, aimed it unsteadily at the Widow, who only smiled.

"I," said James, still out of breath. "I, . . . I . . . know who, . . . what you are . . ."

The Widow said, "Yes, I know you do, dearlet, sweet little wren of mine. After all, are you not also one of us?"

James tried to cock the pistol, while shaking his head as energetically as his exhaustion allowed him to.

"No," he whispered, his breathing returning slowly to normal. "Whatever else . . . I . . . may be, . . . I am, . . . I am not, . . . not . . . of your kind."

"*Tu es adorable*," said the Widow. "*Très adorable*."

She sighed, shook her head and reached out with her bronzey conjure-hands.

"Hold!"

The man in dark glasses, holding a pistol in each hand, advanced up the nave. The Widow spun around.

"You again!" she hissed.

"Never far away," said the man, moving at speed, pistols level. "I killed your children."

The Widow yelled, a sound to scare the magpies from their tower nests, to freeze the marrow of the grey thrushes in the elms.

James fell back, covering his ears, without releasing his pistol.

Hex-fire arced across the nave. The man in the dark glasses threw himself to the epistle side, rose on one knee, aimed one of his pistols and fired. The Widow staggered back but, laughing wildly, she rose up ten feet into the air. As the man raised his other pistol, she descended upon him in the nave, half-chanting, half-laughing an emerald song of destruction.

Another melody answered hers. Bursting into the church, limpid notes of healing blue shattered the witch-song. Maggie ran through the door, followed a moment later by Sally. Both sang, united, a wave of mathematical power.

James shielded his eyes as the dark green chant rallied against the indigo aria.

Maggie ran straight at the Widow Goethals, roaring an unendurable cobalt theme. Sally walked slowly forward, echoing Maggie's song.

The Widow Goethals seemed to expand, becoming a bloated green mass in mid-air, framed by a gorgon's nest of oiled black hair. Her eyes blazed—she was a dragonness of grim proportion. She turned to look down upon James.

"James, your friends arrive to save you," she said. "But what friends are these? Trust them at your peril, my sweet. Their music, *c'est une étude sur la folie*. They will take from you what is rightfully yours. What is ours."

"Fly now, witch," said Maggie. "Or I will destroy you."

The Widow stared down at Maggie.

"Here James is Diana, come to hunt down Actaeon," cold-laughed the Widow. "She will rend you like a stag, nail your skin to the mock-tree."

"*Now*, Owl-mistress," said Maggie. She began to sing again.

The notes sped from Maggie's lips as darts of blue-black fire, taking geometrical shapes as they struck the numinous green mass of the witch.

"I leave you now, James, to your jailer's retinue, in the sickle-sinny drift, as they hie you to the gallows pole," said the Widow. She growled at Maggie, who sang on unaffected.

The Widow Goethals, with a curt laugh, disappeared in a blaze of greens, slates, and mackerel greys, a star fading into the bottom of a very deep well.

Maggie ceased singing.

Into the sudden silence that fell upon the church, walked Barnabas, Sanford, Mr. Fletcher, Billy Sea-Hen and Lieutenant Thracemorton, all with pistols drawn.

The man in the dark glasses stood up, both pistols still in his hands.

Barnabas broke the loud silence.

"Figs and farthings," he said. "Who are you? Declare yourself, friend or foe?"

The man bowed slightly and said, "I am Captain Shufflebottom. I work for the same masters as Lieutenant Thracemorton. He can vouch for me, though he has seen me but once or twice before."

Though greatly puzzled, the lieutenant walked to the captain. The two conversed in low voices for a minute, exchanging passwords.

"Quite right," said Lieutenant Thracemorton, whistling softly.

"This is Captain Shufflebottom. He is on our side."

The entire party looked to the apse. James was no longer visible. He was sitting on the floor, leaning against the altar, facing the sacristy wall.

"James," said Sally. "James, dearest?"

James did not respond.

"James, please. Please? We must talk."

James drew the valise closer to himself. The items within scraped with a muffled sound across the floor.

"Oh, dearest," said Sally, voice shaking. "I never meant you any harm. I wish so much had not come to this pass."

Without rising, James said, "The Widow may be a demon, but that does not necessarily make her words untrue."

Sally let out a small sob and balled her fists. Maggie moved to her shoulder and said, "James Kidlington—you are no fool. We are in the halls of the *Bemmuo*, the mansions of the spirits. You know full well who speaks truth and who speaks falsehoods."

James snorted, "As may be, Miss Collins. But the Widow's enmity for us both does not mean you and I must be friends. You lead the griffins to flay the deer, do you not?"

Maggie started towards the altar. Sally pulled her back.

"James," said Sally. "Please stop. You only make matters worse."

"Oh Sally, I want so much to believe you, my beautiful Sally. But you did not come alone, as I implored you. For your heart's malpractice, Sally, who paid you your thirty silver shillings?"

James continued in a louder voice, "I sense the Admiralty behind this! Do you hear me, Thracemorton and you, the other one, with the glasses? Tell Sir John I am not bought so easily as the McDoons!"

Barnabas moved forward, followed in close order by Sanford and Mr. Fletcher.

"Odd's wrinkles," Barnabas said. "Come out, James, you villain."

"Soon enough, my dear sir—whom I once hoped to call 'Uncle' or the like—soon enough, now that we have a quorum for the final act, in this fane to a God gone missing and a Goddess who slumbers idly by. Sally has a replica of her love here entrapped, a fairy tale hare primed for the skinning, as I suppose she thinks him. How meekly she disembowels me, how softly she prises out my heart for its further disposal."

Shufflebottom signaled to Thracemorton. The two special agents of the Admiralty began to flank the altar.

"Sally, are you listening?" called out James. "The longing continues unabated, doesn't it? Here, there, in your precious Yount, what does it matter? The yearning, always starved, always unsated. Your heart's longing will never be cured."

The McDoons moved towards the altar.

"James, enough, my love," begged Sally. "Return the machinery. Come back to me."

"Oh ho, is that all? Your *Indigo Pheasant* needs its wings, and then I am free to go? Pennons of love and respect she'll fly for me, but she'll not allow a knave loose in her nave."

James cocked his pistol. The sound rang out clearly in the church. The McDoons stopped. The Admiralty men continued to advance.

"Do you know," said James. "I believe this church is in need of a new bell. Sally, do you remember? The curate told us that when we visited him once upon a long time ago. Seemed to think we might contribute to the fund for it."

Sally said, "Yes, I do, James."

"Well, Sally, I think it is time to make that contribution. 'Now fades the glimmering landscape on the sight, and all the air a solemn stillness holds.' Remember, Sally, we read that poem together, you and I, under the elms outside, in the yard to this very church?"

"'Save where the beetle wheels his droning flight,'" whispered Sally. "'And drowsy tinklings lull the distant folds.' Oh no, Goddess, it is still noon, not evening, dear James . . ."

James said, as he heard the Admiralty agents reach the far side of the altar. "Everyone knows that the best-sounding bells need a little blood coursed into their founding . . ."

Many things happened at once then, and no one after had

precisely the same recollection—though the outcome was clear and irrevocable, the interpretation of its proximate cause will forever remain subject to the whims and quirks of individual perceptions.

The main facts:

James stood up.

Sally shouted, "James!"

Five pistols fired more or less simultaneously.

James

fell

back

dead.

James's pistol had discharged. The thought occurred to several that he was attempting suicide, in a flamboyant, melodramatic way that suited his character. Others were more or less charitable, depending on one's views and prejudices, in positing that James was aiming at the McDoons or at the Admiralty men, and simply missed. Or that he could not decide which of several targets to focus upon. The bullet from his gun was not recovered but the hole it left in the opposite wall was on a tangent that meant the bullet passed between Sally and Maggie. No one wanted to dwell on the fact of its trajectory.

Mr. Fletcher, Sanford, Lieutenant Thracemorton and Captain Shufflebottom had also fired their guns. James had two wounds, one to his chest, one to his throat.

The blood spilled on the valise, pooled on the floor, created a small lake around one corner of the altar.

Sally was inconsolable.

Maggie retrieved the valise and would not let it out of her hands until its contents were reinstalled on the *Indigo Pheasant*. When that time came, she was careful to scrub from the stolen gearbox and steam-engine jointure the blood of James that had seeped through the valise. Some blood remained in the narrowest seams, impossible to remove without harming the metal itself, a thin dark script embedded in the technology.

Barnabas leaned on Sanford, both of whom looked old.

"Figs and fiddles, I would have done anything to spare her that, my poor, poor girl."

"We all would have, old friend," said Sanford. "Be not over hard on yourself. No power on Earth could have deterred James Kidlington from cutting open the latter pages of his own book."

Billy Sea-Hen, with Mr. Fletcher, carried James's body out of the church. Billy came back and cleaned the congealed blood from the floor, his hands surprisingly delicate as he wiped the stains from the base of the altar.

That afternoon and in the days to come, Lieutenant Thracemorton and Captain Shufflebottom dealt with the local constable and magistrate, as well as the vicar of Saint Stephen's Church. The Admiralty handled everything. The McDoons were held blameless after a short inquiry.

They buried James Kidlington in the small graveyard by Saint Helen's Bishopgate in the City of London.

In the carriage back to Mincing Lane that afternoon, Maggie held Sally's hand and thought, "Mama, I miss your wisdom. What am I to say? Such a terrible thing, this blood-letting that did not have to be. A rogue he was, and perhaps deprived of his reason when he most needed it, but he did not deserve this end, I think."

Out loud, Maggie said, "Stay with us, sister, the *Indigo Pheasant* needs you. *I* need you."

Sally could say nothing, but almost imperceptibly she squeezed Maggie's hand.

"Women have to be as strong as elephants," thought Maggie.

Two months after the Battle of Blackwall (and the burial of James), in the waning days of September and thus late in the season to be embarking on such a voyage, the *Indigo Pheasant* sailed down the Thames.

Lloyd's List, the chronicle of all things maritime, reported that sizeable crowds gathered, "'curious to see off such a hermaphrodite of a ship, notorious also after the riot that broke out in the Blackwall yard; further, despite the remarkable secrecy that has surrounded the oddly named vessel, we have it on good authority that the *Indigo Pheasant* contains some of the latest in steam-driven machinery, to what purpose is not fully conceived by this paper's editor, though we put our faith in the sagacious heads at Admiralty and the East India Company as to means and ends, for, as Horace has it, we salute a science—even one we little understand—that brings results.'"

We have a good many third-party impressions of the day because the Babbages, the Somervilles, and other members of London's intellectual elite made a special trip out to Blackwall to see the launch of the *Indigo Pheasant* (the pleasant prospect of tea and cakes to follow, at Bromley Hall on the leafy River Lea just north of Blackwall, was surely an additional inducement). For example, the eminent chemist and geologist Arthur Aikin wrote to his aunt, the poet and essayist Anna Laetitia Barbauld, that "most strange—to my eyes at least—was the presence of many females onboard the ship, a fact that will I believe support your own hopes for improvement amongst us." The philosopher and novelist William Godwin, writing to his daughter Mary Shelley (in Florence at that time with Percy Bysshe Shelley), exclaimed "what a sublime sight, dearest Mary, this great ship filled not only with soldiers and the tools of war but with men and women of more intellectual and spiritual propensities together bent on adventure of the highest moral order."

We even have a pencil-and-crayon sketch of the *Indigo Pheasant* itself, by none other than J.M.W. Turner, made as he stood at one of his favourite places, on the Marlborough Terraces at Woolwich. Well preserved at the National Maritime Museum in Greenwich, the drawing clearly shows the indigo-tinted fore topmast staysail, the jib and the flying jib, that is, the three sails rigged between the foremast and the bow, the three giant triangles that lead the ship forward. If one looks very closely, one can discern what must be the "eyes" of the ship, the *qingbao* porcelain plates that Mei-Hua gave as figureheads.

Mei-Hua, on tip-toes, peered down at the *qingbao* pheasant

on the right-hand side of the bow (the "starboard" side, as she had learned to say in her now nearly perfect English). She was elated, seeing the pheasant's glazed eye pointed towards the morning sun. Attached in rows behind the porcelain plate, like scintilla from a racing star, reflecting the sun, were amulets and talismans given by Billy Sea-Hen's adherents; the three mighty masts were also emblazoned with similar tokens, in their hundreds. Also reflecting the sun was a great round gilt-edged clock with a white porcelain face, which Maggie had had attached to the mainmast—a timepiece made by the specialists in Clerkenwell, a timepiece directly connected to the Great Fulginator below decks by corded silver wires, a clock to tell time in timeless places. Mei-Hua hugged herself, wanted to run and hug her brother and even the severe old Tang Guozhi: the voyage, the *real* voyage, had at last begun! Still and always the daughter of a state official in a provincial capital city of the Celestial Empire, Mei-Hua managed to compose herself, but not before she squeezed Maggie's hand.

Maggie stood beside Mei-Hua at the bow of the *Indigo Pheasant* as the ship passed close by Woolwich on the south bank. Maggie admired the three indigo-coloured sails, so distinctive from the regular white sheets unfurled everywhere else on the ship. Colouring the three foremost sails indigo had been her idea, one she had insisted on even when its significant additional cost caused indigestion among the accountants at the Admiralty.

"No other ship in the world has such sails," they'd said. "It's unheard of!"

Moreover, Maggie had refused to allow use of the indigo dyes from South Carolina or from the Bengal, despite their low prices, since in each case the plant was grown and processed by unfree labour.

"Not one item on the *Indigo Pheasant* will be produced by enslaved people," she said with a finality that brooked no rebuttal. She made sure that the dye used for the ship's sales came via the Parsee merchant and Yount-friend Sitterjee, and had its ultimate source in free labour on farms in Gujarat.

"Your scruples as a result have doubled an already unconscionably high cost!" the E.I.C. accountants had wailed. "Most extraordinary and unheard of!"

"My point succinctly," she'd replied, without so much as raising an eyebrow. "The *Indigo Pheasant* is unlike any other ship that has ever been built."

Maggie looked back along the deck towards the stern. The nominal captain, ship's mates, and petty officers, supplied by the E.I.C., clustered near the wheelhouse. Sir Barrow had himself instructed the captain on the nature of the trip, and made it clear that—while the captain and his officers might have command in all things considered traditionally nautical—Maggie was the final authority on all other exigencies and eventualities requiring executive decision-making.

Standing a little off to the side of the E.I.C. men, all on his own and saying little to anyone but watching everyone through his smoked-glass spectacles, was the tall figure of Captain Shufflebottom. Sir John had named Shufflebottom as the Admiralty's primary representative onboard the ship, a supercargo to whom sharp powers had been delegated.

Billy Sea-Hen stood amidships, with many of the men and women he had chosen, his pilgrim-warriors, known as "the sons and daughters of Asaph." They numbered one hundred and twenty-eight, replicating the number of musicians who had returned to the Holy Land from the Babylonian Captivity, the musicians who were descendants of Asaph. (The quarrel with the rival preacher Peasestraw had revolved in part over the accuracy of this number, which is so stated in the Book of Esdras, whereas the Book of Nehemiah gives the number of the post-exilic returnees as one hundred and forty-eight; the Admiralty, caring little for such exegetical niceties but very much about budget and commissary constraints, had only granted space on the *Indigo Pheasant* for one hundred and twenty-eight). Each of the sons and daughters of Asaph wore an armband made of leftover material from the indigo-tinted foresails.

In addition, and despite the warmth of a September sun, Billy wore a long, blue woolen scarf—knitted by the Cook and a gift from her the evening before.

"I know it isn't much, my Billy of Queenhithe—I have a beetle's fingers when it comes to knitting," Cook had said, fighting back tears in the kitchen in the house on Mincing Lane.

"No, no, say not such things, I'll not hear them," Billy had said, likewise struggling to keep from crying.

"Now, you listen well, Billy Sea-Hen. You go wherever it is you and the McDoons are going. You find and fight the awl-rawney until he is good and dead, and then you come straight back, d'you hear? Straight back home. Letting no harm or damage come to you and any of the others, d'you hear?"

"Why," Billy had said, with a slow smile while he clutched the blue knit muffler to his chest. "Might as well try to drown an eel than kill me. This old dumbledore will fly his way back to London, to you. I swear on the immarcessible crown of glory itself, I will."

Reglum Bammary stood further back on the deck of the *Indigo Pheasant*, leading a platoon of Woolwich gunners. Like them, he wore a scarlet jacket faced with slate-grey. In his breast pocket he had a worn copy of Akenside's *Pleasures of the Imagination*, and in a large waist pocket he carried a sketchbook and pencil to capture the likenesses for the *Index of Goettical Creatures* of whatever curiosities the voyagers might encounter on their passage through the Interrugal Lands.

Standing close by Maggie at the bow were—beside Mei-Hua—the rest of the McDoons, as well as Shaozu and Tang Guozhi. Sally, a pale shade, held Isaak. A cage by her feet contained Charicules. Dorentius Bunce leaned on his crutch, his face turned to the cant of the sails and the tilt of the jib-boom, as if trying to read sine and secant on the wind itself. Barnabas, in a vest he described as "like the green-shaded wines we receive from Portugal," was gesticulating to the sailors in the rigging. Sanford, in perfectly pressed black, the few hairs on his head whipped by the wind, scanned the banks of the Thames, already on alert for threats.

As they came to the mouth of the Thames at sunset, just past the spire of Saint Mary Hoo and the clock tower at Sheerness, the ship's shadow lengthening on the swift waters in front of it, Sanford raised his voice in song. Momentarily startled, the McDoons and others nearest the bow could not at first catch his melody (singing not being among Sanford's many talents). Then, one by one, they knew it: "The Seafarer," the ancient hymn that had come down through the Exeter Book and, as translated into modern English by Sir Thomas More, become a standard in the Great Hymnal.

Maggie, who had sung it countless times while at Saint Macrina's Charity School, joined in. She did not fully comprehend Sanford but—at that moment, if not already much earlier—she knew she loved him.

"Now my soul warps out of my breast,
My spirit mindful roams transformed,
Amidst the flood of the sea,
Amidst the realms of the whale."

One by one all but the Chinese joined in (and even they hummed the tune, as best they could ascertain it), from the bow to the stern, from the marines and gunners in the holds to the sailors at the ropes and sails:

"Through all the quarters of the world,
Hungry as the raven, desiring more,
Flying alone, restless,
Shouting on high,
Hurries the heart unhesitant
Onto the whale-roads
Ever over the waves of the sea."

They sang it several times into the dusk, an exultant challenge. Billy and his congregation peppered the verses with "amens" and "selahs." Charicules added his own version of the same, in trills that ran up the masts and along the rigging. They lighted lanterns on the masts and on the bowsprit and along the stern, as night fell, so that the ship was a melody of light, a blazing canticle heard by shepherds minding their flocks in the salt-marshes and by innkeepers in the towns along the estuary.

And as they sang for their final time that evening, just before the last ray of the setting sun fled, the verse ending "Onto the whale-roads, Ever over the waves of the sea," three porpoises leaped out of the water just off the starboard bow. Gleaming in the mingled lamplight, the porpoises splashed and played, to the glad cries of the singers.

Porpoises never left them from that point, not while the *Indigo Pheasant* conducted its sea-trials in the Downs off Kent in the English Channel, not while the ship continued to the Azores, and not while it sailed thence to Cape Town. Even Sally's spirits brightened as she watched the porpoises, mile after mile, pacing the ship on its journey.

At the Cape, they took on provisions, made minor repairs to the *Indigo Pheasant* and otherwise refreshed themselves in preparation for their travels into the interstitial places. The McDoons, with the Chinese delegation, spent much time at the Last Cozy House, where the Termuydens were, as always, exuberantly attentive and gracious hosts. They offered their condolences about James and carefully avoided any further conversation about him. They took special care to give Isaak the food they remembered she liked, and they laughed to see Isaak playing again with their dog Jantje in the garden. The Termuydens took unique joy in seeing Mei-Hua and Shaozu once more. Over steaming cups of well-steeped tea and trays of ever-replenished cakes (to Barnabas's endless delight), the company shared the latest intelligences. They talked of Sir John Barrow, and of Lord Amherst's embassy; they talked with Billy about the sermons he preached; they listened as Mei-Hua explained what the Chinese meant by *kaozheng*, which she translated as "research based on evidence," and by the *shu li jung yun*, or "collected essentials on numbers and their principles." The

Termuydens were most interested in learning all about Maggie, and listening to Maggie's thoughts about the upcoming journey.

On a midsummer morning at the Cape, the McDoons and the Chinese took their leave of the Termuydens. Maggie placed a thick packet of letters in the Mejouffrouw's hands, for posting back to London, the last correspondence the Cook and others would receive from the voyagers for a while. The Termuydens gave to each of their visitors small gifts, tokens to help on the next circuit of errantry.

"For you, Mijnheer Barnabas, I have something *very particularly* special, to sustain you if other stores and provisions run low," said the Mejouffrouw with a merry sparkle in her eye. "Or, as I suspect, even if you face no such shortage, . . . which I of course hope you do not!"

She handed Barnabas a large box, wrapped in a red ribbon.

"Gingerbread cookies," she said.

Sally had to prevent her uncle from opening the box then and there.

Two days out they prepared themselves for the first fulgination into the Interrugal Lands. Reglum and Dorentius—as the only two Yountians aboard—stood with the ship's captain, flanked by the McDoons, Billy Sea-Hen and Captain Shufflebottom, at the bow of the ship. They addressed the assembled ship's company: the officers, mates and crew, the Marines and Artillery Corpsmen, the sons and daughters of Asaph, and—standing at the front, flush by the starboard gunwale—the Chinese trio. Fulmars and petrels circled the ship, dabbing the waves. Several albatrosses soared further up. A pod of whales had surfaced that morning, joining the ever-present porpoises.

Reglum and Dorentius asked for the silver-plated moon to be hoisted onto the spar, and then led the entire body in the Song of the Lamp-Moon, which Reglum had translated into English. As the last echoes of "Our Moon will light our way home!" rolled over the waves, the ship's captain stood forth and led a spirited rendition of "Rule, Britannia!" Everyone sang with exceptional gusto the refrain: "Britons never will be slaves!"

Sanford noted that the Chinese (who had certainly heard "Rule, Britannia!" on innumerable occasions, formal and otherwise, during their long stay in London, and well understood its patriotic vigour) looked discomfited. The ship's captain beckoned Tang Guozhi, Shaozu and Mei-Hua to join the lead party. Tang Guozhi made a short, very diplomatic speech about amity among nations and the Emperor's delight at his friendship with King George, and so on. Then Mei-Hua, who had practised long for just such an opportunity as this, sang her own translation of the great Tang Dynasty poet Gao Shi's work, "The Ruined Terrace," concluding with:

"In silence deep, complete,
I face autumnal wastelands,
    Empty.

The wind, sad, alone
Blows one thousand miles."

Rulers in great capitals such as Peking and London (and Yount Great-Port) can decree whatever policies and strategies as might seem best to promote the aims of the nation, *raison d'état*. But such grand schemes and purposes held little reality for the thousand souls who found themselves alone together on a sliver of wood surrounded by the vast wide pitches of the great southern ocean—and who knew they faced even greater depths of uncertainty on the voyage to Yount. Mei-Hua's voice stirred every heart on the *Indigo Pheasant*.

Maggie hugged Mei-Hua demonstratively and said loudly so all could hear, "The *Indigo Pheasant* is our common home, our *only* home, as we cross into danger. But the ship will protect us, if we protect one another. We shall raise up our voices from the sea, as the Goddess gives us songs in the narrowest night-watch. 'We shall compass you about with songs of deliverance.' Does not the psalmist say so, Billy Sea-Hen?"

Billy raised both arms and shouted back, "Selah!"

"And does not the psalmist also sing: 'Awake up, my glory! Awake, psaltery and harp, for I will awaken the dawn'?"

Billy, joined by the rest of the descendants of Asaph, concurred again.

Maggie sang the "Song of Saint Ann's Translation," and every voice joined the chorus:

"And is it so, that sweet beaded breath will waft us o'er
The Sea of Storm to distant Heaven's shore?
Then bring thy ship of song and singing, that together we
May sail nigh the House of Harmony.
A steadfast friend thou wilt be to me,
Till I imbosom'd am in unity."

Buoyed and ringed by this and many similar songs—some of which Maggie had sung into the wood, flax, hemp and iron of the ship itself, some sung at every watch by those onboard—the *Indigo Pheasant* fulginated into the interstitial lands.

Whether by virtue of these songs or of the power imbued into the Great Fulginator, or because the ship was escorted by the whales and squadrons of fulmars, petrels and albatrosses (besides, of course, the dolphins), the voyage through the Interrugal Lands was more secure than any made before and took a route mostly unknown to those experienced in the trip between Karket-soom and Sabo-soom. The horghoids and jarraries, the cychriodes and ruteles-worms, and all the other loping, gnashing creatures on the rocks and skerries withheld their menace; some aboard the *Indigo Pheasant* said that the monsters were even seen to bow their heads as the ship sailed past. The carkodrillos and asterions and all other broods of swarming, hunting fishes stayed their attack, retreating instead into briny grottoes.

Once only was the ship threatened, and even then it slipped by unscathed. On the eighth day, sudden staunch winds swept the *Indigo Pheasant* in close to a low, marshy shore. Giant sedges pulled at the hull, mud sucked at the keel. The Fulginator could help little in such a pass; traditional seafaring skills alone would save the ship. Gradually, with no small amount of sweat and worry, they managed to tack away, beating against the wind blowing from the salt-side.

As they edged away, they put to flight three enormous herons that had been wading after fish in the shallow waters. While struggling to keep the ship from running a-strand, no one had paid the birds much heed—and distances being deceiving, no one had grasped how large these birds were. Now everyone stared in awe as the three marsh-hunters, wings flapping with a stately thunder, flew past in loose formation. The herons flew—as is their wont—with necks curled back, compressed against their bodies, with the sparse black feathers of their crests bristling down their backs. (Sally thought they looked rather like Sanford might if he were striding down Mincing Lane into a stiff breeze). They were a hazel-green above, with rufous streakings below, their buff-coloured legs trailing far behind them, occasionally shaving the surface of the water. As the herons neared, and were no longer made small by the vast expanse of the empty shoreline, the humans comprehended the bulk of these birds. What most amazed the onlookers were the eyes of the herons—a bright lemon-yellow, each eye the size of a human head—and especially the bills. Each heron had a bill the size of a man. Calculating what damage such a bird might do to the ship, contemplating the fate of anyone plucked off the deck by a body-length bill, the Marines readied their muskets and the gunners took positions at the cannons.

Amazement turned to alarm when the water beneath the herons geysered: a crocodile-whale four times the size of any of the herons shot straight up. With a dishevelled row of piercingly sharp teeth, it seized one of the birds, and fell back thrashing into the sea with its prey. The ripple created rocked the *Indigo Pheasant*. The other two herons, squawking so loudly it hurt human ears and caused the silver moon to rattle against the spar, changed course and flew directly over the ship, just barely clearing the top-sail and rigging.

The sea continued to boil for some time at the place where the monster whale had erupted. The Marines and gunners trained all weapons on that spot. Everyone watched anxiously. Everyone prayed for a quicker change in the wind. The sailors aloft called down that they could see movement in the water, like a shadow that matched the ship in size but had a mind of its own, moving now closer, now farther away.

The crocodile-whale breached one hundred yards to port. It looked like a low-slung island, with eyes.

"Well," said Billy, tying the blue scarf more tightly around his neck, and picking up his long-barreled rifle. "Muck and mire to one side, and a scalavote with too many teeth on the other! I for one don't fancy either choice. Let's see if this old dumbledore can sting the beast in one of its eyes."

As Billy took aim, Maggie walked up and put a hand on the muzzle to lower it.

"Leave be, Billy," she said. "This one won't hurt us. She—it's a she, incidentally—is scared too, scared and yet curious. After all, we appeared in her hunting grounds, not the other way 'round."

Billy bowed his hand and lowered his rifle.

"This creature is very, very distant kin to the whales who accompany us," continued Maggie. "They are attempting to soothe her, reassure her. And so will we. Listen."

The Great Fulginator struck up a different note, a lilting, merry air. Maggie had instructed Dorentius to play "The Prior's Toccata" on one of the keyboards (which were otherwise used as devices to transmit equations into the Fulginator's central analytical engine)—a song ascribed to Saint Bavo but known much more widely in the version edited by C.P.E. Bach.

Billy whistled, shook his head and said, "A tea-tune for a trilly-bite! Well, that's fox-feet on a turkey for sure!"

"She's unlovely to look upon, this giant *agu iyi*," laughed Maggie in agreement. "But she is innocent, Billy, innocent of the malice and intention that characterizes our true enemies. She's a lethal savage, without question, but pure, who acts only as she was made. We can avoid a quarrel with her, and so we shall."

As the *Indigo Pheasant* slowly distanced itself from the quaggy shore and from the leviathan, led by the dolphins and followed by the whales, Reglum took one last look through a telescope at the crocodile-whale.

"Magnificent," he sighed. He had a new species for the Yountian bestiary.

On the fourteenth day, Reglum and everyone else received an even greater shock: they found living people in the Interrugal Lands. They had passed The Cackling Isle (the source of which noise was unknown, and which the *Indigo Pheasant* had no time or brief to discover) and The Dull-Fires (a shingle ever licked by low flames, like a plate of brandy-doused fruit when it is set alight). The Fulginator had sent them into a region of nighs and netherings unknown to any Yountian map, with violent and capricious winds. To starboard they spied a large, hump-backed island, thickly forested except for a thin swath of flower-pricked meadow running abruptly to the beach.

As the ship approached the island, four men burst from the forest and raced across the meadow to the beach, shouting, waving their arms. Their eyes were wide, their beards dendritic, their clothes ill-used. They looked as if they might be shipwrecked mariners from Socotra or Muscat.

Reglum could not believe what he saw through his telescope. He called for the *Indigo Pheasant* to slow, turn about, drop anchor. In the nearly two thousand years since the Yountians had begun their venturing into the Interrugal Lands, in all their several thousands of interstitial voyages, the Yountian tough-ships had never once found another sapient being alive in the places-in-between. A few washed-up corpses, including those of the storkmen with elongated fingers and three nostrils. The deserted towns on Supply Island, empty evidence of other people long gone. Other people! Alive in the Interrugal Lands!

"We must save these poor wretches!" Reglum cried.

All onboard agreed fervently, watching the four men jumping up and down, arms pinwheeling. They hastily formed a landing party and began to lower two boats off the side.

But before the boats hit the water, the wind frowned and the air furrowed. The island was lost suddenly to their view.

"I don't understand, I don't understand," said Dorentius, speaking in the Fulgination Room a few minutes later to Reglum, Captain Shufflebottom, Sally and Maggie. "One moment we are steadily plotted, the next and without warning of any kind we are unfixed."

"The chiasmic equations notwithstanding?" asked Maggie. "The cross-function of the graticules still robust? Our anastomotic derivations on course?"

"Abaxile strings in order?" asked Sally. "Brachistochrones coordinated?"

Dorentius confirmed that all appeared to be in order and yet it was not. For a full day, the *Indigo Pheasant* attempted to return to the island of the stranded mariners. Every time Dorentius, Maggie and Sally re-formulated the coordinates for the island, some force or will other than their own shunted the ship aside. The closer they got to the place where the island should be, the fiercer the wind became, casting gustules of acrid fumes at the ship. They sailed past The Dull-Fire twice more, and heard again the sounds emanating from The Cackling Isle. They were sailing in circles around a void, a hole in the map.

On the morning of the second day after their brief encounter, Maggie held conference in the ship-captain's cabin.

"As my mother would say: '*Chi jibidolu anyi n'uzo*,' which means something like 'Our way has become clouded,'"said Maggie. "Someone or something does not wish us to reach and rescue those poor men. The Owl perhaps, though four men seem few compared to the world he seeks to withhold from us. Maybe Agwu is intervening, balancing on the ball of fortune, disorienting us for reasons we cannot know. Or maybe the Goddess has a hand in this, protecting us but not allowing us to over-reach ourselves."

"But those men implored us, their faces, oh Goddess, their faces—we cannot leave them alone to their fate . . ." said Reglum.

"No doubt," said Maggie. "Yet we are barred. We cannot

fulginate our way back to that island. It is not in our power. Some wall there is, some barrier impervious to the will of our song."

"Those poor devils," said Barnabas.

"'*Kaskas selwish pishpaweem*,'" murmured Sally, choking back tears as she gripped Isaak to her breast. "'"Dear Mother, protect and guide us."'

"We must press on; we have no choice," said Maggie. "My soul breaks to say this, but we must press on."

They sang "The Lamentation of Saint Gerontius" and "The Blessing of the Wayfarer," then continued heavy-hearted on their voyage. The faces of the men on the hump-backed island haunted forever the minds of those who had sailed on the *Indigo Pheasant*. Maggie cried to herself many nights on the rest of the journey. Later, she would say that the decision to end the search and sail on, without having rescued the men marooned, was one of the most terrible she had been forced to make in her life.

Who the men on the beach were, and what became of them, figures into no tale of this Earth.

On the twenty-third day of fulgination, having sailed past "reefs of dragon-horn, on roads with neither hithe nor haven," the *Indigo Pheasant* came into a fog bank of greater than usual proportions. The ship slowed its speed. Dorentius confirmed that the Fulginator had set this course and that his calculations were correct—they would just have to endure the dimness and muffled sight.

As night fell, fostering a darkness oily and nearly opaque, the forward watch spotted at a distance a bobbing light, pale emerald in colour. As the *Indigo Pheasant* cruised nearer, the first light was joined by a second, somewhat larger and higher up. Reglum, Maggie, Captain Shufflebottom and others peered through telescopes. What they saw was a wrought iron lamp-post of ordinary height, from which depended the first light, a lamp swaying in the misty breeze. It illuminated in a pallid green wash the outlines of a jetty protruding from a sloping, rocky shore into an inlet salivary with foam. A wherry (but lacking oars as many noted) bumped steadily against the jetty, attached with rope to a ring. At the edge of the light, as it darkened into tobacco-brown and varieties of dark grey, observers discerned the single mast of a sunken ship, a sloop or ketch, thrusting above the water off the jetty. Lifting their gaze, they saw a set of steep, winding stairs hewn into the rock, leading to a massive house—seen barely in the gloom, and then only because of the second, pale green light glowing from one long slit of a window in the attic.

Reglum said, "Our second encounter with what appears to be humanity, or at least intelligent life, in less than ten days! Remarkable! We travel the moonless tracks for nearly two millennia and never meet anyone else we can converse with, and now on a single voyage, in the span of a few days, we stumble upon others twice."

Captain Shufflebottom (for once not wearing his smoked-glass spectacles) shook his head, "Yet I do not like the feel of this place. Unwholesome, I call it, and that would be putting things charitably."

Maggie nodded her head, and said, "The lamps might be lit as a welcome or set as a beacon for help, yet where then are the people? . . . Oh look!"

A shadow crossed the attic window, causing the glow of pale emerald to flicker.

"Someone is there, right enough," said Captain Shufflebottom. "Reminds me of stories told in the office to which I belong. About the Strange High House in the Mist, for one, and the Lean High House of the Gnoles for another, though perhaps those are the same thing—our knowledge thereof is, you will appreciate, of necessity limited."

Reglum nodded, sadly, and said, "Ah, we have heard such tales as well, or variants of them. The House of the Mewlips. Lures for the unwary far beyond the fields we know. I guess we would not like the conversation we would have with whomever inhabits that house. Miss Maggie, let us quietly away, before something traps us here. We must not tarry. Look, our whales hang back and the dolphins are urging us to retreat, see them leaping?"

Slowly the *Indigo Pheasant* veered away. Maggie and the others with telescopes saw the figure in the attic cross the window several more times, whether it was someone pacing or someone dragging something along the floor or aught else, no one onboard wished to investigate.

The ship continued on its anfractuous journey, "winding through neathes, nighs and flows, into ever-eve across the straits of mourning." The Great Fulginator reckoned steadily and true, producing a densely figured music that held at bay the despair bred by the interrugal lands, and that pierced the folds and margins of xanthrophicius seas. All hearts on board were tuned intimately to the Fulginator's music. The whales and dolphins sang along with it, the birds that surrounded the ship beat their wings in time to it, the clock on the mast ticked and tocked to it.

Charicules, who perched most of each day in the Fulgination Room, created a running melody matching that of the Great Fulginator. Dorentius was convinced that the Fulginator had begun to respond to the saulary's singing, quite independent of any human intervention. Maggie was not wholly convinced, but neither did she dispute the claim.

As the sun set on the thirty-first day, the *Indigo Pheasant* arrived at Sanctuary, on the shoulder of Yount. Those on shore perceived the ship far out to sea, as a gliding palace of light chasing the shadows before it, a choir boat the size of a billowing mountain, pouring out song upon the waters, song that splashed higher than the surf breaking on rocks. Singing "The Thanksgiving Carol" and "The Arrival Song" in several languages, a great multitude crowded the deep-water harbour at Sanctuary to greet the *Indigo Pheasant*—and in the very forefront stood Jambres, the Cretched Man.

"Be most welcome, Lucid Aleph, Primal Music, shadow-stripped archetype of book and song," said Jambres to Maggie and the others as they descended the gangplank from the *Indigo Pheasant*. The choir boat was tied up along side the *Seek-by-Night*, whose masts were adorned with lamps to honour the far-travellers.

The crew and passengers of the *Indigo Pheasant* spent a month at Sanctuary, recovering from the journey and planning the final leg of the expedition. Many were the meetings and reunions, making of the respite a joyous time (if tempered by knowledge of what must come next). Tommy Two-Fingers had baggins on the beach with Billy Sea-Hen, sometimes joined by Afsana and Nexius Dexius, sometimes by Reglum Bammary or Captain Shufflebottom—veterans swapping stories of desperate affrays and brave assaults under different suns. Maggie and Sally spent many hours with Afsana, often including Mei-Hua in the discussions and also the little Malchen (no longer so very little).

Sally and Tom talked long, in the low, short-hand voices of very close siblings. Sally sobbed often, but never in sight of others, unless it was Uncle Barnabas or Sanford.

Queen Zinnamoussea and the chamberlain were honoured guests. There was much talk of the continuing war against the Ornish.

Isaak explored every inch of Sanctuary. She batted at the nose of the knuckle-dog before making tentative friends with the beast. And she enjoyed dining in the company of the Queen.

Charicules played with the parrots and finches in the trees, and sang with the conures and lorikeets in the hedges. He formed a fast attachment with Malchen—the two could be found day and night singing to one another in a language of their own devising.

"Buttons and beeswax," said Barnabas on dozens of occasions. He cried more than once (many times, in fact), and paraded around in the finest vests his thinner purse could afford.

Afsana said to Maggie (the two were friendly from the start) that she thought she had seen Sanford shed a tear as well.

"He's a peculiar old spike, an honest razor," said Afsana. "Whose conscience is so keen it cuts itself."

"That he is; he reminds me of a pheasant, in truth, of the *Indigo Pheasant* itself," agreed Maggie. "'He is come unto the shrine of the blessed, shriven to his meats and mindings.' He will never fail us."

Maggie spent more time with Jambres than with anyone else while on Sanctuary. They talked long about the Owl and the making of the Great Song to liberate Yount. He told her all that he knew of the judgment against Yount and the mandates of an idly irate heaven, a lengthy backward-leaping historiography steeped in woe.

"That you have invaded the Owl's own house, even one of his lesser redoubts, astounds me," Jambres shook his head. "'His are the habitats of misery, abode of sorrows deep-ditched, inhabited by undergraduated creatures whose breath goeth outwards into the void.'"

"He was even more astounded than you," said Maggie, with a grim smile quickly fading. "Yet I could not vanquish him, only put him off a little while, perhaps."

"Such as Strix are not to be vanquished," said Jambres quietly, his gaze fixed on the sea-horizon. "He is immortal, beyond our ability to harm."

"But we can surely defeat him, thwart his will," said Maggie, with such conviction that Jambres turned to look fully upon her.

"I have spoken with the Mother herself," added Maggie. "I respect the immortal order of the universe . . . but I do not fear it, nor will I bow my head to it or any of its less-just laws."

"Was it not Symphorien," said Jambres. "Or maybe Longinus (my mind has too many drawers for rapid retrieval!), who asserted 'to achieve the sublime, we must aspire to a great and vigourous concept, founded upon the rock of never-ending passion'? Such is this mad folly you propose, and now we are come to its final throw."

As they spoke together, day after day, they noticed changes in the Cretched Man's apparel and skin, so subtle that at first they ignored or denied them. Gradually, however, they realized that the sutures of his coat and leggings were beginning to pucker, sag and open. His white skin began to peel in wispy strips, floating up from his body like gossamer caught in the rays of the sun.

"After the embates and blows of a raw fortune, I hesitate to hope," whispered Jambres, his usually distant eyes focused on

Maggie's face, which was equally intent. "My imagination runs me uncommon riot, all my long-locked desires are too easily roused free."

Maggie reached out her hand, stroked his face. He shut his eyes. Neither spoke.

In the final weeks, Maggie rehearsed the Great Song with the choir many times on board the *Indigo Pheasant*, over and over again on the wharves of the little harbour and along the beaches.

"The Seven Singers shall lead us, and the Sons and Daughters of Asaph shall be the first followers," she said. "But the verse is in all of us, all human beings across all of time and wherever we might find ourselves—it is our birthright. In our battle for self-mastery, we here are representatives only of the entire family, not the entire clan or clade itself. Remember that, oh choristers brave!"

In the final weeks, Maggie checked and re-checked the calculations for the Great Fulginator, working closely with Dorentius, Jambres, Sally, Afsana and Mei-Hua. They tested the steam engine and all the connecting, propulsive and relaying machinery.

"Well, Charicules, what do you think?" asked Dorentius, as they concluded their last preparations.

Charicules trained a bright eye on Dorentius and whistled. Even the sceptical Maggie laughed.

That evening Maggie said over a farewell feast on the beach, "We sail tomorrow morning to Yount to confront the Owl. Jambres and a hand-picked crew will accompany us on the *Seek-by-Night*. Otherwise—and besides the beloved whales and dolphins, and some of our friends among the birds—we are quite alone on this endeavour."

Everyone cheered Jambres and the crew of the *Seek-by-Night*.

"And Isaak! We have the cat-warrior on our side!" yelled Tom.

Isaak walked the length of the head-table, her golden coat glowing in the candlelight for the entire gathering to admire.

"The *tess muddry*, the *tess muddry*," chanted the Yountians, and everyone picked up the cry.

"Well cousin," shouted Barnabas, as the chanting subsided. "What's the plan? We're just going to sail right at 'em, is that it?"

"Yes, cousin," said Maggie. "We must be eagles to an owl. We will go right at him!"

More cheers.

"We can handle 'im!" yelled Barnabas, waving an invisible sword in one hand and a bottle of Burgundy in the other (a long-ago gift from the lawyer Sedgewick, brought all the way from Mincing Lane and saved for just such an occasion).

"Remember the *Lanner*!" yelled the many Yountians—most of them refugees from Ornish slave mines and plantations who had escaped to the Cretched Man's Sanctuary.

"For King and Country, for Britons shall never ever be slaves!" yelled many of the travellers from London.

Mei-Hua, Shaozu and Tang Guozhi sang a song from China. Malchen sang a hymn from Germany, Afsana a prayer from Gujarat. Songs from Tamil-land and Mali, from Ireland and Igbo-land, from Yoruba-land and Conakry followed in rapid succession, accompanied by energetic drumming, clapping and the stamping of feet from all quarters.

They were ready.

The following day the *Indigo Pheasant*, together with the *Seek-by-Night* and three-score whales and dolphins, with dozens of petrels dancing along the sea before them and dozens of fulmars and albatrosses soaring the air above them, sailed through the haze and catch-moans that walled Yount.

They arrived in Yountish waters. The waves were calm in an open sea, under a pale-grey noontime sky.

. . . A sky in which, as if a giant had suddenly opened an enormous casement window, a rent appeared, of sharply defined night scattered with tiny bright stars and centred by a large, bulbous moon.

Looking up into the sky, as the albatrosses wheeled away from the slit in the heavens, Maggie and everyone else on the two choir boats could see framed there a dessicated landscape under the impossibly distant moonlight. Row upon row of pillars marched across the undulating bone-plains. Atop each pillar perched a frog or donkey or woodpecker or other creature the size of a house, each winged, each possessing eyes alive with ancient intelligence and unblinking vigilance.

An owl lifted itself off a pillar and flew towards the gap in the sky. It flew through the gap and into Yount, two long pennant tails rippling behind it. One by one and then by twos, threes and fours, others rose off their pillars and flapped their way behind Strix.

Strix hovered just off the bow of the *Indigo Pheasant*. His fellows drifted down in serpentine rows, through defiles unseen in the taut air, braking with their membranous wings, swerving, circling. One of them blurred as it swooped down, became a beautiful woman with jet-black hair swirling in the oceanic breeze. Dressed in an impeccable green gown, the creature known in England as the Widow Goethals and also as Mrs. Hamilton alighted gracefully on the bowsprit of the *Seek-by-Night*.

"Hooo, HOOOOOOM," spoke the Owl, eyes reflecting both Yount's pale sun and the faint gleam of the moon in the marcher-lands outside. "If I commanded you to turn aside now in this very final instance from your arrogant and foolish plan, would you? Nay, you would not—you are committed recklessly to wickedness, the consequences of which you are too small to understand."

No one on either ship said anything. Isaak hissed at the Owl.

"Silence, cat!" said Strix. "Your owners indulge your vanity."

Sally started forward, stood right behind Isaak.

"Oh HOH!" laughed the Owl, his eyes glittering, his bill snapping. "You should know better, *ma petite femme brisée, ébranlée*. You are bereft of authority in this matter. You lost that, well, with James Kidlington, did you not?"

Sally flinched. Barnabas and Sanford stepped to her side.

From the *Seek-by-Night*, Jambres called out a challenge.

"SSSsssssss," hissed the Owl. "You, traitor, have even less authority here. Your mutiny astonishes me only a little less than your measureless impudence in showing yourself to me now.

You will receive no mercy in the Houses of Redemption, that is the only promise I will make to you!"

Jambres said nothing further but he did not alter his stance or drop the level of his gaze.

The green-gowned half-angel on the bowsprit of the *Seek-by-Night* turned and said something to Strix in a language so old that the stars themselves were new when it was first uttered. The Owl flew a figure-of-eight and then laughed so the indigo sails dimpled.

"Indeed," he said to Jambres, in a voice that reached into the souls of all present. "Do you truly believe that the bright, angelic circle will part for you, as a result of your creeping efforts to reconcile yourself with the Redeemer? Oh, tenderest of thy kind, 'last seduced and least deformed,' as your poet has it! Falsely lustrous you have been in all eyes, Jambres. Nay, you will not be granted annihilation, your penance shall be without end and no action of yours can dispel it."

Billy Sea-Hen and Tommy Two-Finger moved forward to flank Jambres. The Widow Goethals brandished her conjure-hands, Astarte summoning the words of permanent exile.

Jambres spread wide his arms and began to sing, a wordless chant, wavering and not entirely in any key. Billy and Tom did their best to join in.

The Widow sang green ribbons of sorcery to bind the Cretched Man. Jambres struggled but withstood the enchantment.

He called out . . . and Maggie answered with a song of her own.

The two sides vied for a long minute, two, three.

Charicules flew at the witch on the *Seek-by-Night*'s bowsprit, circled her with scherzi that delighted the ear as they battled the grinding will to imprison.

Jambres gave a mighty yell. His seething red coat popped open, likewise his trousers, sloughing off him in bloody strips, falling in a pile around his feet onto the deck. Shouting in anguish and hope and disbelief intermingled, Jambres felt his skin pulling off his body.

Maggie sang and Jambres sang, repelling the whorled melody

of the Owl and of the Widow Goethals . . . and reversing an edict pronounced millennia ago in Egypt, when Jambres and his brother were wizards in the court of the Pharaoh, wizards who chose to combat Moses and Aaron.

The white skin of Jambres, the Cretched Man, peeled off in blood-tinged traceries, long thin translucent strips that floated into the rigging and out to sea.

He wept, a naked man, brown-skinned, his hair tight-curly, his eyes their original brown. Jambres was the Cretched Man no longer. He shook and his knees almost buckled, but he regained his strength. Fire was in his eye. Billy took off the blue scarf Cook had knit him, and then his own shirt from his back, and gently laid them around Jambres's shoulders. Tom fetched a coat to cover the rest of Jambres's nakedness.

Maggie shouted, "Behold! The Owl's command has miscarried! Jambres has returned to himself, against all hope—a sea-wearied yet proudful spirit has won against a cold heart's bitter scoring! Selah: he has irrigated the salt-acres with his blood. The springs of the Goddess run in him, our Jambres!"

All the humans roared and cheered.

The Owl and his confederates were furious, yet only briefly nonplussed. Strix boomed louder than the human cheering. With malicious irony, he sang a subtly twisted version of "The Song of Faustus":

"Surely your instruments mock me:
With cylinders, wheels, cogs, and teeth
You push upon the door,
Deftly you wield a key ingeniously wrought.
Yet still no lock will yield
Its mysteries fraught,
No screws or levers will suffice
To open the portal, not above, not beneath."

The Owl's Wild Hunt swarmed tightly around the two ships, singing arias of incarceration, their wings beating a rhythm of submission, of retreat, of denial. Those onboard could barely stand, let alone sing.

Again Maggie shouted from the bow of the *Indigo Pheasant*.

"Strix, wormlet!" she yelled. "We are not daunted, we who have survived the gaunt dwellings between, who have within us the mightiest melody heard since God and Goddess composed the very first notes!"

The half-fallen legions pressed down upon the choir boats, wings like whips and hatchets, eyes like acidulous lamps.

Maggie yelled, "Strix! Hoary hollow worm you are! By our song shall you be thrust through with a dart, and we shall have the government thereof. Goddess has given me leave to tell you that 'yet once more I shake not the Earth only but also Heaven.' Beware!"

The circling demi-angels slowed slightly, listening despite themselves, their barbed and brazen tongues slowed.

"You—who once knew seraphic bliss, who long ago half-turned away—you are here congregated for the assassination of hope and the rape of valour," said Maggie, in a voice that compelled human, animal and angel alike to listen. "*Chi di*, there is yet time for you too! The City of God and Goddess has here and now, on the cope of these waters and the rim of this air, under your creaturely shadows and also ours, conurbated anew."

The winged hordes listened, as they had not listened to a human more than a half-dozen times before in the entire history of the mortal species. They muted their voices, and made their flight more random.

"By Heaven amerced, thus yourselves paying a heavy penalty," said Maggie. "But perhaps one day even such as you may be called home, your melancholy exclusion ended."

The half-angelic chorus fell silent. Around the two ships, the motley hundreds flew on their cold wings, making a sound of rasping wind but otherwise giving no voice, lost each in antediluvian yearning and a secret hope so long submerged the Watchers could scarce give it a proper name. One by one they looked to Strix.

Strix, longest innocent of mercy and most adamant in his cruelty (even when he most injured himself), hoomed and half-sang, "Onward! Do your duty! This one, this little songbird, has no special insight, let alone authority! She paints a vision of freedom and return she has no right to make, and cannot call into reality. Attack, attack!"

Hardened as they were to the dictates of their own fate, most familiar with the portolans of grief and accustomed to the eyeless towers of penitence extracted, the Owl's army resumed its assault on the choir boats.

"Dorentius!" yelled Maggie. "Now, Dorentius! The Fulginator, Dorentius!"

Dorentius manipulated levers, knobs and rods. The Great Fulginator hoomed in its turn, a series of bass notes that rolled through the sea. The whales echoed it back. The Great Fulginator, amplified by the energy produced by the steam engine, began the Great Song.

"Billy, Billy Sea-Hen!" yelled Maggie. "Let the Sons and Daughters of Asaph sing!"

One hundred and twenty-eight men and women, each wearing an indigo-coloured arm-band, neck kerchief or head-scarf, burst into practised song. They sang the opening recital of the oratorio.

"Mei-Hua!" yelled Maggie. "Afsana! Sally! Malchen!"

The four women sang as one, the first aria.

So the battle was fully engaged. As Milton wrote elsewhere, "such music before was never made."

The music surged backwards and forwards, inwards and outwards, roundwards and pointwards. The cantata of opening and emancipation held sway for a while, until the Owl rallied a counter-song, a strident tone of closure and locking. So it went, with ripples of theme and counter-theme spreading across Yount and into the Interrugal Lands and other places besides.

Strix flew down until his long tail brushed the bow of the *Indigo Pheasant*. He glared at Maggie, just below him. He exerted all his power. His voice was a gale that buffeted the ships,

THE INDIGO PHEASANT *Volume Two of Longing for Yount*

driving them back almost into the interstitial crevices. The Widow Goethals and all the other warden-spirits hail-sang the weight of lead and copper, the stillness of antimony and the chill of iron onto the ships, beating down those onboard, smothering the human voice.

But Maggie stood as others faltered and fell to their haunches, some weeping, some unable to do more than moan. Charicules flew to her shoulder. Isaak stood between Maggie's legs, all four paws gripping the deck.

Maggie sang then the main theme from "Saint Macrina's Dream." Mei-Hua, Afsana, Malchen and Sally harmonized.

Maggie sang to the theophanous rhythm of the Great Fulginator. Charicules bent and worried the line of that rhythm. (The Fulginator strained, but its casings of china clay withstood the stress, and the blood of James Kidlington lubricated the threads of the vast machine.) Maggie hit the notes designed to open the door, notes founded on the universal calculus of liberation and the geometry of the spirit.

She sang.

She sang forth.

Invected, her notes bore inwards.

Reflected, her notes flew outwards.

With her song, she re-set a part of the universe.

Suddenly, the gilt-edged clock on the mast of the *Indigo Pheasant* moved ahead by seven minutes.

--

--

At that moment, the same thing occurred on clocks everywhere.

Sir John Barrow peered up from his meeting as the ornate clock in the conference room at the East India House on Leadenhall Street chimed out of sequence . . . and leaped ahead seven minutes.

--

--

Two sharp-faced men—"Mr. I." and "Mr. Z."—in an unnamed office at Admiralty looked up (most unusually, they were startled) when the ormulu clock flanked by ebony hippocamps did the same.

--

--

Cook and her niece jumped when the clock in the partners' room in the house on Mincing Lane gonged out of normal reckoning. "Most unnatural that is," said Cook, eying the clock with great suspicion. "Something's amiss or I have grown wings for ears."

--

--

The Termuydens in the Last Cozy House had perhaps some inkling of the cause of their many clocks simultaneously ringing and displaying a time that made no sense.

--

--

The lawyer Sedgewick was bringing tea to his wife in their house near Pineapple Court when he heard the clock go off irregularly. He puzzled over that and was not relieved to learn from many others of their identical experience. *"Fallaces sunt rerum,"* he said to himself. "The appearances of things are deceptive."

--

--

All over London the rooks fled their bell-towers as the clocks rang at the wrong time. Everyone in the streets looked at the clocks with wonder. Many shouted that the bells presaged the end-time. Panic whispered in ears, anxiety beat a drum in scared bellies. Yet Londoners are nothing if not resilient and they soon resumed their normal rounds. After all, no one had been hurt, and no commercial transactions had been voided as a result, so most people ultimately thought of it as nothing more than a freak episode like sleet falling in July or tulips blooming in December. A few said they were certain the giants on the Guildhall clock had been the cause of all the strangeness, but—as the giants were manifestly still at their stations by the clock—little more could be said on that score.

In one house in London—a wry, half-seen pile just off Hoxton Square, empty of people but full of presence—a long-case clock (with macabre vignettes on its face and sententious proclamations written around its dial) reverberated for nearly an hour and the hands twitched and bucked repeatedly before settling on the new normal time.

--

--

In the House of Design, Saint Macrina waved her hammer and chisel in the air and shouted when the four brass-figured clocks, each one atop a column, each column at one point of the compass, moved ahead together.

--

--

The clock on the column above the garden of the Mother answered to the change more serenely, making a sound like a flute as it advanced the seven minutes. Goddess put down her knife and fork (she was in the pavilion, enjoying a dish of hara masala), laughed heartily and long, and slapped her hands on the table so the cutlery jumped.

"Little daughter has done it," said Goddess. "And found my husband too, I do believe! Well done, little eagle!"

--

--

(Incredibly far away, the notes Maggie sang chimed from a pocket-watch carried by God, waking him from his self-imposed amnesia. His companions, fellow musicians in a Harlem jazz-loft in 1928, forgave him for the interruption during their jam session. "That's a cool riff," said one. "What do you call it, Lennox?" "Man, I don't know," said God, holding up his pocket-watch. "But I am just dying to find out.")

In the seven minutes no longer recorded on the clocks of Yount and Earth (and who knows where else besides?), Maggie's song changed the world. The Great Fulginator opened the gate, freeing Yount from its abandonment in the interstitial regions. With the delicacy of an oystercatcher prising forth the most valuable pearl in the world and the diligence of a master-chef removing a souffle from the oven, the Great Song as enhanced by the Great Fulginator gently transported Yount . . . back to Earth, from where it had been ripped millennia earlier.

The Owl bellowed his rage in vain. He and his troops dwindled. The Great Song shoved Strix and the other Watchers back through the window sliced in the sky, sent them to ponder their defeat while gnawing bones and viscera atop their timeless pillars.

Seven minutes of blinding light passed, shot through with shafts of utter darkness. There was no sound whatsoever. Music needs silence to exist: point and counterpoint, upbeat and downbeat, inhale and exhale. The Great Song propelled the *Indigo Pheasant* and the *Seek-by-Night* through a corridor shrouded in the Ancient Silence that preceded the First Fugue, with the music as their conveyance and their protection. They carried behind them the entire sub-world of Yount, all its several countries, its archipelagos, its surrounding seas, all its people and buildings, all its flora and fauna, encased in the bubble of its life-giving atmosphere.

Seven minutes after Maggie sang the notes of freedom, Yount slid with barely a wave or surge onto the surface of the Indian Ocean. Hardly a cup fell from a cupboard, scarcely a window was cracked or tile broken, so soft was the arrival of Yount. As if it had never been gone, displacing nothing, Yount re-rooted itself to the sea floor. Yount had returned to its original position, where it sits today: a series of islands stretching from just south of Sri Lanka west towards the Maldives, southwest to the Chagos chain, northeast towards the Andaman and Nicobar Islands, and eastwards almost to the coast of Sumatra.

As sound returned (like a mild curtain of rain, and undergirding all a distant hum, like bees plying a meadow), all those on the *Indigo Pheasant* and the *Seek-by-Night* laughed and cried, sang and prayed. They bathed in the warm sunlight washing the choir boats rolling on the swells of a calm Indian Ocean. They dove into the sea to swim with the dolphins. They kissed and made love. They drank and they ate. For that day and night, Heaven held court in the Indian Ocean.

Exhausted, Maggie had to hold on to Jambres through most of the celebration.

The other McDoons similarly said little, spent from their exertions as they were. They sat together, smiling in disbelief and from sheer joy.

Only Barnabas, revived somewhat by a glass of Burgundy and the last of the Mejouffrouw's gingerbread cookies, could muster more than a sentence or two.

"Beans and bacon, she sang the Owl right out of the sky, she did! Had right at 'im, just like Rodney with the French. Better than! And so did my daughter—if only I could know her better—the bold Afsana! With Tom, who has lost his fingers but found all the courage in the world (he had better, haha, if he is going to keep pace with Afsana!). And our poor, sweet, shattered Sally. I grieve so for her in the middle of all this festivity. Really, what shall we do there, Sanford?"

Sanford put a hand on Barnabas's shoulder and said only, "As we have ever done, old friend, we will love her until we die. More we cannot do."

Barnabas paused a very long time before saying, "You are right, of course. Cook will help us there."

A little later, after another glass of the Burgundy, Barnabas said, "So here we are: Yount collected and brought home. A fairy tale, only more so, because it is real and we are in it. D'you hear, Sanford old friend? We helped make some history. Invented— well, *she* did—a machine that roped a world. Remarkable! If my uncle could just see us now. No, not him, brrrr, *Quatsch*! But my mother, the Belladonna born Brownlee! This is her kind of story entirely. She'd be proud of us all!"

Sanford stirred himself and said, "And your aunt Eusebianna born Brownlee. Mustn't forget her. She would be most proud of all, to see what her granddaughter Maggie Collins did."

The low, gentle sound of humming soothed their ears.

"Yes, too right," agreed Barnabas, sipping his wine on the uproll of the ship.

"Nothing will ever be the same now, not for us and most certainly not for Maggie," said Sanford, undertones of melancholy belying the briskness of his words. "King Solomon spoke 3,000 proverbs and had 1,005 songs, but Maggie has more. No, nothing stays the same for her."

Barnabas finished his wine and, feeling as if his happiness would explode his rose-and-slate calicosh vest, he flung his wine-glass into the sea.

"Ah hah, now the sea really *is* wine-dark!" he chortled.

Barnabas surveyed the McDoons gathered around him. He smiled, hummed a scrap of the Great Song that echoed in his mind, and then said loudly, "Buttons and beeswax! Maggie, you did it! You brought Yount home!"

Maggie smiled and said, "No, cousin, *we all* brought Yount home, not I alone."

Barnabas slashed an imaginary cutlass through the air, bowed slightly, and said, "Fairly spoken, dear cousin, though you led the effort! And now, if I may speak for everyone: home for us as well! I yearn at last for nothing more than to sit by the fire drinking a glass of my best Cahors, and to muck about growing smilax root in the garden . . . at home on Mincing Lane!"

As every schoolboy and schoolgirl knows, Barnabas did not entirely get his wish. The McDoons had become—whether they would or not—very public figures. Sanford was right: nothing was ever the same for them, least of all for Maggie.

Inevitably the sudden and unlooked-for return of Yount changed global history. In the nearly two centuries since the Return, every sphere of human inquiry and every plane of human activity have been radically altered. Most profoundly, we now understand that we are not alone in the universe: others—some like us, some not—are out there.

Sir John Barrow, almost immediately upon the *Indigo Pheasant*'s return to London, began sending British exploratory expeditions into the Interrugal Lands. Among the most famous of "Barrow's Boys" was Captain Shufflebottom, who led the ill-fated voyage in search of fabled, sunken R'lyeh. Shufflebottom's final message, sent by ansible-telegraph from a coordinate near the Cackling Isle in 1831, has been parsed endlessly since its sending: we remain baffled by its meaning, just as the existence (let alone the location) of haunted R'lyeh continues to elude us.

Many consider the discovery of the Interrugal Lands and the history of Yount (its Loss & Return, as we now style it) to be unalloyed positives for humankind—in some quarters, what we have learned is deemed a divine revelation. Others are much more sceptical; some reject, deny, refute, attack. A cost-benefit analysis of the Return must be impossible, but that has not stopped philosophers, politicians, economists, theologians and thinkers of every sort and persuasion from making the attempt. How does one draw up a meaningful balance sheet, using counter-factuals and speculative hypotheses as part of the evidence? Wars have been fought as a result that might not otherwise have been fought, but most likely wars never happened that would otherwise have been fought. The Return saved many millions of lives when it was discovered, in the mid-nineteenth century, that the Yountians were immune from cholera (that terrible pandemic scourge of the 1800s), which led subsequently to the hugely successful vaccine based upon various Yountian antigens. On the other hand, the Yountian weasel-rat as an invasive species has caused great damage to rice crops across southern Asia, and remains a durable, if mostly contained, pest. And so on and so forth.

More directly, the Return sparked a global political crisis in the 1820s, one that reshaped the world into the channels we know today. As is well known, Great Britain claimed Yount as a protectorate, based initially on its role in financing and equipping the *Indigo Pheasant* and then also on its key role in supporting Farther Yount in the civil war against the Ornish. When Farther Yount defeated the Ornish and Queen Zinnamoussea named Afsana and Tom her heirs and successors, Great Britain then augmented its imperial claims with the argument that Tom was a British citizen. As is also well known, China contested Great Britain's claim, and the Indian Ocean became the scene of several tense stand-offs between the British and Chinese navies. The fact that the Chinese possessed a blue-water navy by the late 1820s, and one able to resist British assertions, is clearly traceable to the Return: Tang Guozhi made sure that China swiftly adopted Yountian technology and persuaded the Celestial Emperor to overturn the centuries-old ban on long-distance Chinese maritime activity.

In the end, the friendship between Mei-Hua and the McDoons helped defuse tension, at least enough to keep Great Britain and China from outright war. Mei-Hua became one of the most famous women in nineteenth-century China, exerting significant influence over foreign policy. She never forgot her time in London and on the *Indigo Pheasant*. She remembered always the kindness the McDoons had shown her—the Chinese New Year at Mincing Lane glowed undimmed in her memory until the day she died. She remembered that the McDoons, the Sons & Daughters of Asaph, and even British soldiers, had stood as allies and co-combatants with her and her brother (and grim old Tang Guozhi!) in a titanic struggle against otherworldly powers. Above all, she cherished the love with which Maggie had embraced her—she would always be Maggie's "little sister eagle."

Equally important was the active influence of the lawyer Winstanley, who became one of the great reform politicians of the age, serving in Grey's Whig government and drafting elements of the First Reform Act of 1832. Winstanley (strongly supported by his wife) rallied the opposition to British claims in the Indian Ocean and eventually led the anti-imperialist faction in Parliament. Winstanley remembered well and fondly Mei-Hua and her brother, and recalled Tang Guozhi's asperity with respect.

Most scholars, both Western and Eastern, point to Mei-Hua as a chief—if informal—architect of the Anglo-Chinese Trade Treaty of 1840 (the so-called "Canton Concord") that resolved the major issues between the two nations and granted the Chinese trade concessions throughout the Indian Ocean. Winstanley helped draft the terms of the treaty, and he co-sponsored its introduction into the House of Commons. The Canton Concord was the model for the later agreements that ultimately, right after World War I, saw China gain with British support commercial enclaves as far away as Heligoland off Germany and at Naples in Italy.

Other factors were also influential in the confrontations over Yount in the 1820s and 1830s. Tom and Afsana did not accept British suzerainty, nor did they wish to be dependent on a resurgent China. They forged an alliance instead with the Tamil princes in the Carnatic, who were convinced that Yount represented the lost, once-submerged Tamil kingdom of Kumari Kandam. As a Gujarati, Afsana also received aid from that Indian realm as well as from neighbouring principalities (Kutch, Sind,

Baluchistan). The Bengalese Indigo Rebellion of 1826, inspired by the ethos and exploits embodied in the *Indigo Pheasant,* was the decisive event galvanizing the entire Indian sub-continent. Under Afsana and Tom, its armed forces, led by Nexius Dexius, Farther Yount (together with the reformed Ornish islands) assisted the Bengalese, almost leading them into war with Great Britain.

Here, at least, the story has something of a fairy tale ending: the dynasty Afsana and Tom started is, of course, still on the throne in Farther Yount. Farther Yount became a constitutional monarchy in 1908, the same year the British left their last possessions in India, and is one of the Seven Nations of India created in 1920. In a very nice touch, the Empress herself appointed one of Mei-Hua's great-grandchildren to the Chinese delegation that witnessed the signing of the joint constitution at the famed Seven Nations Conference in Calcutta.

The *Indigo Pheasant* also inspired the slave revolts on the indigo plantations of South Carolina and Georgia that helped cause the American Civil War. "Not one iota for indigo," the rallying cry of President C.F. Adams when Confederate troops besieged Washington DC in 1851, is among the most widely known political slogans in the world. Holcroft's Union troops targeted the indigo plantations on the March to the Sea in 1854; when the North finally prevailed over the South, not one indigo plantation remained of any consequence anywhere in the Confederacy.

These sanguinary conflicts were decades in the future when Barnabas, Sanford, Sally, and Maggie returned on a morning to the house with blue trim and the dolphin door knocker on Mincing Lane. Billy Sea-Hen was with them, and also the most unlikely house-guest of all: Jambres, his own skin still reveling in the taste of the wind and the feel of the sun.

"Welcome home," said Cook for the tenth time, tears in her eyes. "Oh, we have missed you, from the beet singling season to the fall of the small moon. Come here, you most particular, Billy Sea-Hen of Queenhithe!"

She crushed Billy to her bosom.

Later, in the partners' room, Cook and her niece (and Mr. Fletcher) asked for a hundred explanations and received a hundred responses.

"And that brainy Mr. Bunce, him so courageous with his one leg missing?" asked Cook.

"In fine form, very fine form, when we saw him last," said Barnabas, enjoying a glass of Cahors. "Has remained at home, hasn't he? With dear Tom and Afsana, and Nexius Dexius, the lot of 'em, in Yount."

Cook looked troubled, glanced at Sally before asking, "With Captain Bammary, as well then?"

Barnabas paused, also shot a glance at Sally (whose face betrayed no emotion) before replying, "That's correct, Captain Bammary has chosen to return to Yount too, and why not? That was part of the point, wasn't it? To find Yount, reunite everyone there?"

Sanford made a low noise like a mule, deep in his throat. The images in the pictures on the wall—the drowning souls spilling out of the wreckage of foundering East Indiamen—seemed to move of their own accord, though presumably that could only have been a trick of the candlelight.

Isaak jumped out of Sally's lap and strode to Cook.

"Well, by Saint Morgaine, you seem no the worse for wear!" laughed Cook, leaning over to pet the cat.

"Where is the beautiful bird?" ventured the Cook's niece. She had so loved Charicules's singing.

"Another migrant to Yount," said Barnabas. So attached had Charicules and Malchen become that the saulary elected to stay in Yount, where it was considered a national treasure. Malchen became Yount's First Ornithologist, establishing the Grand Aviary at the university. In one of their first acts as King and Queen, Tom and Afsana named the saulary as the national bird of Farther Yount—who has not seen the saulary featured prominently on Yountish currency and stamps?

Some semblance of normalcy resumed at the house on Mincing Lane, but no more than a semblance and nothing resembling life before the Return. Matchett & Frew, quick to capitalize on trading opportunities with Yount and staunch backers of forays into the Interrugal Lands, were frequent visitors. The Gardiners of Gracechurch Street also dined often with the McDoons, and sometimes the Darcys when Elizabeth was in town and could persuade her husband to go out to visit. The Darcys escorted Sally on her occasional visits to the Babbages, the Somervilles and other houses. Winstanley dined with the McDoons every other Wednesday evening, often bringing his wife so that the talk at table expanded to include many more topics than Winstanley on his own might have explored. Mr. Gandy frequented the house on Mincing Lane, his eccentric wit never failing to enliven a gathering; he included many Yountish examples in his magisterial *Art, Philosophy and Science of Architecture* (published in 1835).

The Sedgewicks and the McDoons never fully reconciled. Seeking to assert his claims on the *Indigo Pheasant* patents, the lawyer Sedgewick pursued various fruitless suits in Chancery and in the High Admiralty Court, eventually appearing before the Queen's Bench. Thus the ghost of James Kidlington stalked the lives of those he affected so forcefully while he lived.

Mrs. Sedgewick never visited the house on Mincing Lane so long as Maggie resided there, but she did host Sally for tea and meet Sally at other venues.

Sally declined Tom and Afsana's several invitations to join them in Yount, but lived out a life of increasing seclusion in London, surrounded and protected by Barnabas, Sanford, Isaak, Cook, and Billy Sea-Hen. Ironically, while she appeared less and less often outside the house on Mincing Lane, Sally became ever more famous as her central role in the Return became known. Babbage, Somerville, and other leading scientific lights of the era recommended Sally for honours and appointments. For the most part she declined these, shunning public attention, preoccupying herself with her translations of the Yountian classics. In so doing, she—again, ironically—kept herself in public view, not least when she helped start the Saint Macrina's

Library of Yountish Literature, with their distinctive indigo-coloured covers (which influenced Harvard to start the Loeb Classical Library decades later).

Sally corresponded regularly with the Termuydens. When the Termuydens died, and the Last Cozy House was shut, its contents to be dispersed in accordance with their will, the correspondence with Sally filled several very fat folios—which were returned to Sally and later came down to her heirs.

Once a year Sally visited James's grave in the small yard by St. Helen's Bishopsgate.

Among the few outsiders whom Sally habitually sought out was Lieutenant Thracemorton. Sally coveted every scrap of memory the lieutenant had about James, every observation and analysis of James's mentality, scruples, manner, and behaviour. Graciously at first, but with growing depth of feeling, the Lieutenant shared his remembrances and—surprising himself—gradually became a confidante. He and his wife (and eventually their children) were among the very few regular callers on Sally in her declining years.

Isaak died at age twenty-five. Cook found her stretched out in the kitchen, claws extended, as if she had expired while hunting. They buried Isaak in the backyard, the small mound of her grave marked by a carved wooden stele, surrounded by a bed of blue bixwort.

No other cat ever lived at the McDoon house.

Cook married Billy Sea-Hen, and the two of them moved into the back-house at Mincing Lane. While Billy travelled to Yount several times and founded—in Queenhithe—the Society of Asaph (which continues its global social justice campaign to the present day), Cook continued to care for the McDoons.

"Too old to have children," said Cook, whose name was Elizabeth Adelsina Grove. "But the little smee needs lookin' after, and Mr. Barnabas too (though he won't admit it). And Mr. Sanford likewise, though he is even less able to admit it. You have your big flock to minister to, dearest Billy, and I have my own little congelation."

Her niece the maid—Anna Emerentia Grove—finally married Mr. Fletcher. They set up house in a proper street near All Hallows-by-the-Tower, just a few blocks over from Mincing Lane, and were often to be seen visiting at the McDoons. Their daughter, Alice Elizabeth Fletcher, married an ambitious costermonger named Allen, who—through hard work and clever deals struck with Fortnum & Mason and other leading purveyors of specialty foods—amassed a tidy fortune. The oldest daughter of that union was none other than Richenda Mary-Elizabeth Allen, one of the first graduates of Somerville College at Oxford, who helped pioneer the "new biology" based on her discoveries in the Interrugal Lands. Their second daughter was Mary "Zinnamouse" Allen, the eminent historian of the Return, who married the American classicist Edward C. Townsend, joining him on the faculty of Columbia University in New York City.

Elizabeth Adelsina and her Billy, and Anna Emerentia and her Mr. Fletcher, were pall-bearers at Sanford's funeral.

"Oh *Quatsch*," cried Barnabas on that day, leaning heavily on Sally. "What ever shall I do without my oldest friend?"

Less than a year later, Barnabas died. They buried him in his favourite calicosh vest. The Yountish embassy in London reported to Sally that Tom and Afsana did not eat but only drank water for five days upon hearing the news of Barnabas's death, and that they declared an official day of mourning in Yount. Through his tears, Tom wondered if the inscription on his uncle's tombstone included "beans and bacon" or the like. (It does not, as you can attest for yourself by visiting the site at Saint Macrina's Infra).

Sally left the house on Mincing Lane even less often thereafter.

Not many years later, Cook found Sally dead in the attic room, slumped over a sheaf of notes on the Yountish poet Lemmisessurea the Younger. After the funeral (Sally rests next to her uncle, one over from Sanford), after the Yountish representatives had returned to the embassy and the newspapermen had gone to Fleet Street to write up their stories, Cook sat with Billy in the kitchen.

"Little smee flown home for good this time," she said, and then she sobbed.

Cook was startled and even dismayed when Winstanley unsealed the will and informed her that Sally had named her sole heir.

"Oh, fallabarty," said Cook. "What will I do with all this money, and the house, and the garden and all?"

The McDoons having recouped much of their depleted and endangered fortune as a result of very favourable terms of trade with Yount after its Return, Cook and Billy were able to invest large sums in the Society of Asaph and other charitable, humanitarian organizations in London and in Yount Great-Port. They lived in the house on Mincing Lane until the end of their days, caring for it as keepers of a sacred museum, a fane of light and longing in an uncertain world—many seekers and wonderers made what became a pilgrimage, wanting to hear what Billy had to tell them about Yount and the struggle with the Owl and the immarcessible crown of glory, and to hear from Cook all about the McDoons both before and after the Return. Cook took pains to preserve Sally's papers exactly as Sally had left them.

The house on Mincing Lane passed to the Fletchers and then to the Allens in due course. The Allen sisters made the first exhaustive studies of Sally's papers, which today are archived in the special collections at Columbia University.

Most readers will know that the house itself was destroyed in the Blitz, on the very same night that bombs gutted the *Indigo Pheasant*, which had been dry-docked for visitation at the National Maritime Museum in Greenwich. Much has been made of the simultaneous destruction, many claiming that the Owl guided the Luftwaffe on that night—and who is to say that Strix did not?

The Allen family salvaged the dolphin door-knocker from the ruin of the house and had it installed on the front door of their London pied-a-terre, a terrace house on Elvaston Place in South Kensington. That house has passed into other ownership, but a small National Trust plaque remarks upon the door-knocker (still there) for those who care to read it.

Of course, the house and all the rest of the McDoon equity were Sally's to bequeath because Tom and Afsana had long since renounced all claim as heirs, given their status as rulers of Yount.

And because, just over a year after the *Indigo Pheasant* sailed back to London, Maggie had disappeared . . .

. . . disappeared, taking Jambres with her, from London as wholly as if she had never existed there at all, without any clue or evidence for anyone to track her.

She gave no forewarning and left no explanation beyond a short note placed by the sandalwood box in the partners' room. The note read:

> Dear cousins:
> Bear this parting with love and understanding, I ask you. I am compelled; my journey moves me forward, with Jambres as my consort and with the blessing of the Goddess. The Return of Yount is only one more step in the never-ending battle we wage with the Owl—I know this now in my bone and heart. Where I go, not even the *Indigo Pheasant* can carry me. Farewell, and cup the flame of my love within you forever, as I will bear your love with me. Such a song we made!
>
> P.S. For Sanford. I thank you for helping me see the truth of what Saint Anthony wrote: 'spiritual geometry measures dimensions not as quantities but as virtues within the divine.'

P.P.S. For Sally. If I could, I would ask you and Isaak to come with us, but you are needed more in your present time and place. Be well—we women are the strength of the world.

Putting down the letter and pushing aside his ink bottle, quill, blotting paper, and quizzing glass, Barnabas said, "Well, buttons and beeswax. What do we make of this?"

Into and around the ticking of the clock on the mantlepiece, Sanford said, "I think, my friends, that Maggie . . . and Jambres . . . are gone for good, and quite clean out of our time altogether."

Sanford, as usual, had perceived the heart of the matter completely.

Interlude: Farrigine

[From Charles Burney, <u>History of Music</u>, vol. 5, 1803; Maggie read this at the Sedgewicks, who gave it to her as parting gift when she moved to the McDoons; her copy is heavily annotated in her hand]

The mind's operation, when influenced by the emotions piqued through music, is a river of conflicting eddies channelled into one harmonious flow. The system of temperament, whether equal or well, whether founded upon the Pythagorean comma or some other arranging concept, impresses upon us the learning of the affects, such that we—though creatures infinitely small in the thoughts of Heaven—may nevertheless ascend with tentative and trembling souls some distance on the circles that lead to Grace and the Divine. In this regard, some of the more novel approaches taken by the Italians and the Austrians in recent centuries might—with some adaptations to suit the British sensibility—be usefully employed on our shores. I will speak here firstly of the alternative or cross-tuning known in Milan and other Italian centres as 'scordatura,' with reference also to the delightful though today under-utilized *viola d'amore* and the passacaglias of mystery described by H.I.F. Biber of Salzburg in his *Harmonia Artificioso*.

[From Olaudah Equiano's <u>The Interesting Narrative of the Life of Olaudah Equiano, or, Gustavus Vassa, The African</u> (1789), which Maggie read and annotated at the McDoons]

At last, when the ship we were in had got in all her cargo, they made ready with many fearful noises, and we were all put under deck, so that we could not see how they managed the vessel. But this disappointment was the least of my sorrow. [... . . . .]
This wretched situation was again aggravated by the galling of the chains, now become insupportable; and the filth of the necessary tubs, into which the children often fell, and were almost suffocated. [... . . . .]
I also now first saw the use of the quadrant. I had often with astonishment seen the mariners make observations with it, and I could not think what it meant. They at last took notice of my surprise; and one of them, willing to increase it, as well as to gratify my curiosity, made me one day look through it. The clouds appeared to me to be land, which disappeared as they passed along. This heightened my wonder: and I was now more persuaded than ever that I was in another world, and that every thing about me was magic.

Epilogue

"'The history of men's follies,' says the inimitable Fontenelle, 'makes no small part of learning; and, unhappily for us, much of our knowledge terminates there.'"

—**Ephraim Chambers**,
Cyclopaedia, vol. I (1728)

"If I were commissioned to design a new universe, I would be mad enough to undertake it."

—**Giovanni Battista Piranesi**,
c. 1760, as recorded by Jacques Guillaume Legrand in "Notice historique sur la vie et les ouvrages de J.B. Piranesi" (1799)

"It is necessary to make a ruin of a palace so that we have thus rendered it an object of interest."

—**Denis Diderot**,
Salon de 1767

THE INDIGO PHEASANT *Volume Two of Longing for Yount*

"... imaginative metaphysics shows that man becomes all things by not understanding them.... He makes the things out of himself and becomes them by transforming himself into them."
—**Giambattista Vico**,
The New Science (3rd edition; 1744)

Maggie and Jambres ate a tangy chicken yassa with Goddess the Mother in her garden at the crosswinds of the world.

Butterflies landed on the table, flexed their wings nonchalantly.

Nasturtiums crowded the pavilion, chanvre and flax swayed in the breeze. Fig trees, tended each by its jealous tribe of wasps, lined the walls closest to the diners. Prickly thickets of smilax filled the corners of those walls, interspersed with the flowering tea-plants that the Chinese call "cha hua," which the English call "camellias," with their large, ruffled blooms of pink and sabine-white. Hedge-rocket and mustard tempted with their yellows, merony and speedwell with their speckled blues. Bixwort and white evermind dotted the strips of fresh-green lawn trimmed by the brick of walkways. Working the flower-fields, a thousand bees hummed and zussed, some as small and brilliant as copper nail-heads, some as large and bright as oranges from Sardinia.

Water ran gurgling and splashing in dozens of ingenious channels and in many carved fountains of marble.

Overhead the massive clock drummed to the bass of the bees.

Goddess smiled, humming to herself a partita from Maggie's Great Song.

"We have arrived," said Maggie. "As Saint Adelsina sang in 'The Rogation':
  'Lean and ragged as cormorants,
  But undwindled,
  Flame and candle all undimmed.
  Our bodies serving as the reliquaries
  For which we have not the purse,

Our bones wrapped in linen tattered,
For which we slip not the hearse,
Our skin daubed with blood-seeped ash,
For which we scorn not the verse.'"

They finished their meal with sweet-milk rice soup.

"Past all cumbrous snares and walls of trepidation," said Jambres. He made a show of wearing his sleeves rolled up, still marveling at the sight of his own umber skin, whole and alive. Here and there, on his left wrist and around his knees, ran pale milky striations, the scars of his sutures, a subcutaneous reminder of his punishment.

"We will go to New York City," said Maggie. "In the next century. 1928 or 1929, I think."

Goddess smiled even more widely, and said, "Manhattan, around Saint Nicholas Place, I should say."

"Yes," said Maggie. "That sounds about right."

A bird darted right over the pavilion, a flash of deep bottle blue with streaks of rusty-red on its belly.

"The Euhelline Fruit-Pigeon," said the Mother. "At least that is what your little Malchen will agree to call it in English, when she discovers it. It's a native of the Ornish islands, and will one day soon establish itself on Sri Lanka. Quite a beauty."

"Have you . . . ?" started Maggie.

"No, no Indigo Pheasant here since the day you last visited me," the Mother shook her head.

"I am wondering more about another bird," said Jambres.

"Ah, yes," said Goddess. "The Owl. You have made him very angry, you know. Furious, actually. No one has ever done what you did: freed prisoners ahead of schedule, upset the timetable, defied the Rules."

"Strix seems obsessed with rules for one who defied them himself near the Beginning," said Maggie.

"Yes, but also no," answered Goddess. "Strix and his followers, the other Watchers, are not truly like the Fallen at all. The latter: . . . oh my, you should meet one of them sometime, really you should. The Fallen do not believe in rules at all. They mock the very presumption of rule-making. Artists, every one of them: wanton'd Belial; slovenly, shambling Moloch; Mammon the unctuous; Dagon whose witticisms coruscate on their way to their target; Zerustihiel (fastidious poetaster!); and his radiant glory himself, Satan the Lucifer.

Jambres shifted uncomfortably and said, "With utmost respect, most revered Lady, I have seen or else heard something of their artistic eminences while serving in certain precincts of persuasion, and I am not thoroughly certain I would wish to make a closer acquaintance with any of those you name, despite your seeming recommendation."

Goddess laughed a forgiving laugh, and said, "Dear Jambres, I did not mean to thrust you into a salon from which there would be no exit—you have suffered enough. Nor did I mean to elevate the Fallen as such. No, I merely salute them as one artist might to another."

She paused (even gods—especially gods!—have their vanities and understand the impact of the dramatic).

"As artists, however, the Fallen were less accomplished, their song less exalted, their palette less sophisticated and powerful than ours," she concluded. "So, they had to be expelled."

Maggie deliberately listened to the clock overhead and let the humming of the bees caress her ears.

"Strix is . . . ?" said Jambres.

"Ah, I strayed, I know it, a product of too many years on my own, sleep-wandering among the sisymbria and the celandines," said Goddess, shaking her head, waving off a small cloud of butterflies. "Strix and the Half-Fallen are the antitheses of artists. They create nothing. Though they have good taste when I think on it. They are critics and scholars and connoisseurs, you could say, sensitive to the aesthetic but rigorous and inflexible in its application."

Maggie thought of the richly appointed interior of the Owl's house in Hoxton Square, and Jambres thought of the Widow Goethals's exquisite dresses and hats.

"As such, they are about nothing if it is not rules," continued

Goddess. "Rules of decorum and aesthetics, rules to govern the archive and the bureaucracy, rules of what is proper and what is not. Above all, rules that they make themselves. They did not like the original rules, since they had no hand in making those, but they hunger for rules in and of themselves. Oh yes, rules they like very much, so long as they compose and edit them."

"Creation then, of a sort," murmured Jambres.

"Perhaps," conceded Goddess. "Maybe, but a debased sort, among the lowest forms. Authors only of passwords and commands to gate-wardens and timekeepers! Obscurantists! List-makers, cataloguers, anatomists, hah!"

Jambres began to respond but Maggie cut him off.

"Strix knows where we are going?" she asked.

"I would guess so," said Goddess. "Not that he confides in me, of course, the petulant boy! Yet no matter how he shields his thought from me, I can divine it, especially now that I am awake again. That only adds to his anger, and also to his animosity towards you, Maggie- he knows you jolted me from my slumber."

The meal over, Maggie and Jambres made to leave.

"Beware," said Goddess. "I too must observe the rules—how could I not, since I co-authored them!—so can only aid you so far when you return to Earth. Strix—yes, Strix Tender Wurm the Watcher!—is not wrong in all matters. He knows every clause and codicil of the laws, none better."

Maggie and Jambres nodded.

"By the way, the Owl has another one of his outposts, a sentry-house, in New York," said the Mother. "I forget where exactly, but look for it downtown, in Greenwich Village."

"We will," said Maggie.

"One last thing," said Goddess, producing a leather-bound book not much larger than her palm. "Give this to my husband when you find him."

Maggie took the book. Opening it, she saw nothing but blank pages.

"Oh no child," laughed Goddess. "I whispered my words into the book for His eyes and ears only. You won't be able to read it, though you have become mightier than almost any other mortal has yet become."

Maggie put the book away, feeling a little embarrassed but more frustrated, her curiosity surging. She felt a little bit insulted as well.

At the doorway out of the garden, Goddess embraced them, first Jambres and then Maggie.

"Tell God it is time to come home himself," she said. "Tell him his supper is getting cold upon the table. Now, farewell . . . and goddess-speed!"

Looking back just once (Maggie thought Goddess looked small, framed against the garden behind), Maggie and Jambres held hands and walked through the door and down the long, winding stairway to New York City in the 1920s.

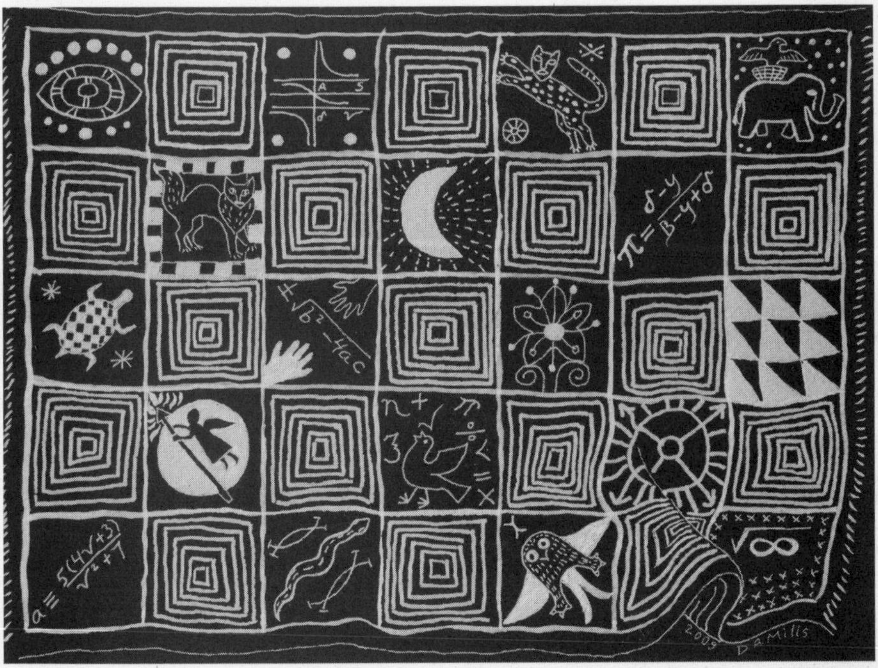
2009
DaMills

Index of Illustrations

"Strix on Column"	9
"Indigo Pheasant Tea Bowl"	11
"Tick Tock"	23
"Disjecta Membra"	42
"Dolphin Door-Knocker"	53
"Videnda"	86
"Conjure Hands"	101
"Qualia"	127
"Maggie vs. Heeg-Owl"	135
"Fontes"	157
"Barnabas Vest and Seachart"	167
"Indicia"	191
"Meissen Ware Isak and Charicules"	201
"Cartulae"	233
"Mei Hua's Qingbai Tile"	236
"Vestigia"	282
"A Great Singing"	286
"Farrigine"	342
"Pheasant and Dolphin Directoire Clock"	344
"Maggie's Ukara"	351

Acknowledgements

First, as always, my deepest thanks to my wife and creative partner, Deborah Mills, whose art adorns the cover and who illustrated the novel itself. Deborah read with a keen critical eye every word—and improved both novels immensely with her comments.

For always helping me pack for my visits to Yount, and eagerly awaiting my reports once I returned: my parents Daniel D. & Kathryn; my brothers Matt and Doug; my sisters-in-law Yvonne and Jenny; my nephews Nick, Patrick, Than, Terence, and James.

For sharing early and often their delight in Yount, my "power readers": Pat McGrath, Dale Smith, Michael & Amy Tuteur, Lise Kildegaard, Phil Sisson & Susan Clark, Tom & Renee Cottrell, Kurt & Alicia Corriher, Regina Swinford, Knut & Iwona Schiander.

For their encouragement, inspiration and advice: Delia Sherman, Ellen Kushner, Matt Kressel, Pam Grossman, Sonya Taaffe, Greer Gilman, Kim Henderson and her creative writing students at the Idyllwild Arts Academy, Shira Lipkin and her colleagues at Arisia, the good folks at the Science Fiction Society of Northern New Jersey, Bill Skees at the Well Read Bookstore (Hawthorne, New Jersey), Terence Craig, Wendy Ellertson, my students at Year Up, Lisa Chin, Lisette Nieves, Rick Taubold, Andrea Pinkney, Doug Smith, and Kate Castelli.

For photographing Deborah's hippocamp, and graciously allowing us the use of the photo for the cover design, I thank Shira Weinberger (and her husband Adam).

Finally, I thank the CZP team: Brett Savory and Sandra Kasturi for believing in this project, Samantha Beiko for editing it, Danny Evarts for the fabulous book design, and Helen Marshall for her general support. I could not ask for a better publisher.

About the Author

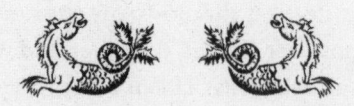

Daniel A. Rabuzzi studied folklore and mythology in college and graduate school and keeps one foot firmly in the Other Realm. CZP published his first novel, *The Choir Boats*, in 2009.

His short fiction and poetry have appeared in *Sybil's Garage, Shimmer, ChiZine, Lady Churchill's Rosebud Wristlet, Abyss & Apex, Goblin Fruit, Mannequin Envy, Bull Spec, Kaleidotrope*, and *Scheherezade's Bequest*.

ALSO BY DANIEL A. RABUZZI
FROM CHIZINE PUBLICATIONS

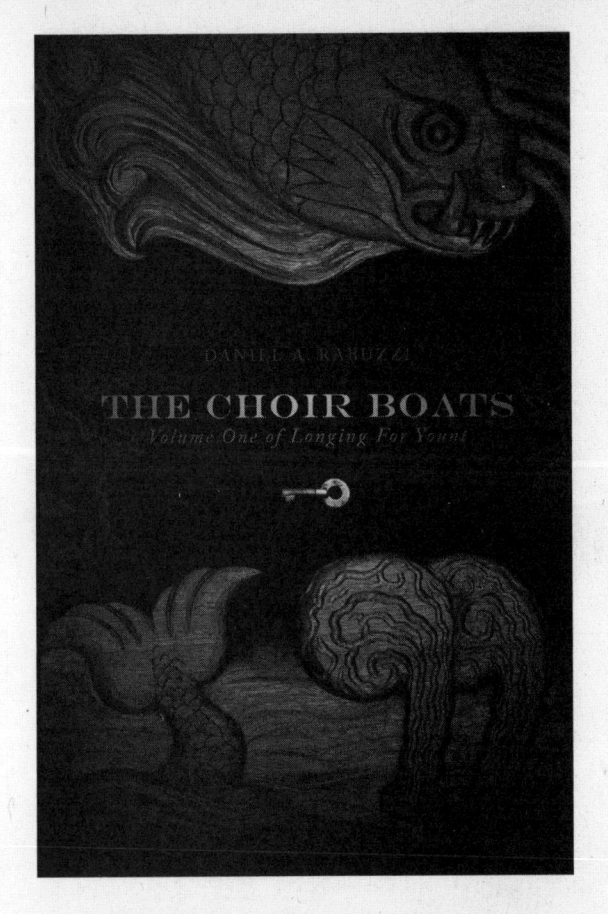

THE CHOIR BOATS
VOLUME ONE OF LONGING FOR YOUNT
978-1-926851-06-8

WITH FULL FLANKS AHEAD, *THE CHOIR BOATS* CHARTS A MAGICAL COURSE OF VERVE AND WIT THROUGH A RICHLY DETAILED NINETEENTH-CENTURY WORLD, SPINNING OFF LITTLE ARABESQUES OF WONDERMENT WITH EVERY TURN OF THE PAGE.
—MATTHEW KRESSEL, WORLD FANTASY AWARD NOMINEE

EMBRACE THE ODD

EDITED BY SANDRA KASTURI & HALLI VILLEGAS
INTRODUCTION BY **STEVEN ERIKSON**
WITH
KELLEY ARMSTRONG
MADELINE ASHBY
CORY DOCTOROW
GEMMA FILES
SILVIA MORENO-GARCIA
DAVID NICKLE
GEOFF RYMAN
PETER WATTS
RIO YOUERS
AND MORE

IMAGINARIUM 2012

the best canadian speculative writing

IMAGINARIUM 2012:
THE BEST CANADIAN SPECULATIVE WRITING
EDITED BY SANDRA KASTURI & HALLI VILLEGAS

AVAILABLE JULY 2012
FROM CHIZINE PUBLICATIONS AND TIGHTROPE BOOKS

978-0-926851-67-9

CHIZINEPUB.COM   CZP

"*Swallowing a Donkey's Eye* is fine, ribald work. There's a futuristic wackiness and bitterness that reminds me of the best of George Saunders's longer stories. It's brutal and hilarious, and Tremblay's narrator holds it all together with an ironic grimace."
—Stewart O'Nan, author of *Emily, Alone* and *A Prayer for the Dying*

SWALLOWING A DONKEY'S EYE
PAUL TREMBLAY

AVAILABLE AUGUST 2012
FROM CHIZINE PUBLICATIONS

978-1-926851-69-3

ALSO AVAILABLE FROM CHIZINE PUBLICATIONS

BULLETTIME

NICK MAMATAS

AVAILABLE AUGUST 2012
FROM CHIZINE PUBLICATIONS

978-1-926851-71-6

CHIZINEPUB.COM CZP

JANUS
JOHN PARK

JANUS

JOHN PARK

AVAILABLE SEPTEMBER 2012
FROM CHIZINE PUBLICATIONS

978-1-927469-10-1

ALSO AVAILABLE FROM CHIZINE PUBLICATIONS

"Ian Rogers' stories are old-fashioned in the very best sense: classic chillers in the spirit of Shirley Jackson and Richard Matheson. *Every House Is Haunted* is full of well-crafted, satisfying twists, a fine companion for any reader of literate horror."
—Andrew Pyper, author of *Lost Girls*, *The Killing Circle*, and *The Guardians*

EVERY HOUSE IS HAUNTED
IAN ROGERS
AVAILABLE OCTOBER 2012
FROM CHIZINE PUBLICATIONS

978-1-927469-16-3

CHIZINEPUB.COM   CZP

WORLD FANTASY AWARD-WINNING AUTHOR

THE BEST DARK FICTION OF ROBERT SHEARMAN
REMEMBER WHY YOU FEAR ME

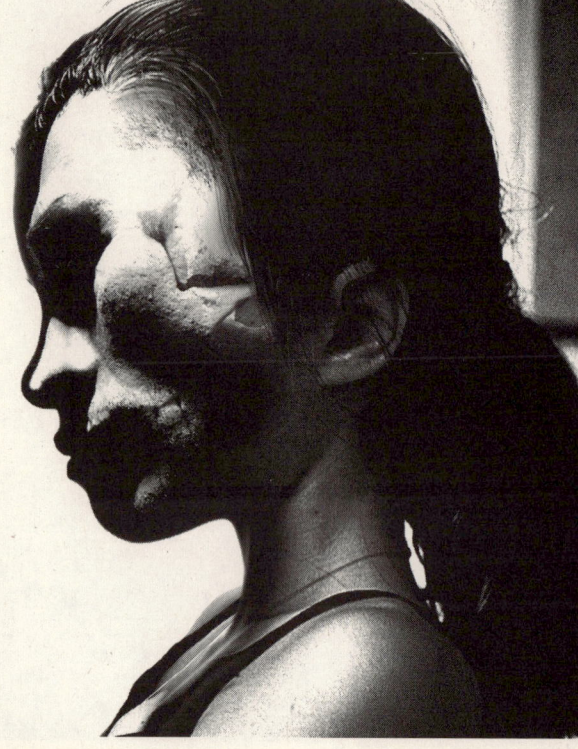

INTRODUCTION BY STEPHEN JONES

REMEMBER WHY YOU FEAR ME
THE BEST DARK FICTION OF ROBERT SHEARMAN

AVAILABLE OCTOBER 2012
FROM CHIZINE PUBLICATIONS

978-0-927469-21-7

ALSO AVAILABLE FROM CHIZINE PUBLICATIONS

THE BOOK OF THOMAS: HEAVEN

ROBERT BOYCZUK

AVAILABLE NOVEMBER 2012
FROM CHIZINE PUBLICATIONS

978-1-927469-27-9

CHIZINEPUB.COM   CZP

HAIR SIDE, FLESH SIDE
HELEN MARSHALL
AVAILABLE NOVEMBER 2012
FROM CHIZINE PUBLICATIONS

978-1-927469-24-8

ALSO AVAILABLE FROM CHIZINE PUBLICATIONS

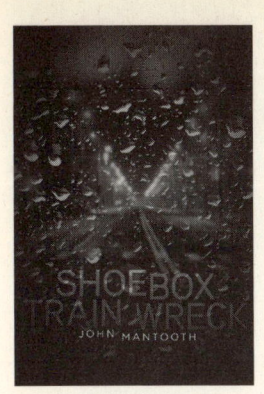

978-1-926851-54-9
JOHN MANTOOTH

**SHOEBOX
TRAIN WRECK**

978-1-926851-53-2
MIKE CAREY, LINDA CAREY
& LOUISE CAREY

THE STEEL SERAGLIO

978-1-926851-55-6
RIO YOUERS

WESTLAKE SOUL

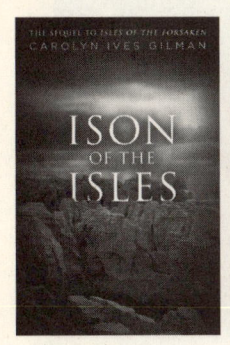

978-1-926851-56-3
CAROLYN IVES GILMAN

ISON OF THE ISLES

978-1-926851-58-7
JAMES MARSHALL

**NINJAS VERSUS
PIRATE FEATURING
ZOMBIES**

978-1-926851-57-0
GEMMA FILES

**A TREE OF BONES
VOLUME III OF THE
HEXSLINGER SERIES**

978-1-926851-59-4
DAVID NICKLE

**RASPUTIN'S
BASTARDS**

"IF YOUR TASTE IN FICTION RUNS TO THE DISTURBING, DARK, AND AT LEAST
PARTIALLY WEIRD, CHANCES ARE YOU'VE HEARD OF CHIZINE PUBLICATIONS—
CZP—A YOUNG IMPRINT THAT IS NONETHELESS PRODUCING STARTLINGLY
BEAUTIFUL BOOKS OF STARKLY, DARKLY LITERARY QUALITY."
—DAVID MIDDLETON, JANUARY MAGAZINE

CHIZINEPUB.COM CZP

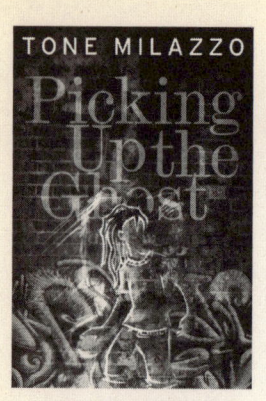

978-1-926851-35-8
TONE MILAZZO
PICKING UP THE GHOST

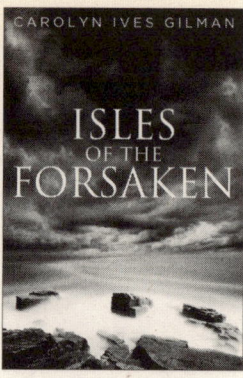

978-1-926851-43-3
CAROLYN IVES GILMAN
ISLES OF THE FORSAKEN

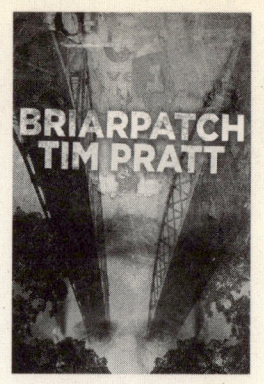

978-1-926851-44-0
TIM PRATT
BRIARPATCH

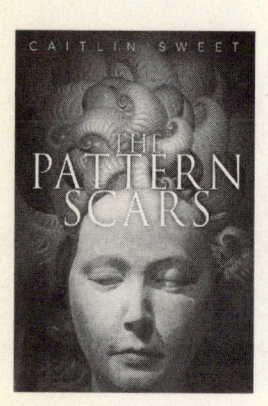

978-1-926851-43-3
CAITLIN SWEET
THE PATTERN SCARS

978-1-926851-46-4
TERESA MILBRODT
BEARDED WOMEN

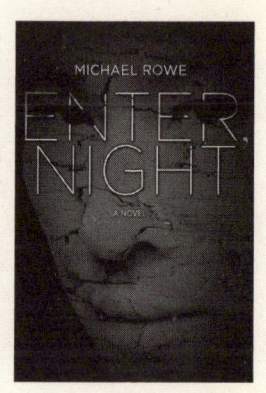

978-1-926851-45-7
MICHAEL ROWE
ENTER, NIGHT

"THE BEST WORK IN DARK FANTASY AND HORROR FICTION THESE DAYS IS BEING PUBLISHED BY SMALL PRESSES, HAUNTED LITERARY BOUTIQUES ESTABLISHED (MOSTLY) IN OUT-OF-THE-WAY PLACES, [INCLUDING] CHIZINE IN TORONTO. THEY'RE ALL DEVOTED TO THE WEIRD, TO THE STRANGE AND—MOST IMPORTANT—TO GOOD WRITING."

—DANA JENNINGS, THE NEW YORK TIMES

ALSO AVAILABLE FROM CHIZINE PUBLICATIONS

978-1-926851-10-5
TOM PICCIRILLI
EVERY SHALLOW CUT

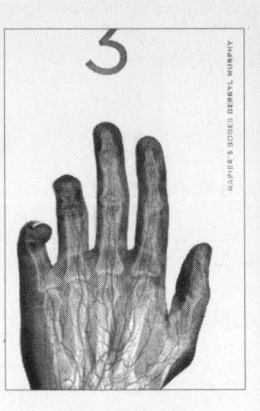

978-1-926851-09-9
DERRYL MURPHY
NAPIER'S BONES

978-1-926851-11-2
DAVID NICKLE
EUTOPIA

978-1-926851-12-9
CLAUDE LALUMIÈRE
THE DOOR TO LOST PAGES

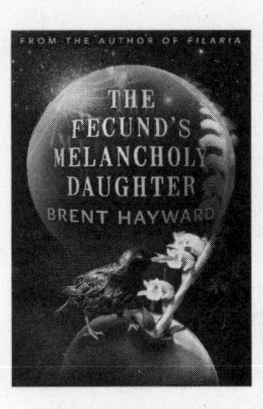

978-1-926851-13-6
BRENT HAYWARD
THE FECUND'S MELANCHOLY DAUGHTER

978-1-926851-14-3
GEMMA FILES
A ROPE OF THORNS
VOLUME II OF THE HEXSLINGER SERIES

"I'VE REVIEWED ALMOST A DOZEN OF THEIR RELEASES OVER THE LAST FEW YEARS . . . AND HAVE NOT BEEN DISAPPOINTED ONCE. IN FACT, EVERY SINGLE RELEASE HAS BEEN NOTHING SHORT OF SPECTACULAR. READERS IN SEARCH OF A VIRTUAL CACHE OF DARK LITERARY SPECULATIVE FICTION NEED LOOK NO FARTHER THAN THIS OUTSTANDING SMALL PUBLISHER."
—PAUL GOAT ALLEN, BARNES & NOBLE COMMUNITY BLOG

CHIZINEPUB.COM CZP

A BOOK OF TONGUES
VOLUME I OF THE HEXSLINGER SERIES
GEMMA FILES
978-0-9812978-6-6

CHASING THE DRAGON
NICHOLAS KAUFMANN
978-0-9812978-4-2

CHIMERASCOPE
DOUGLAS SMITH
978-0-9812978-5-9

CITIES OF NIGHT
PHILIP NUTMAN
978-0-9812978-8-0

FILARIA
BRENT HAYWARD
978-0-9809410-1-2

THE HAIR WREATH AND OTHER STORIES
HALLI VILLEGAS
978-1-926851-02-0

HORROR STORY AND OTHER HORROR STORIES
ROBERT BOYCZUK
978-0-9809410-3-6

IN THE MEAN TIME
PAU TREMBLAY
978-1-926851-06-8

KATJA FROM THE PUNK BAND
SIMON LOGAN
978-0-9812978-7-3

MAJOR KARNAGE
GORD ZAJAC
978-0-9813746-6-6

MONSTROUS AFFECTIONS
DAVID NICKLE
978-0-9812978-3-5

NEXUS: ASCENSION
ROBERT BOYCZUK
978-0-9813746-8-0

OBJECTS OF WORSHIP
CLAUDE LALUMIÈRE
978-0-9812978-2-8

PEOPLE LIVE STILL IN CASHTOWN CORNERS
TONY BURGESS
978-1-926851-04-4

SARAH COURT
CRAIG DAVIDSON
978-1-926851-00-6

THE TEL AVIV DOSSIER
LAVIE TIDHAR AND NIR YANIV
978-0-9809410-5-0

THE WORLD MORE FULL OF WEEPING
ROBERT J. WIERSEMA
978-0-9809410-9-8

ALSO AVAILABLE FROM CHIZINE PUBLICATIONS